DUNCAN MACNEIL is the
pseudonym of a well-known thriller
and suspense writer whose special
interest in the old British Army in
India and the various frontier
engagements of the 1890s and the turn
of the century has led him to research
the period with care and with a
novelist's eye for detail.

Also by Duncan MacNeil

DRUMS ALONG THE KHYBER
LIEUTENANT OF THE LINE

and published by Corgi Books

Duncan MacNeil

Sadhu on the
Mountain Peak

CORGI BOOKS
A DIVISION OF TRANSWORLD PUBLISHERS LTD
A NATIONAL GENERAL COMPANY

SADHU ON THE MOUNTAIN PEAK

A CORGI BOOK 0 552 09366 1

Originally published in Great Britain
by Hodder & Stoughton Ltd.

PRINTING HISTORY

Hodder & Stoughton edition published 1971
Corgi edition published 1973

Copyright © 1971 by Duncan MacNeil

This book is set in 10 pt. Plantin

Corgi Books are published by
Transworld Publishers Ltd.,
Cavendish House, 57-59 Uxbridge Road,
Ealing, London W.5.
Made and printed in Great Britain by
Cox & Wyman Ltd., London, Reading and Fakenham

**NOTE: The Australian price appearing on the
back cover is the recommended retail price.**

THE CHAIN OF COMMAND

Lieutenant-General Sir Iain Ogilvie (James Ogilvie's father)
General Officer Commanding Northern Army at Muree

Lieutenant-General ('Bloody Francis') Fettleworth,
Commander of the First Division at Peshawar

Brigadier-General Preston
Brigade Commander

Brigadier-General
Lakenham, Chief of Staff
to Fettleworth

Lieutenant-Colonel Lord Dornoch
Commanding Royal Strathspeys

Major Blaise-Willoughby
Political Officer

Major John Hay
Second in command

Captain Andrew Black
Adjutant

'Bosom' Cunningham
Regimental Sergeant-Major

Captain James Ogilvie
about to take over B
Company from Captain
MacKinlay but attached
Political Department in
the meantime.

*Captain Edward Healey is officially attached to the Southern
Army Command at Ootacamund in the Madras Presidency.*

CHAPTER ONE

'JAMES, love. . . .' It was no more than a murmur from sleep as the woman stirred a little by his side, but it was enough to bring Ogilvie awake. His head throbbed as though a whole legion of native devils was contained in it, and hammering to get out. Distantly from a cantonment parade-ground, a cruel bugle brought the British soldiers to awareness of yet another day of the ferocious Indian sun. The notes bored stridently through Ogilvie's sick headache. He opened his eyes to see the early morning sunlight beaming through the slats of the shutters across the window of the bedroom; and shut out the sight again as a wave of hideous pain rose from behind his eyeballs.

He groaned. Thank God, promotion didn't come every day. If last night was what happened when one's captaincy came through on the wire from Northern Army Command at Murree, then heaven help the man who attained the rank of major whilst on service in the Raj! Yet India did help to sweat out the drink; the morning's heat would improve matters but if he had taken so much whisky back at the Royal Strathspeys' depot at Invermore in Scotland, James Ogilvie decided now, he would be on the flat of his back for the rest of the day, and that would presumably mean a Court Martial.

Besides, last night had not been merely his own private celebration. It had happened to be a guest night in the Mess – and one of the guests had been no less a personage than Lieutenant-General Francis Fettleworth, the Divisional Commander. Ogilvie broke out in a fresh wave of sweat as he wondered how much of his condition Bloody Francis had noticed. But then, from what he had himself seen of Bloody Francis, he had formed the impression that the Divisional Commander had also been letting his hair down to a pretty considerable extent. Ogilvie's memory was of a large, bloated face, very red in the cheeks – a wonderful background for the white moustache whose drooping hairs totally concealed the mouth – and of bleary eyes cheek-red in the whites.

Memory, after such a night, was unreliable; and there were

blank spots of complete oblivion, periods during which James Ogilvie knew he could have been guilty of the wildest abandon and impropriety. He had had only one such night previously, and that had been nearly three years ago in London, shortly after leaving the Royal Military College at Sandhurst on being newly gazetted to the 114th Highlanders as a subaltern; and, from that one experience, he knew that last night's inebriate must always await enlightenment from other lips before he could truly count his sins. One placed oneself wholly in another person's power; had Ogilvie been unkindly told now that last night he had attacked the guard commander with a claymore, or taken Lady Dornoch, his Colonel's wife, in his arms, he could not have argued the truth of the assertion.

Disliking such placement of himself in another's hands, Captain James Ogilvie, who had not yet physically adorned his shoulders with his extra stars, resolved, as many a man had done before, never, never to drink so much again. . . .

As consciousness came back more strongly, memory stirred a little more vigorously. There were two things, two special things, that Ogilvie now recalled from last night. One was of himself, with Mary Archdale, hidden from view behind a potted palm in the darkness of the verandah outside the Mess, when two men had emerged and conversed, one of them leaning fatly against the railing, the other standing straight and gaunt and obsequiously attentive, listening to the pipes of the battalion marking 'lights out'.

One of those men, the semi-reclining one, had been Bloody Francis. The other, Captain Andrew Black, adjutant of the 114th, also having drink taken. Fettleworth had given a hiccough and had said, 'A wonderful sound – your pipes. Stirring. Warlike. And nostalgic, Captain Black – *immensely* nostalgic. Hrrrmph.' He had then blown his nose, hard. Behind the potted palm, Ogilvie recalled, he had stifled a laugh with some difficulty; for, when last they had been in big-scale action under Fettleworth, a year or so ago on the terrible track to Fort Gazai, the Divisional Commander had, so rumour reported, expressed very different sentiments about the Scots' beloved pipes, and about the Scots as well come to that.

From this point on, memory faded; yet something continued to nag. Something unpleasant; Fettleworth and Black had gone on to discuss him, James Ogilvie. Fettleworth had said something about his early promotion to Captain's rank, and Black

8

hadn't sounded happy. Ogilvie tried to remember more, but couldn't; his chief emotion, as he came back to the hangover-ridden morning after, was a disturbing realization of the next of those few things he could recall in patches. As if to make sure of the facts beyond all doubt, he reached out a hand and touched Mary Archdale's naked body. She was still asleep, sleeping like a child with a small smile of happiness on her face, and he was in her bed. He had no recollection of getting there, presumably in the early hours, but he did remember with a great deal of pleasure watching Mary undress, slowly, and then coming to him with her lips parted and trembling and her arms held wide as if to enmesh him into her very body. And it had been a wonderful, wonderful night; he was grateful that the cloudy mists had lifted for long enough to let him enjoy and remember, so clearly, in so much detail, with so much deep feeling, what they had given each other, lovingly and without any holding back. It was something that for his whole period of service in India they had both longed for, but it had never happened until last night. While Mary Archdale's elderly husband Tom had been alive, such a thing would have been unthinkable, would have meant the end of his career in the army had it come to light; and even during the year subsequent to Major Archdale's death in action, on the march to Fort Gazai, any such close liaison had seemed to Ogilvie improper. One could not bed a widow still in her whole year of official mourning! The twentieth century might not be far from clutching the nine-teenth by the coat-tails, but Queen Victoria, old as she might be, was still sitting like a round fat rock on the throne of England, and her edict and her morals ran world-wide throughout her Empire. One did not flout her standards – not too brazenly at all events. One was an officer and a gentleman, and Tom Archdale, Staff Major, had been a brother officer and gentleman. It had taken a night's heavy drinking to bring down the barriers and cut through the inhibitions of his upbringing, and James Ogilvie didn't know whether to laugh or cry; but his principal regret, he found, was for all the other nights there could have been if he hadn't been so straitlaced; Mary, he felt sure, would have lowered her standards willingly. The delay had been all on his side after Archdale's death.

He sat up in bed. He had a terrible shake in his hands, he noticed. Gingerly he put a foot on the floor and stood, and went over to the wash-stand where he drank some water from a covered carafe and felt the dryness of his mouth depart, though the taste that lingered was still foul and harsh. Then he went back to the disordered bed and woke Mary. He woke her urgently; the day was coming alive, the cantonments would be stirring and he had to make his way back to his quarters in his full Mess uniform. Not an unusual sight, perhaps, for a sub-altern – but for a newly promoted captain?

Mary woke, smiling up at him, her eyes clear and fresh, her breasts, her flat stomach, her thighs, all inviting him to stay. 'Well, love,' she said, resting her cheek on the soft flesh of her upper arm. 'Was it up to expectations?'

He nodded, and went down on his knees beside the bed. He felt tears prick behind his eyelids; she seemed so defenceless, would be so alone when he had gone. 'Mary,' was all he could say. 'Mary, darling.'

'It's all right, love,' she said with a touch of wonder. 'I enjoyed it too, oh, *so* much.'

'I'd do anything for you, Mary.'

'And me for you, love.' She rolled over a little way; he looked down on her buttocks. He couldn't leave her; but of course he had to, and quickly. 'Will you come tonight, James?'

He nodded. 'I've no duties. Yes, of course I'll come.'

'I'm glad, love.' She looked up at him, frowning. 'How much do you remember of last night, James?'

'Little enough,' he said with an attempt at a laugh. 'Only what matters, Mary.'

'I wonder.'

'What do you mean?'

'I think other things mattered too, James. Did you hear, or rather do you remember, the conversation between Fettleworth and your Captain Andrew Black?'

'No,' he said. The nagging worry returned, worse than ever. 'Tell me.'

She said, 'You never did look upon Andrew Black as a friend, did you!'

'Hardly. I'm not much worried about Black now, though.'

It was sheer bravado and she laughed at it. 'Oh, James, you may be a Captain, a very new and very, very dear Captain – but Andrew is still the adjutant and you'd do well to remember that. If he no longer outranks you, he can still be a pestilential nuisance! Company commanders have to toe the line with adjutants, haven't they?'

'Yes, of course. Well, Mary? What was said?'

'Briefly,' she said, 'Fettleworth was sounding Black about you, and Black was being his usual self. Black, it seemed, didn't approve the recommendation for your advanced promotion. He even suggested favouritism – that you owed it to the fact your father happened to be the Northern Army Commander. To give Fettleworth his due, James, he reacted badly to that and Andrew got a flea in his ear. But here's the point, love: Fettleworth has plans for you – unspecified plans to broaden your experience. And, in his own words, for you to acquire much knowledge for yourself and for the High Command as well. The last thing I heard him say was that he would be discussing this with Lord Dornoch shortly.'

'I see.' Ogilvie held his hands to his throbbing head. 'What the devil has he in mind, I wonder!'

'I don't know, love.'

'Well, I'm not shirking any duty ... but I don't much want to leave Peshawar just now.'

She understood what he meant; she kissed him, and said with her lips brushing his ear with a delightfully sensual feel, 'Nobody mentioned you leaving Peshawar, love, so don't cross any bridges just yet.'

'No, of course.' He got to his feet and started dressing. Mary lay and watched him, watched his tall, slim, straight young body, tanned and muscular and hard with the so often rigorous life of the North-West Frontier. Her feelings about him were mixed. She loved him, and more than physically; but marriage, she believed, would not work. In the army young officers did not marry on the whole – and she was eight years older than he, which was quite a lot on the wrong side. Besides, she knew what the Ogilvie parents thought about her – not that it mattered all that much, but it wouldn't help James, and she wanted, badly, to be a help to James. So better let things drift and find their own course ... it was often the only sensible thing to do.

Dressing with more haste than precision, and unshaven, James Ogilvie took his leave, creeping out into the bright morning like a criminal, flitting like a gilded guilty shadow for cover, putting the discretion of distance between himself and Mary's bungalow before he could be seen. In leaving one widow's bed, he yet must not scandalize that other Widow reigning in solemn state half-way across the world.

CHAPTER TWO

JAMES OGILVIE'S return to cantonments in the comparative cool of early morning did not go unremarked, as he had known it would not. The men were about, and already a group of defaulters was marching and wheeling, with full packs and rifles, under the bullying voice of a drill-sergeant. Captain Ogilvie was given a smart eyes right, and a swinging salute from Sergeant MacBean, which, self-consciously enough, he returned. There was a glimmer of amusement in MacBean's face; the men would understand, and sympathize, with the fellow feeling of the rank-and-file for those about to land in trouble. Trouble rose in the form of Captain Andrew Black, watching from a window. Ogilvie was allowed to go peacefully to his quarters, where his servant was waiting. He washed, shaved and dressed in more appropriate uniform, and then went along to Mess for breakfast. Breakfast was a silent meal; in the 114th Highlanders, it was not expected that breakfasting officers should even wish one another a good morning. The *Times of India*, moat-like before the majority of the stolidly munching jaws, proclaimed this as an occasion of privileged solitude. Andrew Black, lifting his dark face for a moment from a plate of porridge, gave Ogilvie one sweeping look and that was all. Trouble would come in Black's own good time, and it did.

Breakfast over, Ogilvie was bidden to the adjutant's office. On the way he met Mr. Cunningham, Regimental Sergeant-Major, a large man whose chest had earned him the nickname of Bosom. The R.S.M.'s salute was as punctilious as ever, his friendliness as obvious, but there was a very slightly disappointed look in his eye.

'Good morning, Mr. Cunningham.'

'Good morning, Captain Ogilvie, sir. And my heartiest congratulations, sir.'

'Thank you, Sar'nt-Major ... but you've already congratulated me.'

'No, sir! Begging your pardon. I'm now congratulating you

upon being able to walk and talk. Sir! Rumour has it you enjoyed yourself last night. You'll not take it amiss from a man of my age, who has your welfare much at heart, if I say that the men talk amongst themselves, sir. It grieves me to hear it. If I were you, sir, I'd watch it in the future. Mind, *I* understand the occasion, sir, and I'm not a man to dislike drink, not at all. But India's India, Captain Ogilvie, and that needs to be borne in mind. Sir!'

Another quivering salute and Cunningham marched briskly away, a cane held at precisely the right angle beneath his left arm. Ogilvie felt a stab of anger, but not for long. The R.S.M. had perhaps overstepped the mark, but there had been a glimmer of humour in his eye, and he meant well. He was a good friend to a young officer, always had been. But his words hadn't exactly calmed the fears in James Ogilvie's mind as he neared Black's office.

The night before, during the conversation with his Divisional Commander, Black had been fairly forthcoming when Bloody Francis had said, 'That young Ogilvie – feller that's just got his captaincy. Good going, that – very early promotion. Course, it was largely on my recommendation,' he had added with a touch of mendacity, for the recommendation, which Fettleworth had merely endorsed and forwarded, had been Lord Dornoch's. 'How's he *really* shaping?'

Black had hesitated at first, but Fettleworth had gone on, 'You may answer honestly, my dear feller ... this is off the record. I know it's a question that should be addressed to his Colonel – but, well, man to man, what?'

'Yes, sir,' Black had answered, and then said, in that harsh voice that Ogilvie knew so well, and had so often suffered from, 'Fair enough, sir. No worse than any other young officer.' Young officers were never popular with Black.

'And no better?'

'In my opinion – no, sir.' He had then, in reply to a further question, indicated that he himself had not approved the recommendation.

'May one ask why, Captain Black?'

'I did not consider him ready for the responsibility of a company, sir. He is young – to some extent he is immature. His early days at a crammer's instead of the rough-and-tumble of a boarding school – it has left its mark. I do not say he is not conscientious. He is. He does his best. And he conducts himself well in action.'

'So I was told, after that damn march on Fort Gazai.'

'In my opinion, sir, a subaltern's future is formed in his early years – while he is still a subaltern. That is where the ground-work lies, where he learns his trade as a soldier, where he learns his profession as an officer, his potentialities as a leader of men. There is more in leadership than a mere ability to face the guns. If you cut short the early years, the apprenticeship as it were, you cut short the training – and you cut short the man in the years to come.'

'Quite – oh, quite. All this was naturally taken into due ac-count. I must say I agree to some extent with what you say. Sound commonsense, very sound. But there is absolutely no reason why a company commander, just as much as a subaltern, should not continue to acquire new and broadening experiences – no reason at all. Why, we all continue to learn – even I! Yes, even I,' Bloody Francis had repeated as if he had suddenly stumbled upon a great truth. 'And I have plans for that young man, Captain Black. . . .'

And now, this morning, the young man in question must needs be dealt with by his adjutant.

'A poor start, James,' Black said. 'A poor start, for a company commander. I was not aware that you had permission to sleep out of barracks.'

'I hadn't.'

'Precisely. And kindly remove that mutinous look from your face, James. You may have a Captain's rank, but I am still the adjutant.' Black was sitting with his elbows on the arms of his chair and was tapping his extended finger-tips together while he surveyed Ogilvie over the tops of them. If his long face had not held its customary bitter, satanic look, Ogilvie thought, he would have looked like a parson interviewing a sinning par-ishioner. 'I am waiting for your explanation, James.'

'I'm sorry. I have no excuse.'

'Oh, I'm well aware of that.' A thin smile appeared, but only momentarily. 'But you must have an *explanation*, must you not?'

Ogilvie turned his head a little, looking out of the adjutant's window across the dust and heat of the parade-ground. Far beyond that dusty expanse and the sweat it brought to drilling bodies rose the foothills of Himalaya with their promise of cool greenness lifting to the everlasting snows on the high peaks far behind. There was a remembrance of Scotland in the very thought of Himalaya; and there were times when James Ogilvie wished for nothing more than a sight of Speyside, and the grandeur of the Cairngorms, and the awesome silences of the Pass of Drumochter so often lost in the mist, with all the memories of clan battles of long ago, and the Tummel water at Pitlochry ... after nearly three years of service in India, Ogilvie found much to hate in the sub-continent – the poverty and the callousness, the cheapness in which human life, British as well as native when it came to action, was held, the dirt and squalor contrasting so vividly – and so viciously – with the extraordinary way of life of the ruling princes and their hangers-on ... all that, and the terrible oppressive heat, and the everlasting dust and grit that found its way into a man's clothing and his mouth, his food and his drink ...

He came back to the present to hear Black angrily repeating that he wished for an explanation. He gave the adjutant an answer – of a sort. He said quietly, 'I'm sorry, Andrew. I can give you no explanation.'

'Other than that you were drunk?'

Ogilvie shook his head. 'I was not drunk. I was not incapable.'

Once again, the thin sardonic smile. 'I would trust not – for the woman's sake.'

Ogilvie started, and flushed. 'What exactly do you mean by that, Andrew?'

'What I say.' Black leaned forward. 'James, you must do me the courtesy of crediting me with some powers of observation, and with some ability to assess a situation. You do not live in a vacuum, in Peshawar, believe me! Your association with that woman is well enough known—'

'That's no business of yours, Andrew, and you know it.'

'On the contrary, when your conduct vis-à-vis Mrs. Archdale impinges upon your duties and responsibilities to the regiment, it is very much my business – and my deep concern. I have much pride in the 114th Highlanders, James, as you should know. Now – are you going to tell me a direct lie – namely, that you were *not* in the woman's bed last night – or are you not? It is up to you.'

Ogilvie snapped, 'I have nothing more to say.'

'Very well,' Black said, shrugging. 'I have no option but to refer the matter to the Colonel.' He took a deep, angry breath and sent it hissing out through his nostrils, which had flared like those of a horse. 'For now, it shall be left to rest. I have other things to say to you. You already know, of course, that you are to take over B Company from Captain MacKinlay before he leaves for Quetta. You will begin at once to acquaint yourself with his duties, and I shall expect you to maintain your company at as high a degree of efficiency as has Captain MacKinlay. You have been long enough with the regiment, James, not to expect to plead inexperience. I shall accept no excuses for any lapses from our standards. Is that quite clear?'

'Quite clear, thank you, Andrew.'

'And you will gain nothing by your insolent bearing. Damn puppy!' Black's veneer, held together with difficulty, had now cracked wide open. 'If I'd had my way, you would not have been given a company for many a long year yet! Why, you're still wet behind the ears, man! And remember this: when you first joined the regiment, butter would not have melted in your mouth. You – you jumped at shadows, you rose from your chair like a jack-in-the-box when an officer senior to you walked into the Mess. You were a child – a child in a subaltern's uniform! I have watched you make some progress towards manhood – not enough, but some – I think I can say that to some extent I have been responsible for your getting a grip on yourself. There should be a little gratitude in you for that, rather than an overweening insolence and – and such a lack of a sense of responsibility!'

'I didn't intend to be insolent,' Ogilvie said, flushing. 'If I was, well, I'm sorry. I'm not ungrateful for anybody's help. It's just that . . . well, Andrew, again I'm sorry, but I'm not going to stand by and let you speak as you have done about Mrs. Archdale. That's all.'

'I see.' Black's eyes glittered; he was still furiously angry. 'If the woman should lose you your company even before you have assumed command, then perhaps you will think differently. Remember, you have yet to hear what Lord Dornoch has to say about your overnight absence. And let me tell you this, young man: Mrs. Archdale is fast acquiring a reputation, and an unsavoury one at that. Do not flatter yourself that you are the only man . . . no, no, you will hear me out . . . and surely to goodness you do not for one moment suppose that any widow who chooses to remain during her widowhood on an Indian military station, is anything but a blasted *whore*?'

Ogilvie jumped to his feet, his fists clenched. 'Andrew, you will withdraw that, and at once, d'you hear?' He stood over the adjutant, his face working.

Black said, 'I'll withdraw nothing. Sit down, Captain Ogilvie. Sit down! That is an order.'

'And I'm disobeying it. Withdraw what you said, and apologize.'

'I'll do no such—'

'Listen, Andrew.' Ogilvie's face was set like a rock, hard and determined. Over the years, that face had grown to resemble his father's; and Sir Iain Ogilvie was every inch the General Officer Commanding. There was something in the face now that scared Black, some inner force that overrode a basically weaker man. Ogilvie himself was not aware of this, but he saw that he was causing the adjutant to have second thoughts. 'We're alone in this office,' he said. 'If you don't withdraw, I intend to strike you. A military offence – oh, yes, I know that, Andrew! But I know something else as well, and it's this: the adjutant who gives a brother officer a personal insult to the point of being struck, does not commend himself to his seniors – and has a black mark against him when his name comes up for promotion. To be struck, Andrew, is to be hurt twice, for by God I'll hit you hard in your face and you won't be a pretty sight . . . and it's going to be said in higher circles that you failed in the first duty of an adjutant, which is to exercise a *tactful* discipline, and not to offer unwarrantable insults! Well, Andrew?'

Black licked at his lips and stared at Ogilvie. For almost a minute they held each other's gaze, and then Black looked away, the first to weaken. Ogilvie felt a tremendous relief; already he had regretted, at least to some extent, his impetuosity. To strike the adjutant would, of course, be the end of his career, whatever the provocation, but evidently he had succeeded in making Black believe he would take even this risk – and, if Black had not capitulated, honour would have demanded that indeed he did take it. But Black said, in a hoarse and strange-sounding voice, 'Very well. I withdraw.'

'And apologize?'

'And apologize.'

Ogilvie relaxed, and found himself shaking all over, a shake he did his best to hide. He said, 'Thank you, Andrew.'

'Now get out, you – you—' Words failed Black. Ogilvie obeyed the order. He went along to B Company's office, where Rob MacKinlay was battling with what seemed to be a vast amount of paperwork. He looked up when Ogilvie entered, and appeared glad of an excuse to sit back for a while. 'You have an air of strain, James,' he said, lifting an eyebrow. 'Rumour has it you've been with the adj. Has that caused the strain – or was it last night?'

'If you mean,' James Ogilvie said carefully, 'have I a hang-over, the answer's yes, a bloody awful one. Anything else?'

'Hold on to your shirt, old man. I'm not prying.'

'So it has spread. Well, Black did hint that you can't keep things secret in Peshawar.'

'Or anywhere else in British India, James my boy!' MacKinlay looked at him hard. 'Has Andrew been on that tack, then?'

Ogilvie nodded and slid onto an upright battalion chair. 'He wanted to know where I'd been – oh, not unnaturally, I agree! I didn't tell him – but he made guesses.'

'I see. And insinuations, I don't doubt. I hope you kept your temper, James.'

'I didn't.' Ogilvie told MacKinlay what had happened, and MacKinlay pursed his lips.

'Couldn't get off to a worse start as a company commander if you'd tried deliberately, James. My word! You threaten Black – and you win! He's not going to forgive you for that, you know!'

'He's never forgiven me for anything since the day I joined the regiment, Rob, you know that. He said he's helped me – but honestly, he never has. Except perhaps by opening my eyes to a few things, a few facts of British Indian life. Regimental life, that is.'

MacKinlay warned, 'Don't go sour because of a bad ad-jutant. I've told you that before, but from now on it's going to be even more important. When I go off to the Staff College, James, I don't want to feel the company's suffering.'

'I won't let that happen, Rob.'

'No, I know you won't, not deliberately. But you'll find that a company commander can be got at through his men, James. Black's not above mucking up a company's spirit so he can report adversely on its officers. It's been done before and it'll be done again, and Black's not the only one in the army to use dirty weapons, you know.'

Ogilvie sighed, listening to the drill sounds coming through from the parade, the tramp of heavy boots, the shouts of the N.C.O.s and then the sharp rattle of hooves as Captain Black rode past the window. He asked, 'Rob, what's up with Andrew Black? Why's *he* gone so sour?'

MacKinlay laughed. 'Sheer, vindictive jealousy, James. After all, he's not one of us and he knows it. Oh, he's a wealthy enough man, but it's all come from trade. You know that.'

'Yes, but is that enough to make him what he is?'

'I think so. I've told you before, James. He started off by feeling inferior, right from the day he joined us. Damn it all, we're a pretty blue-blooded lot in The Queen's Own Royal Strathspeys, you know!' He laughed, with a touch of self-deprecation for what he had said. 'It doesn't make us better soldiers, but there it is, it's a fact. Trade and landed gentry just don't mix, not even now. It started to work on Andrew's mind and the rest followed as the night the day – Andrew being the kind of man he is. He's been hitting back in his own way ever since.' MacKinlay pushed at a pile of papers. 'Well, I'll have to get on with this lot, James, or I'll never hand over. I don't want to leave you with a legacy of loose ends.' He paused, frowning. 'You've pulled something of a boner. That has to be admitted. But don't spend too much time worrying about Black. That way, he'll get you rattled. Just keep your eyes open, that's all.'

'I'm more worried about the Colonel than Black just at the moment, really.'

'Because you were absent last night?' MacKinlay ran a hand across his chin. 'Well, he's not going to like it, but you weren't required for duty. Dornoch's human enough. You'll have to watch it in future, though.' Then he added, 'Look, James. Are you sure you're not being just a little unwise? I think you know what I mean.'

'If I am,' Ogilvie answered briefly, 'it's my own funeral.'

'Oh, quite. But if I were you, old son, I just wouldn't let it get as far as a funeral. And now I've got work to do. Going to sit down and lend a hand, all in your own interest?'

Ogilvie shook his head. 'Can't, Rob. I have to watch Colour-Sar'nt Bruce put a squad of replacements through their paces.'

'Oh, all right. So long, James.'

Ogilvie left the company office and walked out onto the parade, settling his Wolseley helmet on his head as he came into the open. With his kilt swinging the tartan of the Royal Strathspey around his sunburned knees he marched across the wide space, returning salutes as groups of men were brought to attention on his approach, heading for a corner around the angle of the sergeants' mess where the casualty replacements, fresh from home, were being bawled at by Colour-Sergeant Bruce, a raw-boned Highland Scot from the Monadhliath Mountains. As he went he found his thoughts going back to Mary Archdale, and from her to Andrew Black. In any regiment, the adjutant was always a man of influence and power beyond his actual rank. In the case of Black, this was perhaps more so than would normally be the fact. That bitter, satanic man seemed even to have some curious ability to make the Colonel see things his way. Of course, he was efficient, and tireless in the performance of his duties; even after a night's heavy whisky drinking – a weakness of Black's – he was as smart, as punctilious, on parade as might be any soldiering Plymouth Brother or Strict Baptist, with nothing except his bloodshot eyes and a pallor beneath the tan of his face to give away the previous night's excesses. Had he not been efficient, he would not have remained so long as adjutant of the 114th, for he was known as a bully and a man prone to give vent to an evil temper. From a consideration of Captain Andrew Black, Ogilvie's thoughts went by natural process to the conversation Mary had overheard the night before between Black and Lieutenant-General Fettleworth; and he wondered what the Divisional Commander could possibly have in his mind as regards a newly-appointed Captain of infantry.

That was something he would have to wait upon; and in the meantime he would need to face his Colonel.

Lord Dornoch had been about to send for Ogilvie when a runner came in from Division, bringing a message that the Colonel of the 114th Highlanders was required to report forthwith to General Fettleworth, along with all other battalion commanders and brigadiers. Dornoch looked up at Black. 'What does this mean, I wonder?'

Black shrugged.

'I was speaking to the General last night, Andrew. There was no hint of any conference.' Dornoch drummed with his finger-tips on his desk. 'What's in the wind this time? The Waziris? There's been some talk of possible trouble from that direction.'

'It could be that, Colonel.'

Dornoch stood up and reached for his helmet. 'Have my horse brought round, if you please, Andrew. Ogilvie'll have to wait.' He paused, frowning. 'Couldn't you have dealt with that, Andrew? You've said he wasn't required for duty.'

'That is true, Colonel, but—'

'And if he'd asked permission it would have been granted. It's a somewhat technical offence, you know.'

'I have told you, Colonel, he was insolent. I think it import-ant he should not be allowed to get above himself. And it is a thoroughly bad example to the men, in a freshly-appointed company commander, Colonel.'

'The men should have no idea whether or not he had been granted leave for the night. I have a feeling you overstate the crime, Andrew.'

'Other junior officers will know, Colonel, and in a regiment—'

'I know all about the regiment, thank you, Andrew,' Lord Dornoch cut in briskly. 'I shall deal with this, of course, now you've reported it, but not yet.' He gave a nod of dismissal; Andrew Black's hand shot to the salute and he about-turned smartly and went out. Dornoch, frowning still, listened to the adjutant's footsteps clattering down the corridor. A few minutes later he heard the sound of his horse, and he went outside into the brilliant sun, taking over the mount from an orderly. He walked his horse across the parade, and out past the quarter-guard. Once on less hard-trodden ground, he broke into a canter, welcoming the feel of the wind in his face, the wind of his speed, though in all conscience it was a hot and far from refreshing wind. He was vaguely troubled by the sudden summons to Division. On the North-West Frontier, where the Pax Britannica was always a brittle thing, the garrison was almost continually geared for combat and men had much more of an eye to their weapons than had the troops in any other area of the Empire. Here in Peshawar, last garrison on the route to the terrible Khyber Pass and the rugged Afghan hills, the British Army was perched on the very brink of civilization, was the guardian of the ultimate, garrison of the most extreme point of the great Empire that stretched from the walls and lawns of Windsor Castle to embrace and rule a quarter of the world's population. The men, the commanders, carried a tremendous responsibility, and the Queen's Own Royal Strathspeys had done their share as much as had the English regiments, and had suffered grievous losses over the years in dead and wounded. It was this that troubled Dornoch, who was at heart a clansman, a Highlander from a long line of nobility, men who had been the fathers of their people. Some good, and some bad of course, but most of them well aware of the strong paternal responsibility. Each time a man fell to the native bullets, Dornoch felt it keenly and personally. The 114th were very much a family regiment, and almost totally recruited from around the depot at Invermore, though their officers came to some extent from a wider field – Andrew Black, for instance, though a Scot, had the blood of the Bessemer steel family, also, and had lived his life in Birmingham. Because of this family element Dornoch knew his men with a fair degree of intimacy. Many of them were the sons of men who worked on his own estates on Speyside, or of his own tenant farmers. In the past months of Indian service he had had many difficult letters to write to wives and mothers, and would have as many painful visits to make when at last the 114th Highlanders detrained at Invermore, and marched back once again into barracks at the depot, with himself, God willing, still riding at their head behind the battalion's pipes and drums. But he was a soldier, and they were soldiers, and their trade was war, and trade they must. It was, perhaps, simply that after two-and-a-half largely action-filled years in India, after half a lifetime of service in other spheres, and earlier periods here on the Frontier as well, Dornoch no longer needed to look in the glass to recognize in himself the signs of age ...

Riding past the General's guard at H.Q., Dornoch saw Colonel Hennessey of the Connaught Rangers dismounting ahead of him and handing over his horse to an orderly. Other senior officers were present as well – several Colonels, and Brigadier-General Preston who had commanded the column marching from Gilghit to join Fettleworth's advance from Peshawar upon the rebels outside Fort Gazai. Since then, to General Fettleworth's great annoyance, Preston had been appointed on the C.-in-C.'s recommendation to command the brigade composed of the 114th, the Connaught Rangers and a native regiment of the Indian Army. Catching Preston's eye, Dornoch gave a punctilious salute, which was somewhat sketchily returned by the Brigadier-General. Preston, who had an impish face and a friendly smile, was in fact dressed not in uniform but for polo.

He said, 'Hullo there, Dornoch. I suppose you're wondering what Bloody Francis has in store for us this time?'

'Yes, sir,' Dornoch answered, a shade formally. He liked and admired Preston, but was not himself the sort of man who would speak disrespectfully of his commander to anyone junior.

Preston laughed and said, 'Frankly, so am I. He's spoiled my morning and damned if I won't tell him so to his face!' He took off his hat, a floppy affair of a green material that looked incongruous in such surroundings as Divisional H.Q., and fanned his face. 'Well, we'll soon know the worst, no doubt.'

'Yes, sir,' Dornoch said again. He nodded at some of his brother Colonels. A moment later an A.D.C., very crisply turned out, very smart with the gilded tassels of his appointment, emerged, glanced with some distaste at Preston's clothing, and said loudly, 'Gentlemen, the General's compliments. He is waiting for you.'

'The devil he is,' Preston murmured. 'He usually keeps *us* waiting. This must be important!'

They went in, following the immaculate A.D.C. along a corridor paved with cool tiles, its walls hung with tapestries. They entered a room at the end, a large room with tall windows looking onto a cool, shady courtyard where a fountain played beneath the overhanging trees white with the terrible gritty dust of India. Birdsong came through, and beyond the fountain three young children played under the care of an *amah* dressed in flowing white. Preston whispered, 'Bloody Francis's long-suffering grandchildren, Dornoch.'

'I didn't know he had any.'

'No more did I till a few days ago. His daughter's staying with him, God help her. Tell you what—' Preston broke off as the General, who had been seated behind a trestle table on the dais at the end of the room, rose to his feet, short and stubby and paunchy, with a large turnip-shaped gold watch held ostentatiously in one hand.

'You have kept me waiting, gentlemen.' Sharp eyes roamed his audience. 'Brigadier-General Preston?'

'Sir?' Preston stood up.

'Kindly sit down at once, then we shall not be so aware of your dress, which I consider highly inappropriate to the occasion. Before you leave, you will give me an explanation of why you thought fit to attend upon me dressed for a game.'

'I—'

'Afterwards, afterwards!' Fettleworth lifted his head and addressed his next remarks more generally. 'Gentlemen, we are all soldiers, sent here to preserve the Queen's peace, not to dilly-dally on the field of sport. The way we dress is important, if we are to impress the enemy with our intentions and our serious purpose – as I'm glad to note that all the rest of you have realized. I've never heard of such a thing in all my life.' Fettleworth said pompously, raising and lowering his body on his heels as if to give himself the intermittent advantage of greater height. 'But no more of this.' Importantly, he paused. 'Gentlemen. You will all be aware that for some weeks past there has been some indication of restiveness among the Waziris. No more than this – until the early hours of this morning, when a man, a native, was apprehended in an attempt to break into my headquarters. It appears he was after information – that he was trying to steal copies of my confidential assessment of the Frontier situation and of my plans to deal with any emergencies. Yes, Brigadier?'

Once again displaying his inelegance, Preston had stood up. 'He admitted this under questioning, sir? Was he a Waziri?'

'Yes, he was a Waziri. Why d'you ask?'

'Because in my experience a Waziri never talks, sir. Never! Whatever else they may be, they are fanatically loyal to their leaders.'

Fettleworth snapped, 'I never *said* he talked.'

'Then, sir, how do you know what he was after? Or am I wrong in thinking that you said the man had been apprehended in an *attempt to break into* your headquarters?'

'You are impertinent, Brigadier-General Preston—'

'I'm sorry, sir.' Preston sat down again.

Fettleworth, red in the face, glared at him and then, with an obvious effort, proceeded. 'Very well. The man was caught in – in the act. He was rifling my desk. I need hardly say that such a thing will *not* occur again. Of course, the man was questioned, but he has said nothing. The questioning will continue – my Political Officers are currently carrying out my orders to this effect. We must not expect a great deal of help. It is true that the Waziris do not talk easily. Therefore, we must now act in a precautionary manner, to safeguard our position along the Frontier, gentlemen. For, taking last night's events in conjunction with the many rumours that have been filtering through, it is my opinion that the Waziris may intend to rise. I say *may*. But if they do, God alone knows what other tribes and disaffected elements they will carry with them! Cornforth-Jarvis, the map.'

The A.D.C. stepped forward, bearing a rolled-up map. He hung this over a blackboard set upon an easel to the General's right, and unrolled it. Fettleworth took up a pointer and laid its end on the map. He laid it upon the mountains of Waziristan, south-west of Peshawar, a territory that ran contiguously with the Afghan border from Thal southwards to the Gomal Pass from Largha Sherani into Dera Ismail Khan. He said, 'Terrible country, gentlemen, treacherous country for men to fight in. In that territory, according to Lord Roberts's estimate, are no less than forty thousand wild tribesmen – warriors to a man! Other estimates put their strength higher – up to fifty thousand and possibly more. And think – think of what other strength might join a rising that appeared to have any hope of success!' The pointer lifted and fell, dotting its way north along the frontier with Afghanistan. 'Kurram, Tirah, the Mohmands, Bajaur, the Shinwaris, Kohistan, Chitral. An endless list.' As though contemplating infinity, Fettleworth remained staring for some moments at the map, pointer in hand, before swinging round to face his audience again. 'If the worst happened, gentlemen, the rivers would run with blood, the North-West Frontier would vanish, the hordes would sweep through the passes from Afghanistan, we would be in danger of submersion beneath a storming tide of Asians . . .' He stopped abruptly, feeling, perhaps, that he might be overdoing it a little, though Dornoch knew well enough that the element of exaggeration was not very great. To some extent Fettleworth might be allowing himself to be panicked by the action of a thief, but so easily, so very easily, could north-west India become a bloodbath. One error of judgment, of handling . . . they were all sitting on the edge of a volcano, every moment they spent in India was heavy with threat and potential danger. The smallest sign must never be ignored – India's history taught that. The tribes sat far from easily under the benevolent yoke of the Raj. 'From the first probe by the enemy, gentlemen, the whole Peshawar garrison would be instantly committed. In current conditions it would be the gravest mistake to regard any thrust, however small, as a mere border incident, a raid. Our reaction must be instantaneous and overwhelming. We shall need the immediate support of Northern Command at Murree and I intend to inform the Commander-in-Chief of this at once. I also think it likely that reinforcements from Ootacamund would be needed fairly early.' There was another pause, while Fettleworth moved back towards the trestle table and Captain Cornforth-Jarvis obediently rolled up the map on the General's abrupt nod. 'Now, gentlemen. You will at once prepare your commands, your brigades and your battalions, for possible action at any given moment. We shall not be caught napping. No leave off the station will be granted from now on until further orders, and any officers or men presently away are to be recalled immediately. Your quarter-guards are to be doubled, all sentries, wherever they are posted, are to be warned to be fully alert at all times. Any case of dereliction of duty, of any lack of this alertness, will be reported to me and will be dealt with most severely – *most* severely! You will all see to it that your weapons and ammunition supplies are checked and brought up to the full authorization – likewise, of course, your provisions for a march. Bear in mind that we may have to sustain ourselves in the field for a considerable time, with possibly very extended lines of communication. Watch your sick lists, gentlemen. Your medical officers are to furnish detailed reports daily for transmission to this headquarters, and the smallest signs of any epidemics are to be treated with the gravest concern and nipped smartly in the bud. Skrimshanking will be severely punished – I will tolerate no malingerers. Training programmes are to be stepped up and the men given every opportunity for rifle practice. When your commands are ready, gentlemen, ready in all respects for war, you will report accordingly – and you will be expected to stand by your reports. No excuse will be accepted for any shortcomings after that. Thank you, gentlemen. That is all. You may go about your duties. Lord Dornoch, you will remain behind.'

As the various officers departed amid a low buzz of conversation, Dornoch remained seated. So, alongside him, did Preston. Fettleworth busied himself with the A.D.C. until the others had gone, then he looked up and beckoned to Dornoch. 'Come to my study, if you please, Colonel,' he said, and moved off the dais towards the door.

Preston, standing for the third time, brought himself to his General's attention. 'You wished for an explanation, sir,' he began. 'I—'

'Yes, yes. Later. When I have finished with Lord Dornoch, Brigadier.'

'Sir, I have a brigade to administer and prepare for active service—'

'Dress is also a part of war, Brigadier,' Fettleworth said evenly. 'You must wait until I have time to attend to you,' and he moved away with his head in the air, followed by Lord Dornoch. He was being stupidly childish, Dornoch thought irritably, and he wondered at Preston's forbearance; but by now the senior officers had grown accustomed to Fettleworth, and let his insults flow over them more or less unheedingly, for he had his good points and in all conscience he was little worse than many another old-time General Officer. He had had a distinguished past, and was as brave as a lion in battle. One could forgive a little pompous assininity – unless and until stupidity increased the casualty lists, and it was there that Dornoch, whose regiment had suffered badly a year ago because of Fettleworth's insane dislike of using his artillery, parted company with his own forbearance. Reaching his study, Fettleworth told Dornoch to sit. A native servant appeared, and stood expectant of orders. Fettleworth asked, '*Chota peg*, Colonel?'

'Thank you – no, sir.'

Fettleworth grunted. 'Oh – very well. You won't mind if I do. Thirsty work – these conferences. I'm not much of a man for spouting, y'know, Dornoch. Prefer to get at those black blighters in battle – one, two, one-two!' He made a couple of thrusts as if with sword in hand, then nodded at the servant, who went out of the room silently, bowing his way out backwards as if leaving the presence of the Queen-Empress herself. General Fettleworth went across to a window, one that, like the conference chamber, looked out onto the courtyard. His grandchildren had gone by this time and the place was empty but for an ancient, wizened gardener bent over some plants in a rockery, and silent but for the slight, cooling sound of the fountain. The General stood with his hands clasped tightly behind his thick, plump back, his khaki tunic showing sweat-stains around the underarms. He turned when the native servant glided back and handed him the whisky on a silver salver. Fettleworth took

27

the glass in silence, nodded a dismissal, and walked across the dark room – the furniture was that of an English study, chiefly old oak, and the courtyard trees gave plenty of welcome shade – and stood looking down at Lord Dornoch.

'Ogilvie,' he said abruptly. 'I want to talk to you about Ogilvie.'

Dornoch sad, 'Yes, sir?' and thought, not for the first time, that everyone seemed to want to talk to him about young Ogilvie – for he was assuming, and rightly, that it was the son and not the father who was to be the subject of Fettleworth's interest.

'Time he had his horizons widened, don't you think?'

'Widened, sir? He's seen plenty of action, more than most, in the time we've been out here.'

'Action, yes. That's just what I'm coming to. He has yet to learn that the army isn't all action – action of a physical, fighting kind, that is. *Overt* action – you'll understand, Dornoch – death and glory. Military bands in support. Heroics, and tumultuous welcomes when marching back to cantonments. D'you follow?'

'Not entirely, sir. Oh, I take your point that no officer or man should think of the service entirely as – as a hero's return! But could you be more explicit, General?'

'Yes.' Fettleworth turned away, rasping at his cheek with a pudgy hand, and took a few turns up and down the room while Dornoch watched him in silence and with some apprehension. He himself had plotted James Ogilvie's career for a few years ahead, at any rate in so far as it lay within his limited scope to do so. Ogilvie was going to make a first-class fighting soldier and Dornoch was not keen to have him side-tracked, which was what he now suspected Fettleworth of organizing. Suddenly, the General halted in front of him. 'There are things,' he said, 'that I need to know, Dornoch. Vital things.'

'About Ogilvie?'

'No! About the Waziris.'

Dornoch started. 'Do you mean spying, sir?'

'Well, I don't like the word. We British, Dornoch – we don't *spy*. We – er – use Political Officers, but—'

'But Ogilvie is not attached to the Political Department, General, and would not wish to be.'

'It's not what he wants that matters,' Fettleworth said tartly, 'but what the Queen's service requires of him. An attachment –

28

a *temporary* attachment – could be arranged with the greatest of ease. It would be most excellent experience for him.'

'I think he needs other experience than that. He has done well. He needs the fulfilment of his efforts – he needs his company. I consider him well fitted for it – I would not have recommended him for promotion otherwise—'

'Of course, of course—'

'—and moreover, I need him as a company commander in the room of Captain MacKinlay. This is doubly important if we are to move into action. Ogilvie has the ability to lead men in greater measure than any of my other younger officers, General.'

'But not more than Captain MacKinlay, one would presume?'

'No.' Dornoch paused, looking carefully at the Divisional Commander. 'Sir, may I ask you to come to the point of your proposal?'

'You may, Colonel. I propose to delay MacKinlay's appointment to Quetta for the time being, and to ask you to be good enough to give him back his company. And to release Captain Ogilvie for formal attachment to the Staff for secondment to the Political Department – on a purely temporary basis.'

Dornoch's face stiffened. 'I see, sir. To be used in the capacity of a spy?'

Fettleworth snapped, 'I've told you, I don't like that word! To be used to obtain certain information from the tribes. I see from his records that he is fluent in the dialect – this is a qualification, though it may not be used in a direct sense. I shall require him to infiltrate the enemy villages, to infiltrate the enemy's confidence, and report back to my headquarters. You understand, Colonel?'

'And if I refuse, sir, as I think I am entitled to do in all the circumstances?'

'It would be unlike you to refuse to obey an order, Lord Dornoch.'

'This is an order, sir?'

'Indeed it is, indeed it is!'

'In that case, of course, there is nothing more for me to say.' Dornoch stood up, his face hard. 'I shall inform Captain Ogilvie of your wishes as soon as I return to my regiment. Is there anything else you require of me, General?'

'No, that's all,' Fettleworth said, rubbing his hands briskly together. 'Ogilvie's detailed orders will be notified within the next day or so.'

'Then good-day to you, sir!'

'And to you, sir!' Fettleworth seemed in a high good humour, Dornoch thought as he left the headquarters building and mounted his horse. He usually was, when he had won a point; but Dornoch had a nagging feeling there was more behind it this time. Fettleworth's total disregard of his, Dornoch's, own recommendations had gone beyond even his normal mule-like obstinacy. He had clearly been quite determined to hook Ogilvie out of the regiment and send him on this dangerous mission – this highly dangerous mission of, to say the least – in Dornoch's opinion – doubtful practical value. The Waziris were up to all the tricks of the trade and if Fettleworth's idea was to send Ogilvie in dressed up as some mendicant native selling beads or whatever, that young man's goose was well and truly cooked from the start. It was much too naïve – if that *was* his idea. Possibly it was not, possibly he had something else up his sleeve, but if so Dornoch couldn't fathom it out. The trouble with Fettleworth was his virtual submersion in the past, in all the old outworn ideas. He had failed totally to move with the times – as witness that curious dislike of artillery. About sixty years before, some other pot-bellied General whose name had been lost in the mists of the years had similarly disdained artillery, and, in his case, with success. Bloody Francis still went along with that. And the same in other things. Once, British officers had indeed infiltrated enemy encampments dressed as beggars or holy men and had got away with it – possibly because they had taken a childish delight in dressing up, and playing games, a glorious extension of nursery charades, so they had managed to be convincing! Even the Waziris were a little too sophisticated to be taken in by those antics any more, surely?

What was behind it?

Fettleworth had a devious mind. Had Preston given the order, Dornoch would still most likely have disagreed with it, but at least he would never have suspected the motives. But with Fettleworth . . . and all at once Dornoch remembered, and went cold at the very thought, that James Ogilvie had been one of a very small number of officers who had known – and none better than he, since he had been the prime mover in the affair –

that Lieutenant-General Fettleworth had been in a fair way to losing Fort Gazai and the remnants of its garrison until the moment that the despised artillery had so surprisingly, and so shatteringly, opened from the flank and sent the native hordes flying in total disorder. As surprised as anyone else, Fettleworth had been sufficiently all there to turn the botched orders to good account, and had smugly accepted the lavished praise and honours as his due for a notable victory. But since then – this was no more than rumour, and quite possibly malicious rumour but at the same time entirely believable – Bloody Francis had harboured certain antagonisms against those officers who had known the truth. Rumour or not, there must always have been a nagging worry at the back of his mind that, one day, someone might let something slip. And it was a fact that his then Chief of Staff, Brigadier-General Forrestier, had since been promoted out of harm's way – on Fettleworth's glowing recommendation; *he* would keep his mouth well shut! Dornoch recoiled from the conclusion that his thoughts led to. No British General, surely, would sink so low! No ... it was impossible, not to be thought of, a most scandalous slander on a brave officer. Nevertheless, he could not stop himself facing the undoubted fact that James Ogilvie was the one officer who, in a sense, was the living *proof* of Fettleworth's mendacity, if ever he cared to speak. He would not speak, of course; but Fettleworth could not be sure of this.

His mind in a turmoil, Lord Dornoch cantered back to barracks. On arrival, he sent first of all for Captain Black; the arrangements for B Company had now to be reversed, and, before calling a meeting of his officers to give his orders for the action preparations, the Colonel wished to settle this rather alarming affair of Ogilvie.

There being no reason why he should not, he informed the adjutant of all that Fettleworth had said, though naturally voiced none of his own suspicions at the hidden motives that might exist. He asked, 'What's your opinion, Andrew?'

'I'll be glad enough to keep MacKinlay in B Company,' Black said at once.

'I've nothing against MacKinlay whatever, though he's going to be disappointed about Quetta. That, however, wasn't quite what I asked you, Andrew.' He paused. 'Tell me frankly – you've never got along with Ogilvie, have you?'

'I have not, Colonel.' Black's long, sallow face contrived to look at the same time disapproving and forgiving; also judicial. 'Oh, I'll not disguise that I'll not miss him! I wish to be perfectly open about this, perfectly sincere, as it is my duty to be. He and I have not seen eye to eye – this has to be confessed, and I'll not argue that some of the fault may have been mine. All this, however, I am able to set aside. And even when I have set it aside, I am bound to say . . . yes, I agree with the General. The experience, the very different experience, would be invaluable to any young officer. Invaluable. The Political Department is one that can lead to promotion for those lucky enough to be attached to it, Colonel.'

'Yes, true. I don't know about lucky, though. They've always struck me as a shifty lot, but I suppose that's their job, after all.' Dornoch sighed, and rubbed hard at his eyes, trying to dislodge the dust. 'Well, you'd better make your arrangements accordingly. I'll see MacKinlay later. Then I'll want to see all officers and senior N.C.O.s. In the meantime, you'd better send Ogilvie along, Andrew.'

'Very good, Colonel.' The adjutant withdrew. Dornoch sat on behind his desk, reflecting that there was no reassurance in the fact that one other person who seemed to have, or fancied he had, cause to dislike James Ogilvie had not only been in favour of that young man's new assignment but had – for him – leaned over backwards to be polite and fair and frankly honest about his dislike . . . almost disarmingly so! And he remembered, with more gnawing anxiety, that at the party last night in the Mess he had seen Andrew Black in some apparently earnest discussion with Bloody Francis.

Dornoch's anxious reverie was interrupted by Ogilvie himself. Bidden to enter, Ogilvie crashed to attention and gave a swinging salute. 'You sent for me, Colonel?'

'Yes, James.' He motioned Ogilvie to a chair. "Sit down." Too late, Dornoch remembered that a rebuke was to precede the intimation of new orders. Rebukes were best given with the victim standing at attention, but no matter now. In the circumstances as Dornoch saw them, the rebuke would be purely perfunctory. 'James, the adjutant reports that you slept out of cantonments without permission last night. Do you dispute this?'

'No, Colonel.'

'H'm. What have you to say?'

'I'm sorry, Colonel. It will not occur again. Next time, I shall ask permission.'

There was a glint of humour in the Colonel's eye. 'With no assurance that it will be granted. James, had you been required for duty last night, even unexpectedly, I would have had to take a very different view, as well you know.'

'Yes, Colonel.'

'I think you have been lucky. Don't abuse your luck, James. Now, on your apology and your assurances for the future, I'll say no more. Except this: watch your tongue, especially with Captain Black. D'you understand me?'

'Yes, Colonel.'

'All right, then. Now I've something else to say.' He paused, leaning across his desk. 'I've been talking to the General about you – or rather, he talked to me about you. I'm sorry, James, but for the time being you're not getting your company.'

'Not—?'

'Now, don't jump to conclusions. You'll get your company later on, there's no aspersions being cast at you, James, none at all. But you have another job to do first, on the General's direct order. You're to be seconded via the Staff to the Political Department.' With many inward misgivings he told Ogilvie the facts as known to him, and with more misgiving saw that Ogilvie, in spite of an obviously keen disappointment that he was not yet to command a company on active service, was intrigued by the idea of the proposed mission. There had been plenty of lesser-scale action and many, many patrols since Fort Gazai and Dornoch supposed, with the hindsight of middle age, that to a young man eager for variety even fighting could in the end become boring. . . .

There was, however, one hope left. He, Ogilvie's Colonel, could not prevent what he considered this miscarriage of an appointment, this ridiculous interruption of a regimental officer's career – and Fettleworth must have plenty of young men in the Political Department who could do the job as well if not better, which was yet another disturbing thought – but there was someone who, if he should happen to see things in the same light, most certainly could: Ogilvie's father. Fettleworth's plans would need to be submitted to the General Officer Commanding in Murree – this indeed was why there was to be a delay in the notification of detailed orders – and Lieutenant-General Sir Iain Ogilvie, himself a former Colonel of the 114th Highlanders, might well nip them smartly in the bud.

33

CHAPTER THREE

A HUNDRED miles away in Murree, headquarters of half of the sub-continent's military forces, the General Officer Commanding, Northern Army Command, read next day the dispatch from the Commander of the First Division in Peshawar. He noted with approval that Lieutenant-General Fettleworth was reacting with commendable promptness to the early rumblings from Waziristan, rumbles whose echoes had also reached Murree and had in fact formed the subject of a confidential memo from Army Command to all divisions in the area.

Sir Iain Ogilvie was frankly as worried as Fettleworth as to the implications of the rumours, and of the reports from the Political Officers attached to his headquarters; and though he paid little attention himself to the activities of the thief who had penetrated Fettleworth's defences, giving the affair its due weight in his mind, he could well understand that in the circumstances Fettleworth should take the matter much to heart and react accordingly. After all, it was Fettleworth who had been caught with his trousers down – not him. And the thief *could* well have been after secret information as Fettleworth had suggested.

Nevertheless, Sir Iain chuckled as he read the dispatch.

'Poor old Fettleworth,' he observed to his Chief of Staff. 'Dammit, he's not going to like being broken into! His office'll be submerged in bumph from Calcutta after this – memo after memo from the damn Civilians about locking the back door after the cat's been put out for the night. In fact I'll be obliged myself to give him a formal warning about his sentries.' He looked up. 'See to that, Leith, if you please.'

'Very good, sir.'

'Tactfully. You know what Fettleworth is. I have to keep reminding myself he's the same rank as myself now.' His gaze went down again to the dispatch, reading on. Then he said, 'Well, I'll be damned!'

'Sir?'

'He means to repay the Waziris in their own coin, Leith. Send in a spy – a thief to steal men's thoughts!'

'It's been done before, sir.'

'I know, I know, I'm not saying it isn't necessary, but I detest the idea behind that sort of thing. Not straight-forward, not British, Leith.'

'No, sir, I agree, but war is war.'

Sir Iain rustled irritably. 'I know that too, you fool. Dammit, man, you're full of platitudes this morning!' He jabbed at Fettleworth's dispatch. 'Point is, he wants to send my son in as his damned spy!'

Leith was slightly jolted. 'Really, sir?'

'That's what he says.'

'Well, sir. It's all new experience, and valuable experience too, for a young officer. There's no way better of getting to know the native mind—'

'Certainly – if you don't die first.' Having said that, Sir Iain instantly regretted it. He would much have liked to tell Fettleworth to find someone else to do his dirty work and leave his son to get on with soldiering; now, never mind all the other considerations that would be involved, he could scarcely do that. In the eyes of his Chief of Staff, any interference on his part with a subordinate commander's decision would smack distinctly of an attempt to keep his own flesh and blood out of harm's way. And such news would travel fast in India. The Army Commander scowled and snapped irritably, 'My dear Leith, the next Chief of Staff I have is going to be a yes man. They're much more comfortable to live with.'

It was a highly personal matter, so, before giving final approval to Fettleworth's plans, Sir Iain took the step, unusual for him, of talking it over with his wife after luncheon. He placed the whole thing before her, calmly and unemotionally, and asked for her comments.

Lady Ogilvie felt an icy grip around her heart; her husband's action was so uncharacteristic that the mere fact of his confiding in her was thoroughly alarming. When James had been sent into action before, nothing specific had ever been so much as mentioned to her. But she fought to keep her anxiety under control and said. 'Tell me one thing, Iain. Are you saying that you could stop this?'

'Dammit, I'm the G.O.C., am I not? Of course I could!'

'But it wouldn't be a good thing.'

'It would be a damn bad thing.' Not for the first time, Sir Iain was grateful that Fiona was a soldier's daughter as well as a soldier's wife. She 'understood' in a very positive sense; but at the same time Sir Iain himself was wise enough to realize that his wife's third position – that of being a soldier's mother – was perhaps the hardest of all and certainly, in this case, the most relevant. In a way he was being unfair, he knew, in asking her to share the burden of decision, if there was any decision to be made in so delicate a matter, but he felt instinctively that she would prefer to know the facts on this occasion, so that, whatever the outcome, they as husband and wife, they as parents, would have given joint thought to what was really best for the boy – and even as he thought that, Ogilvie pulled himself up sharp. Why, really that was his answer: James was no longer a *boy*. He was a man, a full-blown Captain in a Highland regiment – the best of Highland regiments and one that had been commanded already by two generations of Ogilvies. He could make his own decisions, and probably had. Sir Iain repeated, 'A bad thing, Fiona. But on the other hand, if you felt...'

'Felt what?'

Ogilvie looked down at his wife, lying on a long couch behind the shutters. Those shutters let in just a little of the afternoon sun, and the beams, falling irregularly on her cheek, showed her suddenly as she had looked when they had married, so many years ago. Young and defenceless, and a little apprehensive of her future, for in her father's house she had led a fairly sheltered life, whilst the Ogilvies, whose clan she had now joined, were a rumbustious, full-blooded lot not much given to doing things by halves; and he had seen the apprehensive look again from time to time when she had held the young James, a baby in her arms, as though her mind was projecting for him through troubled years ahead. Possibly it was just a trick of the light today, but possibly – indeed almost certainly – it was more than that.

Sir Iain cleared his throat gruffly and said, 'I dare say I'm making a mountain out of a molehill, but if you really feel I should, I'll find a way of countermanding Fettleworth's order. I admit I'd rather see James as a regimental soldier... taking his chance in open combat in the field.'

'How dangerous is this mission going to be?' she asked directly, watching his face.

36

He shrugged; his tunic was open at the neck, and she saw the sag of his throat, the wrinkled flesh of many chins. Iain was no longer a young man, she thought sadly; he would not have much longer to go in the service, just a handful of years to close a chapter, and a very honourable one. He was, she knew, devoted in his soldierly, undemonstrative way to his son, and the last ambition left to him now was to see his son command the family regiment as a lieutenant-colonel; but even so, he must not be allowed to close his chapter of service with any suspicions of string-pulling or favours attaching to his name. It would be so obvious – so very much too obvious! He must know that in his heart.

He answered her question carefully. 'It would depend largely upon James himself, Fiona. It would depend upon how convincing he could make himself, and on his ability to assess situations as they arose and decide when the moment had come for him to withdraw in the knowledge that his usefulness was coming to an end. It would also depend on luck. I won't disguise that it could be extremely dangerous, but on the other hand, it is an accepted practice of war on the North-West Frontier. That is to say – it has been done many times before. Successfully.'

'Always successfully?'

'No, Fiona. Not always.'

'And when it is not?'

He spread his hands, eloquent in his silence. She looked away; it had been a stupid question. She asked another: 'How do you assess the chances, Iain?'

'Fifty-fifty. That's all I can say. Well, Fiona? I'm not asking you for a decision, you know. Only an opinion. The decision will be mine entirely.'

She closed her eyes against the shutter-filtered sunlight, the hard sunlight of a savage land, an unfeeling land, even a sadistic one. For what seemed an age, she thought while her husband waited patiently – which in itself was unusual for that impatient man. But she already knew what she must say; command decisions must not be interfered with on personal grounds – never! She believed that in fact Iain's mind was already made up, and she would not weaken his resolve. Opening her eyes at last, and sitting up, she said, 'It must be left as it is, Iain. If we were to interfere . . . we might very well regret it. Don't you see that?'

He did, and he nodded. Like many a Highland man or woman, Fiona Ogilvie had a fairly strong belief in fate. If harm should come, as come it always might, to James in the field, then she would blame herself if that harm should come as a result of any interference with what had been decided for him. Sir Iain took a deep breath and said, 'Very well, Fiona, I'll formally approve Fettleworth's plans. And I feel sure it'll all turn out for the best. Have no worries, my dear.'

She said, almost involuntarily, 'I do think it might be better for him in many ways, to be away from Peshawar.'

Their eyes met, and Sir Iain nodded again, and they knew that each of them was thinking of Mary Archdale. The G.O.C. left his wife and went back to his duties, working through the hot afternoon when he should have been taking his siesta, and next day confirmation of James Ogilvie's temporary posting reached Lord Dornoch. When he read this Dornoch shook his head fretfully, still not liking the business. Naturally enough, he appreciated the enormous difficulty of a serving father, but he found it ironic and sad that that father should be the third in a chain of men who, for one reason or another, desired James Ogilvie's departure from Peshawar. For Dornoch, of course, was by no means unaware of the situation in regard to Tom Archdale's widow.

Feeling that perhaps he should have taken decisive, if interfering, action much earlier in that direction, he sent for Captain Ogilvie with a heavy heart.

'I'll give you the background first, Ogilvie,' the Political Officer said later that day. 'It's somewhat involved, like everything else in India.' He giggled; Major O'Kelly, late of Skinner's Horse where his sack-of-potatoes figure had made him more than a square peg in a round hole, was a giggly man with a high-pitched voice, irritating mannerisms, and a way of looking sideways instead of full face at people to whom he was talking. There was a curious greasiness about him, and an air approaching furtiveness that suggested to Ogilvie that he liked things to be involved. If involvement was his bread-and-butter, that was possibly quite natural; but Ogilvie fancied it went beyond that and that involvement was, as it were, his mistress too. It was a love affair with double dealing. Even this interview had its furtive side. It was being conducted, not in Major

38

O'Kelly's office at Division, but in his quarter. Here there was no wifely influence, for O'Kelly was a bachelor and a slovenly one at that, with no obvious ability to cope with his native servants. The room in which they sat was seedy and threadbare and on the table between them there was still the evidence of O'Kelly's last meal: a loaf of bread on a white kitchen plate, and another plate with a remnant of smelly cheese and a crust. There was also a bottle of whisky that had been half emptied by the Political Officer himself, and there was a smell on the air of stale alcohol. On O'Kelly's shoulder a tiny monkey perched, staring at Ogilvie from black beady eyes while one hand lethargically searched its body for fleas. Without in the least disturbing the monkey – Ogilvie fancied it was in fact a marmoset – O'Kelly slopped more whisky into his glass with a well-kept white hand, a small hand like a woman's. Then he went on, 'You'll have heard of Nashkar Ali Khan, of course.'

'The Waziri leader?'

'That's him.' O'Kelly reached up and stroked the marmoset, laying its body against his cheek. 'A Pathan, of course – and you know what that means.'

'A warrior?'

'Well, certainly a warrior. They're all a bloody-minded lot, the Pathans – I don't need to tell you, you've fought them in open battle. You'll do your fighting a different way from now on, my lad, and jolly good luck to you! But there's more in the word Pathan than just a knife in the gut, Ogilvie. Tell me – what do you know of *Pukhtunwali*?'

'Isn't it a kind of religion, the Pathan religion?'

O'Kelly shook his head and giggled. 'It's not quite that, no. You could possibly say it *amounts* to that, I suppose. *Pukhtunwali* ... it's a generic term really, embracing all men who speak Pushtu – and by the way, I gather you have the dialect yourself?'

'Yes.'

O'Kelly gabbled off a question in the hill dialect, and Ogilvie answered. They conversed in this tongue for a minute or so and then O'Kelly said, 'Yes, quite good. Who taught you?'

'The *Munshi* sahib.'

'I'm surprised he didn't brief you on *Pukhtunwali*. Put concisely ... well, as I say, it included all Pushtu speakers, and

39

they're split up into literally dozens of tribes, all strong and some immensely strong, which are divided again into *khels*, which you could more or less call clans I suppose. That should make you feel more at home, what?' He giggled again, then moved his head suddenly and looked at the marmoset. He seized it and held it at arm's length, getting to his feet. 'Excuse me one moment, I'll have to attend to Wolseley.'

'I beg your pardon?' Ogilvie asked, looking about him in startled astonishment.

'Not the Whitehall one, this one,' O'Kelly said, indicating the marmoset. 'I'm a Roberts man myself, that's why I called this little bugger Wolseley. Sorry – he wants to pee.' The Political Officer made an ungainly dash for the door, and disappeared, returning a couple of minutes later with Wolseley, who was still scratching. 'Now we'll get on, shall we? I was talking of *Pukhtunwali*. Now, an important element of *Pukhtunwali*, and the one that concerns us, is *badal*.'

Revenge?'

'Good for you – yes, revenge. Revenge is obligatory, it's a *commandment* to the Pathans. Which, of course, is why the Frontier is always more or less in flames, dear boy. The Pathans take revenge extremely seriously, as I dare say you know.'

'Yes, I do know, sir.'

O'Kelly flipped a hand. 'Don't call me sir, dear boy. It ages me terribly.'

'I'm sorry . . . Major.'

The Political Officer looked disconsolate, but said, 'Well, yes, I s'pose that's better. Now.' He leaned across the table. '*Badal*, of course, is behind this current business, or anyway that's how I assess it. The General, by the way, agrees with my assessment. Mind you, I claim no originality for seeing the revenge motive,' he added, pouring himself another glass of whisky, 'that's sheer routine, really. But the rest of it is rather interesting if you're a student of Frontier affairs – which I am. However, I'll try to keep to the main points and be as brief as I can.' He sat back for a moment, and screwed up the flesh around his eyes, evidently assembling his thoughts. Then he said, 'I dare say you know the Pathans are a very, very old people. Basically, so far as we can say, they're Turko-Iranian with a dash of Indian blood – other affinities too, Dinaric for example. Even Herodotus knew them and spoke of their being the most warlike of all the Indian tribes, and went on to say that they lived around the city of Kaspaturos.' He looked up at Ogilvie. 'Well, does that convey anything to you?'

Ogilvie shook his head. 'I'm afraid it doesn't, Major. Where's this – what did you say – Kaspaturos?'

O'Kelly said with the air of a conjurer, 'Here, dear boy. Right here!'

'In Peshawar?' Ogilvie felt bewildered, and showed it.

'Not exactly *in* Peshawar. I've formed a theory: *Peshawar itself was once known as Kaspaturo*s. Startling? Anyway, that's what I've come to believe. I won't bore you with all the details of my studies, I'll just ask you to accept the proposition. If you do that, you may begin to see what I believe to be behind the unrest in Waziristan, and you'll see that we, the British, are very much hurting the susceptibilities of all the Pathans along the Frontier by sitting right smack in what their forefathers looked upon as paramount among all their cities, the absolutely sovereign city ... in a sense, I suppose, very much as the Muslims look on Mecca. Well, not *quite*, of course, but that'll give you some idea. D'you follow?'

Ogilvie said, 'I follow to the extent that I can see they wouldn't like it, but is there anything new in the idea?'

'New?'

'I mean, couldn't this have been said to be behind all the Frontier wars, for years past, Major?'

'Oh, no. No, not at all! Didn't I expressly say, this is *my* theory. What?'

'Yes, you did.' Ogilvie paused, then went on, trying to be tactful, 'But surely – if you're the only one who knows this – the Pathans don't realize they have anything to be upset about?'

'Ah!' O'Kelly said, not at all put out but looking vaguely triumphant. 'I'm not saying I'm the only one who does know this. In fact, I'm pretty sure I'm not. I've heard things in the market place, as you might say. Little things mostly, but things that add up, you know. I believe someone else is propounding this theory about Kaspaturos, and is inflaming the tribes thereby.' He hesitated, biting at his lips, and giving Ogilvie a series of covert glances; some inner struggle seemed to be going on in his mind, then he came to a decision. 'I have to be honest, dear boy, I have to be *fair* to you and give you the *facts*. These little things that I've heard ... it's them that really gave me the first ideas about Kaspaturos. Do you see? Just those vague hints, as it were, set me thinking and since then I've done an enormous amount of study. Enormous. So it's really quite fair to call it *my theory*.'

Ogilvie concealed a smile with some difficulty, but conceded O'Kelly's honesty of purpose. Gravely he said, 'Oh, quite. I can imagine the hard work, Major. But who d'you think is selling the idea to the tribes?'

O'Kelly said, lowering his voice instinctively now he appeared to be reaching the point, 'I've heard talk of a holy man, up in the hills. I believe, somewhere around Gumarshah, near the Waziristan-Kohat border, though I can't pin-point him closer than that. I believe he shifts around quite a lot. Now I don't know that he's our man, but it seems likely that he is, since rumour has it that he's been having talks with Nashkar Ali Khan. And I believe he's filling the tribal ears with war talk – talk of Kaspaturos, and the perennial desirability of hoofing out the British – but, this time, with more of a bite in it. I expect you can see that. We're occupying the ancestral home in a very positive sense.'

'But we've occupied the Frontier – and Peshawar – for years!'

O'Kelly nodded. 'Yes, true. But Kaspaturos — and the *knowledge* of its location, don't you see – is quite, quite different. Possibly you wouldn't understand without a deeper feeling for the Pathan mind and heart. It's something you'll have to take my word for, dear boy. Once a place has been *identified* as being your long lost Mecca, to use the simile again – well, surely you must *see*?' He spread his hands. 'Anyway, those are the facts as I see them, not without evidence to go upon, as I've tried to say. But I'm not saying those facts are complete. There's another thing I might add, and it's this: Waziristan holds the seed of whatever is happening and there have been signs that the other tribes, those outside Waziristan, are harbouring jealous thoughts about the Waziris—'

'Because they've got the holy man and the others haven't?' Ogilvie gave a short laugh. 'A little childish, isn't it?'

'You can laugh,' O'Kelly said, his own face solemn, 'and I agree the childishness – the Pathan *is* childish in some ways, at any rate when seen against our own standards of civilized behaviour. But it's nonetheless serious to them. I don't know that the jealousies *are* to do with the ground chosen by the holy man for his soothsaying, but they might be – they might well be. Now, we of course don't mind the jealousies since they're clearly divisive, but I don't believe this state of affairs will last. The very opposite will come about in time. The word about Kaspaturos will spread like a fire, dear boy, like an all-consuming flame, and that holy man will become the unifier. And when that happens – well, God help Peshawar and all its inhabitants!'

Ogilvie nodded; he could see the dangers if O'Kelly was right. Fettleworth would have the devil's own job to defend the garrison against a concerted assault by all the Frontier tribes, fanaticized by retold dreams of past glories and a past home, presented with an embodiment of that splendid past, a target for attack. Abruptly he asked, 'So what is it you want me to do, Major?'

'Go into Waziristan and make contact with the holy man. Find out exactly what is going on, what precisely is threatened, and how far this thing has already gone. Find out also the enemy's plans in as much detail as possible – it's really that, of course, that the General requires of you so I have to advise you to make that your first objective. But do not make the mistake of disregarding the other objectives. They're vitally important for the future. Have you ever killed a man, dear boy?'

Ogilvie was startled by the unexpected question. 'In the field, yes.'

O'Kelly said, 'You'll find a vast difference. Killing a man of whom you've made a friend, killing him in cold blood, well, it's not very pleasant. But it has to be.'

'Am I expected to do that?' Ogilvie asked.

'Yes. Depending on what you find out – depending, that is, on how far events have moved . . . if this is only at its start, a still-birth can be induced. To induce it you must kill the holy man. How you do this is your own affair, and the only stipulation is, the body must never be found afterwards.' O'Kelly leaned again across the table and grasped Ogilvie's arm, a sudden movement that caused Wolseley to utter a shrill cry of near dislodgement. 'You'll be doing it for the Raj, dear boy. In the name of Her Majesty.'

It sounded horribly hollow and even insincere and pretentious. Ogilvie wondered how good Queen Victoria, assuming she was not a complete imbecile deaf and blind to what went on in her name, could ever find sleep in her great bed at Windsor Castle.

He was not to enter the fastnesses of Waziristan in the guise of a native. O'Kelly said, and said rightly Ogilvie thought, that such things were of the past, though it seemed there had been some disagreement on that point from General Fettle-worth. Instead, he was to go in as an Englishman, a renegade Englishman selling arms to the warring tribes, a man who cared nothing for the fact that his arms would be used against British soldiers but was interested only in his profit. He would, of necessity, go in under discreet cover. His route would be given to him within the next twenty-four hours, after various ar-rangements had been made with his battalion and with Div-ision. Whilst in Waziristan, or wherever else his journeyings might take him, he was under no circumstances to attempt communication even if such were possible, with Peshawar. He was simply to come out as soon as his investigations were com-plete – and the sooner the better, of course – and make his full report to O'Kelly and General Fettleworth. If anything should go wrong, if he should have the grave misfortune to be un-covered, he would get no help from the British Army or the Government in Calcutta. He would be disowned. Naturally, no matter what the pressures put upon him, he was never to reveal his mission. And, equally naturally, he was not to breathe a word to anyone before he left Peshawar.

O'Kelly said, with an embarrassed cough, 'I apologize for saying this, dear boy, but it has to be said, and you must know very well that any garrison town has its gossippers – besides which, it's my plain duty to acquaint myself with the full back-ground of an officer who becomes attached to my Department.' His eyes – Ogilvie had noted this as a habit of his – revolved upwards so that the pupils were lost and only the white showed. 'I'm referring to a certain lady – no names, I'm a gentleman, damn it! You must not tell her anything, of course, but she will have to be given some explanation for your absence. You will tell her that you are going on a temporary Staff assignment in Murree, attached to your father's headquarters. This has been agreed with your father, as a matter of fact, and he will see to it that nothing comes unstuck. It will also give the lady an address to which to write should she ask.'

'And what about replies?'

'There will be no occasion for replies. You will in fact advise the lady, as no doubt you would do if the Staff job was real, that it would be better if she did *not* write. On the other hand, you

44

see, if she *does* still write, the letters will be delivered care of your father and not sent back as undeliverable or anything of that sort. It's the best we can do, and I think it will be all right. Now, have you any further questions, dear boy?'

'Not at the moment.'

'If you have any before you leave, get in touch – here, not at Division.' O'Kelly got to his feet and reached out his hand. 'Good luck to you. Thank you for your co-operation.' When Ogilvie shook that outstretched hand he found it surprisingly firm and was also surprised to see in O'Kelly's eyes a clear, straightforward meeting with his own and even a look of compassion. He didn't like the implications of the compassion but he felt the Political Officer could after all be trusted for what that might be worth. Leaving O'Kelly's bungalow, he reported again to his Colonel, and found Lord Dornoch non-committal when he told him, without specification, that he now had his orders. Dornoch clearly disapproved, however, in general terms, though he went no further than to say that he would be delighted to see Ogilvie back in due course and that his command of his company was assured the moment he rejoined the battalion. That evening Ogilvie went round to Mary Archdale's bungalow and gave her his cover story as instructed. There being no reason for her not to do so, she believed him; but was nevertheless surprised that Fettleworth's 'plans' for Ogilvie had turned out to be an appointment to his own father's Staff. 'Not at all what I'd have expected of General Fettleworth, James,' she said wonderingly. 'Is it some deep plot, whose exact cleverness escapes me, to attach you to your mother's apron strings, and forget me?'

He laughed at that. 'I doubt it – and he wouldn't have a hope anyway!'

'Your father, then?'

'No. He would never do that. I don't suppose he likes the prospect any more than I do.' To his own surprise, he found he was being totally convincing, even to the point of convincing himself that he was bound for Murree. He hoped he would be as efficient in his duties once he had crossed into the gaunt hills of Waziristan. 'It won't be for long anyway, Mary.'

'I hope not, love. Oh, I'm going to miss you so terribly, James.' She paused, her eyes searching his face. 'You don't think this has some connection, do you, with your being out of cantonments? That you're being sent away from me because of *that*?'

Again the feeling of self-convincement came to him as he answered, 'I don't know, Mary dear, but, well, I suppose it might be that. We're being awfully dangerous, you know. Nothing's secret.'

She pushed herself at arm's length away from him on the sofa where they were sitting. 'Has it never occurred to you,' she said with spirit, 'that there's really nothing to be secret *about*? I'm no longer another man's wife!'

He flushed; he hadn't paid her much of a compliment, to be sure. He said lamely, 'Well, you know what we've discussed, Mary.'

'Yes, love, your career. Oh, it's important, of course it is, to me as well as you. But all these damn gossippers, these dreadful bitchy old women – why, even your Lord Dornoch's as much an old woman really as that Bates woman who saw us together at Annandale months and months ago! Why can't men ever be realists?' She added fiercely, 'We're both free to marry, if it comes to the point. We're not doing anything illicit!'

He smiled at her, and moved towards her. She came into his arms and let herself relax slowly. He said, 'Aren't we? Doing anything illicit?'

'Only if you're a Bible-thumping prude, love!'

'Which I'm not. I leave that to Andrew Black.'

'Whom you won't be seeing for a while.'

'Thank God for that, at all events.'

'You won't be seeing me either, love.' She kissed him on the mouth; a long kiss. 'Well?' It was full of meaning.

He understood, and he nodded. 'No more absences from cantonments, though. Not yet, anyway.' Nothing more was said; they got up and went through to Mary's bedroom, and she closed the shutters. Already the daylight was fading outside; the bedroom became shadowy but he could still see the gleam of white skin as she undressed. This time there was no drink to make his head reel, to dull the edge of his emotions and his appreciation, as in fact, he now realized, it had done on the last occasion. He took her in his arms and lifted her, and carried her, and set her gently on the bed, with a kind of reverence. She spoke only once, breathlessly, urgently, but with a deep intensity of feeling. She said, *'Oh love, my love,'* and that was all. It was something he would carry with him in his remembrance and in his heart, distantly into the wild Waziri hills.

CHAPTER FOUR

'I'M very sorry to hear you're leaving us, Captain Ogilvie, sir, even though it's only temporarily. You'd have made a fine company commander, sir, if I may say so.'

Ogilvie smiled. 'Thank you, Sar'nt-Major. I'm sorry too, but it can't be helped. As you say – it's only a temporary appointment, and not of my seeking.'

'Aye, sir. You have my best wishes in the interval. I'll be obliged if you'll give my best respects to Sir Iain Ogilvie, sir.'

'Thank you again, Mr. Cunningham. I know my father'll be glad to have news of you.'

'Then good-bye for the time being, sir.'

Ogilvie held out his hand; Bosom Cunningham's grip was warm. A Sergeant-Major of the old school, Ogilvie hated lying to him, even by inference, even as the result of orders; Cunningham was the sort of man who made one feel ashamed of an untruth. Cunningham and his father – and Cunningham's father as well – had in the past given their service together to the Royal Strathspeys, and Sir Iain Ogilvie himself had more than once put his trust in that large, tough Highlandman.

It was a circuitous business – much more circuitous than Ogilvie had imagined it would be, and time-consuming. But in India's lazy heat there was, it seemed, time in which to take even war easily. O'Kelly's route orders indicated that the important thing was authenticity. So Ogilvie went first to Murree with two metal trunkfuls of kit, by train and bullock cart. A hundred or so miles by the flight of a carrion bird, Murree was considerably more when the creaking railway carriage took its passengers by way of Nowshera, Attock and Rawalpindi. At Nowshera Ogilvie's solitude was interrupted by a gaunt-looking Major of the Green Howards, but not for long. After an abrupt good-morning the Major flapped open a *Times of India* and went to ground behind its pages, with long thin legs thrust out beneath the deaths, births and marriages, the human events that signposted an army's and an Empire's tenure of the East. Ogilvie stared in silence out of the window as the train jolted fussily along the track. Under a burning sun he inhaled the age-old smells of the sub-continent, the unmistakable smells that told a man, if nothing else did, that he was in India. It was a stifling morning and Ogilvie, each time the slow old train stopped at a halt, swatted at innumerable flies, vicious brutes with what his father would have called blue arses. He beat at them with waving arms till they buzzed away and joined others crawling over putrefying matter by the side of the track, or over decayed beggars lying totally inert in the shadows cast by the wooden platform of the halt, men still as death despite the irritation of the wandering hairy legs and probing mouths, their thin, stick-like limbs thrust out into the dust, the eroding marks of disease inescapable in their pitiful faces. Beggars . . . without the strength in their sinews to lift a beggar's dish or whine for alms.

Reaching Murree at last, Ogilvie left one of his trunks at army headquarters, a trunk ostentatiously painted in white with his name, rank and regiment. Then, without a sight of his father, he proceeded in accordance with Major O'Kelly's orders to the house of a Civilian, a Mr. Totness, a gentleman from the finance department of the Government in Calcutta, attached for duty with Army Command in Murree. Here, Ogilvie changed out of uniform into mufti from his second trunk, putting on a cream tussore suit and a civilian topi. When Mr. Totness had given him a bulky package that included a number of documents, and had indicated which he was to keep on his person and which he was to read, memorize and then destroy by fire, he proceeded, after a good meal and half a bottle of French wine, again by bullock-cart, out of Murree to the small town of Abbottabad in the Hazara district of the Punjab. This terrible progress took him right through the night and deposited him, just as a splendid dawn came up over the hills, at a hostelry run, as he had been told by Mr. Totness, by a former *havildar* – major of the native regular troops of the Indian Army – a man, Mr. Totness had said, absolutely to be trusted for his loyalty to the British Raj. Here, Ogilvie was given a clean room and breakfast. After breakfast, he studied his documents with more care than he had so far been able to do. His new identity was that of a Mr. Ernest Wilshaw, travelling arms salesman, representing a large British combine – Dilke-Braybrook-Chalmers of Birmingham. There was a *curriculum vitae* of Mr. Wilshaw attached, fully comprehensive as to background; and there was a great deal of useful arms-sales information designed to give him all he needed to know in order to keep his end up. Having read and memorized all of this, he struck a match and set fire to it in the safety of an earthen vessel which he found beneath the bed; and with some difficulty, for the receptacle was not large enough to be entirely safe, he restrained the flames from total destruction of the loyal *havildar*'s property. Then he read the literature which he was to keep, and found it consisted mainly of leaflets descriptive of the virtues of the Dilke-Braybrook-Chalmers products. There was also what seemed to be an order book and a book of cheques, some of which had been used, drawn on the London branch of a British bank; and, in addition, some ready cash – no less, indeed, than ten thousand pounds equivalent in five-pound notes drawn on the Bank of England and in rupees. This was for his personal expenses and for any bribery that might become necessary once he was inside Waziristan. Study over, he slept – with the money securely beneath his pillow. After some hours another meal was brought and the next act took place when at 5 p.m. the ex-*havildar* bowed an entrance to his room and said, 'Sahib, there is a person below who wishes to see you.'

'His name, Ram Sadar Singh?'

'He says his name is Jones Sahib.'

'Then send him up, Ram Sadar Singh.' The *havildar* bowed himself out again, and Ogilvie grinned to himself. The appellation of 'sahib' had come with reluctance from the hostelry-keeper's lips; his description of Mr. Jones as 'a person' was much closer to his real feelings. Not for the first time, Ogilvie reflected that there was no snob like the British-orientated Indian in British India; Mr. Jones – which was not in fact his real name, as Ogilvie had been warned – was clearly not a gentleman.

The man appeared, smiling, and bounced into the room, full of bonhomie. He said, 'Mr. Wilshaw, I'll be bound! Eh? Nice to meet you, sir, nice indeed.'

'Thank you Mr. – Jones. That's a compliment I return.' He shook the man's hand. Jones was middle-aged and short and fat, and wore a heavy brown moustache, its waxed ends drooping in the close, stuffy heat. The door closed; they heard the *havildar*'s footsteps receding down the stairs. 'We can talk, Mr. Jones. Ram Sadar Singh's to be trusted, I'm told.'

'That's right, Mr. Wilshaw, that's quite right. I've heard he's a good old scout – never met him before, mind, not myself, to be honest he don't like my trade, but I know all about him.' Mr. Jones, without being so invited, sat himself on the bed and hooked his thumbs into his braces, which he brought out like catapults and then released to twang back against almost woman-sized breasts. 'Nice to sit down,' he said, blowing out his cheeks. 'Lord, Mr. Wilshaw, I feel just like my old lady – haven't sat down all day. I dunno, life's a rush sometimes. Still, I can't complain, not really, I make plenty of money and that's what counts, eh? Not that I wouldn't give a lot of it to be back in Brum right now, I can tell you, Mr. Wilshaw.'

'Brum?'

'Ah, that's it – Birmingham, as if you didn't know. What's the matter, Mr. Wilshaw? Got a nasty smell or something, have I?'

'No, I—'

'Well, you look as if I have.'

Ogilvie flushed. 'I'm sorry,' he said. 'It's just that . . . oh, well, never mind!'

'Come on, out with it, let's be honest.'

Really, Ogilvie decided it was the only way so long as it could be done without giving offence. He smiled. 'It's a little different from the service. I'm not used to this sort of thing, you know.'

'Not quite like the Colonel or the Major, am I?' Chirpily, Jones returned his smile. 'Wouldn't know what to do with me serviette at supper an' that's a fact. I admit it. Still, it takes all sorts to make a world, Mr. Wilshaw. I hope I'm going to be of service to you, that's all. That's my job for now, and believe me, I'm not used to your sort either.'

'I'm sure we'll get to know one another,' Ogilvie said diffidently.

'We'd better, seeing we've to spend quite a little while in each other's company, Mr. Wilshaw. When'll you be ready to leave?'

'As soon as you like.'

'Right. We'll get old Ram Singh to give us some supper, then we'll be on our way south and west. I'm taking it you know the drill?'

Ogilvie nodded. 'You're the real salesman for Dilke-Bray-brook-Chambers ... this is in fact your last tour of duty in India, and you're showing the new man the territory. Correct?'

'As ever was,' said Mr. Jones. 'And believe me, it's dead lucky for yours truly that it *is* my genuine last tour, cos I'd never dare come back after this lot. I'd be the deadest duck you ever set eyes on, Mr. Wilshaw. I dare say you know what sort of memories the tribes have!'

'Yes, I do. Well ... it's a pretty decent thing you're doing, Mr. Jones.'

'So what's that supposed to mean? Eh?' Jones looked, for no reason that Ogilvie could see, suddenly angry. 'All it means to me is that it's very curious a dirty bastard like me should do anything decent. Talk about condescension. Why, you're all the same! Don't interrupt, it's bloody rude, didn't nanny tell you? Look, Mr. Wilshaw. Don't you make the mistake of seeing everything in black and white. I'm an arms salesman by profession and it's made me a good living. Oh yes, I know how the guns and the bullets are used sometimes, but if I didn't do it, somebody else would, and I have a living to make same as anyone. I've a wife and seven kids in Brum, five of 'em grown up and off my hands, true, but what I've sold out here's helped 'em grow up. Believe it or not to look at me, I've got an old mother as well. Eighty-eight she is, and blesses me for keeping her. A man has to do what he can, and this is what I dropped into. It doesn't mean I can't be decent, Mr. Wilshaw. But you've only to say the word and I'll ride back to Kagan with pleasure and leave you to explain to your precious Colonel—'

Mr. Jones's voice had risen and Ogilvie had almost to shout the words: 'For God's sake, man, shut up! You'll be heard all over Abbottabad!'

'Oh – sorry!' Mr. Jones's hand flew to his mouth. 'You're quite right, Mr. Wilshaw. Very sorry.'

'So am I,' Ogilvie said in immense relief. 'You've misunderstood me entirely, but I apologize very sincerely. I only meant to thank you, that's all.'

'Ah, but you were wondering what had made me *decent* all of a sudden, and don't deny it, Mr. Wilshaw. What's more, I'm going to tell you.' He struck an attitude. 'The Queen, God bless her! The British Empire on what the sun never sets, the good old Raj, the memsahibs and the squire and his relations, and us all in our proper stations, Rule Britannia and the British Grenadiers. So help me God.' He dabbed at his streaming face with a bright green handkerchief.

'Tripe,' Ogilvie said, half smiling. 'You don't mean a word of that!'

'No,' said Mr. Jones complacently, 'but you'd like me to, and it's what makes *you* tick. Now I'll tell you the solemn truth.' He used the handkerchief again, this time to dab at a tear that had suddenly trickled from his right eye. 'My old dad . . . he was the Regimental Sergeant-Major of the 14th. What they call the West Yorks now, the Prince of Wales's Own. Yes, sir, a British Non-Commissioned Officer.' Mr. Jones glanced towards the ceiling, reverently. 'He's up there somewhere now, looking down and not liking what he sees. I'm going to shift his sights for him, Mr. Wilshaw.'

As suddenly as the tear had sprung, Mr. Jones winked. Taken in conjunction with the apparent emotion of that tear, the wink was quite incongruous, and all at once Ogilvie realized that the arms salesman was slightly tight. He didn't for the life of him know how to take his new companion, or what to believe, but he could foresee certain elements of danger in the mission if he was to remain long with Mr. Jones.

They left Abbottabad after the evening meal, heading south-west out of the little town through mean streets of sleazy hovels and past the inevitable beggars, making towards the Indus River to cross into Kohat south of Khushalgarh. Mr. Jones had provided his own transport – a bullock-cart, covered, with a horse ambling along behind. The horse was for Ogilvie's onward transportation once they had parted company, which they would do shortly after they had entered Waziristan, and in the cart was a small tent which Ogilvie would take with him. Jones said, 'All I need do, Mr. Wilshaw, is to make you known to a few of the *khel* leaders, the *maliks* they call 'em, and after that the word'll spread fast. You'll be all right with my say-so behind you. I'm – trusted.' He used the word with an odd inflexion, almost diffidently. Ogilvie understood why; he was about to break another trust. Ogilvie wondered mischievously what Mr. Jones's old dad would have to say when he looked down from above on *that*, but assumed that approval would be the order of the heavenly day in the circumstances.

'As for me, I'll get to hell an' out once I've established your *bonafides*, Mr. Wilshaw, if you'll forgive the term. After that, well, you're on your own.'

They jogged along a rutted track, slowly, uncomfortably, with Jones driving. Ogilvie sat alongside him on a hard bench-like piece of wood, soon aching in every part of his body and wishing he could stretch out in the back. This was impossible, or if not precisely impossible, pointless; for the back was filled with the hard stuff – literally – under a tarpaulin. When Ogilvie had inquired what was there, Mr. Jones had said laconically, 'Samples, Mr. Wilshaw, samples. Under the trash, that is.'

'Trash?'

'Beads and trinkets. I do a nice little trade with the women. That's me perks. It's also good cover. I'm well known to the authorities as a trader in rubbishy jewellery, and officially, that's what I am.'

'And the . . . samples? What are they samples of?'

'As if you didn't know, Mr. Wilshaw. Guns, of course. And ammo. Junk very largely, like the trinkets, but impressive to the tribes. Gatling parts . . . Colts, Mausers, Mannlichers, Lebels, Rosses.' He glanced sideways at Ogilvie, as the last of the light faded from the sky. 'We haven't got around to the new pieces yet. The automatic rifles, and the Long Lee-Enfield that's replacing the Snider and the Martini-Henry in the British Army.'

'Thank God for that!'

'Thank my old dad,' Mr. Jones said, winking again. 'He's up there keeping an eye on God, jogging his elbow just a little way in the right direction . . . keeping an old sweat's eye on God an' me and his British troops.'

A few minutes later Ogilvie broke the silence by asking, 'What happens if we run across a British military patrol . . . with all that lot in the cart?'

'You'll have to talk us out of it, Mr. Wilshaw.'

'I can't do that. I'm under orders not to talk to anyone not directly involved.'

Mr. Jones shrugged. 'Don't cross your bridges, Mr. Wilshaw. I've always found that a good rule of life. If I hadn't, why, I'd be dead from worry by this time.'

'It should be thought about, though. We should be ready.' He grinned. 'Perhaps the R.S.M.'ll see us through!'

'R.S.M.?'

'Your father, Mr. Jones.'

'Oh – my old dad. Yes. Well, reckon he will.' Mr. Jones lapsed again into silence, leaving Ogilvie to wonder if his old dad was no more than a figment of his imagination, though it could certainly be assumed he'd had one some time or other. Another thought came into Ogilvie's mind as well, an unkind one that asked him how much Mr. Jones was being paid by the minions of Calcutta to make this journey worth his while. Somehow, the ring of the cash register seemed more germaine to Mr. Jones than did any lofty-dwelling, haloed R.S.M.

The bullock-cart and its attendant impatient horse forded the Indus three dawns later and came into Kohat. They made their tedious way along the valleys, around fifty miles south of Peshawar itself as they headed, westerly still, towards Teri, whence they would drop down into Waziristan by way of Bannu. It was during the fifth night, some thirty-two hours of actual driving time after fording the Indus, that the trouble came, and came a little to the north of Bahodur Khel as they were about to cross the old caravan route leading north to the mouth of the Khyber Pass.

CHAPTER FIVE

'Now, what the hell was that?' Mr. Jones asked suddenly, pulling the bullock-cart up short. It was pitch dark now, with no moon at all, and there was a chilling wind coming down on them from Himalaya.

They listened.

Ogilvie said, 'I didn't hear anything, Mr. Jones.'

'Call yourself a soldier!' Jones's voice was low, no more than a whisper. 'Good Christ, Mr. Wilshaw, I reckon I've done more Frontier time than you have when it comes to the pinch, nipping out of here and there. And I tell you now, there's a patrol not far off.'

'How d'you know?'

'I heard a rattle of equipment, that's how. Hark!'

Ogilvie listened again. At first he heard nothing to break the heavy, brooding silence of the darkness beyond the occasional cry of a night bird; then, distantly still, he fancied he heard what the arms salesman had heard: a thin jingle of harness. Mr. Jones had very sharp ears; there was no sound of horses' hooves. The indication was that the horses were moving at a walking pace and on soft ground, and that the patrol, if it was a patrol, was in fact closer than he had thought.

'Well, Mr. Wilshaw? What do we do now, eh?'

Ogilvie thought fast. He believed the horsemen were closing them, that they were probably right in the line of advance. To stay would mean their arrest and the end of the mission for the time being; to move would lead to the same end, for they could obviously never outrun a military patrol. He asked, 'How well do you know the lie of the land, Mr. Jones?'

'Like the back of my hand.'

'Is there anywhere we can pull off the track, and get lost?'

'Maybe, but not just hereabouts.'

'How far, then?'

'Too far. Around a couple of miles ahead there's a dry gully, off to the right – if we cross that there's—'

55

'As you said – too far. We'll have to think of something else.'

'For Christ's sake, why not stop and *talk?*'

'I told you why not.' Ogilvie scrambled down from the cart. 'We'll get out on the horse. It'll carry us both.'

'What, and leave my stock?'

'Yes. It can't be helped now.'

'But it's capital—'

'Move, Mr. Jones! Come now – I'm in charge. You'll obey my orders, and without question.' He ran around to the back of the bullock-cart and untied the horse. Mr. Jones joined him. The harness-sounds from the rear had stopped now; perhaps, Ogilvie thought, their own sounds, quiet as he had tried to be, had been heard and the patrol had halted for a listening space. They would not have much longer, but Mr. Jones, though inclined to protest still, was amenable to orders. Ogilvie mounted, and the arms salesman climbed up behind him, puffing and blowing. Jones was hardly securely seated before Ogilvie sent the horse fast along the track. Stones flew from beneath it hooves. Jones gave a gasp and clung on tight around Ogilvie's waist. Ogilvie at first heard no sounds of any pursuit, but a few seconds later there was a crackle of rifle fire. No bullets came near them, and quite soon the firing stopped.

Jones panted, 'They'll have got to the cart. My bloody stock, Mr. Wilshaw.'

'I hope it keeps them busy for a while, that's all! Keep your eyes skinned, Mr. Jones. Tell me when to turn off.' They rode like the wind, trusting to luck and the horse's survival instinct to keep them clear of obstructions in their path – the darkness was thick and the sides of the track visible only as faintly lighter blurs against the deep black of the night. It was not long before the shooting started again, but their luck held and the bullets went as wide as before; and by the time the first of the pounding hooves was clearly heard coming up fast behind, Jones had found what he was looking for: a break in the high rock side of the track.

'Pull off!' he yelled into Ogilvie's ear. 'Down into the gully!'

Ogilvie brought the horse up sharply, feet slithering on loose stones and small rocks. They turned to the right, and galloped on, starting the descent, a sharp one, into the dried-out gully. Ogilvie felt twigs and branches scrape across his face, and the horse slowed. They were coming into a certain amount of cover, which should be useful, but Ogilvie felt disinclined to linger in it.

'Where to now?' he asked.

'Left a little way, Mr. Wilshaw. That is – south. After a while we'll come to a break in the west bank. When we go through, we'll come to a hillside with caves in it. A lot of caves, Mr. Wilshaw, all honeycombed inside.'

'That could be a trap.'

'It won't. You wanted to get lost. We'll get so lost we could stay there for ever.'

Ogilvie urged the horse on through the scrubby growth in the gully. He heard sounds away to his left as he turned along the hard backed watercourse, sounds as if someone were riding along the bank, but there were as yet no more shots. He didn't much like the idea of heading into a network of caves – his recollections of hiding out in a cave before the march on Fort Gazai were not happy ones – but recognized that currently such a course probably offered them the best hope of concealment. Now and again he heard voices, British voices. He had started to wonder if they were being chased, not by a British patrol, but by a band of tribesmen; but no doubts were left now. Probably, had their pursuers been natives familiar with the terrain, they would in any case have been caught up with by this time. Ogilvie thought with sympathy of the officer commanding that patrol, possibly some green young subaltern, such as he himself had been not so long ago, gaining experience of a night probe into what was virtually hostile territory. It was never a pleasant thing, to have to report failure to one's Colonel; but Ogilvie, as Mr. Jones's voice in his ear informed him that they were now coming up to the gap in the farther bank of the gully, prayed fervently for that patrol's failure this time. Such were the ways of the army, he reflected, that the patrol's success in apprehending them might in the circumstances rebound on the head of the unfortunate leader in any case.

The horse scrambled up a steep bank, reached flat ground, and was directed left again. By the time they reached the hillside that Jones had spoken of, there was no sound of the patrol. Ogilvie pulled up the horse beside the first of the cave mouths, which yawned blackly, a darker patch in the faint lightening of the rock.

He said, 'We'll dismount, Mr. Jones, and reconnoitre on foot.'

Jones slid down over the animal's rump and brought out his green handkerchief. He rubbed away at his sweaty face. 'Let's get inside quick,' he urged. 'No point in hanging around, is there?'

'There's the horse,' Ogilvie pointed out impatiently. 'We can't leave him outside like a signpost.'

'Never suggested we should, Mr. Wilshaw. Lead him in.'

'I'll check for headroom first. The horse can't very well get down on hands and knees! We may have to go on farther.' Ogilvie turned away and made for the indistinct loom of the cave's mouth, bending and going a little way inside with his arms outstretched in front of him. There was width and height enough to accommodate the horse; it would do. He turned about and made his way back to the entry. When he reached it, Mr. Jones was no longer alone; he was surrounded by shadowy figures. They were not British soldiers; they were wild and ragged men carrying old-fashioned long-barrelled rifles, but Jones appeared happy enough. He was talking to them in Pushtu, urgently and rapidly, and Ogilvie realized that the fat little arms salesman had a far greater grasp of the dialect than he had himself. Ogilvie was able to make out that Jones was explaining their situation. All the time more and more hillmen seemed to be crowding in, emerging from out of the night. They had been, it seemed, bent on a probe against the British positions around Peshawar and had been attracted by the sound of the rifles earlier.

Ogilvie reached Jones's side and interrupted the flow of dialect. 'Just a moment,' he said. 'Aren't we being indiscreet? We'd better do as you wanted and get hidden – the cave's big enough to take the horse.'

'The situation's different now, Mr. Wilshaw.'

'Oh? How? Who are these men – d'you know them?'

'I know their *malik*. They're from a *khel* that lives just over the Waziri border. I've done business with the malik before now. They'll trust us, you needn't worry.' Jones's voice was hoarse, and Ogilvie, close enough to him to make out the expression on his face, was alarmed by what he read in it. It was a kind of obstinate determination mixed with fear and, in spite of the keen chill of the wind off the far northern snows, beads of sweat were clustering on Jones's forehead. 'Just leave this to me, Mr. Wilshaw,' he said. 'All right?'

'I told you before, I'm in command. Get rid of these men and join me in the cave, Mr. Jones. That's an order – and just remember we haven't all night. The British patrol will be here any minute.'

'Yes,' Mr. Jones said. That was all. He stepped back a pace and the next Ogilvie knew was the feel of the arms salesman's fist on the point of the jaw. His head rocked backwards and before he could make any recovery another fist had landed smack in his stomach; and as his body doubled up in agony a third blow took him, again on the point of the jaw, and he went down flat on his back. Unconscious, he was dragged by two of the Pathans into the mouth of the cave, followed by Mr. Jones leading the horse. Half a dozen of the hillmen went inside with them, and the rest dispersed, fading into the night behind the jags of rock and skeleton-like trees.

They did not go far away and that night there was a massacre in which an entire British patrol, provided by mounted infantry of the King's Regiment, was wiped out. Ogilvie, struggling through the mists after a while, heard the firing and guessed what was happening. When he moved his head a sharp point of steel pricked into his throat. Jones was kneeling beside him, holding a knife against his adam's-apple. In a low voice Jones said, 'Don't open your mouth, Mr. Wilshaw, if you value your own life. I've sent the natives away, but they're not right out of earshot.' He lowered his voice still more. 'I'm sorry about the patrol, believe me. But it was the only way, since you'd said you couldn't explain matters to the officer if he caught us up. And it's just as well you didn't, seeing as how this bunch wasn't far away. Now, don't start shouting the odds – take it like a man! You don't know it yet, Mr. Wilshaw, but this is what war is all about. If we're going to win, we have to be as dirty as the bloody natives and that's a fact of life out here. As it is, we're on a very good wicket. We've proved we can be totally trusted – you as well as me, see. All you've got to do now is to convince *yourself* that you're Mr. Ernest Wilshaw of Dilke-Braybrook-Chalmers, Birmingham ... not an officer of Her Majesty's bleeding army. All right?'

Ogilvie didn't answer. Jones went on, 'You'll see it my way when you think about it, son. God knows, I didn't like doing it – that is, *allowing* it to happen. But you got to be convincing. From now on, it's vital, Mr. Wilshaw. You simply mustn't react like a soldier any more. That's out – right out! Get me?'

Ogilvie nodded an aching head, and swallowed. 'Yes, I get you.'

'It's for the greater good of the greater number in the end, Mr. Wilshaw. Hold fast to that – and hold fast to your duty. To that extent, you can be a soldier still.'

Ogilvie found he was shaking like a leaf. 'How much do you really know about all this, Mr. Jones?'

'About what?' The knife was still at Ogilvie's throat, and he could smell Jones's rancid breath.

'About – what my orders are.'

'I don't, Mr. Wilshaw, I don't. Why?'

'You spoke about it being for the greater good in the end.'

'Just an assumption, Mr. Wilshaw, that's all. The nobs wouldn't be sending you into Waziristan unless they had something big in mind, now would they?'

'No. All right. I wish you'd take that knife away.'

Jones said, 'You won't do anything foolish, Mr. Wilshaw?'

'No, I won't.'

'Have I your word on that?'

'Yes.'

The knife was withdrawn from his throat. He sat up, feeling his jaw. It was stiff and felt bloody, and his whole stomach was rawly painful. The cave was beginning to take on shape now; there was a faint lightening outside. The firing had ceased, and the tribesmen from Waziristan were gathering again by the cave's mouth. Jones got to his feet, and went to talk to them. After a moment he came back to Ogilvie. 'We can go on now,' he said. He met Ogilvie's eye. 'We'll even have an escort into Waziristan. The auguries are good, Mr. Wilshaw. You've started on a very favourable footing.'

'Perhaps,' Ogilvie said. He felt weak and sick, and not from physical causes. But he made an effort; he had a job to do and it hadn't really begun yet. 'You had to knock me out in order to get away with it, remember. Doesn't that look odd, to the Pathans?'

'Not so.' Mr. Jones shook his head emphatically. 'It was a private affair, just between you and me. You were trying to tell me what to do. You're just my assistant and you got too saucy, Mr. Wilshaw. It's not the first time, and I lost my temper.'

'And they accepted that?'

'Yes.' Jones was emphatic. 'And it wouldn't hurt to repeat it. Just for authenticity's sake. I'll give you the tip, when.'

They got on the move as the day grew lighter under a blood-red orb of sun. The tribesmen brought up the bullock-cart, its contents opened but otherwise unmolested, to the farther bank of the gully. Tactfully Jones refrained from expressing any satisfaction at the recovery of his stock. He even helped Ogilvie in his self-appointed task of concealing the British dead beneath piles of stones against the attentions of the vultures, already circling bleakly overhead, foul black symbols against the rising sun. The Pathans understood the desirability for the British renegades of doing what was possible to erase the signs of battle; and also, as warrior themselves, possibly understood that even traitors were bound to have some feeling for their own compatriots. As they moved off, Ogilvie, back alongside Jones, who was once again driving, studied the escorting Pathans. They were a stiff-faced, self-contained lot, some fair, some dark, all with dirty tattered garments and shaggy hair, hard men who lived hard lives, men to whom death in the act of battle was a thing to be welcomed. They were as rock-hard indeed as their own terrain, a bleak land of hot sun and sand and dust and mountain crags. Jolting along the track for the Waziri border, Ogilvie was silent and preoccupied; Mr. Jones didn't interrupt his thoughts, for which he was thankful. Had the man from Birmingham done so, he would have had his head snapped off. Ogilvie was feeling keenly to blame for what had happened to the men of the King's Regiment. Possibly, after all, Mr. Jones had been right. Perhaps he should have regarded his orders with more elasticity, even though they had been perfectly clear and unequivocal: under no circumstances was he to tell anybody about his mission. Heavy-hearted, he knew that in fact there was no way around those orders and if he had disregarded them and revealed himself to the officer of the patrol, the result would very likely have been the same in any case. The act of telling would not have dispersed the tribal force, which vastly outnumbered the small patrol, and after the attack he, Ogilvie, would have suffered the added bitterness of self-blame for disobedience of orders. This appraisal of the situation, however, failed to bring him comfort. It merely pointed the basic unpleasantness of his task and he wondered how he had ever come to look upon the assignment with anticipation and zeal.

However, no more trouble was encountered. At nightfall, close now to the border a little way south of Gumatti, they were joined by more tribesmen and shortly after this they crossed into the desolation of the Waziri hills.

Late that night Lieutenant-General Fettleworth's Chief of Staff reported to the Divisional Commander that a patrol of the King's Regiment had failed to return to cantonments in accordance with orders.

'Why tell me?' was the General's snappish response. 'Surely this is a matter initially for their Colonel, and after that, for Brigade?'

'Yes, sir. Brigade, of course, is aware of the situation, but has made reference to Division. The reason for this, sir, is the special mission into Waziristan.' The Chief of Staff, who had sins of apparent omission to confess on behalf of someone down the chain of command, looked worried. He gave a discreet cough and a gentle reminder. 'Captain Ogilvie of the 114th Highlanders, sir, if you remember—'

'Of course I remember!' Fettleworth rustled angrily beneath his pyjamas. Sometimes, the Chief of Staff reflected, Bloody Francis seemed to break down into the role of a music-hall General, all bounce and bluster. But not for long this time. Collecting himself rapidly, Fettleworth sat up straight, meeting his informant's eye. 'Lakenham, where precisely was this patrol functioning?'

'From Nowshera down to Bahodur Khel, sir, with, I gather, particular orders to clear the area of the Rawalpindi to Mianwali sector of the railway line of bandits.'

'God damn!' Fettleworth said explosively. He pushed his feet over the edge of his bed and thrust them into carpet-slippers. 'Did I, or did I not, give perfectly clear orders that the whole blasted area was to be kept free of patrols until such time as the special mission had passed through? Don't interrupt, sir! I expressed the opinion, which was never contested, that it *would not do* to maintain patrols and warn their officers about Ogilvie. Secrecy – I made the point quite plainly – is secrecy. One does not make *broadsheets* out of things like the special mission! I said all that.'

'Yes, sir. Obviously, there has been a case of – of an error of judgment. I understand it was as a direct result of a request from the railway authorities—'

'Error of judgment be damned, blasted disobedience more like! When the stationmaster at Rawalpindi takes over as Army

Commander in Murree he will be able to supersede my orders. Not until. Damn it – someone's going to pay for this, Lakenham!' Fettleworth was furiously angry, but he was functioning. 'But that's for the future. What makes you think there's been a clash with Ogilvie's mission – hey?'

'I don't say there has been, sir. I simply suggest there *may* have been some incident – as a matter of fact the idea was Major O'Kelly's. In the circumstances I feel it should be investigated.'

'H'm. It's a pretty long shot, Lakenham.' Fettleworth gnawed for a moment at the drooping ends of his moustache. In bed, Lakenham thought with sudden irreverence, he resembled a walrus, a red and gingery-white one. 'Any amount of ground out there, y'know, any amount! What?'

'Yes, sir. I still think it should be looked into with half an eye on Captain Ogilvie.'

'H'm, well, yes.' Fettleworth stared blankly in the light from the guttering oil lamp carried by his Chief of Staff. 'I've an idea you're panicking over nothing ... however, there's no harm in a probe, I suppose, and the patrol will have to be looked for as a matter of routine. How long overdue are they?'

'Six hours, sir.'

'Good God, man, what's *six hours* on the Frontier! Why wake *me* up?'

Lakenham began again, patiently. 'Captain Ogilvie's mission,

'Yes, yes, yes! Oh, all right. Should Ogilvie have cleared the area by this time, assuming he's still intact?'

'Yes, sir.'

'Very well, then. You're my Chief Staff Officer, aren't you? Get on with it, Lakenham. Use your initiative!'

Pointedly, General Fettleworth got back into bed and settled his balding head on his pillow. Lakenham shrugged and left the room. Within the next few minutes a runner had been despatched from headquarters and shortly after this a squadron of the Guides was moving south into Kohat. They returned to cantonments the following evening with word that they had come upon what had obviously been the site of an action – they had found a good deal of dried blood and some spent cartridges. Upon investigation they had discovered the concealed bodies of the British soldiers, and later had found some of the dispersed horses. There were no British survivors. There was no sign of any tribesmen and the area was now quiet. Divisional Headquarters, after receipt of this intelligence, was quiet no longer. An enraged Fettleworth sent at once for the officer commanding the squadron of Guides and received his detailed report in person. He then told this officer that he was to keep his mouth firmly shut about the concealment of the dead, and was to see to it, on pain of wholesale Courts Martial, that his troopers did likewise. As he remarked in private to Brigadier-General Lakenham, no one but a British officer would have thought of concealing dead men's bodies. 'It's scarcely an old Pathan custom,' he said scathingly, 'to be so solicitous. They're more likely to cut off their testicles and sew 'em into their mouths. And I do not want the whole of Peshawar and Nowshera to be buzzing with rumours. You shall see to it, Lakenham. If you fail me, you'll be out on your ear!' And he added, 'I'll have that young man's hide for this, if ever he comes back!'

That evening the bullock-cart and its escort rumbled into the tiny village of Janda Khel, thirty miles inside the border and perched in the foothills of the Waziri mountains extending out of Afghanistan. Dirty by now, sweat-soaked, weary, Ogilvie looked forward to nothing more than rest from the jolting cart, a long sleep in the evening cool. But this was not to be. Some men of the escort had gone ahead of them to spread the word of their coming – or rather to confirm their imminent arrival, for from time to time in those hills Ogilvie had seen lean bearded figures on the peaks, clutching the long-barrelled rifles and watching the movement along the pass, and reporting ahead, no doubt, to the village. Now, as they rumbled the last hundred yards or so towards the rough huts of the tribesmen, the villagers were emerging, lining the sides of the track to welcome the conveyors of arms, arms for use against the British. Hawk-faced men, dark eyed warriors, met Ogilvie's stare boldly. They made no sound, but their gaze raked the bullock-cart with avid interest; Ogilvie felt they were almost licking their lips. Here and there, well in the background of events, a Pathan woman was to be seen. Some fat and grotesque, others slim and comely, all in their appointed places – a physical and moral step behind their menfolk. But above the veils their eyes held the same look of eager interest in the uncovering of Mr. Jones's wares of war, a look of anticipation and a look of cruel, vengeful triumph. Ogilvie felt a shiver of real fear run along his spine; he was not surprised General Fettleworth was a worried man. If the men and women of Janda Khel were typical of the inhabitants of all Waziristan, then – with the dreadful assistance of men like Mr. Jones to arm them – the prospects were bleak. Ogilvie, now that he was ostensibly at one with Mr. Jones and had been doing his best to force all his thoughts and actions into the mould, found that he was already viewing these passionate fighting tribesmen with an eye very different from that of a remote regimental officer, an officer who saw them as it were at rifle's length. In a curious way – since they were obviously accepting him at face value as a renegade acting on their side – he could identify with them. And, as a result, could the more closely and instinctively sense and appreciate the threat of their intentions. It was far from pleasant. He had enough action experience behind him to know very well that Waziristan's hordes, thousand upon thousand of men like these, reinforced by similarly minded men right along the North-West Frontier, would have little difficulty in carving a wide swathe through the Raj, and decimating the Peshawar garrison with its women and children en route.

Jones, interrupting his mental imagery, gave him a hard nudge in the ribs. 'Try and look happy,' Jones urged. 'You're about to do yourself a bit of good, Mr. Wilshaw.'

'Good?' For a moment Ogilvie looked puzzled.

Jones lifted a hand and rubbed his thumb against his forefinger. 'Oodle,' he said softly. 'Sponduliks. *Money!*'

'I wouldn't touch it, thank you.'

'Yes, you will. Oh yes, you will, Mr. Wilshaw. You'll take your share and look happy. God's teeth, Mr. Wilshaw, do remember you've got a bloody job to do!'

They rumbled on, behind the flicking tail of the ruminatory bullock. Bullock speed – dead slow and stop. Soon a man came out and stood in their path, bringing them to a halt. 'The *malik*,' Jones whispered. 'He's the top bloke in the *khel*, kind of clan chief. Name of Gojun Khan.' As he spoke, he got down nimbly from the cart. Ogilvie followed him. 'Greetings, Gojun Khan,' Jones said, giving an obsequious bow. 'My visit, I think, was expected?'

'You are welcome, seller of arms,' Gojun Khan answered. The conversation was in Pushtu, and Ogilvie could follow it well enough – well enough to recognize the note of contempt in the tribal leader's voice. He was a tall man, and leanly hard,

65

and he was expressing the warrior's contempt for the traitor and the tradesman with his body as well as with his voice. It was the same the world over, black or brown or white, the warrior talked with the warrior and despised all other manner of men. Then Gojun Khan's cool gaze flicked like a lash over Ogilvie. 'This man – who is he?'

'Rumour has not flown ahead of us, Gojun Khan?'

The man smiled briefly, a mere flash of very white teeth in the dark, close face. 'What reaches ahead of you is my concern, seller of arms. I have asked a question, and you have not answered it.'

'I am sorry,' Jones said. 'This man, Mr. Wilshaw, is my new assistant who will shortly take over my territory – I'm retiring, you see. Going home at last, for good.' He sweated, and glanced at Ogilvie. When Ogilvie, standing straight and still, did not move, Jones, with an edge to his voice, said in English, 'Come, Mr. Wilshaw, Gojun Khan is a good customer.'

He had said 'customer' in a meaningful way. Ogilvie, unused as he was to dealing with 'customers' and not fully realizing the magic of the very word to all engaged in selling, be it manufacturing, wholesale, retail or tuppenny market stall, yet took in what it was his current superior was telling him to do. With as good a grace as he could muster, he did it. He bowed to Gojun Khan, seeing as he did so the man's contemptuous face as a target for a British bullet, his body as good exercise for the cut of a claymore. Using every effort of his will, Ernest Wilshaw then predominated and Captain James Ogilvie of the Queen's Own Royal Strathspeys, Her Majesty's 114th Highland Regiment of Foot, was sunk without trace – though not without a few backward glances at a long family tradition of military service to the British Crown in the whole course of which an Ogilvie had never bowed his head to any man save the King of England always – since 1603 – and God on Sundays; let alone to a native whose black arse, he thought with a sudden savagery which was totally unlike him normally, had been specifically provided by God for kicking practice. Having bowed, he felt physically sick.

Gojun Khan merely said, 'You also are welcome, assistant seller of arms,' and beneath Ernest Wilshaw's veneer, Ogilvie Sahib squirmed. After this the tribal leader turned his full attention to Mr. Jones, who moved to the back of the bullock-cart and demanded Mr. Wilshaw's immediate assistance in the unloading. Ogilvie brought out case after case of dismantled machine guns and rifles, box after box of British ammunition which he was told to stack beneath the shade of some trees. He worked hard, and as he worked he became more and more aware of the smell of the village, which stank to heaven of dried urine and human excreta and foul cooking smells coming from the dilapidated huts. Gojun Khan's disdainful eyes flickered hungrily over the stock, counting Mr. Jones's offerings, warily assessing a price in his mind. Along the route Mr. Jones had explained to Ogilvie that he never brought a vast quantity of arms at any one time, no more did any of his professional colleagues. 'No question of travelling with some bloody great caravan,' he had said, 'even though small deliveries tend to up the overheads and cut the margins. Oh, no, Mr. Wilshaw, *never* a big delivery.'

'Why's that?' Ogilvie had asked in his innocence.

Jones had laughed heartily. 'Because I value my skin. Give the bastards just a small consignment, and they want to see you back again with more. Give 'em enough to mount a campaign, and you're a dead duck. Works out cheaper for 'em that way. You don't pay dead men, Mr. Wilshaw.'

Ogilvie remembered that as he saw Gojun Khan's glance rest for a lingering moment on Jones's back. As he looked at the arms salesman, Gojun was fingering a long, thin knife thrust into a dirty sash at his waist. It was fairly obvious that Mr. Jones's life hung on a promise – a promise of a couple of hundred or so rifles next time; a time that henceforth would lie within the supply capabilities of Mr. Wilshaw (but only so long as the prudently forward-looking Mr. Jones was allowed to make his unmolested way back into British India, by which Mr. Jones, who had explained this also to his new assistant, meant, course, British *held* India.)

Once the stock was unloaded, there was some haggling over the price. Eventually Jones agreed, with a show of reluctance, to twenty thousand rupees for some seventy-five percent of his cargo, a rapacious demand for what Jones himself had called a load of junk; and this sum was handed over in hefty bags of cash which, except for one which he handed to Ogilvie with the words '*Cumshaw*, Mr. Wilshaw,' Jones hung on hooks attached to a leather belt around his waist. Then he said he and his assistant would be grateful for food and lodging for the night, a request to which Gojun Khan acceded; and announced that he wished to discuss future supplies of arms after the two salesmen had eaten and refreshed themselves.

'We are at your service, Gojun Khan,' Jones said, and gave Ogilvie one of his meaningful glances. 'Since it will be the last time I'll have the pleasure myself, I'll look forward to a good talk with you.'

When the *khel* leader had turned away the man from Birmingham took Ogilvie's arm and led him into the lee of the bullock-cart, speaking into his ear. 'Tonight's the time you lay your ground-work, Mr. Wilshaw,' he said. 'You get yourself into Gojun's good books, and believe me, you're half-way home. The Pathans are like that, see. It's *melmastia* – hospitality – partly. They're hot on *melmastia*, Mr. Wilshaw. Means a lot to them. The stranger within the gates – you know what I mean. Can't do enough for you, once you're trusted. Get along with Gojun, and believe me, the word'll spread fast. It's largely up to you, but I'll be putting in all the help I can, of course.'

'Thank you.'

'Don't worry about the thanks,' Jones said with a chuckle. 'Do you know, Mr. Wilshaw, there's times when I've hated my job. Bloody detested it, and myself for doing it – but I've already talked enough about *why* I've done it. The thing is . . . well, don't you see, I'm getting a bit of my own back now as well as doing something to right a wrong. Atone's the word for that, I s'pose. Revenge is nice, too!'

'*Badal?*'

'Ah, *badal*!' Jones chuckled again. 'Pay 'em off in their own coin, like. So don't you worry your head about me, or about feeling grateful for what I do to help. Just keep your mind right on the job, and learn to live the part. The key-word is authenticity and convincement, see? And just to aid that, we'll have a repeat tonight of our little disagreement earlier, like I said before. That'll scotch any possible feeling these lads may have – and myself I don't think they have – that you got laid out for a purpose. All right?'

Ogilvie nodded. 'I'm in your hands still, Mr. Jones.'

Jones clapped him on the shoulder. 'Well said, Mr. Wilshaw. Take advantage of those hands while you can. Tomorrow, you'll be on your own. I'm coming with you to just one more village, and that's the lot. I've another customer waiting for the rest of the stock, which is by way of being bespoke. From then on, your job is to fix up contracts.'

They walked slowly back towards the clustered huts of the villagers, the target for many curious eyes, and a few discreet smiles from the women, the younger ones among them seeming interested in Ogilvie's tall, tanned figure. His own thoughts being elsewhere he noted them with no more than half an eye, but registered that there were some beauties among them, with very desirable forms, girls who, little more than children now, would all too soon swell and droop into the ungainly replicas of their mothers, and whose hair, now soft and fine, would straggle into the matted, sleazy, smelly coverings of those older women. As he and Jones walked along, a man came up and directed them to a broken-down hut on the village outskirts, a hut now empty but for a frugal meal of maize and a handful of unappetizing roots, together with a pitcher of goats' milk, sour and horrible.

Jones laughed at the sight of Ogilvie's face. 'You'll have to get used to it,' he warned. 'You'll be glad enough of it after a week or so. Our own rations won't last forever, which is why I asked old Gojun to help out. Tuck in, Mr. Wilshaw!' He rubbed his hands together hard, as if dredging up an unwilling appetite from the depths. 'At least it's nourishing.'

Gojun Khan, though every inch a warrior and a man of an innate dignity, was no cleaner than his tribesmen, and his hut stank of a lack of washing water. He sat cross-legged on a filthy mat, and behind him, while he talked with his arms suppliers, two of his wives sat, women as unclean as himself, and with half visible, sagging breasts that were no more than flaccid pouches of empty skin whose nipples fell slackly into the tops of their filthy garments. These women bickered together in low but sharp voices until bidden by their master to be silent; after which they contented themselves with mutually venomous glances.

'Continue with your story, arms salesman,' Gojun Khan said when he had dealt with his womenfolk. 'Why are you leaving us to this beardless young man?' His dark eyes flicked towards Ogilvie.

Jones said, 'Gojun Khan, it is because I am not so young as I was and I am tired, and I wish to stay in my own land with my own family. For me, the fight is done.'

The native gave a brief nod. 'I understand this, but I think that when the fighting is done, then the man also is done. I shall fight to my death. Assistant arms salesman, are you a man of spirit?'

'I think so, Gojun Khan,' Ogilvie answered.

'You do not look like your superior,' Gojun Khan said ruminatively, stroking his beard. 'Why do you sell arms to your country's enemies?'

'I need to make a living,' Ogilvie answered carefully. 'I am doing nothing wrong in the eyes of the law. My company is permitted to sell its products wherever a market can be found, Gojun Khan.' He added, 'It is not for me to inquire what my customers do with what they buy. That is their own concern.'

'So you ask no questions, assistant seller of arms?'

'None.'

'Yet as an intelligent man, as intelligent as your superior, you must surely ask questions of yourself?'

Ogilvie hesitated. 'Perhaps, Gojun Khan. Perhaps.'

'And what are these questions, and the answers you give yourself?'

Steadily Ogilvie gave the obvious answer: 'I ask myself if the weapons we supply may from time to time be used against the British. And then I give myself this answer, Gojun Khan: what the eye does not see, the heart does not grieve over.'

'This is a saying of your country?'

'Yes.'

'A strange race, the British. Yet this outlook I have observed before, many times. The British like to be assured of what they wish to believe, and are able to pretend to themselves that the unacceptable does not exist. Like the ostrich, with its head in the sand, they are safe from what they cannot see. A strange thing, and unaccountable to a Pathan such as myself. But it takes many breeds to people the earth.' Gojun Khan was silent for a while, then he spoke to Mr. Jones. 'When you leave us, seller of arms, with no wish to return again, what will happen to you?'

Jones shrugged. 'Nothing. I'll take a ship home to Brum, and draw the company's pay-off. I've made enough money to live on, Gojun Khan.'

'You will need no addition to this money?'

Jones gave a sly smile. 'Gojun Khan, I am wise enough to guess your thoughts. You are thinking that during my travels along the Frontier, and here in Waziristan, I have picked up many secrets. I have – that's true, dead true. But I'll not be telling them to the authorities, Gojun Khan. That way leads to trouble. You've rightly said that the British prefer not to see . . . but when they have seen, they grow angry and they act. Like Mr. Wilshaw, I have done nothing against the letter of the law . . . but the spirit, now that's a different thing! My countrymen are not so different from yours, Gojun Khan, when it comes to *badal*. There would be reprisals against me . . . we in the profession never, never talk about our work – and in addition to that, we have our colleagues to consider. If one of us did as you suggest, Gojun Khan, how welcome would the others be in the Frontier villages in the future?'

Gojun Khan grinned. 'Not welcome, seller of arms.'

'What would happen to them?'

The *malik* grinned again and, wordlessly, drew a finger across his throat.

'Well, exactly!' Mr. Jones said amiably. 'And if I were responsible for one of my colleagues getting the chop like that, well, I'd find a reception committee waiting for me when I got back home to Brum, wouldn't I? But don't forget something else, Gojun Khan.'

'Yes?'

'It cuts both ways. I know I'm now at a certain amount of risk, and I'd never have taken the risk of telling you I wasn't coming back if it hadn't been for the fact my company's paid me a good deal of money to introduce Mr. Wilshaw here. Now, I want to minimize that risk. How do I do it? Here's how, Gojun Khan: I cross your frontier safe and sound, with no impediments, or Mr. Wilshaw sells you no arms. You'll have observed for yourself he carries no stock of his own. He just takes orders this first trip. No safe conduct for me – no arms for the *khels*. Your scouts'll report back when I've crossed out, and they'll take back my own personal message to Mr. Wilshaw. When he gets that, and not unless and until, he'll fulfil his contracts. And not only that. I said this whole thing cuts both ways. If I don't get out, the word'll spread – you know how it is. After that, no arms salesmen will enter Waziristan again. Wouldn't be worth the risk, would it?'

Gojun Khan bowed his head. 'We think alike, seller of arms. You will leave our land in peace and safety. This I promise.'

'And for that I thank you, Gojun Khan, and as one man of spirit to another, I accept your assurance.' Jones hesitated. 'And my assistant, Mr. Wilshaw?'

Gojun Khan said, 'Your assistant must prove himself.'

'But in the meantime you will give him your help, and your trust, Gojun Khan?'

'This I will do, until such time as he gives cause to the *khels* to withdraw this trust.' He looked keenly at Ogilvie, who was surprised to find a trace of friendliness in the native's eyes. 'Go in trust, assistant seller of arms, who is now a seller of arms in his own right.' Then he laughed. 'Go also in blindness, Englishman, for as blind men are the British happiest!'

When they had left Gojun Khan, and were once more in the privacy of the hut allotted to them, Ogilvie asked why Jones had not given him the tip to start the argument he had said would be necessary. Jones said, 'Why, Mr. Wilshaw, because I saw it wasn't necessary after all. Old Gojun trusts you and likes you.'

'I hardly said a word to him.'

'Maybe that's what he liked. Anyway, take my word for it, you're in good, Mr. Wilshaw.' He looked reflectively at Ogilvie. 'Don't ask me why, because I don't know the answer, but you're the sort of young chap people *do* like. Why, even I've come to like you, in spite of your classy attitudes. I'll miss your company, going back. Now, coming from me, that means a lot.'

The speech, obviously a sincere one, embarrassed Ogilvie. To cover his embarrassment he asked Jones how confident he was that any interference with his progress to safety beyond the Waziri border would lead to a total withdrawal of sales labour. Jones guffawed at that. 'Load of tripe,' he said. 'We have a kind of rough-and-ready code of honour in the profession, mind, but we all have to live. Before long, somebody'd be back ... some other company'd cough up enough sponduliks to make it seem worth the risk involved. Competition's competition, results are results, and the sack's the sack. Get me, Mr. Wilshaw?'

Ogilvie nodded. 'I suppose I do, yes. But for your part, do you believe Gojun Khan means what he says about safe passage out?'

'Oh yes,' Jones answered. 'Course I do! These Pathans, they do keep their word once they've given it in friendship. It'd be beneath their warrior instincts to rat.'

And we British? Ogilvie thought – but didn't say it. That night he slept only fitfully, tossing and turning on a pile of skins on the earth floor of the hut, the stink of the village thick and

72

heavy in his nostrils, Gojun Khan obtruding into such night-marish dreams as he had. Many people at home, and in Peshawar as well, would say that a Pathan was only a native, an enemy to be used as best one could when the opportunity arose, a heathen whose mission in life should be to bow the knee to Calcutta and Whitehall and the race of sahibs above. Others, like his own father and his Colonel, would respect Gojun Khan as a warrior but still consider him basically as material sacrificeable to the Raj. Ogilvie could not consider him in quite this impersonal manner. Gojun Khan was a man as well as a fighter, a man who had apparently given him his trust and his liking, and to kick him in the teeth was reprehensible and un-gentlemanly. Strange indeed, the split mind of the British, who could so easily, so calmly and so damned insolently select those to whom their military officers should also behave as gentlemen! On the verge of another spell of sleep, Ogilvie sighed disconsolately. He was no longer an officer, he was a spy, and by the very nature of their existence spies were reprehensible, and he had better just make up his mind to be as reprehensibly successful as the best of them . . .

Next morning he and Mr. Jones set off, leaving Janda Khel with the bullock-cart, now only a quarter loaded, and the horse tied on behind. Gojun Khan himself came to see them off, and gave them an escort for a little way. Thereafter they negotiated the mountain passes on their own, seeing now and again those silent, watchful figures on the high crags, lean brooders on the silence who gave them a wave of recognition as they passed along the track below.

'We'll be reported ahead,' Jones said. 'Roses all the way, now! You should have a nice, easy run . . . up to a point.'

'How d'you mean, up to a point?'

'Well, Mr. Wilshaw, I still don't know what your job is, of course, but like I said before, or words to that effect, it's not to sell ladies' underwear. One thing I do know is, or if I don't exactly *know* it only a fool wouldn't be able to guess it, and that is, you're no more Mr. Ernest Wilshaw than I'm Mr. Ewart Gladstone. So the point in question, is the point you throw off your cloak of disguise, or when it's thrown off you, eh, Mr. Wilshaw?'

They jolted and rumbled onward, deeper into Waziristan, into tribal and very hostile country, as the sun crept up the sky and sent down the full blazing heat of the day, heat that

73

parched the land almost into very fire. Later, dust-covered and hot and weary, they pulled into the next village, Mr. Jones's last port of call. Here they were well received; word had been sent ahead by Gojun Khan, via the bush telegraph, fantastic communications system of a fantastic land. As soon as his deal had been successfully completed, Mr. Jones handed over the horse and the tent and took his leave of Ogilvie, shaking him warmly by the hand, and then climbed up into his empty bullock-cart.

'The best of luck to you, Mr. Wilshaw,' he said, easing his belted bags of rupees into a comfortable position.

'Aren't you worried about all that money?' Ogilvie asked.

'No, Mr. Wilshaw, not one little bit. You can always trust the Pathans once they've given their word, if I may repeat myself, at any rate, when it's in their best interests. Good-bye, Mr. Wilshaw, once again.'

'Good-bye, and thank you.'

Mr. Jones jerked the stately bullocks into movement, and slowly and ponderously set off, back along the track towards the border, his mission ended. He turned once, and waved, and Ogilvie waved back. The rays of the setting sun struck fire upon Mr. Jones's retreat, turned the dust raised by his wheels and the animals' hooves, to a golden haze, painting a many-coloured picture across the evening sky. Ogilvie watched the cart out of sight around a bend in the track, then turned away, back to the village and the task that lay ahead, on his own now, alone and lonely, with a horse for company, in the Waziri wilderness.

Six days and three villages later James Ogilvie, now coming deeply into the southern mountains, had begun to suffer from a stifling feeling of uselessness and frustration. His discreet probes, very discreet probes, into the confidences of the various *khel* leaders had produced nothing but one blank wall after another. He was not so far even in a position to make a useful report, when eventually he returned to Peshawar, upon the state of readiness of the tribes for war. He had in fact seen no such preparations at all; and the only real evidence he would be able to offer was the avidity of the *maliks* for arms and as much ammunition as he could promise to supply – they seemed, those *maliks*, to have access to vast amounts of money, and it would be interesting to know where the money was coming from – but then, no doubt, the Pathans were always anxious to acquire arms and possibly nothing specific could be read into their current desires.

These were, perhaps, early days; and yet on the other hand time was running out, and delay would be found firmly on the side of the Pathans. The British could not be more ready than they already were, aside from a top level request for heavy reinforcements to be provided by Whitehall in the fastest possible troopships and then hastily trained in the ways of Frontier fighting so that ignorance should not render them too quickly into mere cannon-fodder; while the Pathans, in spite of Ogilvie's having seen no overt signs, were very likely advancing their readiness every day.

In the meantime, Division awaited his report. In a sense, the Empire of the East hung upon him now. This was not too great an exaggeration, for Lieutenant-General Fettleworth was the immediate executive link with the start of action, and Bloody Francis, though impetuous in battle – and often enough hankering *for* battle too – was the kind of officer who liked to have the fullest possible reports before he committed himself to actual movement. The reason for this was easy enough to find: Fettleworth needed to present a cogent case to his superiors. Divisional Commanders were no longer, in the nineties, quite the free agents they once had been.

As if physical speed would of itself help to solve his problems Ogilvie urged his horse, as tired as he, faster along the rock-strewn, dusty pass.

The leader of the local *khel* in the next village, a small man named Ram Surangar, was of a very different type from Gojun Khan or indeed from the other leaders with whom Ogilvie, in his guise of Mr. Wilshaw, had done business. For one thing, instead of using the impersonal style of 'seller of arms', he addressed Ogilvie as Wilshaw Sahib; and he was light-skinned, as were so many of the Pathan people. Admitted, Ram Surangar was a greasy little object, full of cunning, and with a fawning manner, and the little eyes were as shifty as quicksand. Nevertheless, Ogilvie believed he was genuinely anxious to please, and he was undoubtedly greedy for weapons. The time had come for probing to go a little deeper and Ram Surangar was the most pliable material that had so far offered itself.

'My company,' Ogilvie said expansively when, as was customary, he was discussing business in the privacy of the *malik*'s dwelling, 'is a large one, and important. Its business interests are widespread, Ram Surangar.'

'Yes, Wilshaw Sahib.'

'Yet there is always room for further development. Many favours await those who bring about this development.'

'Yes, Wilshaw Sahib?' The small eyes took on an avid look.

'I refer, of course, to myself. I have not been long in my company's employ, as you know. I wish to grow large with the company. However, as I realize very well, I can grow only at the pace at which my customers give me orders. If those orders are large, my commission is large too.' He paused. 'It would be possible for me to allow certain of my customers a share in this commission.'

'By way of smaller prices, Wilshaw Sahib?'

'Perhaps not so.' Ogilvie eased his uncomfortable position on the floor; he longed for nothing so much as to sit once again in a chair, rather than on a floor or the back of a horse. 'Ram Surangar, I do not seek to pry into the ways and means by which you raise the payment for arms. It is not my concern, but yours alone.' He returned Ram Surangar's bow of assent to this proposition. 'Nevertheless, I believe it may be that certain precise sums of money are sent to you for expenditure upon these arms . . . or it may be that you raise a levy from your villagers. I do not know. But I have no doubt that a little extra money coming your way by means of a commission quite separate from the price, would not necessarily have to be made known to your financial sources, your sources of revenue. Do you understand me, Ram Surangar?'

'Perfectly, Wilshaw Sahib.'

'Excellent! Then I feel sure we can reach some agreement, Ram Surangar. Now I shall proceed a little farther.' Ogilvie leaned forward, aware of the caution and greed mixed in the old native's face. 'The arms which I supply to *you*, Ram Surangar, will not of themselves be enough to admit of my sharing my commission with any third party. I need very much bigger orders than any *khel* could give me. And along the frontiers of the British Raj I have heard the whisper of a name, the name of a man who might well be able to place very large orders indeed.'

'This name, Wilshaw Sahib?'

'Nashkar Ali Khan.'

Ram Surangar sat very still, but the sudden flicker of his

eyes, which Ogilvie was watching carefully, gave him away. That flicker revealed his fear, his sudden desire, perhaps, to dissociate himself from any discussions of Nashkar Ali Khan, the man O'Kelly in far Peshawar had said was the overall leader of the about-to-be-embattled Waziris. Still watching that crafty, wizened old face closely, Ogilvie saw the small signs of an inner conflict, the wonderment as to how much his visitor knew, how much he could say without revealing more, how far he could simulate innocence; how far he would need to go in order to advance the matter of a little personal pocket-lining.

Plainly, he needed more help; more persuasion.

Ogilvie said carefully, 'Ram Surangar, the question of arms supply depends to a large extent upon mutual co-operation, as I have tried to indicate.'

'This I understand, Wilshaw Sahib.'

'I am glad to hear this, Ram Surangar, for it would be in the best interests of neither of us if I should be forced to pass by your village on my next trip into Waziristan.' He shrugged, and sat back, fanning his face with a sheaf of leaflets that gave the specifications of various small-arms. He hoped he was giving the impression of a likely loss of interest in Ram Surangar as a customer; but quickly found that Ram Surangar was equal to the occasion.

The old man said, 'Wilshaw Sahib, I too am sorry if this should happen. Something, however, tells me insistently that it will not.'

Ogilvie considered the point, meeting Ram Surangar's apparently guileless smile. Reaching certain conclusions, he asked, 'And this something, Ram Surangar?'

There was an indifferent shrug. 'There are other sellers of weapons, Wilshaw Sahib. Some from your country, some from America, some from other lands across the mountains.'

'Yes, this is true—'

'And if word were to spread that it were better for us to deal with these other suppliers, Wilshaw Sahib, your commissions would fall like the ebbing tide that I am told washes the land-world clean with astonishing regularity.'

Ogilvie grinned. 'True, Ram Surangar. But there's a tide in the affairs of men as well! Do you not see, Ram Surangar, that this is an opportunity that will not occur again? Do these other sellers of arms offer you a share in their commission?'

77

Ram Surangar didn't answer, but there was something in the shrug of the old man's skinny shoulders that told Ogilvie he had scored a point. Ram Surangar was filled with bluff like an egg with nourishment. For more long minutes the bargaining, or the jockeying for the commanding position, continued; and then, with obvious reluctance, Ram Surangar asked, 'What do you wish to know about the man you call Nashkar Ali Khan?'

'His whereabouts, Ram Surangar.'

'This is all?'

Ogilvie nodded. 'It is.'

'This is, I think, more information than I possess.'

'Ram Surangar, I would think more about this. I can bring much help, and I would be grateful for my commissions. As I have promised, I would show this gratitude.'

'It is a promise?'

'Of course. You have my word.' Ogilvie said this with some difficulty, and found himself unable to look Ram Surangar in the face as he did so. Subterfuge was far from second nature as yet. He added, as if in some atonement for a promise to be shattered, 'I can offer a token sum by way of an advance, Ram Surangar.'

The eyes glittered. 'The amount, Wilshaw Sahib?'

'A thousand rupees.'

A little bargaining extended this sum to fifteen hundred rupees. Ogilvie reached into an inside pocket for some cash. He counted out a sum roughly equivalent in Bank of England five-pound notes. 'The place where I can find Nashkar Ali Khan?' he asked, holding on to the money.

'The town of Maizar. I can say no more than this.'

'It is enough. Thank you, Ram Surangar.' Ogilvie handed over the notes. 'I am confident that you and your men will respect the safety of my possesssions,' he added, in reference to the obvious fact that he was carrying very much more than fifteen hundred rupees on his person. 'I know that Nashkar Ali Khan would take his revenge were I to be molested.'

Ram Surangar bowed his head gently. 'There is such a thing as *melmastia*, our law of hospitality. You will go in peace, Wilshaw Sahib, and for tonight you shall rest in my village. In the morning, my scouts will put you upon the road for Maizar. Do you,' he asked solicitously, 'wish for companionship meanwhile? As an honoured guest, Wilshaw Sahib, you shall be accorded your choice of a woman.'

'No, thank you, Ram Surangar. Please forgive me if I seem discourteous. I do not mean to be. The fact is, I . . . have my own woman outside your borders.'

'But,' Ram Surangar pointed out with unanswerable logic, 'your woman is not here, Wilshaw Sahib.'

'That is true,' Ogilvie said in some embarrassment, 'but she expects me to be faithful. For my part, I wish to be so. It is the British way, Ram Surangar.'

Ram Suranger spread his hands. 'This, of course, I have heard, but am still lost in wonder. Do you drink only from the one well, do you refuse drink from a well upon a journey, rather than offend the one that is a thousand miles behind? I feel only sorrow for the British people, for they have ideas that are most strange and curious . . .'

That night, on his uncomfortable bed of skins, a replica of the others he had slept on during the past week, Ogilvie reflected that it was quite refreshing to see his countrymen through purely native eyes with no possibility of restoring an accustomed perspective by talking to a fellow Briton. He was perfectly willing to admit to himself that he would have welcomed a woman to share that dreadful bed of skins and would not, in the process, have felt it to be an act of unfaithfulness to Mary Archdale. Looked at logically, it was totally absurd to deny a strong appetite its satisfaction, especially in the situation in which he was currently placed. In such a situation there was really little value in faithfulness, the rupture of which would be a purely physical and in no sense a mental act. His feelings for Mary wouldn't change because he bedded a woman here in Waziristan. Yet in a sense he would have regarded it as an act of callousness when he thought how recent had been that first union between himself and Mary, a union towards which every part of him had been urging him since they had first met. For the rest, the objections were purely social and conventional. It wasn't done, one would lose caste if one slept with a native girl. It was all very silly, he thought sleepily, and come to that, not everybody kept to the rules. He'd have wagered any sum that Major Tom Archdale had done his Indian wenching since marriage . . . and then remembered that Mary had told him her husband had no time or even ability for sex. This brought him to a fresh awareness of all Mary must have gone through during her years of wedlock with that ageing Major, and how prodigal of the passing months they had been in not consummating their passion long, long before they had. Eventually sleep came to him, bringing him tantalizing dreams of Mary, of their bodies lying so close together, of the play of hands, of that wonderful rush of deep feeling and of her equally deep and vigorous response. He heard her cry: *'Oh love, my love,'* and it seemed to carry from out of the military splendour of Peshawar, across the great dividing hills and through the passes, over the unkempt heads of watchful, waiting Pathans with long rifles and unpolished bayonets, to seek out its target with its heartfelt message that he was to come back safely to British India and his own kind of woman.

CHAPTER SIX

MAIZAR at last, Maizar in the late evening after a weary journey, and a hungry one during which Ogilvie had existed largely on such fruit and berries and nuts as he could pick; and had supplemented his water-bottles, with a certain degree of risk, by drinking direct from the water-holes along the way.

He walked his horse through the gateway and past the meanly-built dwellings inside the walls, heading towards the bazaar, central place of Maizar. Men and women looked at him curiously and children scattered from his path. Even the chickens ran, fluttering confused feathers at the stranger on horseback, the man from another world. Few British people, Ogilvie guessed, had ever come to Maizar; probably none except for the occasional official, ordered out into the wilds from Calcutta to supervise some Government survey or census. He himself would, and did, stand out.

The crowd surged along the roadsides, filling the road itself, impeding his horse. There was an unfriendly sound, a kind of low but rising murmur of suspicion; the horse grew restive. Ogilvie had a strong feeling that he was about to be dragged down and beaten, even kicked to death, or stoned beyond the walls. But he struggled through and reached the bazaar, past the beggars with their importunate dishes, their outflung pleading arms, past hungry-looking men with heavy bandoliers slung across their chests, dark men and light, almost gingery men. Here and there, treated with respect by the milling crowd, a holy man sat contemplating infinity and the hereafter. Ogilvie wondered, not for the first time, how he was ever to find one particular holy man in a land abounding with holy men, largely nameless – but the first task was to find Nashkar Ali Khan, who was not nameless.

He approached an old white-bearded man, a soothsayer by the look of him, seated cross-legged in a booth, a man staring into space like the holy men. 'Old man,' he said, cutting sharply into the reverie. 'I seek your help. Do you know where I can find Nashkar Ali Khan, with whom I have business?'

The eyes stared back dully. 'I cannot help you, Sahib.'

'You do not know of Nashkar Ali Khan?'

'I do not know of him.'

Ogilvie had no doubts that this was a lie, but knew he would not be able to shake the soothsayer. Once again the crowd was showing its displeasure at the stranger in its midst. Ogilvie shrugged and pushed on, slowly, carefully through the throng. He stopped at other stalls, at the snake charmer's pitches, at gymnastic displays, and repeated his inquiry. Always he was given a similar answer: Nashkar Ali Khan was not known in Maizar. But after a while Ogilvie became aware that he himself was an already marked man. Shortly after passing on from the booth of the soothsayer, he had noticed an ungainly man, tall, thin and completely bald, with no ears, and with a nose almost entirely eaten away by some revolting disease.

This man was keeping close to him.

His interest in the stranger was quite obvious; even though he was giving no overt sign that he wished to speak, Ogilvie began to feel that this was what he wanted. He made his way, with the ungainly man keeping his station, right through the bazaar until he began to come out on the farther side of the town. Here the crowd thinned, though Ogilvie still had his group of hostile attendants. He saw that he was approaching a gateway, another exit from the town, and it was as though he was being herded towards it. But just before he reached it, he turned and saw that the crowd had fallen back and that the ungainly earless man was standing between his horse and the crowd, which was now silent, and that this man was standing straight and tall and, somehow, dominating; and that he appeared to have cowed the townspeople by his very glance.

Ogilvie reined in his horse.

As the crowd dispersed, moving away, with an occasional backward look, into the teeming bazaar, the earless man turned and walked towards Ogilvie. He walked with a curiously measured tread, halting close by Ogilvie and looking up into his face. In English said, 'You are Wilshaw Sahib, the arms seller?'

Ogilvie was beyond feeling any surprise. He answered, 'Yes, I am. No doubt word came ahead of me?'

'Many words have come ahead, Wilshaw Sahib, one of them being a message for you from a friend.'

'Jones Sahib?'

The earless man bowed his head a fraction. Ogilvie looked in fascination at the naked ear-holes. The wounds of removal looked fairly recent. The man said, 'Even so. He has left Waziristan in safety.'

'I'm glad.' Ogilvie was indeed sincerely pleased; in spite of Mr. Jones's profession and lack of ethics, there had been something open and decent about him from time to time and he had been a cheerful, friendly companion.

'Rumour has it,' the earless man went on, 'that you wish to do business with Nashkar Ali Khan.'

'Bazaar rumour, from here in Maizar?'

'That, and rumours from farther away, Wilshaw Sahib.'

'And you know of Nashkar Ali Khan – and where he is to be found?' Ogilvie swatted at the viciously buzzing flies rising from the heaps of refuse that gave pungency to the air. 'You will tell me?'

'Nashkar Ali Khan is no longer in Maizar, Wilshaw Sahib.'

'No longer—?' Ogilvie's sense of frustration returned; already, he felt, he had been for too many unproductive days in Waziristan – yet he knew that in India it was always senseless to talk of speed. 'Then where is he? Will you tell me?' He hesitated. 'If you seek payment, I can pay.'

'I seek no payment, Wilshaw Sahib,' the earless man said, looking hard into his face. 'From the talk that has reached me, I think Nashkar Ali Khan will wish to meet you, and for facilitating this, my reward will reach me from Nashkar Ali Khan himself.'

'Then you'll take me?'

'I will take you.'

'Where?'

'Nashkar Ali Khan has gone into the hills, not far from Maizar, Wilshaw Sahib.' The earless man lifted long, thin brown arms from an enveloping white garment, and pointed with both outstretched hands towards the west, away beyond the Maizar walls to where the high peaks of Afghanistan reared majestically, their light brown ranges thrusting into the shimmering but now darkening blue of a cloudless sky. Ogilvie thought of the nub of Major O'Kelly's briefing: 'I've heard talk of a holy man, up in the hills,' O'Kelly had said that day in Peshawar. The Political Officer's holy man had apparently been then in the vicinity of Gumarshah near the Waziristan-Kohat border – but O'Kelly had added that he couldn't pinpoint him and he was believed to shift around quite a lot – moving about, spreading the gospel of Kaspaturos, the supreme Pathan city, rousing the tribes – and having talks with Nashkar Ali Khan.

This earless man could unwittingly lead him to the heart of what he had come to find. Ogilvie asked an innocent question: 'Why has Nashkar Ali Khan gone into the hills?'

'This I cannot tell you. I can say no more than I have said, Wilshaw Sahib. If you wish to speak with Nashkar Ali Khan about your trade in arms, you must put your trust in me to lead you to him, and plague me with no questions. This is agreed?'

'This is agreed,' Ogilvie said. 'Are you going to tell me your name?'

'I am known as the Earless One.'

'Very well, Earless One, when shall we start for the hills?'

'At once. You will ride out from the gateway now, Wilshaw Sahib, and in a little while I shall join you as you ride slowly along the westward track. I go now to obtain a horse, and will be very quick, I promise you.'

He turned away, the setting sun striking fire from the shining baldness of his head, and stalked off, making his way back into the bazaar. Soon only the bald head was visible, moving purposefully through the crowd, and then this too vanished from sight. Ogilvie urged his horse into movement, turning for the gate, and a few moments later rode under the stone archway, past more beggars and swarthy armed tribesmen, out into the open country along the track descending in twists around the hillside, down into the valley. He rode slowly as instructed by the earless man, feeling that at least he had made a little progress, or at any rate was about to make some, but feeling frankly sick at the thought of more interminable miles of jogging through passes and valleys, tired, hungry and thirsty, nagged at by flies and insects and the appalling bite of the sun by day and the sharp cold by night.

It was a full hour later, and dark, when he heard the sound of a horse's hoofbeats behind him and, looking round, saw the earless man coming to join him with his long white garment flying out along the breeze made by his own speed. Ogilvie halted to await the man's approach, moved on again as soon as contact had been made, and inquired about the direction they were to take. 'We follow the track, Wilshaw Sahib,' the earless man said. 'Now let us ride and not talk.'

'As you wish, then.'

Ogilvie shrugged, and urged his horse on a little faster. This was going to be a gloomy ride, he thought, if they were not to talk – and he would have welcomed talk for other reasons than to break the solitude of the hills. No doubt the earless man was, from his own viewpoint at this stage, wise enough to take no chances with his tongue!

They jogged on, not hurrying, scarcely exchanging a word; the earless man seemed unaccountably on edge after a while, casting glances at Ogilvie continually, sometimes furtive, sometimes open and challenging and filled, Ogilvie could have sworn, with sheer hate. He was a most uncomfortable companion for a lonely journey. Ogilvie wondered what could possibly have turned him like this, whether, after all, he had begun to suspect something amiss. This was highly unlikely, and even if such was the case, then the earless man could scarcely have much to worry about since he was escorting the stranger, not out of the country to make his report, but to the very eyrie of Nashkar Ali Khan.

So Ogilvie believed.

They came out from a long pass, a narrow defile whose high sides would mercifully cut out the sun in daytime, and emerged in the first of the moonlight on to a wide, flat plain, a barren plain that appeared devoid of any habitation or any human kind; and a little after this, as the moon grew stronger, the earless man dropped behind and a few seconds later said, 'This is far enough, Wilshaw.'

There was no 'sahib' and the tone of the voice was utterly changed. At first Ogilvie quite failed to take in the meaning of this change. Startled, however, by it, he halted his horse and turned in the saddle to find the earless man holding a British Army revolver pointing at his chest.

'What does this mean?' he asked. 'You promised to lead me to Nashkar Ali Khan. I expected to be able to trust the word of a Pathan warrior, Earless One!'

The man grinned. 'Did you, indeed! Damn you to hell, I'd have shot you earlier if it hadn't been necessary to make sure there were no witnesses. You'd better say a prayer – if you have any God at all, you renegade bastard.'

The voice was now unmistakably English and Ogilvie broke out into a drenching sweat. He said, 'You're making a great mistake—'

'Cut it out, Wilshaw. The bush telegraph doesn't go too wrong, you know! You don't deny – you can't possibly deny – that you've come in to sell arms against British troops?'

'I don't deny the obvious part of what appear to be the facts, no.' Ogilvie was in a terrible dilemma. A glimmering of an explanation was coming through to him – a belief that this man was in fact a British agent, probably sent in by the Civilian side on some mission or other – but he couldn't possibly take this for granted. The earless man, who indeed looked every inch a Pathan, could so easily be a genuine follower of Nashkar Ali Khan who was putting mere suspicion to the test; or carrying out what would be a perfectly sensible probe of Wilshaw Sahib's credentials even if he had no actual suspicions at all. But what to do? For one thing – if the man *was* a British agent – he, Ogilvie, was still under absolute orders not to reveal his mission to anyone whatever the circumstances; though he doubted if O'Kelly had ever envisaged these particular circumstances.

'You'd better tell me the whole truth,' the man said. 'All of it. I want to know who else is making a profit out of the deaths of our soldiers.' He moved closer, holding the revolver very steady. 'Talk, Wilshaw, or you'll be sorry.'

'I won't talk if I'm dead.'

'No. But you'll talk before that point is reached, my dear traitor! See my ears – or lack of them?'

'Yes.'

'The Pathans did that to me – to satisfy themselves I was trustworthy enough for Nashkar Ali Khan's purposes. I learned how painful it was – and I learned how to do it, with the highest degree of pain, to other people! My nose too. It looks like disease, doesn't it, but it isn't, Wilshaw. It was done with a red-hot iron.'

'Who are you? Tell me that, and I may answer your questions. I like to know who I'm talking to.'

'All right. It doesn't really matter now. My name's Healey. Captain Edward Healey, late the Bengal Lancers, attached as a Political Officer to Southern Army Command at Ootacamund. I can offer no proof of this – it's not the custom of Political Officers to enter native territory bearing evidence of their identities. But I assure you it's all very official! No one's going to question my decision to wipe out a dirty little rat like you, Wilshaw.'

Ogilvie gasped in astonishment but made a fast recovery as the hammer of Healey's revolver clicked back. This time, he thought, military compartmentized secrecy had surpassed itself. With admirable coolness he said, 'Really? Don't you think you're a little off your beat, Healey, old man? This part of the world is Murree's pigeon, surely?'

Healey lifted an eyebrow. 'Well, well! Do go on.'

Reaching what in fact was the inevitable decision to disregard his orders this time, Ogilvie, who no longer doubted Healey's identity, grinned into his face and said, 'Captain James Ogilvie, 114th Highlanders, on temporary attachment to the Political Department of the First Division at Nowshera and Peshawar. Let me add to this by way of establishing my *bona fides*. My Colonel is the Earl of Dornoch, my Divisional Commander is ...' he was going to give the latter's full rank but thought of a better way, '... is Bloody Francis Fettleworth, of whom I'm sure you've heard. My father commands the Northern Army at Murree.' He stopped.

Captain Healey stared hard into his face for a moment, then rode forward, pushing his revolver into his robes. 'How d'you do,' he said solemnly. 'I must admit I had an idea you were a gentleman, which a damned tradesman wouldn't have been. We've not really been properly introduced, but I dare say you won't mind stretching a point?'

He held out his hand and Ogilvie shook it.

Then they burst into laughter.

'What now?' Ogilvie asked when the laughter had subsided. 'Where do we go? Do you really know where Nashkar Ali Khan is?'

'Indeed I do,' Healey said. 'I told you – I'm trusted now! The baldness, by the way, was there before I came in. Some sort of hair disease – but never mind, the women seem to find it attractive, rather to my own surprise. But Nashkar Ali Khan. What I told you, Ogilvie, happens to be true. He's in the hills on the Afghan border—'

'With a holy man?'

'Oh, so you know about that?'

'A man called O'Kelly told me. I gather he's of pretty vital importance.'

87

'Correct, he is. Filthy, no doubt, like all *sadhus*, but vital. More so than O'Kelly! We were at Wellington together, incidentally, O'Kelly and I. Bit of a squirt, but he's done well enough, I suppose. We'd better be moving on, Ogilvie.'

'Right.' They moved on together, towards the next range of hills, into the sunset spreading its many colours over the grim, harsh outlines of the land. As they went, they exchanged mutual information. Edward Healey had been sent in some months earlier, on a slightly different mission – a mission to make inquiries into the fate of some men from a Southern Army division who had been captured on a patrol and taken, it was believed, all the way north into Waziristan. Being a fluent speaker of Pushtu and a man of much greater than normal knowledge of the country, he had gone in as a native and had fairly quickly worked his way into the confidence of some of the *khel* leaders, and had gone on from there to establish himself with Nashkar Ali Khan's hangers-on as a fanatic who could be useful to the cause. He had successfully completed his mission in so far as he had been shown the bodies of the British patrol, tortured and mangled before death in an effort to make them talk about the strength and disposition and intentions of the Imperial forces in the south, and their potentialities as re-inforcements for Northern Command. 'I spat on those bodies, Ogilvie,' he said in an almost toneless voice. 'It was a difficult thing to do, but it helped.'

'You stayed on in Waziristan, even though you'd found what you came to look for? Why was that?'

Healey said, 'My interest had been aroused by the other things I'd found out along the way.'

'Anything specific?'

'No, I'm afraid not. Just a general unrest among the tribes, a feeling they're approaching a break-out. Of course, there'd been rumours in Ootacamund—'

'And in Murree, and Peshawar—'

'But you know as well as I do, Ogilvie, that we're never without rumours in India, and especially up here on the Frontier. All the same – it's a different thing this time. I feel it in my bones – I'm damned sure there's something big in the air, though I've not been able to discover what.'

Ogilvie asked, 'What do you know about Kaspaturos, Healey?'

'Kaspaturos? It was an old Pathan city, the centre of the old-

88

time Pathans' very life.' Healey looked across at him shrewdly. 'Why d'you ask?'

Ogilvie was still conscious of the rigidity of his orders, but having broken the major part of them already he saw no good reason for not confiding wholeheartedly in Healey who was, after all, of the same Department as O'Kelly. He said slowly, 'Kaspaturos and *badal* . . . it's a theory of O'Kelly's.'

'Yes?'

'He believes Kaspaturos was originally on the site of what is now Peshawar. How far would you go along with that?'

Healey reined in his horse suddenly, and sat staring across towards the Afghan mountains. 'My God,' he said softly. He looked at Ogilvie. 'I don't know how that fits the historical facts, but as a theory it could have a mighty big explosive power! It could also explain a thing or two.'

'Such as?'

Healey said, 'Well, I *have* heard talk of Kaspaturos among the tribes. Nothing definite, nothing precise, but it's been running through the country just lately. You know the sort of things – tales of the glorious past, of long ago when the Pathans were on top of their world, when in the fifteenth century they even invaded Delhi successfully under a leader named Bahlol Lodi, and back before that as well. And you're right – it's all linked with *badal*, Ogilvie.'

'Is that holy man behind this?'

'I believe so, in concert with Nashkar. The holy man supplies the fervour and the spirit – and the history – while Nashkar supplies the force of arms. The intelligence and the brute strength. It's a dangerous combination. Where did O'Kelly dig up his theories from, d'you know?'

Ogilvie told Healey all that O'Kelly had said, and Healey nodded thoughtfully. 'He always was a clever little bugger – too clever, some said. Didn't really go down at Wellington, or the R.M.C. either, but he's got his majority before anyone else in his term. If he's right over this business of Kaspaturos, Ogilvie, we're going to be right in the dead centre of the biggest cyclone you ever saw!'

'Do you think he is right?'

'I don't know. I suppose it's possible. But even if he isn't – I mean, if he's wrong about Peshawar being, in effect, the ancient city of Kaspaturos, he could still have hit on something vital, something central to what's brewing in Waziristan.'

'How d'you mean, Healey?'

'I mean this. Look at it this way. As I've said, there's a strong feeling running through the *khels*, its unmistakable, and there's been this breeze, this pervasive general talk of Kaspaturos emanating from Nashkar's holy man. That's fact. The tribes are being stirred up for what begins to feel uncommonly like a holy war – which is why I've stayed on beyond my orders, of course, intending to get to the heart of things before I pull out and report – if I can! But the stirring-up must be leading to some identifiable act, some concrete plan, obviously, and it's that that I've not been able to pinpoint. Now, suppose, once the full pressure has been built up, with Nashkar and the holy man sitting on the valve, the whole lot is released, crystallized as it were, in the word that the idenity of Kaspaturos has been revealed? That Peshawar, no less, is Kaspaturos? What happens?'

'The attack, presumably.'

'Quite. And what an attack, Ogilvie! All the bottled emotions that have been fermenting, the frustrations, the hopes of reviving past glories – all suddenly released, and not only released but channelled on to Peshawar and the British interlopers who occupy the city! It'll be the biggest massacre of all time, a total outpouring of all the tribes, riding hell-for-leather across the border, right the way along! It'll be unstoppable! And that, you see, is why all the talk I've picked up has always been broken off at a certain point – broken off because no one has been allowed to know any more until the pressure has been built right up. Then, and only then, will the holy man release the news about Peshawar. So even if O'Kelly is wrong factually, it doesn't matter. The tribes will believe the holy man.'

Ogilvie said, 'It's all theory still, isn't it?'

'Yes, but it holds together, old man! Didn't you say O'Kelly's advice was for you to concentrate on contacting the *sadhu*, the holy man?'

'Yes.'

'That was sound advice, Ogilvie. If what you've said is right, he has to be stopped before Kaspaturos and Peshawar are connected in the tribal mind. In the light of what you've said, I think that's vital.'

'Why haven't you had a go at the holy man yourself, Healey?'

90

Healey laughed. 'Lack of opportunity – I've never had so much as a smell of him until now, and smell's the right word I expect. And besides, you've only just made me aware of this Peshawar theory, haven't you? But let me repeat: stop the holy man, and you won't need to bother with Nashkar Ali Khan.'

'I'm also under orders to find out all that's going on and what the precise threat is. And the enemy's plans. That's what General Fettleworth wants – and that means Nashkar Ali Khan.'

Healey laughed. 'If I were you, I wouldn't worry too much about Bloody Francis! My instinct would be to follow O'Kelly. Frankly, in spite of what I said earlier, it could be that we have all we need about the threat that's building up, and a good enough general picture of the plan – a bloody great outpouring across the Waziri border, a rising to be joined probably by all the Frontier tribes. All I've lacked has been the *reason*. It's always important to try to follow the Pathan's line of thought. Now we have that as well – and we should act accordingly.'

Ogilvie shook his head. 'It's still only a theory, you know.' He added, 'I've been concentrating on finding Nashkar Ali Khan, to sell him arms and get his confidence – and get him to talk. Talk *fact*.'

'In other words, Bloody Francis carries more weight, even in your subconscious, than O'Kelly. Well – that's not surprising! But as it happens, I believe you'll find Nashkar and the *sadhu* both together, which you can regard as a stroke of luck.' Healey urged his horse forward again, towards the mountains. 'You won't mind if I come all the way with you? I could give you directions that'd put you inside Nashkar's scouts, but it'll give me some kudos in old Nashkar's eyes, if I lead in the man who can back up his armament supply.'

'I'll be glad to have you with me, 'Ogilvie said. Then he frowned. 'It's a lucky meeting, but I've a feeling it wasn't just chance. Was it?'

Healey laughed. 'Not entirely, old man, not entirely. The bush telegraph had informed me – I told you – that you'd been put on the track for Maizar, seeking out a good customer. I was determined to find you, I confess.'

'That was why you came to Maizar, too?'

'Yes. And my intentions, I assure you, were strictly lethal.'

'What about my Mr. Jones?'

'What about him, old man?' Healey, bathed in the cold light of the moon, stared into the gloomy mountains ahead.

'*Has* he got out of Waziristan? Was that the truth?'

'Oh yes, that was true – so far as my information goes, he was observed by some tribesmen beating it through a little-known pass south of Gumatti – between there and Bannu.'

'That's the way we came in.'

'I imagine so. Waziristan's a land of difficult entry until you know it well. Which one would suppose your Mr. Jones did.'

'Well, I'm glad he got out, Healey. He wasn't a bad sort, and he's done us a good turn, at least.'

'I still wouldn't mind seeing him swing for all he's done in the past. That sort – the sort who put profit before country – damn it all, Ogilvie, I've no time for them at all. To put no finer point upon it – they're filthy swine! And yet, when he's at home, I'll wager there's no one more respectable. A keen churchgoer, as likely as not! Fears God, and honours the Queen. Damned hypocrite.' Ogilvie, looking sideways at Healey, saw that his companion's face was cold and hard, forbiddingly framed by the black, flapless ear-holes and the totally bald head, cruelly ravaged by the mutilated nose. After a pause Healey asked suddenly, 'Know what it is, a week today?'

'I beg your pardon?'

Healey stared. 'I see you don't. You should. It's Her Majesty's official birthday.' Ogilvie fancied he detected a faint irony. He had, in fact, quite forgotten; though, had he been still on regimental duty in Peshawar, he would have been thinking of nothing else for some days past. For there would be spit-and-polish in the air of Peshawar, and much brisk activity on the parade-grounds, and an overhauling of full-dress scarlet and pipeclayed belts, all the brilliant trappings of Empire going on display to impress the natives with the far-flung authority of the little old lady with the bun, the bosom and the slightly scornful eyes. Regimental Sergeant-Major Cunningham would be busy supervising the Colour-Sergeants with their pace-sticks, Pipe-Major Ross would be rehearsing the pipes and drums of the battalion in all the appropriate tunes, including no doubt his own composition *Farewell to Invermore*, to tickle the ears of Lieutenant-General Francis Fettleworth as he rode along the ranks of the Royal Strathspeys on the day, in honour of the many years of his Queen-Empress. Out here in the oppressive splendour of the Waziri hills, so close now to Afghanistan, the Queen's Majesty seemed dimmed, even to falter before a more awe-inspiring majesty of nature; and yet, somehow, the very thought of that black-clad figure was comforting to James Ogilvie. In contrast to his wild surroundings, she was almost homely – though no doubt she would have been indignant at such a thought – the mother of a large family, with a mother's concern for all of them, and would guard each one of them with all the resources open to her. His image of her brought back familiar scenes . . . of the Court at Balmoral – James Ogilvie, as a child, had taken tea there with his father at Her Majesty's command – of the little black bundle disembarking from the London train at Waverley Station on one occasion when the Royal Strathspeys, then quartered at the Castle, had provided the Guard of Honour; of the royal carriage bowling along the Mall, and the gentlemen along the way uncovering and bowing, the ladies curtseying, drooping silk into the dust uncaringly as aloof dignity trotted past. In a very positive sense, Queen Victoria, who had been on the British throne for ever as it seemed, was home. Beneath the splendid Royal Standard floating over Buckingham Palace or Windsor she was warped and wefted into the very fabric of society and the family, the fount of all the virtues, all the graces, braveries and sacrifices – and of a host of odd tradition. Ogilvie gave a sudden explosive laugh as he recalled how an old servant at his father's ancestral home of Corriecraig Castle had once told him, with evident seriousness, that the new-fangled royal lavatories were furnished, not with rolls of paper as in lesser establishments, but with five-pound notes.

Healey asked, 'What's the joke, old man?'

'Oh – nothing. I was thinking of the Queen, Healey.'

This was received in reproving silence, rather squashingly.

Up in the hills, almost on the Afghan border north-west of Maizar, the decaying *sadhu*, the holy man, sat gazing out over a thousand years of history, of bloody tribal warfare, of which he had personal memories extending over some ninety of those turbulent years. The old *sadhu*, Nashkar Ali Khan reflected as he sat at the skinny feet, reverently, was like the walking dead. His eyes, red-rimmed where they were visible, were set in deep pits under shaggy white brows that were the sole evidence of hair on the long, fragile body. The nose was immense, the lips full, the chest scraggy, with corpse-like dark brown flesh stretched as tight as parchment over the rib-cage. The legs had a withered appearance and were thin from much sitting about,

93

and the *sadhu* had little self-motion, relying mainly upon the good offices of a succession of devoted attendants to move from place to place. Mostly he remained in these hills now, though he had recently been on his travels to the eastern part of Waziristan, talking to the tribes there and along a circuitous route that had brought him back at last to brood upon Afghanistan from whence all Pathans came. Frail he might be physically, and neglected in his person, but fervour and a deep inner power burned in his eyes and his influence was truly immense, truly far-flung, out of all proportion to an appearance that Nashkar Ali Khan would have considered it a heresy to describe as unprepossessing; and no jealousy had ever invaded the soul of Nashkar Ali Khan that, despite all his own worldly riches, despite his undoubted warriorcast leadership and his splendid palace outside the town of Maizar, the decaying old *sadhu* possessed a far greater power than he over the minds of men, an influence incomparably more insidious. For was not Mahomet, whose mouthpiece the *sadhu* was, good and wise and all-seeing?

'What thoughts, Master, are passing through your mind now?' Nashkar Ali Khan asked suddenly; the eternal brooding bored his own active mind intolerably, highly though he respected and valued the holy man. He had, after all, made his current pilgrimage in order to consult.

The *sadhu* moved no part of his body other than his lips; he was like a talking statue. He said in a far-off voice, 'My son, I think of other times . . . of days when the world was younger, of the great power and fame of our race.'

'Before the British came?'

'Long before the British came, my son. Before the Mongol Empire, before Kubla Khan, before Genghis Khan even. I see back into our remote past, into the days of great glory.'

'Which will come again, Master?'

'They will come again, my son. Many times have I said this.'

'I know – and I am glad.' Nashkar Ali Khan, more finely dressed than the *khel* leaders but still basically a Pathan warrior, with a face that proclaimed his calling, allowed a trace of impatience to escape into his tone. 'But the men of the tribes cannot be kept at a high pitch for too long without action. The fervour will depart. I have this very much in my mind. Success in fighting depends upon the heart and the spirit, and this time the British must be completely destroyed, all along the Frontier. You know what this means, Master?'

'Yes, my son, I know well. I promise you success, but we must yet await the sign.'

'You are convinced of success, when this sign comes?'

'There will be complete success. The city the British call Peshawar will fall, and will be destroyed by fire and by the sword, and all its men, women and children will be put to death. Yes, my son, I am convinced of success, for it has been promised to us by the prophets, even by the very tenets of our faith.'

'No more than this?'

'It is enough.' The holy man made a sign, and two attendants came forward and lifted him, holding the thin tall body between them so that the fragile legs dangled clear of the ground. He directed his carriers towards a flat, projecting ledge some yards away to his left. There was a long drop below, clear into a scrub-lined cleft through which the pass ran; it looked dangerous for so frail and old a man, but there was a most excellent view into Afghanistan and an equally good panoramic one of the whole orb of the sky above the surrounding peaks. The *sadhu* told the bearers to set him down on this ledge. They did so, then backed away in reverence; the *sadhu* called for Nashkar Ali Khan to join him.

'From here,' he said, 'I shall not miss the sign.'

'How will it come?'

The old man lifted a skinny brown arm and pointed into the Afghan hills. 'From that direction,' he said.

'And what form will it take?'

'I do not know, my son. But when it is revealed, I shall know beyond all doubt, and I will send for you.' He sounded wholly confident. 'I wish you and my bearers to leave me now, my son, to watch and wait in solitude.'

'It shall be as you say, Master.' Nashkar Ali Khan hesitated, surveying the comparatively narrow rock ledge and the terrible drop only a matter of feet away from where the *sadhu* sat. Old men, even old holy men, could become suddenly ill, and might try to move for help, and the *sadhu*, despite his frailness and the semi-motionless legs, might drag himself . . . the Pathan went hot and cold by turns as he thought of all his dreams of conquest vanishing, not in a puff of smoke, but in a heap of shattered bones far below in the pass. The tribes would not move if the *sadhu* should die before the sign was revealed. But the *sadhu* was his own law and his words were Nashkar Ali

Khan's commands, and argument, however reasonable, might, for all the Pathan knew, militate against the speedy revelation of signs. The mind, to be receptive, had to be composed, peaceful and remote from worldly things. Without further speech, Nashkar Ali Khan bowed and left the *sadhu*'s presence, making his way alone down the side of the mountain. From a bend in the pathway when he was nearing a group of his horsemen in the pass so far below the ledge, he stopped and looked back. He saw the distant, lofty figure of the *sadhu* sitting motionless on his perch, like a lonely old eagle frozen into stone, remote and immensely dignified. So much depended on the old man. Shaking his head, then prostrating himself to mutter a prayer, the Pathan turned away and hurried down to join his followers.

'We'll not have long to go now,' Healey said. 'At least, we shouldn't – if my information's correct, we should pick up friend Nashkar at the end of the pass.'

'Or he'll pick us up.'

'Yes, as a matter of fact that's more likely. He'll have sentries posted, and scouts out as well.' Healey yawned. 'My God, Ogilvie, a man gets bloody tired at this height! I'm still tired, even after a good night's sleep.' They had bivouaced shortly after midnight, and prepared a frugal meal from the remains of Mr. Jones's provisions, and then slept in their clothes in Ogilvie's small tent. They had moved on again after a dawn breakfast.

Ogilvie agreed about the tiredness; the thin air made the smallest movement into something of a conscious effort, and he was aware all the time of his breathing. But he was able to take this more or less cheerfully, for he felt that every step now was bringing him closer to the centre of events and that before much longer he would be on his way out of Waziristan. He asked Healey if he thought O'Kelly had been right in saying that there was rivalry between the tribes, between those in Waziristan and those in, say, Tirah and Bajaur to the north. Healey thought that was accurate enough.

'There's always rivalry,' he said.

'But jealousy – because Waziristan has the prophet, the holy man?'

'Very possibly. Yes, I'd agree with that. But it won't help us when the time comes.'

'They'll unite?'

'You bet they will! The eternal bickering and jockeying for position'll come afterwards – and by that time, old man, we won't be around to watch!'

'You sound as though you expect defeat.'

'Oh, I don't know,' Healey said. 'We British have pulled through bad patches before now, and I dare say we'll do so again. But it's going to stretch us to the limit, you know. We'll need lines of communication out to all points of the compass – unless we can bring about an abortion of the whole thing between us!'

Soon after this, Healey, who had been scanning the surrounding peaks through Ogilvie's binoculars – another legacy from Mr. Jones – pulled his horse up short. Ogilvie also halted. At first Healey didn't say anything, but just went on looking intently at one point far above and still some way ahead. Then he gave a short laugh and said, 'Bag of bones. Here – you have a look.'

Ogilvie took the glasses. 'Whereabouts?'

Healey showed him.

'I don't see ... oh, wait a moment – on a sort of flat ledge?'

'Yes. What d'you make of it?'

'Looks like a – a carving out of rock. Isn't there something in America – the Grand Canyon, isn't it, with all the presidents of—'

'On a rather larger scale, old man, and this isn't America. And that's no carving. Have another look.'

Ogilvie did so, taking his time. 'Whatever it is, it's not moving, I'm certain.'

'Quite right. Perpetual unmotion.'

'Oh, for heaven's sake, Healey . . . what *is* it?'

'It's your holy man,' Healey said calmly.

Ogilvie whistled in astonishment, but felt a thrill of excitement stirring his blood. 'What's he doing up there?'

'Ruminating. *Sadhu* on a peak, staring into the face of heaven. Also, if I'm not much mistaken, plotting something nasty. I'll tell you something else.'

'What?' Ogilvie was still looking intently through the binoculars, watching that distant immobile face set against the clear blue of the sky.

'Nashkar Ali Khan won't be far away. I told you before, we're already in the pass where he's to be found. For my money, we're under observation already. We'll get on, Ogilvie, and await developments. From now on, watch your step carefully.'

'I'll do that, all right!'

They moved ahead, jogging along the pass, avoiding falls of rock and boulders, keeping their eyes skinned for any movement ahead or to the sides. There was a curious feeling in Ogilvie's stomach, a vague loose wateriness, the feeling that always came to him before action but this time with an indefinable difference. This time he was moving, knowingly, into what could be a particularly nasty trap, the most dangerous ambush of his career so far. Whether or not he came out alive would depend not upon skill at arms or upon good tactics, nothing so soldierly as that, but upon the use for good or ill he could make of his tongue. For backing he would have no trained troops or comforting N.C.O.s, but only Captain Healey, who was very much an unknown quantity still. And he was a long, long way from base with no line of communication open and no guns handy; to say nothing of the total lack of a supply column!

The very air seemed still – seemed hostile in its very stillness and the surrounding jagged solitude. He felt that a thousand eyes were watching, that a thousand rifle-sights were bringing him into sniper-shot. They were deep into the pass by this time, and its high rock sides were shutting out the sky, bringing coldness and gloom and fear. The sounds of the horses' hooves rasped at his nerves as they sent their message of approach echoing off the cavern-like rock.

Then minutes later the first movement showed itself.

Ogilvie failed at first to see it; but heard Healey's warning voice beside him, kept low: 'We've made contact. Just keep going.'

'Where's the contact?'

'Left, and a little ahead. Sniper behind a boulder, on a ledge.'

Ogilvie looked from the corner of his eye. He saw the long, thin barrel pointing downwards. Soon after this, more became visible, and then two heads showed. Those two heads presaged the multitude; Nashkar Ali Khan was well guarded in his mountain retreat, however temporary a headquarters it might be; and now his quarterguard, as it were, was streaming nimbly down the side of the pass.

Healey halted his horse, reaching out to Ogilvie's bridle. 'Leave this to me,' he said.

As the first of the tribesmen came up, wearing what seemed to be livery of a sort, Healey spoke to them in their own dialect. Ogilvie could follow most of it without too much difficulty. Healey, who was obviously known as someone already in brotherhood with their leader, was explaining Ogilvie's desire to trade with Nashkar Ali Khan. He said, 'Wilshaw Sahib brings the promise of much comfort to our leader, the comfort of many weapons and bullets.'

A dark, sinewy hand was laid on Healey's bridle, another on Ogilvie's. 'Earless One, you will come with us.'

'Even so, brother.' They allowed their horses to be led forward along the pass. The war-equipped Pathans surged around them, hemming them in. The very air was heavy with the smell of their bodies; Ogilvie saw lice crawling on the skin of more than one of them. For the first time thoughts of disease came into his mind: typhus, cholera, dysentery the triple scourges of the British Army in India. He felt unclean, more unclean than he had felt even in the village huts, in the bazaar at Maizar. To some extent he believed this was mental, because he had come to do an unclean thing. He had come to kill a defenceless old man, the *sadhu* on the mountain top, that ruminating rock-carving. But possibly that immobile figure was far from defenceless; Nashkar Ali Khan's garrison was his as well.

The finery was tinsel, rubbishy. Cheap decorative jewellery such as Mr. Jones might have made a handsome profit from – and very likely had. There were few of the outward trappings of power or authority or imminent conquest of a part of an Empire about Nashkar Ali Khan as he sat like a spider in a cave leading off a rock fissure beside the main pass. Ogilvie, at first, had been conscious of a sense of disappointment. He had half expected some romantic storybook character, a Genghis Khan or an Atilla the Hun from out of the history text-books. There was nothing of romance or legend about Nashkar Ali Khan, who was almost as dirty as his common soldiery, and smelt as much too. His hair was dank and matted and his beard and moustache were greasy from food not yet washed off. But there was no doubt about the fact that the man was a leader. It was in his eyes, in the cut of his face, in his manner and in his speech. Wash him and starch him, give him a bun and a bosom, cut a foot or so from his height . . . yes, this man was of the stuff of emperors as well.

Greeting Healey, the Pathan swept his gaze curiously over Ogilvie. Then his attention went back to Healey. Incisively he said, 'Your story in detail, Earless One.'

Healey gave it. He described the meeting and the journey, with obvious exceptions, and also described how he had heard that the seller of arms had been wishing to contact the leader and that he had already made agreements with some of the *khels* in the eastern part of the country.

'A man to be trusted, Earless One?' Nashkar stroked a hand along his greasy moustache.

'This is my belief, Highness. Rumour speaks well of him.'

'Rumour speaks that he is willing to provide arms against his own countrymen?'

'Even so, Highness.'

Nashkar scanned Ogilvie again; the face was expressionless, but Ogilvie, perhaps through his own sensitivity, felt the scorn like the lash of a rawhide whip. 'Describe your wares,' the Pathan ordered in a harsh voice.

Ogilvie did so, in detail; bringing out his printed pamphlets in support.

Nashkar said, 'I, also, have heard the talk that says you have impressed my *khel* leaders. I, also, have heard the talk that says you wished to trade with me, with Nashkar Ali Khan. Why is this, Wilshaw Sahib?'

'Highness, my commissions. Clearly your orders will be large. I am only starting in this trade, as perhaps you also know. I must make money.'

'So you come to me, to provide your living for you?'

'I shall give you good service, and fast delivery.'

'And competitive prices?'

'We must discuss a price, Highness, but it will be a fair one.'

The cold eyes went into him like slivers of ice. 'And this fast delivery, Wilshaw Sahib. How fast? Where are your arms? In your English city of Birmingham?'

'Yes, Highness—'

The Pathan laughed scornfully. 'Come now, Wilshaw Sahib! Six weeks for your message to reach England, six weeks for your British merchants to delay, and six weeks for your promised cargo to reach Bombay – or longer, to come more safely overland through Persia and Afghanistan. Four months – which is four months too long!'

'Highness, you forget that I can cable to England, which is fast. And our merchants are not slow. But better than this: I have arsenals concealed in Abbottabad. My supply can be very quick, I do not need to await replenishments from England, indeed, your *khels* will be supplied from Abbottabad.'

Nashkar nodded slowly, as if interested; he went on nodding for a while, with a curious glitter in his eyes, a wily glitter that worried Ogilvie, and then he said, 'I am told that you are well spoken for by the other seller of arms – Jones Sahib, a man whom the leaders of the *khels* have come to trust. This is so?'

'I am grateful to Jones Sahib for speaking well of me. I have come to take his place.'

Surprisingly, Nashkar Ali Khan roared with laughter at this; he shook and rumbled, he slapped at his thighs, he gasped with merriment. His entourage, grouped around Healey and Ogilvie, smirked politely. When the laughter had run through him Nashkar said, 'Wilshaw Sahib, you speak the truth perhaps – more, I believe, than you yourself imagine. It has been interesting to exchange words with you – words exchanged in fun, in play only. Mere teasing.'

Ogilvie said, 'I don't understand, Highness.' He glanced sideways at Healey, saw the quickly extinguished flicker of warning in his face. He was aware of a rustle running through the assembled Pathans, a rustle of what seemed to be anticipation. Something clearly, had gone wrong.

Nashkar Ali Khan, smiling coldly, said, 'Wilshaw Sahib, I have a surprise for you,' and made a signal to a member of the entourage. This man left the cavern with two others, all three of them heavily armed. With fear pricking into his very guts, Ogilvie waited in a heavy silence. A few minutes later he heard footsteps and he looked towards the mouth of the cavern. The three men were coming back, with a fourth. A stout, short, ragged figure with a heavy brown moustache, a figure trying hard to keep its end up by means of a cocky bounciness that had lost its mainspring – Mr. Jones of Brum.

CHAPTER SEVEN

'WELL, well, if it isn't Mr. Wilshaw. Well, now, isn't that nice? How've you been making out, may I ask, Mr. Wilshaw?'

'I've got where I wanted, Mr. Jones.'

'That's fine. I hope you bring off a nice deal, Mr. Wilshaw, I do indeed. Retiring I may be, but I've not lost interest, far from it.' Jones stopped and brought out the green handkerchief. He mopped at his face and neck. It was cool, almost cold, in the cavern but the arms salesman was sweating like a pig. 'Yes, well. What do you want of me, Highness?'

Ogilvie looked across at Nashkar Ali Khan, who was standing with folded arms, watching Jones. The Pathan's face gave nothing away but there was now no doubt that everything had taken a wrong turn somewhere along the line. Glancing quickly at Healey, Ogilvie found the same lack of expression but was aware of a vein pumping hard in the side of Healey's neck beneath one of the naked earholes.

Answering Jones's question Nashkar said, 'Tell Wilshaw Sahib what has happened so far.'

'What has happened, Highness?'

'To you.'

Jones drooped pathetically. He lifted his arms, let them fall again to his sides, and said, 'They stopped me, Mr. Wilshaw. Just as I was about to cross the border out.'

'Why was that?'

Jones said, 'I don't know, really. They've always trusted me, and I've always trusted them. I told you once, you can rely on the word of a Pathan because in his own way he's a gentleman. Or was. Times have changed – seems like.' He gave Nashkar a hurt look.

'It was necessary to detain you, seller of arms, at this moment of history, as I have already told you. It would have been necessary to detain anybody attempting to leave our country – just in case he had learned certain things that I do not wish to be made known yet beyond our frontiers.' He paused. 'I think you know to what I am referring, Jones Sahib.'

'No,' the fat man said. He looked lost, not at all the confident Jones Ogilvie had known. 'I really don't know, Highness. I – I just sell for my firm, that's all, I don't meddle.' Once again Ogilvie looked at Healey; he recalled that officer's words about Jones, the man who lived on dirty money and in effect traded with the lives of British soldiers. In this unexpected situation, Healey's reactions might not be entirely dependable; in spite of training and discipline, something might show.

Then, once again, and as suddenly as before, the situation changed, growing more menacing. Nashkar Ali Khan smiled and said, 'But – and this I have not yet told you – you have a loud voice, Jones Sahib, a voice that is easily overheard, even so far away as Abbottabad,' and then Ogilvie remembered how he had tried to silence Jones that evening, so long ago it seemed, when the arms salesman had bellowed angrily about decency and his own motives.

'You were allowed to enter Waziristan without hindrance,' Nashkar Ali Khan said softly, a hand falling to the curved knife at his waist, 'but, as you have already found, the leaving is not so free.'

So, Ogilvie thought with a heavy heart, they had been expected all along and, no doubt, watched every inch of the way thereafter.

The Pathan gestured towards Healey. 'You have seen the Earless One. Pain proved his trustworthiness. Much more pain is coming your way, Jones Sahib, and yours, Wilshaw Sahib, but not to prove a trustworthiness that is not there. It will be to make you talk, and I shall start with you, Jones Sahib. Fat men talk faster when the flesh is pricked, the wind escapes as from a pricked pig's bladder!'

They were ordered to walk through to the back of the cavern, whence they climbed a steeply ascending passage to emerge into the open. They came on to a wide expanse of flat, table-like rock. The tribesmen formed a rough circle, with Jones quaking in the centre. A blade was pressed into Ogilvie's back. He watched Edward Healey, standing a little apart from the others, his face still without readable expression. Ogilvie wondered how it was that Captain Healey, so close, apparently, to

Nashkar Ali Khan, had not known the wind's direction better than this . . . and that he had been so sure that Jones had crossed the border into safety.

A fire was started, and long irons were brought to red heat. Jones sweated more than ever, and made great play with the green handkerchief, which was by now no more than a dirty wet rag. He was ordered to strip, and he did so with alacrity and obsequiousness, as though obedience could propitiate the Pathan. He looked grotesque and pathetic, a lump of quivering lard. All the same, there was an obstinacy about his face, or it could have been bravado, that said he was going to do the decent thing this time. In point of fact, as Ogilvie knew, he had little enough to tell beyond the one damning fact that Wilshaw Sahib was not Wilshaw Sahib at all.

That, and that alone. But it would be more than enough to shift the torture on to Ogilvie.

Jones gave a loud cry as a tribesman brought a heated iron from the fire and pushed the red-hot end towards him.

Nashkar Ali Khan lifted an inquiring eyebrow.

Jones said in a high voice, 'No, no!' Then, as the iron jabbed suddenly into his buttocks, he leapt screaming into the air. Landing again, he received another jab. Clapping his hands over his bottom he ran, still screaming, desperately seeking escape, trying to break the circle of wild Pathans. He was hurled back into the arena by brutal hands, to become an object of derisive laughter, as he scuttled and cried and twisted away from the searing, searching iron.

Ogilvie felt sick, really physically sick to retching point. He knew he could save poor Jones further pain and that indeed there was little point in his not doing so straight away, since Jones would obviously break before long. He looked across at Healey, seeking some sort of sign, some guidance in what he ought to do. But there was nothing – nothing in Healey's face beyond a horrible kind of fascination in Jones's painful indignity, as if Captain Healey were only too delighted a spectator of the profit motive getting its just punishment. There was no pity, and there was also no fear. But then Healey had no cause for alarm in a personal sense – Jones knew nothing about *his* identity; and even if Ogilvie should be uncovered and sacrificed, Healey's work as an agent would continue and once he had his facts he would run out and make his report to his superiors in Ootacamund.

The screams continued and so did the terrible jabbing of the red-hot iron, branding Jones for all time. Tears were streaming down his face now, and he was gasping for breath as he ran and twisted, fell and got up again almost like a comedy doll with a bias base. But it was Ogilvie himself, who, a fraction before Jones, reached his limit. As he saw the man's bloated, tear-stained face turned towards him, as if in pleading, he stepped forward and opened his mouth to make what he now saw as an inevitable confession. Jones, however, beat him to it in the end.

The arms salesman called out, 'No more, Nashkar, I'll tell you what I know. So help me God, but I can't go on, Mr. Wilshaw.' He fell in a heap on the ground, and the rest was a mumble. 'Not you, Mr. Wilshaw. You wouldn't be able to live with yourself after, I know your sort, not like me. You're a sahib and I know what that means. So I'll stay true to type and do the dirty to save you doing it.' He lifted his head. His mouth was like jelly, wobbling and trembling. There was a tense silence, during which once again Ogilvie glanced at Healey. Healey's hand was moving inside his robe, where Ogilvie knew he had a revolver. For a moment he wondered if Healey meant to shoot Jones before he talked, and then try to break the two of them out; but guessed that Healey wouldn't risk that, since his own cover was safe.

Jones said, 'Nashkar, Mr. Wilshaw isn't Mr. Wilshaw. I was told to bring him in as my makee-learn assistant.'

'Told?'

'Paid.'

'By whom?'

'A man. I don't know who he was. He gave me cash.' Jones shook. 'That's all I know. I swear it. I swear it before God. I can't take any more of that iron. If I knew any more, I'd tell you, but I don't. I don't!'

Nashkar nodded. A cold wind had started to blow around the group of men, and the sun, though high now, brought little warmth to the mountains. Thin streamers of milky cloud trailed over Afghanistan to the west. The Pathan said, 'I think you speak the truth, seller of arms, but your supposed assistant clearly has much to say.' He gestured to his followers. 'Bring him to me.'

Ogilvie was seized and hustled towards Nashkar Ali Khan.

The Pathan lifted his right hand and gave him two stinging slaps, back-handers, across the cheeks, blows that rocked his head badly. 'You will talk.'

'I will not talk.'

The Pathan smiled. 'You sound very sure of yourself, Englishman, but I am far from sure. I watched your face a few minutes ago ... you were ready to talk but you were saved the necessity. You do not like witnessing pain. I believe, as I have said, that Jones Sahib knows no more than he has spoken of already. It is you alone who can save him now.'

He gave an order in Pushtu and two of the tribesmen went towards Jones and picked him up, setting him on his feet and holding him steady. Jones was blubbering like a baby, all control gone. Healey was still watching with supercilious lack of concern; but Ogilvie fancied he saw a more wary look in his eye, the beginning of a fear that Ogilvie might well break, and, in so doing, give away his own cover after all.

But Ogilvie knew that whatever might happen now, he must never do that. He must shut his eyes to Jones's weeping, his ears to the terrible cries that tore at him and rang across the peaks, echoing into the Afghan hills as the dreadful proceedings were resumed. The time for burning was past now, the embers of the smouldering fire kicked out in a shower of sparks. Fresh implements were brought, irons of different shapes and uses. To some extent at least, this was the Pathan creed of *badal* in action, an exercise in the stark cruelty of war-minded men, of a race that held human life as cheap as dirt and who, as fighters, scorned the fury of any gods. Ogilvie closed his eyes, but was made to open them again. Afterwards, he found his memory for detail unclear, as though his subconscious had drawn a protective veil over the images that had moved across his vision. His memories were a blur of demented screaming, of gushing blood as Jones's tongue was drawn – not cut – from his mouth, drawn out by an iron clamp that extended it until something gave way and the bloody remnants were cast on the ground at his feet. He remembered the empty eye sockets, but without a conscious remembrance of the act that had put out the eyeballs. He could see the stumps of arms and legs after the hackings of a curved blade had severed them, one after the other, so that Jones was reduced to a twitching, sightless, speechless but still moaning trunk only just about alive. Cruelly, death would not come to him, though it was only a matter of time before he bled to death. Equally cruelly, Ogilvie could remember the actual end with terrible clarity: the sight of Jones finally being flayed with long whips that ripped the living skin from all that was left of him, of the shattered bloody mouth sending out bubbles of red blood that turned the whimpers and moans into grotesque gurgles, and the body bouncing up from the ground, into the air, propelled by desperate levering movements of the stumps, as it tried to evade the all-seeking, all-finding lashes of the whips.

When Jones was dead Ogilvie expected the same kind of treatment and wondered how long he would take to break. But he was wrong. Nashkar Ali Khan, showing no discomposure that he hadn't talked, turned to him and said, 'For you – whom I shall still address for the time being as Wilshaw Sahib – for you, a different treatment.'

'Why so?' Sick to the stomach, Ogilvie still had his head up, though his face was as white as a sheet beneath his tan. 'Different in what way?'

'You will see. I do not wish to kill you. I may have a use for you. I believe you are a British officer, sent into Waziristan to spy upon me.'

Ogilvie shrugged. 'Believe what you like. I can't control your thoughts.' Although the idea of continuing to live as a British officer, rather than die like Jones, had its attractions, his duty was still plain: he must scotch any suggestions that he was what he was.

'Why do you persist in a denial of what is obvious?'

'I do not know what is obvious, Nashkar Ali Khan. Except that I am a seller of arms.'

The Pathan made a gesture of irritation. 'Come, you cannot expect me to believe this now!'

'It is nevertheless the truth. The man who paid money to Jones Sahib . . . he was from another arms firm. A rival. I was to be planted on Jones Sahib's territory . . . to take over his contacts. I am employed, not by Jones Sahib's firm, but by this other one. I can still arrange for a supply of arms.' It was all he could think of, and it was as useless as he had expected it to be.

Nashkar laughed loudly, lifting his arms to the sky. 'I am taken for a fool, a child! If this is true, why did you not speak before?'

'Because to do so would not have saved Jones Sahib any

suffering, as well you know, Nashkar Ali Khan. You would have continued with the torture whatever had happened.'

The Pathan nodded. 'It is true I do not like being deceived by any man, but I think the true reason why you did not say this earlier is because Jones Sahib would have failed to order his thoughts in time to back you convincingly, and for him to die suited you better. Or that such fantasy has only at this moment flown into your mind, Wilshaw Sahib.'

'I repeat, you must think your own thoughts. I cannot make you believe me if you do not wish to, Nashkar Ali Khan, but it takes a fool to turn away help before complete certainty is reached.'

The Pathan laughed again. 'Then to such extent, Wilshaw Sahib, I accept the name of fool!' Impatient now, he swung away on his heel, striding to the edge of the flat rock with his garments blowing out along the cold wind, and stood for a moment gazing out, like the *sadhu* on his high peak overhead, at the brown and purple Afghan hills. He was a commanding figure, Ogilvie thought, and a very confident one. He had seemed in fact little troubled about having a spy in the camp, an attitude that seemed to indicate his plans as being so far advanced towards fulfilment as to be unassailable by any spying. Nevertheless, Ogilvie was surprised to note an air of frustration about the Pathan leader as Nashkar Ali Khan turned his back on the panorama of the hills and once again faced his prisoner. He walked almost moodily towards Ogilvie, and stopped in front of him. Fingering his beard he said, 'A little subterfuge in your case, Wilshaw Sahib. A provocation, something to agitate the minds of your British soldiers. Many times throughout our history it has been of benefit to cause doubt and anxiety in the heads of the enemy.'

'I have no connection with British soldiers, Nashkar Ali Khan. There is no enmity in my thoughts.'

The Pathan laughed. 'You are a foolish man, Wilshaw Sahib. So foolish! Were it not for the fact that I believe you to be a British officer, you would already be dead. As dead as Jones Sahib who – a mere seller of arms in very truth – had the temerity to bring you into my land! But as a British officer, Wilshaw Sahib, you may have a very welcome use.'

It was true, Ogilvie thought. Bargaining, holding him as a hostage, using him as a threat in so many possible ways – he was much more use alive than dead, clearly. Jones hadn't been.

He said, 'Very well, then. If you wish, regard me as a British officer. It'll do you no good, of course, but it's entirely your decision. What's this subterfuge you spoke of?'

'For now it remains known to me alone. Brooding upon this will do you no harm, Wilshaw Sahib, and you will do your brooding here, in the solitude of the mountain-tops.' The Pathan had words with his followers after which three of the tribesmen, with the long-barrelled rifles in their hands, took charge of Ogilvie and led him away. Nashkar Ali Khan laid a friendly hand on Captain Healey's shoulder. 'Come, Earless One,' he said. 'For the time being, the fleshpots of Maizar once again – and you shall join me. If we are lucky, the time for fighting will come soon now.'

Ogilvie's last sight of them, as he looked back on starting a descent from the flat expanse of rock, was of the two men engaged in an amicable conversation. In close company with his escort, Ogilvie walked through the cavern, out into the fissure and across the pass, after which he was told to follow a path running up the mountain-side. They climbed for a long way, no easy matter in the rare atmosphere, stopping at last beside a hole in the hillside that reared above the lonely, barren track. To Ogilvie's right the landscape fell away, to give the same outlook, but a much longer one, as had faced the flat rock where Jones had died: a splendid view into Afghanistan, home of the Pathans. And, looking upwards to a higher peak in the range where he stood – looking, as though his eye had been drawn involuntarily to the spot – Ogilvie saw what he had seen earlier, at a greater distance through his binoculars; the old carven face and skinny frame of the *sadhu*, Nashkar's holy man, keeping his unending vigil for Ogilvie knew not what. It was a remarkable sight, almost a frightening one. There must surely be some sinister objective behind that cold and lonely vigil.

The men of the escort party pushed Ogilvie towards the hole, ahead of the long, snaking bayonets, rustily projecting from the barrels of the rifles.

'Into the cavity,' one of them said in Pushtu.

'There is no room.' The hole was scarcely two feet in height, and little more in depth from the track. 'I could not even curl up like a dog.'

'There is room. See!' The man pushed his rifle and bayonet into the hole, prodding downwards into darkness. He appeared not to touch bottom. Ogilvie, realizing the hopelessness of resistance, shrugged and moved forward and carefully lowered himself into the hole. It was a fearsome business, for anything might lurk in that pit, but he was fortified by Nashkar Ali Khan's expressed desire to keep him alive. There was bottom, as his feet told him when his head was just about on a level with the tribesmen's knees. This bottom felt like dry rock, with a thin covering of rubble. Tiny things, lizards probably, scuttled over his groping feet. His head, he found on looking upward, was an inch or two clear of the roof of the hole.

The Pathans bent, and looked in on him; then turned away, and he heard grunting and straining noises, and the clumping, dragging sound of something heavy being brought towards the hole. It was a boulder, oval in shape, and weathered by its long sojourn in the hills to an overall smoothness like the egg of some colossal nightmare bird. This boulder was rolled and pushed towards Ogilvie, into the mouth of the hole, where its poles slotted neatly and very firmly into grooves on either side. Ogilvie's eyes were just clear of it, and he was able to look out; but it formed a very effective key to a very effective prison.

When the boulder was in place there was some low chatter outside and soon after this Ogilvie heard footsteps going away. He was not, however, to be left alone. More footsteps, slower ones close at hand, told him this; and a moment later he saw the feet and the hem of the dirty garment of the Pathan who had been left on guard.

He could still see the holy man, as motionless as before.

The silence of the high hills was intense, a living force of nature. Occasionally and startlingly, it was broken by the raucous squawk of a bird, or the horrible slow flap of greedy vultures' wings as the birds of prey circled expectantly overhead, foul birds bent upon a foul meal – carrion birds that, oddly, seemed not to go near the lonely *sadhu*, so far as Ogilvie could see.

Hours passed in this silence; the sun went down into the distant Afghan hills. There was a crack of a rifle from somewhere; the vultures, crying out, wheeled away, flapping off for a look. Perhaps, in the silence, a man had died. There was no apparent human reaction, and even the Pathan, sitting down outside the hole, showed no interest; he didn't even move the scrawny legs thrust out before his body. But soon after this he stirred, and held a water-bottle through the hole, putting it to Ogilvie's lips.

'Drink,' he said.

Ogilvie did so, though he guessed the water would be far from clean. 'Food,' he said.

'Patience, Englishman.'

More time passed, then once again the guard rose to his feet stiffly and pushed some tough substance into Ogilvie's mouth – it tasted like meat of some kind, but had the consistency of india-rubber. Ogilvie retched, but forced himself to swallow. Life had to be maintained. As night fell, he dozed, slipping into uneasy nightmares, into disordered thoughts. The constriction of the elongated hole was of itself painful; he longed to stretch his limbs, which shook and twitched with inaction and restlessness; but he could do no more, in what was in effect a sheath that enclosed him in as glove-like a fashion as any sword's scabbard, than wriggle his fingers and shuffle his feet. It was a claustrophobic feeling that could soon bring panic – and almost had already. Each time he had felt that panic encroaching Ogilvie had taken a deep breath and forced his thoughts away from the hole, away from his body, to roam in the free world.

Next day as the sun came up, invisibly behind him, to lighten the grandeur of the hills, the guard provided breakfast: a drink from the water-bottle, and some crushed maize which the dirty hands once again fed directly into his mouth. At least it was nourishment; if he was not to be feted, he was not to be totally starved. It was proof that Nashkar Ali Khan had meant what he said, and it was proof to be held on to as an earnest of eventual release.

Munching maize, he looked upward at the *sadhu*'s peak. The old man was still there, still motionless. 'What does the *sadhu* eat?' he asked his warder. 'Manna from heaven?'

'The *sadhu* is fasting,' the man answered. He turned away from Ogilvie to stare upward. 'A fast of indefinite length, it is said, but he will survive.'

'How do you know?'

'It is written.'

'What is he waiting for? Is that written, too?'

'All is written, and men have only to read and follow. Or listen to the words of the wise men, the men who read, and then follow. The *sadhu* awaits a sign.'

'I see.' Ogilvie hesitated. 'What is this sign, then?'

'No man can say what form the sign will take, but when it comes, the *sadhu* will know.'

'Is it the sign for fighting, for war . . . war on the British?'

The tribesman said, 'Yes, even so, Englishman. It will be the sign for deliverance, for the throwing-off of a yoke for too long strung about the necks of my race. When the sign shows itself. there will be a most mighty upsurge that will overwhelm the usurpers and cast them into the sea whence they came.' There was fervour in the man's eyes and voice, dedication in his whole being. 'It is this for which the whole Pathan nation now waits.' He lifted a lean, hard arm. 'Up there, upon the peak, the *sadhu* sits as you see. Upon our loftiest peak, from where he watches over the land of our ultimate birth. It is he who soon will light the lamp, and when he lights it, Englishman, its glow will instantly be seen along the borders of the British Raj, and all men will follow it.'

'And Nashkar Ali Khan?'

'He is our leader, and we will follow him.'

'But only on the word of the *sadhu*?'

The man nodded. 'Even so.'

Ogilvie found this interesting; evidently O'Kelly had been as right as Healey had thought. Without the *sadhu*, Nashkar Ali Khan might well dwindle to the status of a mere *khel* chieftain. Without the *sadhu*, the fervour would go out of the tribes. He asked, 'And the sign which the *sadhu* awaits . . . if this does not come, what then?'

'The sign will come,' the man said with firm conviction.

'But if it should not?' Ogilvie persisted.

'It is a useless speculation. The sign will come. The *sadhu* has promised this.'

There was no doubting his sincerity and his utter, single-minded belief; but there was equally no doubting the content of the answer he would not give: no sign, no rising. It was as clear as if he had shouted it aloud from the mountain top. And, if the sign should in fact fail to reveal itself, the impact of its failure was going to be the more catastrophic to Nashkar Ali Khan's hopes by simple virtue of the overwhelming importance already accredited to it.

Ogilvie looked up again at the *sadhu*. At any moment, presumably, the sign might be revealed. It would not be overtly revealed to Ogilvie, or indeed, perhaps, to anybody but the *sadhu* himself. History, very bloody history, would assemble its legions in the processes of an old man's mind; and the subcontinent would move inexorably to war.

CHAPTER EIGHT

THE day had come at last, the day of the Queen's birthday parade, the official celebration delayed until after the rains; and from the Himalayas in the north to Cape Comorin at India's southern tip the loyal subjects of the Queen-Empress had gathered to pay her homage, and to show their love and respect. The sound of trumpets was in the very air hanging over city and village, swamp and mountain, forest and fertile plain, over sacred river and desolate, empty gorge. Even the gaily-decorated elephants, lumping along in the parades beneath the lurching *howdahs*, seemed to be rejoicing.

In the Peshawar garrison a splendid extravaganza had been mounted; cavalry, infantry, artillery and support corps were to march their might past Lieutenant-General Francis Fettleworth. Three squadrons of the Guides would lead, followed by the Bengal Lancers, moving past the saluting base at a walk before cantering off with a rattle of harness to the strains of Bonnie Dundee from an artillery band. After them, leading the infantry, would come the 114th Highlanders, the Queen's Own Royal Strathspeys, behind Lieutenant-Colonel Lord Dornoch and the pipes and drums. The guns, so disliked by General Fettleworth, would rumble past behind their horse-drawn dark-green limbers after the last of the infantry but ahead of the menials of the support corps. There had been some high-level complaints from the artillery commanders about this virtual down-grading, and plenty of tooth-sucking from lowly sergeants and bombardiers and gunners; but all to no avail. Fettleworth, as was his custom, was adamant.

There had been complaints on another matter also. Lord Dornoch himself, never a man to be overawed by rank, had spoken out strongly at the conference called by the Divisional Commander to settle the plan for the birthday parade. He had got to his feet and he'd stated his opinion. 'Sir, as you before all of us know, we're likely to be having trouble with the tribes.'

'True, Colonel. Why do you bring this up now?' Fettleworth plucked irritably at his Sam Browne belt.

'For this reason, sir. I doubt if this is the time to concentrate virtually the whole division upon one parade-ground. Can we not reduce the strength of the parade, in view of our possible commitments?'

'It would be a slight upon Her Majesty, Lord Dornoch.'

'I think not, sir, I think not! I think I know where Her Majesty's closest interest lies, and, given the choice, it would not be found to lie in pomp and ceremony.'

'Pomp and ceremony, fiddlesticks! A parade's a parade, a simple mark of respect – and besides, it's always been done.' Fettleworth snapped his teeth angrily. 'If I *must* justify my decisions to my Colonels, let me say this: in full assembly, no enemy can possibly catch us unawares, which is what you seem to be suggesting – hey? We'll be all ready for 'em!'

'In scarlet, sir – in full-dress scarlet, with ladies in the stands? Why, damn it to hell, sir, we'll be all but caught with our breeches round our ankles! We'll have the guns firing into the backsides of the infantry, and the infantry climbing up the cavalry's tails!'

Dornoch had overstated his case; Fettleworth had not liked the rustle of amusement that had run through the assembled officers, and he had snapped Dornoch's head off. His decision stood; there would be a full muster on parade and no excusals except for men on the various fatigues who could not be clean in time to march.

And now, here they were. Fettleworth, impressive in his scarlet coat and white breeches, shining spurred riding boots, white feathers cascading down his cocked hat, breast colourful with the medals and stars of past campaigns, stood four-square to the thump of the music on the saluting platform. Behind him Brigadier-General Lakenham, Chief of Staff, and his Brigade Commanders and aides-de-camp, plus certain high-ranking departmental officers, and a representative Civilian from Calcutta sweating into clerkly black cloth. Behind again, the senior ladies in the stand – Mrs. Fettleworth, Mrs. Lakenham, Lady Dornoch, Mrs. Colonel this-and-that. Fettleworth rose and fell slightly on his beautiful polished bootheels, feeling the heat but feeling a surge of emotion too as the squadrons of the Guides approached amid the clash and thunder of the gunners' band crashing out patriotic and traditional tunes. As his right hand began quivering, ready to return the salute of the officer commanding the cavalry, he thought of Her Majesty and his chest swelled. When the cavalry had passed, his hand came down, rose again to acknowledge the lifted claymore of Lord Dornoch, riding behind the barbaric wail of his pipes, the colourful kilts of his highland men swinging behind. As the sloped rifles and the gleaming bayonets went past to the tune of The High Road to Gairloch, guarding the resplendent battle-honoured Colours of the Royal Strathspeys, a runner from Division hastened on to the parade-ground and made his way below the stand towards the saluting base. He caught the eye of an A.D.C. and saluted. The young officer bent towards him, impatiently.

'Urgent message for the General, sir.'

'Great heavens, man, he can't possibly take it now!' The A.D.C. gnawed at his moustache, anxiously, gilded ropes and tent-pegs dithering at his left shoulder. '*How* urgent?'

Music blared brassily across the vast sandy space, seeming to echo as far as distant Himalaya frowning grandly to the north; heat pressed down, rose again from the ground to make men swelter into thick full-dress uniforms. The runner had to shout; the message was something about a man called Wilshaw. 'It'll have to wait,' the A.D.C. said irritably. 'I'll inform the Chief of Staff after the march past.' Fettleworth's view on interruptions to solemn occasions were well known to all his officers, and so were his patriotic emotions. His eyes were always a trifle moist after a surfeit of martial music and subaltern-borne Colours, and his inner thoughts about the Monarch were not so private as he fancied. It was the same on every royal occasion, and an A.D.C. had once been heard to remark in the Mess that Bloody Francis ought to send a picture postcard to Windsor Castle reading 'having a wonderful time, wish you were here'.

The arrival of the message at Division had ended a journey as circuitous as had been Ogilvie's own meanderings from Peshawar to Waziristan by way of Abbottabad. It had been ridden across the border by a fast horseman out of Maizar, and taken over by another in a tiny village in Bannu, and hastened north into Kohat. In the town of Hangu it had been transferred to an itinerant knife-grinder who had brought it more slowly to Peshawar and handed it over to a friend of the same calling who knew Peshawar intimately. This man had wrapped the roughly scrawled message around a stone and, whilst pursuing his trade in the vicinity of the British military officers' married quarters, had deftly hurled it through the first unshuttered window he had found, knowing very well that it would reach its ultimate destination in safety. The window had happened to be that of a bungalow occupied by a Surgeon-Major of the Army Medical Staff who had prudently placed himself on the sick list for the duration of the parade, he being a man who disliked great heat; thus he had been at home when the message arrived, and, supposedly sick or not, he knew his duty. He had personally taken the message to Divisional Headquarters and had handed it over to a Staff Captain on duty. It was another three hours before General Fettleworth's mind was free to concentrate on the message from Waziristan and when he did read it at last, back in his residence, he announced loudly that it should have been brought to his attention much earlier.

'Could be serious,' he said, easing the sweat-soaked neckband of his scarlet tunic. Glory was still circling in his head, reducing his concentration. 'With a *tum, tum, tum, tum, tum ... tum*. Yes. Damn serious – I don't like it, Lakenham.'

'Nor I, sir.' The message was simple enough, baldly put. *This is written on behalf of a British officer, Wilshaw Sahib, held prisoner as a spy in Waziristan. He asks help before he is tortured.* There was no signature.

'It's a trap, of course.' Fettleworth sat down and drummed his fingers on his desk. 'What do they take me for – hey?'

'I'm not inclined to agree entirely, sir.'

'*Not* a trap?' Fettleworth snorted. 'Fiddlesticks – of course it is! Ogilvie wouldn't ask for help – no officer would in the circumstances.'

'Again, I can't agree. The message speaks of torture—'

'Torture! Damn it, this isn't the Middle Ages!'

'No, sir, but it's the North-West Frontier. We know very well that the tribes indulge in torture.'

'Yes, but it's so damn melodramatic, isn't it? Overplayed. *Asks for help before he is tortured.* Sort of thing a damn *native* would write!'

'Exactly, sir.'

Fettleworth looked blank. 'What d'you mean – hey?'

'A native *did* write it, sir. Surely that's obvious?'

'No need to be rude, Lakenham.'

'I'm sorry, sir.'

Fettleworth scowled at the message, pushed at it with his hand, with distaste. 'A native, eh? A *friendly* native! A damn courageous native – to take such a risk! No, Lakenham, I'm convinced it's a trap of some sort. Very fishy.'

The Chief of Staff blew down his nostrils, heavily. 'Very good, sir. What do we do about it?'

Fettleworth pondered, fingering his chin. Then, 'Send for Lord Dornoch,' he ordered. 'Tell him to report at once.'

'Very good, sir.' On his way out of the General's presence, Lakenham turned. 'Is Ogilvie's father to be informed?'

'Good God, no, certainly not ... not *yet*.'

'But—'

'That's all, Lakenham. *No one* is to be informed of anything in this connection. Oh, except Major O'Kelly, of course. He'd better come along with Dornoch. See to that, Lakenham.'

When Dornoch and the Political Officer arrived, Fettleworth showed them the message and repeated his belief that it was a trap. In opposition to the Chief of Staff, they both agreed that it probably was, though neither could suggest what the purpose of a trap might be. Lakenham made his point once again about torture. He said, 'No man can be sure how he's going to stand up to the sort of thing the Pathans can dish out. Dornoch, you say Captain Ogilvie wouldn't explicitly request help, that he'd simply – well, sit down and take it. But—'

'That's my opinion,' Dornoch said. 'The Ogilvies have a long military tradition and I've served under his father myself. I think I can forecast what young Ogilvie's attitude would be and it's as I've stated.'

'I don't agree—'

'You never do,' Fettleworth put in angrily.

'—I think, if he found the opportunity to ask for help, he or any other officer might use it, just in case he should break under stress. I confess, *I* would. And I would do it in the best interests of my orders, what's more! Surely, it's better to ask honestly for help than run the risk of giving away information?'

'A British officer,' Fettleworth began as expected, 'would never—'

'One moment, General,' Dornoch cut in brusquely. 'Brigadier, I take your point, of course. But in *Ogilvie*'s case ... I don't see him doing so. I have an idea that the older you get – the more *senior* you get – the better a sense of these things you develop. You and I have seen for ourselves what the Pathans can

117

do – we've seen the results. Ogilvie isn't so experienced on the Frontier. And I think any young officer who's only just been given a captaincy . . . no, his reactions would be different. He'd feel, very likely mistakenly, that he could pull through it on his own – and that he *must*, what's more!' He shook his head. 'I don't see him initiating such a call for help. I have to agree with the General.'

'Thank you,' Fettleworth said with a touch of sarcasm. 'O'Kelly, I think you also agree?'

'Yes, broadly. Mainly, I think, for this reason: I told him he was on no account to communicate with Peshawar, and I also put it to him before he left that he wouldn't get any help anyway. He thoroughly understood *that*. It's part of my routine, of course. It's nasty, but there it is.' He flapped a hand in the air, dismissing conscience.

'Nothing *nasty* about it,' Fettleworth snapped. 'It's a case of duty, no more, no less. Now then, what about this trap? No ideas at all, gentlemen?'

Glances were exchanged, shoulders shrugged, and it was left to O'Kelly, as the expert in subterfuge, to answer as best he could. Pouting doubtfully he said, 'You never know which way the Pathan mind is going to turn, of course. Wily devils all of them, and Nashkar Ali Khan has a reputation for not even being consistent in his inconsistency – if you follow me, sir?'

'Of course, of course.'

O'Kelly gave him a sardonic look. 'Sorry I can't be more help, but you know how it is. Never try to out-think a Pathan is my motto – he'll *always* contrive to come up behind you!'

'Then what *would* you do, O'Kelly?'

The Political Officer pondered again, fingering the small cigar that Fettleworth had obstinately refrained from giving him permission to light. 'Well, I'd take it that the *obvious* thing to think would be that Nashkar's trying to lure an expeditionary force inside his borders – don't ask me why, unless it's so he can cut it up as a warning to us and an encouragement to his followers. But then, d'you see, that's *too* obvious – so I'd disregard it.'

Fettleworth muttered, 'God give me strength.'

'I think, on reflection, I'd adopt the old precept of maintaining a masterly inactivity. Do nothing.'

'Ah, ha,' Fettleworth said, liking the sound of that in all the circumstances. 'Wait for something more positive to show itself?'

'Yes, sir.'

Dornoch said, 'Wait for Ogilvie to be brutally murdered, you mean.'

'Colonel you—'

'I'm sorry, sir, but Ogilvie is one of my own officers and a very promising one. The message itself may be a trap, but I think we all know the threat of torture is likely to be real enough. I cannot sit by and – and connive at Ogilvie's abandonment!'

'Connive! You're under orders, Dornoch! My orders – and I'll take the responsibility!' Fettleworth's face had reddened dangerously; but suddenly he underwent one of the curious changes that his officers had so often remarked in the past. He said with obvious sincerity, 'You must never think such responsibility is easy, Dornoch. I detest the idea of possibly sending a young man to his death, but I have no alternative. It grieves me a great deal ... the son of an old friend too. But even you would not expect me to place these considerations – weighty as they are – before my duty to the Raj. Would you, Dornoch?'

Dornoch lifted his hands and dropped them again with a gesture of great weariness. 'No, sir,' he said.

'I'm glad to hear you say that, Dornoch. I understand your concern for your officers. It does you great credit, and I would not have it otherwise. But as the Divisional Commander, I am forced to take other views. Now I have something else to say to you – to impress upon you all, gentlemen.' He leaned forward heavily, his stomach riding over the lip of his desk in a surging thrust of scarlet and gold. 'There is to be no mention of what we have been discussing. No one is to know the position Captain Ogilvie is in. I shall now speak personally to Surgeon-Major Warrender, who brought the message to this headquarters, and to all others concerned – nothing will be said from that quarter, I assure you. I need hardly remind you, gentlemen, of a vital fact of military life: *we do not acknowledge espionage.*'

They did not acknowledge espionage, even though the enemy knew full well that espionage was carried on every day of the year to the greater glory of the British Raj. Spies were spies and ladies and gentlemen used the word with a shudder of repulsion, while they lived and drank and gorged and fornicated and rode arrogant horses and stuck pigs in Peshawar and Nowshera and enjoyed the cool of the Simla hills – safe behind the curtain of security held in place by officers acting as spies. Dornoch's mood was savage as he rode back to his regimental lines that afternoon. James Ogilvie was to be abandoned, written off the regimental rolls, his name never to be mentioned, an officer who had vanished and left a query marked against him. That was what it had all sounded like, anyhow. Dornoch's lip curled as he thought of the dexterous O'Kelly and his girlish manners. *Wait and see!* Wait for something to show – when they all knew nothing ever would, before it was too late to save Ogilvie! Of course, it wasn't Fettleworth's fault – except for having dreamed the whole ridiculous mission up in the first place. It was that for which Dornoch would never forgive him in his heart. He had a sudden dangerous fancy that on arrival back at the lines he would send for his second-in-command, his adjutant and his bugler, and parade his regiment, and march them, every man, for the Waziri border, behind the pipes and drums. He knew that every man would have gone willingly, with the Highland blood-lust singing high, to hack their way through the Pathan hordes as generations had done in India before them ...

The vision faded, leaving bitterness behind. Even he could baulk the issue when the point was reached. A Nelson would indeed have marched the regiment out and to ruddy blazing hell with his superiors! To such a pusillanimous pass did the habit of obedience and the training of years reduce a man.

On the way in he met Andrew Black, and gave him a nod. 'Well, Andrew.' He could think of nothing else to say.

'Good afternoon, Colonel. May I ask what the General wanted?'

'You may, Andrew. It was mere routine, nothing more.'

'To do with the Frontier situation, Colonel?'

'Yes – to do with the Frontier situation.'

'There are no fresh orders for us?'

'No, Andrew, none.' Reaching the door of his office building, Dornoch dismounted and handed his horse over to an orderly. He wished Black would go away; he was a persistent fellow and more than usually unwelcome just now.

Black said, 'I wonder how Ogilvie is getting along, Colonel.'

'Yes – I wonder.' Turning his back, Dornoch went inside. To his relief the Adjutant did not follow him. Dornoch's face was stiff with anger and dislike, and he found to his alarm that he was shaking all over, so much so that it must surely be noticeable. Black was one of the men, one in the chain of circumstance Dornoch was positive, who had been responsible for sending Ogilvie into Waziristan; and would be the first to acquiesce, with a loathsome joy, in his obliteration.

The news, released at last in an upward direction by Fettleworth, who could not sit on it for ever, reached Army Command at Murree in a secret despatch addressed only for the eyes of the General Officer Commanding personally.

To read it in bald black and white was an immense shock; to read Fettleworth's decision was another. It took a moment or two for the impact to strike, and then Sir Iain Ogilvie gave a deep sigh. His head seemed to swing, and he fell forward a little way, across his desk. Only for a moment, and then he had regained control; but not before his A.D.C., who had brought Fettleworth's despatch to him, had noticed that something was wrong.

'A glass of water, sir.' The A.D.C. moved to the door.

'What? Don't be an ass, man. Something much stronger.'

'Of course, sir.'

'I'll see to it myself, thank you, Elliott. My compliments to Brigadier-General Leith. I'd like to see him – at once.'

'Sir!' Captain Elliott left the room. Sir Iain Ogilvie sat for a minute or so, staring across his desk and out through the wide windows, across an immaculate and well-watered garden to where chairs and a table stood in the cool shade of dusty trees. His wife was there, chatting to Barbara Leith, wife of his Chief of Staff; a native servant stood discreetly at a distance, awaiting orders. Sir Iain closed his eyes, then opened them again and blew his nose hard. He got to his feet, slowly, and went over to a cabinet where he kept a bottle of good Scotch whisky and some crystal tumblers. He poured himself two fingers, and took it neat. Whisky was a good friend to a Scot so long as the companionship was sought in moderation; but this time, the comfort was not there, only the bitter lees. To be a General, to be a General Officer Commanding and responsible only to the Commander-in-Chief in Calcutta, brought very many advantages over lesser men, advantages, obvious ones enough, of station, autocracy and physical comfort; but not the one that thoughtless people, ignorant people, the little men, usually took it for granted one had: one could distribute favours to other men's sons but could never single out one's own son for positive military assistance.

His Chief of Staff came into the room. 'You sent for me, Sir Iain?'

'Oh – yes, Leith. A matter's come up. My son – supposed to be attached to my staff, as you know.'

'Yes, sir?'

'I gave him leave, as you also know.'

There was a pause. Leith, puzzled now, said, 'I'm aware of all the facts, sir.'

'Not all of them, Leith. Not all of them.' Ogilvie gave a short, hard laugh. 'The damn natives have got him, Leith. He's been rumbled. You'd better read Fettleworth's despatch.' He handed it over with a hand that shook. 'This is to go no further, you understand – no further at all. My son's ... leave is extended. See to that, if you please.'

'Of course. I'm very sorry, sir.' Leith's face was full of concern.

'Thank you. That's all.'

'Yes, sir.' Leith hesitated, but didn't leave. 'Would it not be possible to mount an—'

'I said, that's all, Leith.'

'Very good, sir. I'll be available whenever you want me.' The Chief of Staff turned away and shut the door quietly behind him; but not before he had heard Sir Iain say, in a voice that sounded dragged from his very heart, a voice of bitter regret, 'I'd like to wring Fettleworth's bloody neck!'

Later in the morning, just before luncheon, Sir Iain Ogilvie walked into his wife's drawing-room and found her, much to his relief, alone.

'Fiona,' he said, staring at her, holding out his arms.

She smiled. 'What is it, Iain?' She patted the sofa beside her. 'Come and sit down. I'm so tired, and we'll have people arriving any minute.'

'People? What people?' He remained where he was, staring down at her.

'Surely you've not forgotten? The Benhams, Lord Dunstaffnage, Colonel Hawke . . .' Her voice died away, and when she spoke again there was a sharp note of anxiety. 'Iain, what's the matter?'

He shook his head, lifted his arms in a hopeless, beaten gesture, and then sat down beside his wife. Holding nothing back, he told her such facts as Fettleworth had revealed. He expressed no opinion as to what he believed might happen to their son, but knew he had no need – unfortunately perhaps – to do so. Fiona, as a soldier's daughter and a soldier's wife, with much past experience of the Frontier, could make as accurate a guess as he. He had scarcely finished when a servant announced Lord Dunstaffnage, who came in smiling and elegant and jovial, smelling of good soap and expensive linen and cracking the joints of his fingers as he advanced towards his host and hostess; a habit that his colleagues at the India Office in Whitehall found irritating in the extreme. After Dunstaffnage, closely, Major-General Sir Hugh and Lady Benham; and then the rest of the luncheon party. It was a partly gay, partly serious occasion. The Ogilvies kept up appearances and their manners did not slip. Sir Iain was fully attentive to Lady Benham on his left, to Lord Dunstaffnage on his right; at the other end of the table, while her husband expressed dutiful and thoughtful opinions to Dunstaffnage on Indian affairs ranging from the military to the civil by way of the railways and the drains, Fiona Ogilvie responded to the heavy, antique witticisms of Colonel Hawke, a venerable gentleman who had served in the Mutiny and had not yet ceased talking about it and recounting endless and pointless funny stories connected with it.

Afterwards, all the guests said, sincerely, how much they had enjoyed the luncheon. There was a great deal more to being a G.O.C. than simply commanding an army. Noblesse, that long day, obliged through heartache. It was not until the late evening that Sir Iain Ogilvie was able once again to talk at length and privately with his wife. Knowing the answer, she nevertheless asked if there was anything that could be done.

'Not a thing, my dear, not a thing. It's too late now. What could have been done, should have been done before he started for Waziristan.'

'You mean over-ruling General Fettleworth, Iain?'

'What else? I *could* have done it, I suppose. I wish I had.' He stumbled for the right words. 'What's position, set against the boy? H'm. Come to that – what's duty? That's really what I meant to say, Fiona,' he added quickly. 'God! I'd never have for one moment considered the pomp and ceremony as being in any way important, as against James.'

'Oh, my dear man, d'you imagine I don't know that?' Her eyes were filled with tears that sparkled in the soft glow from the oil lamp. 'But whatever happens you must never lose your sense of duty, Iain – that's a different thing. It's so deep in you. Without that . . .' She didn't finish; without the prop of his stern concept of duty, her husband could crumble – any soldier could. It would be like an archbishop losing his faith in God. She returned to her original question. 'We have to think of the present now, and the future, not the past. Are you quite sure nothing can be done, Iain?'

'Yes. That oaf Fettleworth does happen to be right, damn his eyes! He *can't* act – neither can I. It *could* be a trap. One can't commit troops on that basis. Besides, there's another angle, though I doubt if Fettleworth thought of *that*.'

'Well?'

He said, 'To send in an expedition might be his death warrant, Fiona. They would never let him be found alive. Hard as it is, my dear, we must face the fact that disregard, total disregard of the Waziri message, is the only possible way.'

'Just – leave him? Leave him all alone, at those brutes' mercy, if they even know the word?'

He nodded, his face set. 'Yes, my dearest, yes!' He held her close to his chest, clumsily moving a rough hand up and down her arm. 'Don't cry, Fiona. It doesn't help. We can help best by showing nothing. It's very important in my view as in Fettleworth's, that no word should get back to Waziristan that anybody knows anything about a man called Wilshaw.'

That night, in his bedroom adjoining hers, the G.O.C. lay awake listening to his wife's crying. His clenched fist beat continually at the sheets by his side as he listened. He did not realize that she was blaming herself, that she was bitterly regretting her earlier insistence that a father should not interfere. Iain had said, and now the words seemed to burn like fire in her mind, '*if you really feel I should, I'll find a way of countermanding Fettleworth's order*'. And her own eventual decision – although Iain had stressed he would regard her answer as an opinion only – had been that matters should be left alone. She had probably been right in basis, for such interference would have done husband and son no good in the long run; but, now as then, she doubted her own real motives. Lying in her bed, fearful of the next news that might come from Peshawar, she ached with a terrible longing to tell James that Mary Archdale would be more than welcome to Murree and, eventually, to Corriecraig Castle on Speyside as a daughter-in-law.

Three days later another message, of a sort, reached the garrison at Peshawar: an unrecognizable lump of rotting flesh and bone, an armless and legless trunk bearing on a strip of cured goatskin attached to the neck the inscription, *Jones Sahib, British spy*, was found by a patrol a little to the south of the entry to the Khyber Pass. Trundled in a commissariat cart to Peshawar, Mr. Jones's sordid remains were examined with clinical detachment and professional interest by Fettleworth's Staff Surgeon, and with revulsion by the Political Officer, Major O'Kelly. Little useful information was gleaned from the corpse, but it was hierarchically inevitable that the item's receipt should be reported to Sir Iain Ogilvie in Murree. Brigadier-General Leith was present when Ogilvie read the despatch, and he remarked afterwards to the A.D.C. that he was worried about the General.

'Watch him,' he advised. 'We don't want him to crack up, Elliott.'

'It wouldn't be surprising if he did, sir. What's new?'

'His reaction to a report from Peshawar.' Briefly, the Chief of Staff recounted the grisly details. 'In a way, I suppose it was characteristic, but in another sense, it was far from being so. Sir Iain's *never* been a man to speak out against his subordinate commanders in front of officers junior to them.'

'What did he say, then?'

Leith rubbed at his jaw. 'He said he wished to God it had been bloody Fettleworth. It's not like him, you know, not like him at all.'

Elliott laughed. 'I'm afraid I don't agree, sir. It's only too like him. My guess is, he's fighting back – and that's the best possible sign, isn't it?'

From where he was still imprisoned in the hole behind the slotted boulder, Ogilvie realized that he had a commanding view of a track leading through a mountain pass out of Afghanistan. He realized this only when, after many days of increasingly painful inactivity, he saw a long straggling line of men and mules coming through below him. The mules looked heavily laden, and the men were many. No doubt the mules carried supplies, and also arms and ammunition. After a while no more mules came through, but still more men. More and more as the day passed towards evening. These must be the tribes, joining Nashkar Ali Khan for the grand assault, which could not now be long delayed. The old *sadhu* was still up there on his peak, as stark and as lonely as ever, still fasting, still waiting for his sign to come to him. Ogilvie's guard had been changed many times over during the past days, but there could be no replacement for the *sadhu*. Ogilvie wondered how the old man would announce the advent of the sign. Would he blow a horn, or a trumpet, would he yodel out his message across the mountain tops? Or would Ogilvie's guarding warrior be sent scurrying down the hillside with the tidings, and start a relay to carry them to the lord and master, Nashkar Ali Khan? Even if he were to be left unguarded, Ogilvie knew he would still be unable to escape. From time to time the guard had risked official displeasure by falling asleep on his post, and Ogilvie had tried desperately to shift the boulder by pushing against it with face and chin, but it had been hopeless. It wouldn't budge a tenth of an inch, and there was no room to draw up his arms.

During one long night of his imprisonment the mountain around him rumbled and trembled to a brief but deep shock, something far off. Ogilvie's heart leaped with fear. He called out to the guard, asking in Pushtu what had happened.

'It is a shock of the ground, an earthquake.' The man had bent to speak to him, and there was a bright moon that night, and Ogilvie could see the glitter of excitement in the eyes. 'It is perhaps the voice of the gods, the sign awaited by the *sadhu*!' The Pathan stood upright then, leaving only his legs on display. Ogilvie looked up towards the peak. The holy man was as still and as silent as ever. They watched for a good ten minutes, at the end of which time the Pathan said gloomily, 'No, it is not the sign, Englishman. We must still wait, and wait.'

'Perhaps it's a sign the other way,' Ogilvie suggested unkindly.

'How so?'

'A sign that the gods disapprove of Nashkar's schemes. A warning to him to retract – or a warning of what will happen to him if he doesn't. An earthquake that will shatter Waziristan.' Then he put in a touch of propaganda for himself. 'It is certain

126

that without my weapons he cannot succeed. Many guns will be needed against the British troops.'

'We have guns enough already.'

'No army ever has that, brother!'

'You are a spy,' the man said, and spat contemptuously.

'Believe what you wish,' Ogilvie said, trying to sound casual about it. 'I speak only the truth, but while I'm here I can't prove the truth, can I? If I should get out, I would bring much help to you and your brothers in arms. I would thus become rich myself. These riches I could share with those who had helped me. Do you understand?'

The man's bayonet came down, silvery in the moon, snaking into the opening above the boulder. 'A Pathan warrior does not stoop to bribes, Englishman, son of a pig!'

The rusty steel snicked his nose and he felt the blood run. It was no use. He went back to a silent contemplation of the silent *sadhu*, one kind of prisoner studying another kind. And many miles away in Maizar, enjoying the fleshpots as promised, Captain Edward Healey, late of the Bengal Lancers, was a little later making a different kind of study – a study of soft and yielding flesh, a dusky smooth skin pinnacling down to a triangle of duskier hair whose geometric symmetry was destroyed as the light touch of his hand widened the legs.

'Earless One, man of my heart,' the girl whispered into the hole at the right of his head, 'why did you leave me so long?'

'His Highness is a man of generosity, Flower of mine,' he whispered back. 'And I am a man of catholic tastes. I like different women for different satisfactions. One woman cannot be all things to any man, nor one man to any woman for that matter.'

A moment later she murmured, 'You smell of sweat.'

'I'm not surprised. So do you. And I like it.' He nuzzled her again, and she giggled in delight.

'There was an earthquake,' she said a little later, 'and I was so frightened.'

'So was I,' said Captain Healey. 'So was I.'

'But it was not serious?'

'Stop worrying yourself about it. No, it was not serious. The one tremor only. It is not unusual.'

Soon the girl slept, curled like a vital young kitten in his arms, but Healey remained wide awake, staring into the darkness.

CHAPTER NINE

PESHAWAR, hothouse garrison of rumour, of intrigue, of long gossiping tongues whose owners, not always female, had too much time on their hands not to indulge in the small cheap thrills of prying into and then dissecting other people's lives verbally, was vastly and infuriatingly intrigued by Mary Archdale.

Her slightly improper friendship, so obviously a close one, with Captain James Ogilvie had been widely known and much commented upon in confidential conversations at tea-parties, dinners, balls and those other occasions when the ladies of the garrison forgathered to shred each other's and their menfolk's reputations in that delicious intimacy of infelicitation. There was, of course, a strong element of green-eyed jealousy when it came to Captain Ogilvie and his presumed mistress, for James was a good-looking man, and becoming more of a catch for unmarried daughters with every passing month. Had it not been for the wicked, brazen Mrs. Archdale, who should by all decent standards have departed the station after her gallant husband had been killed in action, Captain Ogilvie – so many a fond military mama told herself – would have been a dutiful son-in-law enhancing his wife's father's promotion prospects as a result of the alliance with so famed a regiment as the Queen's Own Royal Strathspeys and so illustrious a father as the General Officer Commanding, Northern Army. Instead of that, what had happened? This wretched woman, this widow, this baby-snatcher seven (at least!) years older than the innocent soldier, had come like an evil witch, a harridan, yes, even a *harlot*, to snatch away the gilded prize, one of the expected perquisites of the parents of daughters on military stations from Colchester to Hong Kong.

And what had been the result? Why – the more-or-less expected one! Captain Ogilvie was lost to them altogether now; he had been withdrawn by a wise father from the dangers of Peshawar, to serve more circumspectly on his father's Staff to the, no doubt, inordinate glee of the Murree mothers. And very possibly he would not return to his regiment until he was safely and respectably married off to some dull girl who would not be able to hold a candle to the daughter, of say Mrs. Brigadier-General Kintoul, Mrs. Colonel Maitland-Cornish, or Mrs. Major Evans. And yet there was mystery, a nagging uncertainty; for rumour had come back from Murree that Captain Ogilvie was presently on leave of absence. Well, perhaps that was natural; he had earned a respite, he had seen a good deal of action, and there was always plenty of leave going in Murree and Ootacamund and Simla. You were not 'on duty' in the same sense as in the Peshawar garrison, with its proximity to the Khyber Pass and the constant necessity of maintaining patrols.

Still – the Mrs. Colonels and the Mrs. Majors clucked – it was a great pity, a great shame for Ida and Olive, Ellen and Susan and Mildred ... and it was rather odd too, really. On leave he might be; what was certain was that he was not with his light-o'-love in Peshawar.

It became very considerably odder after Mrs. Surgeon-Major Warrender had allowed an indiscretion to pass her lips.

'A *spy*? I can't believe it, Margaret. Surely you're mistaken!'

'No, I'm not.' Margaret Warrender shook her gingery curls. Normally overawed by Mrs. Carmichael, who was bigger and louder and more senior – her husband was Director of Medical Services at Division – Mrs. Warrender was feeling the power of superior knowledge and was emboldened thereby. 'Oh, I assure you I'm not mistaken, Mrs. Carmichael. I saw the message myself – it was I who gave it to my husband as a matter of fact. It startled me so much – it came through the window quite close to me. I was very upset. I thought at first it must have been one of these dreadful agitators, and on the dear Queen's birthday of all days.'

'Just the day they would choose,' Mrs. Carmichael stated, heaving her chest. 'They should be herded together and used for pig-sticking, in place of innocent pigs. That's *my* opinion. Now, what about this – this *spy*? Such a terrible word to use! Was there a name?'

'Yes. Wilshaw Sahib.'

'Wilshaw? Was the regiment given?'

'No.'

'Wilshaw.' Mrs. Carmichael absently pulled down the pince-nez secured by a thin gold chain to a spring device in a button-shaped case on her breast, then let the glasses bound back again. 'I don't think I know any Wilshaw, either here or in Nowshera.' She reflected, mentally reviewing the regiments and corps of the Division. 'Possibly he's from H.Q. in Murree, Margaret.'

'Yes, I suppose he could be.'

'And he's in danger of his life?'

'In danger of torture, the message said.'

'What a very terrible thing.' Mrs. Carmichael clicked her tongue and looked distressed. 'How dreadful for his family. I suppose nothing will be done about it.'

'Nothing?'

'Well, I should imagine not! I've always heard that people who do *that* sort of job don't expect help. It's understood, I believe.'

Margaret Warrender nodded, and her somewhat weak blue eyes filled with sudden tears. 'How dreadful! What a *brave* thing to do, though.'

Mrs. Carmichael gave a sniff. 'To ask for help?'

'Well, I meant to undertake such a job really.'

'Oh – yes. Yes, *brave*, very. Not *quite* the thing, though. Not the kind of thing a gentleman would take part in. One doesn't wish to sink to the level of the natives, Margaret.' Mrs. Carmichael, who always gave the impression of being an instructress in all things military, social and worldly, leaned towards her friend, or subordinate, with her hands clasped in her lap. Her voice become formal. 'I think you should not be telling me any of this, Margaret. What did your husband have to say on the subject?'

Margaret Warrender looked down, away from the hard and accusing, yet interested, eyes. 'He did say I wasn't to. But I haven't really, have I, Mrs. Carmichael? I mean, telling you is *quite* safe. Naturally, I wouldn't dream of saying a word to anyone else.'

'Quite so, quite so. Yes, of course, it is safe with me. But I hope you'll be careful. If General Fettleworth had wanted this known, I imagine he would have said something in orders. There must be a good reason for secrecy. It is up to us to respect it.'

'Oh, of course, Mrs. Carmichael, of course, you're *quite* right. Another cup of tea?'

Mrs. Carmichael inclined her head graciously, keeping her back straight. 'Thank you.'

Margaret Warrender reached out and jerked a bell-pull, and a native servant came in, bowing, to attend to the ladies' needs. From then on the conversation, though still tête-à-tête, was of a more general nature concerning polo and pig-sticking, and *petit-point,* and home, and then, inevitably, of promotion; and even more inevitably of the Queen, and Windsor, and what a trial the Prince of Wales must be to his mother with all his gallivanting and unconventional ways and his love of horse racing, and of the Dukes of Cambridge and Connaught and how standards had slipped since the former had departed from the Horse Guards and his office as Commander-in-Chief of the Army. The name of Wilshaw was not mentioned again, nor, naturally, was espionage. And thereafter both ladies were most conscientious and dutiful in their strict control of their tongues when talking to other people, except perhaps in the case of their most *intimate* and *bosom* friends, those in whom they could trust *absolutely* and who would never reveal a confidence – other than in confidence. For it was all very intriguing to ladies with not enough to fill their days; and after a little while, as the story, though never talked about, somehow managed to make the rounds out of earshot of the menfolk, a touch of fantasy began to weave its way into the strict truth, and the vague theorizing of some of the ladies – the drawing-room ponderings of who, why, what, when and where – began to slot into the story and into the original message. Within little more than a day or two the keen ears of Mrs. Colonel Bates of the Supply and Transport had picked up the information that the strange Mr. Wilshaw, now missing, had been attached to Army Head-quarters in Murree.

When she had digested this information fully, and had had time in which to think it over, put two and two together, and invent a few conclusions, she made it her business to pay a friendly call on Mary Archdale. Mary, though more than aston-ished, was pleasant enough, and offered her tea, which was accepted. Mrs. Bates spent half-an-hour in innocuous chit-chat before approaching the point, and then she approached it obliquely. She said, 'That nice young man I saw you with – oh, a long time ago now, it must have been – at the race meeting in Simla. Do you remember, Mrs. Archdale?'

'Yes. That afternoon at Annandale. Of course I remember!'

Mary gave a sudden laugh. 'James had told you the night before that he didn't care for racing, and then you saw us there!'

Mrs. Bates flushed angrily. So typical, she thought, of the woman to be tactless – tactless and insulting. A lack of breeding of course, always showed. 'I really can't remember everything a subaltern says to me, Mrs. Archdale. However – I do recall that he was a nice young man . . . what's the matter now?'

'I'm sorry,' Mary answered. She had laughed again, remembering the look, all that time ago, on Mrs. Bates's face when she had seen them – caught them would be how she would have regarded it herself – and had referred to James as 'your Mr. Ogilvie', and how her own reaction to Mrs. Bates had been the remark to James that she was an extraordinarily ugly woman, an opinion she had seen no reason to change since. 'Do go on.'

'Yes.' Mrs. Bates bit her lip angrily, and decided to hurt well and truly now. 'As I say . . . a nice young man. Mr. Ogilvie, was it not?'

'He's Captain Ogilvie now, as a matter of fact.'

'Really? I'm so glad. Such *quick* promotion. Of course, his father's the G.O.C.'

'There's no connection, I assure you, Mrs. Bates.'

'Oh, but of course not – *what* a suggestion – kindly do not credit me with having made it, Mrs. Archdale.'

'Very well, Mrs. Bates.' Mary poured tea, smiling sweetly. 'What suggestion were you making, then?'

'None,' Mrs. Bates snapped, reddening unattractively. 'I was merely going to say that I understood he had been appointed to his father's Staff, and—'

'In other words, you know very well he'd been promoted, and you know very well we're close friends, and have been for a long time, so we'll take all that as read, Mrs. Bates. I'm flattered that you've been keeping your eye on us all this time, which I'm quite sure you have. I expect you've come along to commiserate with me in my – shall we say – grass widowhood?'

Mrs. Bates gave a gasp. 'I consider that a little brazen,' she snapped. 'What you do is your own affair—'

'Indeed it is.'

'—but it is in the worst possible taste to – to *flaunt* your conquests under the garrison's noses in the way you do. And what,' she added viciously, 'have you to say to *that*?'

Mary kept her temper and laughed in Mrs. Bates's face. 'I say that jealousy does more harm to the possessor than to the victim, Mrs. Bates. Your jealousy's been showing in your face for a long time now. Another cup of tea?'

Mrs. Bates stood up, shaking all over. 'You can keep your tea, Mrs. Archdale. I've *never* been so insulted.' The feathers in her bonnet waved and dipped as though giving support to her indignation. 'I came to give you a friendly word, some information about Captain Ogilvie's whereabouts, and look at the reception I get!'

'Give me the word,' Mary said. 'Since I'm sure it's far from friendly, it should help relieve your feelings. What is it, Mrs. Bates?'

'I'll not utter—'

'Oh, yes, you will, Mrs. Bates!' Mary got to her feet and swept round the S. and T. colonel's lady, putting herself between the agitated woman and the door. 'I'm sure you don't want a scene. You can certainly rely on my servants listening to any racket, and spreading it all over Peshawar. I know you look on me as the Scarlet Woman, Mrs. Bates. Let me tell you, I'll live right up to my reputation if you don't finish what you started to say about James!'

Mrs. Bates was not without a kind of courage in the face of adversity, in the face of having an unkindly meant intrusion somehow turned it back again much more unkindly than she had originally intended. She asked disparagingly, 'You have heard no rumour?'

'None.'

'I must say I'm scarcely surprised. You naturally have no friends, as I would speak of friends, in Peshawar. You are out of things. That is why I came – trying to be a friend.'

'Please come to the point.'

'Very well, since you insist, that young man is no better than a spy. That's what he is – a spy. That's why he went to Murree. It explains the rather curious appointment. Now he's got his deserts. He's been captured by the Pathans in Waziristan.' Mrs. Bates panted. 'I call it the vengeance of God.'

'And I,' Mary said between her small white teeth, 'call you a bitch,' and suddenly her hand shot out and took the Colonel's lady once on each sallow cheek, hard.

For Mary, that night was torment.

She had not let Mrs. Bates go until the woman had told her all she knew, or had made up in order to hurt. Having spoken, Mrs. Bates, clutching her draggled dignity and lifting the hem of her dress clear of the floor, had swept out muttering threats. Mary hadn't even listened to the nature of the threats, knowing they were so much wind. In point of fact, Mrs. Bates, having opened her mouth far too wide for safety, was a very frightened woman. She had laid herself open to Mary Archdale, and Mary, by saying a few words in the right places, could make life very hard for Colonel and Mrs. Bates. Colonel Bates might even be forced to leave the station, or at the very least to send his wife away. Mary, however, had no intention of hounding anyone as pitiful as Mrs. Bates, anyone as sunk in their own spiteful thoughts as was that unfortunate ugly hag. Mary's own thoughts were all of James Ogilvie, and they revolved in a distressing circle of uncertainty, of a wonderment as to how much was true and as to how she could ever find out for certain. Racked with this worry and uncertainty, she paced her bedroom most of the dark hours. To some extent, what the woman had mouthed at her had had the ring of truth, and also it held together. James had indeed gone to Murree, or so he had said; and yet he had been vague about it, not as forthcoming as usual, and there had been the instruction not to write, and the uncertainty as to how long he would be away ... and there was the basic fact of his having been appointed to Sir Iain's Staff. She had always been a shade worried about that, seeing it as an attempt on Lady Ogilvie's part to bring about a separation. Perhaps there had been a more sinister reason behind it, a more dangerous one for James.

It made sense and it could be true.

Flinging herself on the bed, she gave way to tears, and she cried herself to sleep. She woke in the morning, luckily before she was called by her servant, to find herself still dressed, and stiff and rather cold and with a hollow-eyed face that stared back at her from the looking-glass, when she got up from the disordered bed, like death itself.

She could eat little breakfast, though by the time the meal was ready she had done her face and looked considerably better. She drank strong coffee, and Scarlet Woman that she was, imperilled the blood-pressures of Peshawar by lighting a cigarette. She made a wry face as the blue smoke spiralled into the air, crossing a shaft of sunlight that streamed through the opened slats of the shutters. She had no right to be getting in such a state over James Ogilvie; she had no claim upon him, nor him upon her. It was unlikely enough that they would ever marry, and she was in fact unsure if she would even welcome the idea. She had never been in love with Tom Archdale, whom she had married as a result of parental pressure; but even so, marriage to him had only made her detest him more – things had worsened rather than improved with close and constant familiarity. Not that James Ogilvie could ever be compared with poor Tom, of course; but her experience of marriage had been unpleasant and it was all she had to go upon, except for her parents' marriage and that had been a fiasco too. Marriage hadn't done much for Mrs. Bates either. She would start with much love and devotion for James, but she would not wish to watch it dwindle, to see the spark go out. She loved him, in a sense, too much for the stifling deadweight of marriage with all its conventions and attitudes and formal reactions, and its certainties. There was a wonderful excitement in their present relationship – or there had just begun to be, when he had been posed.

Mary sat for a long time, just staring into space while, a little later, the servant noiselessly cleared the table around her. What, she had wondered again and again, of James himself? What dreadful things is he undergoing? She had heard so many terrible stories of the cruelties practised by the Pathans – Tom had told her a few, bolstering his own image by recounting the daily dangers he had been up against. The soldiers never even left their dead behind, never mind the wounded, when fighting the Pathan. James might not even be left with the outward and visible symbols of his manhood.

She gave a loud cry, quite involuntarily: *'Oh love, oh love.'*

White-faced but unshakeably determined she hired a carriage and went to see Lord Dornoch, privately, in his quarter. She was conscious of some constraint from the stately Lady Dornoch, who, though kind, was formal in her manner. The image of the Scarlet Woman seemed to have preceded her; but Lady Dornoch was a very different kettle of fish from Mrs. Colonel Bates and it was she herself who suggested, with innate tact, that perhaps Mrs. Archdale might prefer to talk to her husband in his study.

135

'Thank you so much, Lady Dornoch,' she said. 'That is kind of you.'

'You're in some trouble,' the tall, rather gaunt Scotswoman answered. 'I know you'll find my husband understanding.'

Mary smiled a little, gratefully. 'Oh, dear,' she said. 'Does it show?'

'It would be unnatural if it did not,' Lady Dornoch said.

'Then you know—?'

The Colonel's wife laid a hand on her arm. 'Off you go, my dear girl,' she said crisply, 'and tell my husband all about it.'

In Dornoch's study she asked the question direct: 'Lord Dornoch, please tell me, where is James?'

Dornoch shook his head and looked away from her searching eyes, his own eyes sadly worried. 'He was posted, as you know, to Murree, Mrs. Archdale.'

'Yes. But – after that? Where is he *now*?'

'One would imagine – in Murree.'

'Oh, dear,' she said, 'you're going to be difficult.' She made use of her eyes, just for a moment, before she realized that with Dornoch this would be quite the wrong tactic. 'Have you heard the rumours?' she asked.

'What rumours, Mrs. Archdale?'

'Why, about James.'

'I never listen to rumour,' Dornoch said sharply. Then he leaned towards her, resting his elbows on the huge old arms of the leather chair that he had brought from his home in Scotland. 'And if you're wise, Mrs. Archdale, neither will you. Please believe me when I say that so far as is known officially, you have no cause for anxiety about Captain Ogilvie, and—'

'So you *have* heard the rumours?'

Dornoch blew out his cheeks. 'I suppose there's no harm in saying I've *heard* them. I am taking steps to have them checked. Take no notice – I repeat this – take no notice of rumours, my dear girl. They're terribly unreliable things!'

'But do you believe this one?' she persisted.

His answer was quick and final. 'By no means. It's a lot of poppycock.' Once again he looked away, this time under cover of a pretence of feeling for his cigar case. 'Captain Ogilvie is in Murree – or more precisely is currently on leave – and in due course will rejoin the regiment.'

There was a sudden gleam in Mary's eye. 'That is all you will tell me, Lord Dornoch?'

'It's all I *can* tell you,' he corrected.

'Then I thank you. You've been more than helpful.'

When she had gone Dornoch moodily joined his wife in the drawing-room. 'Mind my cigar?' he asked absently.

'Yes, but you know very well you'll smoke it just the same—'

'No, no, my dear—'

'Oh, go on with you, Alastair!' She patted the sofa. 'Sit down and tell me all about it.'

'All about it?'

'Yes! Your little tête-à-tête with that very attractive young woman. I've always admired her looks.' She paused. 'Well?'

He examined his cigar. 'I've let something out, damn it! I said Ogilvie was on leave.'

'Well, Alastair?' she asked again.

'She obviously hadn't heard that.'

'I doubt if it's very important, Alastair. Anyway, that's the official truth, isn't it?'

He gave a short laugh. 'Official truth – yes! But it does go against the grain to tell barefaced lies to a girl who so obviously loves him, my dear. God, how I wish I'd resisted Fettleworth right from the start!' He blew smoke for a while, a fragrant smell, then asked, 'What do you think of her?'

'Mrs. Archdale? I suppose I've been a little swayed by what's supposed to be her reputation—'

'A lot of gossiping old harridans who'd be all the better for the attentions of a man—'

'Hoity-toity! Never disregard the garrison ladies, Alastair, for if you do, it'll be at your peril! I see you've fallen for her charms yourself. But as for what I think . . . I may sound catty, Alastair, though I'm sure I don't mean to, but she puts me in mind of the saying, always the blushing bridesmaid, never the—'

'Oh, nonsense.' Dornoch shifted irritably on the sofa. 'She's been a bride, she's been married—'

'I know, I know. I have the thing wrong in my head anyway. What I meant to say was, she's the perennial blushing mistress, and not noticeably blushing really. But – yes, I think I like her, Alastair.'

Dornoch said, 'You've no reason to call her what you just have, my dear, no reason at all. There's been far too much loose talk.'

137

Lady Dornoch sighed. 'I dare say. It's possibly just her appearance, her personality ... she looks the part! Too attractive.' She thought, but wouldn't say, too sexy. 'I like her, but I can quite understand any anxieties Fiona Ogilvie may have.'

'Possibly. But I'll say this without fear of contradiction: she's very much in love with young Ogilvie.' He couldn't quite interpret the look his wife gave him when he had said this. The matter went out of his mind soon after, when Captain Black was announced on regimental business. By this time Mary had ordered her carriage elsewhere; alarmed by Dornoch's revelation that James was on leave, she had made up her mind to go to the top. If James had genuinely had leave of absence from Murree he would have come to see her. Of that she had not the slightest doubt in the world. But he had not done so. *Ergo*, he was not on leave, and lies were in the air. James had talked a good deal about Lord Dornoch, and she had met him herself many times – indeed it had been Dornoch who had introduced them in the first place, at that dance before James had gone off with his regiment to besiege Jalalabad in Afghanistan. Lord Dornoch was an honourable man, none more so. If he was being forced to lie, to conceal something, then it began to look very much as though Mrs. Bates had somehow managed to hit a nail firmly on the head. Impetuously, Mary decided that there was only one thing to do: she must talk to General Fettleworth, upon whose own Staff Tom Archdale had served as Staff Major.

Fettleworth, when she was admitted to audience, was attentive and polite. He had always had a bulging eye for a pretty woman and the mere presence of one in his immediate vicinity tended to give him a slightly roguish air. 'I'm delighted to see you again, Mrs. Archdale,' he said. 'I have many memories of poor Archdale, of course. A first-rate officer, if I may say so.' He hadn't been; he'd been a confounded nuisance on the march, with that blasted field-lavatory of his trundling along with the commissariat in the charge of his frivolously-named bum-*havildar*: Fettleworth hummed and ha'ed for a few moments, then leaned close. 'My dear gel, is something the matter?'

'Yes, General Fettleworth, there is. Captain Ogilvie of the 114th Highlanders.'

'Oh. Really? But I don't see—'

'I'll come to the point,' Mary said, a handkerchief clutched in her hand. She was feeling unusually nervous, and this was sharpening both her voice and her attack. 'I've no doubt you, as well as everybody else in Peshawar, have heard talk about Captain Ogilvie and myself. I have nothing to say about that beyond the fact that I – am very fond of Captain Ogilvie.'

'Ha,' Fettleworth said, closing his eyes. Mrs. Archdale, he had been quick to note, was wearing an exceptionally low cut dress, quite outrageous really of course; and he was being given a delectable view, a grandstand one; the dangerous nub of this interview having been reached, he realized with a pang of regret that on no account must he allow temptation to sway his judgment and his tongue. The woman was after something for which she would be willing to pay heavily, and as Divisional Commander he could not, in this particular case, afford the cost. Hussy!

'I want to know where he is, General Fettleworth.'

'To the best of my remembrance, Mrs. Archdale, he was posted to Murree.'

'I'm aware of that, but where is he *now*?'

Fettleworth mopped at his face with a handkerchief. 'Really, my dear young lady. I do not wish to sound pompous, but it is beyond my capabilities to keep track of the movements of every junior officer in my command. I'm sorry, but I really can't tell you where he may be at this moment. I—'

'If he's on leave of absence,' she burst out, 'which I'm told he is, why hasn't he come to see me? Why? Can you tell me that?'

'No, I can't. Surely this is a personal matter? I can't possibly answer such questions!'

'You could if you wanted to,' she said hotly. 'I know you could. I believe he's in trouble. If he is, I want to know.'

'God bless my soul,' Fettleworth said in alarm. He blew out his cheeks. Tricky! Of course, he was aware of the rumours that had been circulating; they had worried him a good deal, but he had seen no other course but to disregard them and hope they would die down as all rumours did in the end. To issue explicit denials would do no more than exacerbate the situation and, in a sense, confirm that something *was* up. This business of Mrs. Archdale would have to be handled with similar negativeness, he decided. Nevertheless, he had to keep his reactions in proper order, so he asked, 'Now, what has given you that idea, my dear gel?' and he managed to strike just the right note of amused, tolerant disparagement. 'I see no special dangers in being on leave of absence in Murree!'

She told him about the rumours; he dismissed them with a laugh. 'You need have no fears,' he said in a fatherly way. 'I'm quite sure all's well with Captain Ogilvie—'

'Then who is this man Wilshaw, General Fettleworth?'

He checked her on that, sharply. 'You must not ask me military questions, Mrs. Archdale. I have nothing to say on the subject.' Realizing that he had made a boob, he tried to cover up. 'Wilshaw, as I had already been given to understand, is simply part of these stupid rumours. I've no knowledge of any Wilshaw, none at all.' He stood up. 'Now, Mrs. Archdale, you'll appreciate I'm a busy man, and I'm sorry I can't be of more help to you. I feel sure all will come well, however, and you really mustn't worry.'

He went with her to the door and assisted her into her carriage. He held her arm as he walked, and his grip was hot and lecherous, but he was undeniably throwing her out. Mary had no doubts in her mind that to bring Bloody Francis into bed would be child's play normally and that his hot desire could be made to tempt him into indiscretion – but not, definitely not, this time. And that spoke far more truly than had any words from Bloody Francis's lips.

She drove away, through the dust and the heat, past the military sights and sounds of the cantonments, the sweating soldiers drilling under the loud screams of the sergeants. A short distance from the Divisional H.Q. building her carriage passed a military cart coming from the direction of the hospital. She scarcely noticed the square-shaped hump beneath a pile of sacking, nor the dried bloodstains, and was not near enough to catch the sharp smell of fomaldehyde and antiseptic, and naturally Mr. Jones would not have meant anything to her in any case. Her thoughts drummed through her head, circling uselessly. What was she to do? Should she go herself to Murree? But if she did that, and everything was indeed all right, she would make a fool of herself and James might even be furious, to say nothing of the Ogilvie parents, whose strictures might rebound on James himself. It was a quandary without solution, and she had the feeling of a brick wall, of a conspiracy of total silence surrounding James Ogilvie and blotting him out of her life, as though there was an implicit determination to be done with him.

'We can't let it go on,' Fettleworth said. He said it with force and obstinacy, slamming his first down on his desk. He glared round at his Chief of Staff, at Lord Dornoch, at Captain Andrew Black, and at Major O'Kelly, for all of whom he had sent, after Mary Archdale's departure, to help resolve his dilemma. 'Can't any of you suggest one damn thing we can do?'

Lakenham shrugged. 'It's difficult, sir. I do agree, he can't just be left at Murree as it were. Officers do return from leave, after all!'

'Well, exactly. That's the trouble, isn't it? I've had that damn woman here interrogating me, and I tell you, I don't like it! I don't like it at all! Half Peshawar will be laying siege to my headquarters before long. What do we *do*!'

Black said, 'If I may say a word, sir . . . the problem seems to be, to decide upon some permanent and logical disposal for Captain Ogilvie—'

'Yes, yes.'

Dornoch protested angrily. 'Oh, come! We really can't have that. I certainly haven't written him off, I assure you. I've every confidence that he'll return – with an understandable feeling of having been cruelly let down.'

'By whom, sir?' Fettleworth demanded angrily.

'By you, sir,' was Dornoch's sharp answer, 'among others – myself included—'

'Damned impertinence—'

'None was intended, sir. I apologize.'

'So I should damn well think.'

'But the facts remain. We're abandoning a British officer to Pathan hands, and whatever the military necessity I consider that a scandal to the army and the Raj, sir.'

'Pish – to the last part. For the sentiment regarding abandoning a British officer, though I do not accept the word abandoning, for he will still be doing his duty as an officer of this garrison – for *that* sentiment I need hardly say I have the highest personal regard.' Pointedly Fettleworth swung away from Dornoch and faced Andrew Black. 'You were about to make an observation, I believe, Captain Black. What was it, pray?'

'A permanent and logical disposal for Ogilvie, sir.' Black looked down, studying his fingernails. 'It is not a welcome suggestion, General. I realize that, but needs must, I think, when the devil drives. It would appear to me obvious, in that light. There must be a funeral. A weighted coffin. It would, of course, be a delicate matter to broach to the parent.'

There was a silence, the silence of shock. Even Fettleworth was shocked. 'Good God!' he said. 'A funeral. Bless my soul – a little drastic, don't you think, Captain Black?'

'But effective, sir, very.' Black leaned forward. 'It would be the end of all gossip, of all rumour. And if we cast from our minds all thoughts of – how may I best put this – of *reality* in the occasion, then there will be no *effrontery* in it. No insult to the Lord.' Black hesitated, his dark eyes scanning the group of senior officers. 'This does not commend itself, gentlemen?'

Fettleworth said, 'Dornoch?'

'I think it's wholly preposterous, sacrilegious, unfeeling – and scandalous!'

'I must say, I'm inclined to agree with your Colonel, Black. Oh, I acknowledge it as effective, but we have to bear in mind that Ogilvie *may* return. Should he do so, I think you can see the complications for yourself, without my detailing them.' He drummed his fingers on his desk, unhappily. 'Some other solution must be found, and quickly!'

The talk flowed around Dornoch's more or less unheeding ears. Brigadier-General Lakenham made some vague suggestion that Northern Army Command be asked to give the absent officer a further posting, say to Calcutta, but Fettleworth found difficulties in the way of this. Dornoch was thinking of Black, thinking that his revolting proposal had been born of murkier depths than would have been obvious to Fettleworth. Fettleworth may have had his reasons for wishing James Ogilvie off the local scene, but Fettleworth was not a vindictive man at heart and he had that human side that kept coming to the surface at unexpected moments. He would not knowingly – and here was the essential difference between him and Black – he would not knowingly and with deliberation act in so despicable a manner as to rid himself of a possible embarrassment by leaving a junior officer or anybody else to the mercies of the Pathans. Black, Dornoch had come to believe, was capable of this, at any rate in his innermost thoughts. Black had a kind of death wish for Ogilvie, and it was this wish that had fathered the idea of the funeral. As for Fettleworth, he must have some other reason for that headstrong, stupid insistence that a Political Officer should not, after capture, be acknowledged. Certainly this was normal military practice – under normal conditions, if any conditions along the Frontier could be described as normal; but there was surely a difference in this case! *Once that message had been received, firm action should have been taken.* Further secrecy was pointless. Now that rumour appeared to have caught up with the truth, action was more than ever the only right and proper course. To dither and hedge in the changed circumstances, to abrogate a General's responsibilities, would be, once the whole thing came out, to bring the greatest possible discredit upon the whole military institution.

Forced by his inner conflict into speech Dornoch said as much, cutting across a further contribution from the Chief of Staff. It did not the slightest good. Fettleworth, made only the more obstinate by opposition, treated him to an angry speech on military necessities and expediencies and the over-riding importance of not being seen to be engaged in espionage, *et cetera*. Dornoch, who had heard it all before, listened in boiling silence. In the end the officers dispersed without a real decision having been taken. The day was won by the policy of wait and see. Or, in O'Kelly's phrase, more masterly inactivity . . .

James Ogilvie's continued inactivity was far from masterful; it had become so intensely painful that he doubted his ability to hold out for many more hours. Day after day, with only the guard-changes to relieve the desperation of his monotony, only the distant mountain tops and the old *sadhu* and the occasionally perambulating legs of the sentry to watch, he had borne his confinement and he had no idea when it would end; but he kept going, kept his sanity as his limbs, his whole body, trembled uncontrollably, by telling himself that Nashkar Ali Khan must have a genuine use for him and, in his own good time, would order his release. It would have been quite pointless to keep him here under guard if that statement had not been genuine; death would have been more effective securitywise, and visible torture more fun.

Thoughts of Jones tormented his hours, more especially when sheer exhaustion brought brief and nightmare-ridden sleep. Then he could see that poor tormented body gradually

143

dwindling to a trunk, could hear the terrible shrieks and the high, sighing moans that had burst from the tongueless mouth in those last horrible moments of bouncing up from the flat rock. Jones himself could never have remotely visualized the way his life would end, when he had first set out from Brum to make his money. To make it by a dirty and unworthy trade, certainly – Healey was only too right about that. He had deserved punishment, but not torture and degradation. He had got far, far more than his deserts, and it was ironic that this should have come about as the result of an act of patriotism at the last. For Jones had done a brave thing, and had done it to the best of his ability and in full awareness of the risks involved. He had not been a soldier, he owed no military allegiance to the British Raj; he was acting under no orders. Poor Jones had been a true volunteer, even though possibly a well-paid one. And no one in Peshawar or Nowshera or Murree would mourn his death; he was expendable, an easy sacrifice to the greater good. Some Staff Officer, some O'Kelly who had initiated Jones's participation, would have been wining and dining carelessly enough in some depot Mess the night Jones had bounced his screaming way to death and to whatever recrimination awaited him when once more he made contact with the late Regimental Sergeant-Major of the old 14th Foot.

Ogilvie found that this thought of Jones's father brought the relief of a smile and temporary forgetfulness of horror. Jones had been a character, however disreputable, and their journey together had had its lighter moments. He was thinking of some of these moments, and seeing Jones in wily conclave with Gojun Khan, first of the *khel* leaders with whom they had made contact, when he became aware of things happening outside his rocky prison. The dawn had reached across the hills and the Pathan on guard had scraped himself to his feet and had moved some distance away, so that Ogilvie could see the whole of his tall, rangy figure and the rifle that was pointing down towards the track leading up from the pass.

Men were coming up the track; three men, Pathans. When they reached the hole one of them bent down and Ogilvie saw that it was Healey.

Healey gave him a warning wink, with his face close, and spoke in Pushtu. 'Wilshaw Sahib,' he said, 'you are to be released and you will come with me.'

'By whose order?'

'The order of Nashkar Ali Khan, who is in Maizar.'

'What does he want of me?'

'This you will see.' Healey stood upright again. Looking at
his lean brown legs, Ogilvie heard him talking to the guard and
his two companions. Soon after this two of the men bent and
dragged away the securing boulder. Hands reached in and laid
hold of his shoulders, and heaved. It was a painful business, and
his head banged hard against the rock roof of the hole and he
lost some skin from his arms and body, but the feeling when he
was stretched out on the open track was one of sheer relief and
joy. Healey bent and gave him water from a goat-skin, and
forced him to take more of the rough food on which he had
lived over the past days. His limbs were twitching still, and he
was cruelly stiff in his joints, so much so that he doubted if he
would ever move again. But Healey was patience itself. He was
well prepared to wait until Wilshaw Sahib was fit to move.
This was as Nashkar Ali Khan himself wished it.

'Then he wishes me no further harm, Earless One?'

'In certain circumstances, under certain conditions, he
wishes you nothing but good. Now, Wilshaw Sahib, I shall
bring life back to your limbs.' Healey squatted beside him on
the ground and started massaging, rubbing warmth into arms
and legs, easing away the stiffness and the restlessness that was
making him twitch so badly. Healey's hands were strong, and
this massage worked effectively. After half an hour's hard
sweaty work, Healey sat back on his haunches and said, 'Now
try to stand, Wilshaw Sahib.'

Ogilvie did so, but staggered. Healey and one of the Pathans
caught him and steadied him. Panting with the effort, he tried
to take a step, but his legs crumpled. Over the next two hours,
no less, he learned to walk all over again, and at last Healey was
satisfied, but said he would be carried down the track to the
pass by the two bearers. 'Horses are waiting,' he said. 'The ride
to Maizar will not take too long.' Shading his eyes, he looked
upward at the holy man on the peak. 'Up there is someone who
has a longer wait than you have had, Wilshaw Sahib. Truly a
man of patience, and of a godly strength.'

'Still there is no sign?'

'Only the *sadhu* can say, and he has not spoken.'

'And Nashkar Ali Khan?'

'Still awaits the sign.'

'All else is ready, Earless One?'

'All else will be very ready, Wilshaw Sahib, when you have played your part.' Healey, who happened to have his back to all three Pathans at that moment, gave Ogilvie another wink, accompanied this time by a cheerful grin. Ogilvie was much intrigued by this, but had to wait in patience for some explanation. 'You are ready to start now?'

'Yes.'

Healey signed to the bearers and Ogilvie was lifted like a baby and the procession, losing no more time now, started the descent. Now the sun was high, spreading a harsh glare over the mountains, and the clarity of the atmosphere was such that Ogilvie could see many scores of miles into Afghanistan and could pick out the crevices like old scars on the hillsides, and the deep rocky gorges that formed the high sides of the passes, the ancient caravan routes. Along those passes, for centuries before the British Raj and its regiments from every corner of the British Isles had arrived like a roll of drums along the Afghan border, wild men had surged on their expeditions of plunder and rape and killing, men who had formed the spearheads of the rise of empires or the destruction of dynasties. In his mind's eye he saw them again – or their descendants, equally wild and bloodthirsty men – marching and riding along those same age-old passes to wage war against the present enemy, the most persistent and presumptuous enemy of all, the men from the west, the soldiers of the Queen, men with womanish white skins and a curious way of dressing that made them all look alike. The thunder that could come out of Afghanistan to join with that of the Waziris and the tribes to the north could all too possibly rise to the crescendo of a storm that would tear the British flag from its pre-eminence in the Empire of India, rip it from cantonment and residency and fortress and scatter its defenders, as one of the Pathans guarding his prison-hole had said, back into the seas over which they had come to conquer.

He took a last glance upward at the *sadhu*. It was all in his hands. Eagle faced, old bag of bones, skinny, clad only in an animal's skin, with sandals on his feet, probably sitting in his own excreta if his foodless vigil had left him anything to excrete, you could knock him to oblivion with the gentlest push – yet, if she were a wise woman, Her Majesty Queen Victoria herself would have the greatest respect for his potential.

Had Ogilvie had the strength in his body at that moment, he

would have kicked the Pathans down the hillside and climbed to the peak to do O'Kelly's bidding. But the moment passed and with it passed his disturbing vision of the embattled tribesmen. Why, they were all poorly armed and equipped, and surely to goodness all the fervour in the world was not enough to arm them against the power and might of the British Army in India? There would be slaughter, yes, wickedly long casualty lists and much human misery and heartache, and no doubt many more Joneses screaming in their death agonies on the parade-grounds of Peshawar. But – surely – the final issue could never be in doubt!

They reached the pass, gloomy between its rock sides. The horses were waiting, tethered to scrubby trees. Healey asked, 'You can ride now, Wilshaw Sahib?'

'I'll try.' He did; and successfully mounted and sat, though it was a painful process still. When he was ready they moved off in procession along the pass, and after a while Healey announced that he wished to discuss their master's business in private with the Englishman. The Pathans went ahead obediently, out of earshot. When it was safe to do so, Healey spoke. He said, 'So far, so good, old man. At least you're out of the frying pan!'

Ogilvie grinned. 'Where's the fire – and what are the chances of falling into it, Healey?'

'The fire is all Waziristan, but I suppose you could say it's likely to be burning more brightly in Maizar. As to the chances ... how does fifty-fifty strike you?'

'Fair enough, I suppose.'

'Quite. It's all I can promise you, anyway.' Healey chuckled. 'I've been a busy man the last few days.'

'Doing what?'

'Ingratiating myself further, chiefly. Nashkar's a damn sight simpler than he imagines, actually – not that it's been child's play. It hasn't. I've worked like a nigger, if you'll forgive something of a pun.'

'It's come off?'

'You bet it has, old man. Nashkar thinks the sun shines out of my backside. Some of that has rubbed off on you. I've built you up, my boy! Very trustworthy, and likely to blossom into a first-rate supplier of arms. I took my cue from you – what you said about belonging to the rival firm and all that. I insisted that it sounded absolutely genuine and now Nashkar's willing to take a chance. Your case has been aided by something else as well: Nashkar's put out feelers towards Peshawar.' He glanced sideways. 'You've been disowned, it seems. I don't know how that feels to you, but it's worked wonders with Nashkar, who has been put in a very believing frame of mind – you see, the way he put out the feelers was pretty subtle.' He outlined the facts. 'All the same,' he added, 'it's going to be up to you and you alone to produce the pudding that gives the proof.'

'Well, I'll try! You'll have to give me some more information to go on, Healey.'

'Of course.' Healey drew his horse back a little, for they were catching up with the Pathans. 'Between us, Ogilvie, we're going to find out the entire plan of campaign and also we're going to inhibit the long awaited sign before it materializes. Right?'

'Right!'

'But to do it, we need time. Time, time, time – that's the thing. And that's where you come in.'

'How?'

'You guarantee an arms supply from Abbottabad. I know I've said I've done the groundwork, and that's true, I have. But it's you yourself Nashkar has to trust. You'll need all your wits about you to keep his trust while you're milking him of full information, but I've a feeling it's our last remaining hope and I can promise you one thing for sure: Nashkar won't move till he does get your arms delivery, or someone else's! We know he'll not get yours, but at least *we'll* get the time we need if you talk convincingly.'

'He said he had all the arms he needed for the assault, Healey.'

'Quite right. He had – when he said it.' Healey seemed full of mirth. 'Did you – er – happen to feel a small ground tremor a few nights ago?'

'Yes. I suppose it was a minor earthquake somewhere.'

'You could call it that,' Healey said modestly as they jogged on through the pass. 'As a matter of fact it was me – blowing up Nashkar's biggest arsenal, a few miles this side of Maizar.' Ogilvie gave a whistle of surprise. 'It's a long story, of course, but in point of fact the actual deed was quite easy. The place was virtually wide open – in a guard sense I mean, the actual site was underground, and simply vast. No wonder you thought it was an earthquake! So did a certain maiden – wrong word, that – whose bed I beat it to afterwards at breakneck speed.

The dump was guarded by just a handful of rather seedy Waziris on whom I was able to practise my *thuggee*.' He clasped his fingers around his throat. 'You know – army boot-laces. I thought they might be useful and I brought them into the country made up into a sort of net arrangement to support an indecent part of my anatomy. Next day, Nashkar went ber-serk, but he never connected the business with me. And now, you see, he's in the market for arms, and fast.' He glanced at Ogilvie's anxious face. 'We have to beat the *sadhu*, old man. God could well be in His heaven if things go right for us, but in the meantime His rival's self-styled prophet is very much on earth. If the sign comes before we're ready ... well, Nashkar will march, buggered-up arsenal or not. Frankly,' he added, '*I* wouldn't consider the loss vital, though I've persuaded *him* it is, naturally.'

'So it's still back to that confounded holy man!'

Healey nodded. As if he had connected in some way with Ogilvie's earlier thoughts, he said, 'The Queen-Empress, long may she live, is by way of being up against Allah or whoever it is that communes with our holy man. I should have said Maho-met. It'll be like a clash with the Dean of Windsor, if one regards the *sadhu* as being of the same sort of seniority.' He paused. 'Shall we join the Pathans?'

Healey seemed in a very good humour, and full of confidence, which was more than Ogilvie felt. They sent their horses ahead faster and caught up with the tribesmen, and with a practised ease of manner Captain Healey reverted to the severe gravity of the Earless One.

CHAPTER TEN

BACK into the smells of Maizar; but not for long. Nashkar Ali Khan, whose liveried mounted escort met them outside the western gate and conducted them arrogantly through the crowds of men and women, occupied a splendid fortress-palace built on high rock away beyond the town to the north-east. The Pathan leader looked out of place here, Ogilvie thought, as though he and his garments were more suited to the rigours of the open mountains and the freedom of the plains. It was possible, he imagined, indeed likely, that Nashkar had seized this palace by force from some princeling whose power and followers he had usurped.

They walked, soon after arrival, on the battlemented roof of the building – Ogilvie, Nashkar Ali Khan, and Healey. The Pathan, who had apologized for the lengthy imprisonment, was polite and friendly, though there was still a reserve about him in his dealings with a man who had yet to offer conclusive proof of his trustworthiness.

'You will, of course, have been told by the Earless One, Wilshaw Sahib, that a further shipment of arms would be welcome. I have enough, and more than enough, to put my immediate plans into full effect, but . . .' he shrugged 'avenues of supply are never to be lightly turned away.'

'They are not too easily come by, Highness?'

The Pathan laughed good-humouredly. 'You wish to prepare the ground for bargaining! I shall not be ungenerous in my offer, Wilshaw Sahib, but first I shall want to know what you can supply, and how quickly.'

'Yes, indeed.' Ogilvie paused. 'Your plans are, of course, against the British positions along the Frontier?'

'Yes. Does this cause you to have second thoughts, Wilshaw Sahib? Do you not understand, as a seller of arms about the world, that to have your products used against your own people is a risk you must take, you and all other sellers of arms?'

'Yes, certainly. I do understand that. It is never a welcome thought, though.'

'You prefer to forget it?'

'Let us say, it is not necessary to stress it, Nashkar Ali Khan! I asked the question because it occurs to me that after your first assault you might well find yourself able to take over arms captured from the soldiers, and will not need a replacement supply.'

Again the Pathan laughed. 'Such honesty does credit to your gentlemanliness, but scarcely to your pocket, Wilshaw Sahib! I shall not rely, however, on such imponderabilities. Your British soldiers seldom leave their arms behind, and have a habit of destroying what is not transportable in a retreat. No, I must be assured of my own independent supply-line, Wilshaw Sahib.'

'Very well. What kind of quantities are we discussing, Highness?'

'All you can promise.'

'Quite so, but I would like a basis to work on, Highness. If you would, perhaps, indicate, however roughly, the size of your armies in the field, this would help.'

'My armies?' Nashkar Ali Khan stopped his measured pacing. He waved an arm towards the peaks surrounding the brooding palace. 'Here in Waziristan I command sixty thousand warriors. Along the North-West Frontier of your Raj – from Kohat to Chitral – I have the promise that another eighty thousand men are ready to march. From Afghanistan a virtually limitless number, of whom some fifteen thousand have already crossed the Frontier to join me. Does this help?'

'Yes, Highness.' One hundred and fifty-five thousand already, plus that inexhaustible reservoir in Afghanistan – a continual reserve to flow in like a mighty river. The whole of Northern Army Command contained some one hundred and seventy thousand troops, consisting of forty thousand British plus native troops, native reserves, volunteers and Imperial Service troops. A mixed bunch, and not all of them fighting men. Many were medical orderlies, many were clerks, cooks, storekeepers and so on. And they were spread around all of the northern half of India, whereas Nashkar Ali Khan's fighting hordes were nicely concentrated, poised, probably, for a pincer movement on Peshawar and Nowshera. If those two great garrisons fell, the hordes would sweep on to Murree and Northern Command would disintegrate. In spite of Fettleworth's awareness of the threat, Nashkar's attack could carry him right through the British positions unless Fettleworth had already acted to reinforce his Division. Speed was essential now. Admitted the British garrisons were grouped around the railway system so as to facilitate movement, but the railways could handle only a certain number at any one time. And if troops had to be sent north from Southern Army at Ootacamund in the Madras Presidency, why, then the request for them, and the first entrainments, should already have been made. That would be up to Ogilvie's father, of course, but Fettleworth was the man first responsible for notifying Army Headquarters of his needs. Ogilvie found he had broken out into a heavy sweat as he thought of the numbers the Pathan had so lightly quoted.

He asked, 'And the men from Afghanistan? Do they come with their own arms?'

'In most cases, yes. There is a supply from the Russians, but their pieces are old-fashioned, and I prefer the British rifle and the British machine-gun. Now, Wilshaw Sahib. Can you supply such an army as I have described?'

'Not all of it, Highness – at any rate, not quickly. But I can help. In and around Abbottabad I have some eighty thousand rifles . . . and perhaps five thousand machine-guns, and much ammunition. Also explosives, and loose powder.' He could only hope he had not over-quoted unreasonably.

'These can be delivered, Wilshaw Sahib?'

Ogilvie tried to say it casually: 'Of course, Highness, if I go to make the arrangements.'

Once again the Pathan laughed, and laid a hand on Ogilvie's shoulder. 'My dear Wilshaw Sahib, you cannot for one moment think that I would let you cross my borders into British-held India! Do you take me for a madman?'

'You don't trust me enough to let me help you?'

'Of a certainty I do not trust you enough to let you leave my country, which is a different thing, and a natural thing with which you must agree. Come, Wilshaw Sahib, let us walk again.' He let his hand fall from Ogilvie and they resumed their pacing of the battlements, looking out across the barren peaks reaching skyward in solemn and barbaric majesty. 'The Earless One believes you are to be trusted, and I trust the Earless One. There is another thing also, but even this is yet not enough for me to let you go, Wilshaw Sahib.'

'What is this other thing, Highness?'

Nashkar said, 'I have trailed what you, I think, would call a red herring into your garrison at Peshawar.' He repeated what Healey had already told Ogilvie about the goat-skin message hurled through Surgeon-Major Warrender's window. 'Enough time has elapsed, but the British have neither replied nor made one single move. I believe – all my past experience tells me – that they would not leave a British officer to be tortured and broken by the tribes who are their enemies. This heartens me, Wilshaw Sahib, in my trust. I believe the name Wilshaw is perhaps genuinely not known to the British command.'

'I can assure you it is not,' Ogilvie said earnestly. He had in fact had very mixed feelings ever since Healey had told him of his disownment. Fettleworth's apparent non-activity on his behalf suited his book of subterfuge well enough, certainly – but at the same time left him with an alarming sense of aloneness and abandonment. He had expected no less if such circumstances had ever arisen, but now that they had, he'd still found it a shock to be told that his predicament was being officially ignored. He was aware now of a sudden blinding and unreasoning hatred for Fettleworth and O'Kelly and the whole vast, unwieldy system of the British Army in India that could send any man into the unknown, into terrible danger and distress and the certainty, if caught, of an end like Jones had met – and then wash their hands of him, shrug him off, cable his family with formal regrets after the worst had happened, and then carry on with the meaningless ritual of military social life with no more than one backward glance of pity. God damn them all. Then he steadied, and looked objectively at the facts. Perhaps Fettleworth had been dead right – or his advisers had been. Perhaps, even, Fettleworth had handed him salvation on a plate. At least, the British non-action seemed to have led to a wondrous buttressing of trust!

He said, 'Highness, you have said you do not trust me enough, even so, to allow me to leave Waziristan, but without my doing so, there can be no supply of arms.'

'Another way must be found,' Nashkar said. 'In your country you have a saying, have you not, that to Napoleon there is no such word as cannot?'

'I am not Napoleon,' Ogilvie said, smiling. 'I am one of the shopkeepers that Napoleon charged the British with being!'

The Pathan smiled in return. 'Nevertheless, Wilshaw Sahib, a way will be found. Have you not an agent, someone in the town of Abbottabad who can make the arrangements ... if a discreetly worded message reaches him from you?'

'The whole conduct of my affairs lies in my hands alone, Highness. You will appreciate a need for great secrecy.'

'Naturally! But you cannot operate entirely on your own, Wilshaw Sahib. There must be people whom you can trust. It is in the nature of things that this must be so.' Once again he laid a hand on Ogilvie's arm, drawing him across towards the battlements on the north side of the palace. 'Think well, Wilshaw Sahib. Your arms must reach me before the *sadhu* speaks. The Earless One, whom as you know I trust, tells me that I need extra weapons before I am ready. This attack must not fail, and it will not fail. The *sadhu* will speak the moment, I will bring out the strength. In unison, we shall sweep the Frontier clean. It is written. The chance will not come again.'

They had reached the north battlements now. 'Look down, Wilshaw Sahib,' Nashkar said, and Ogilvie looked. He gasped. He looked out over seemingly boundless ranges of hills and mountains, melting into a vast distance under a noon-high sun; and then down the sheer side of the rock pinnacle on which the palace sat, into a valley a very long way below. It was the most tremendous drop, right down that sheer hard side, that he had ever imagined. He was linked to the floor of the valley in a straight line of wall and mountain with not so much as a tree or bush to break it. Nashkar Ali Khan said, 'You are an honoured guest of my house, Wilshaw Sahib, and will be treated as such. There will be many delights. But as in any other house there are rules, and guests are expected to obey them. If they do not, then they cease to be guests.' He lifted an arm and extended it over the battlements. 'Arms from Abbottabad in the north, Wilshaw Sahib, or I shall order you to be thrown down from this spot. You understand?'

White-faced, Ogilvie nodded. He stepped back from the embrasure, involuntarily. His head swam; he had a feeling, for the first time in his life, that he had no head for heights – such heights, anyway. He said, 'I understand, Highness, but I cannot see the means whereby I can obey.'

The Pathan shrugged and said, 'It is for you to think of the way, and then for me to approve. But we have not much longer, Englishman!'

'How long?'

'As I have said so many times, this depends upon the *sadhu*. At any moment the sign may come. So, Wilshaw Sahib the arms, and quickly!' Nashkar Ali Khan, in a sudden movement of impatience, swung round on Healey. 'What think you, Earless One?'

For the first time Captain Healey spoke. 'Wilshaw Sahib has talked to me of a woman, who assists him in his work. He does not want to involve this woman . . . but perhaps he can be persuaded it is for the best.'

Ogilvie stared; he gave a gasp of astonishment, of alarm and indignation. This reaction seemed, he fancied, to please Healey; and instinct kept his own mouth shut until something clarified. But he wondered how the devil this Political Officer from far-off Ootacamund could possibly have heard anything about Mary Archdale, who was the only woman he could be presumed to refer to.

It was instinct again that provided him with the right reaction. He became very British. 'I can't involve a lady,' he said stiffly. All the while his mind was working fast. In point of fact Healey had given him a first-class opening and had given it under the best possible conditions of authenticity; it all had the appearance of being dragged from Ogilvie, something he had not thought of for himself. And it was just possible that Mary might interpret a message, and pass it on to Lord Dornoch, who would contact Division, who would consult O'Kelly . . . it could work if he was damned clever in the way the message was worded! It would go against his orders from O'Kelly, of course, the order that he was on no account to communicate; but O'Kelly was not here, and he was. Expediency must dictate, initiative must take a firm grip. Campaigns had been lost before now because of an officer's blind obedience to orders. If Division, as result of a message, could organize a decoy arms caravan, with a strong force covering it and nicely hidden . . . but in God's name what could they *do*? A force big enough to achieve Nashkar's rout on his own territory would need to be so big it would be reported to this peak-perched palace before ever it moved out of cantonments!

Ogilvie's heart sank again, but, for what it was worth, he followed the given lead. 'It is true I have a friend of whom I have spoken to the Earless One, perhaps too lightly. She means much to me, and I to her.' He decided to amend this a little; and to help the process he gave a slight, knowing smile. 'More, perhaps, I to her, though I would not care that she should know this. I – find her useful to me.'

'In your selling of arms?'

'Yes.'

'Explain fully, Wilshaw Sahib.'

As if with reluctance still, he did. 'She is the widow of a British officer, formerly of the Peshawar garrison, killed in action some while ago – before I myself came to India. She . . . blames the British Army for her husband's death. She was devoted to him. Despite this devotion, there are things that, having been a married woman, she misses.'

'These things you supply, as you supply arms?'

'That's right,' Ogilvie said steadily, giving another realistic smutty smirk. 'In return she – well, she tells me things. She is still much in touch with the military, and military affairs are talked about a good deal. She keeps me informed of the movements of patrols – things like that. Also where the soldiers are likely to be operating, so that I can avoid those areas for my trade missions, and go to them when it is safe again.'

'She knows where your arms are hidden, this woman?'

He hesitated, but not for long. 'No. I have never told her that. It isn't that I don't trust her. But the less a person knows, the less they can reveal under pressure if anything goes wrong. This I believe you will understand, Highness.'

'Assuredly, and you are wise! Continue, Wilshaw Sahib. How, then, can she assist you now?'

Ogilvie said, 'She can take a message – personally, to Abbottabad. You are right that I have associates, not many but a few – men who are mere subordinates, who will not act except on a personal message. This is a rule of all arms companies who trade in areas of the world such as this – you must understand that there are many people against us, and many ruses are used to trip us. Thus, all orders except those from the representatives such as myself are disregarded.'

'And the woman? They will trust *her*?'

'Yes. One man will, a man whom she has met.'

Nashkar looked at him hard, penetratingly. Ogilvie, tense from the concentrated thought and lightning-like verbal processes and decisions that this conversation had forced upon him virtually unawares, looked back and met his eye squarely. He was aware of approval emanating from Healey. The Pathan leader asked suddenly, 'This man. His name?'

'He is called Cunningham.'

'Cunning-um.'

'That's right.' It was unlikely, but possible, that the name of Dornoch was known to Nashkar Ali Khan; it could be taken as reasonably certain that that of the Regimental Sergeant-Major would not be. And old Bosom Cunningham was a good friend and as dependable as a rock. If a message could be got to him, it would reach the Colonel at the double, or at least as fast as the heavily-built R.S.M. could move.

'You can trust this woman not to give your message to anybody but Cunning-um?'

Ogilvie gave an easy, assured laugh. He felt the tide running his way quite strongly and he was filled with a surge of optimism. 'Absolutely! You do not imagine any woman on a military station is likely to admit friendship with a man who provides arms for the tribes? I have even to be careful not to see this lady in Peshawar, or to be seen there myself. She comes to me in Abbottabad . . . or sometimes we meet in the hills that lie between.'

Nashkar nodded, then turned away. He stalked along below the embrasures, deep in thought, moving up and down with his arms folded in front of his body. At last he stopped, and once again faced Ogilvie. 'Very well, Wilshaw Sahib,' he said. 'You shall prepare a message, which I shall read. If I approve it, I shall have it delivered to this woman – and then we shall see. You will be your own hostage, Wilshaw Sahib.'

'And in the meantime, Highness?'

Nashkar laughed. 'In the meantime you are still my honoured guest and you have the freedom of my palace. This state of affairs will continue for so long as I am given no cause to change it. Do you understand, Wilshaw Sahib?'

'I understand,' Ogilvie answered gravely.

'Good! Then we shall meet again later, when you have decided upon your message. The Earless One will take you to your apartment now, Wilshaw Sahib, where you will be provided with pen and ink and paper.'

It was a splendid apartment, on the side of the palace looking northward, over the long drop into the valley beneath the battlements. Ogilvie and Healey approached it by way of a thickly-carpeted corridor whose ends were guarded by Pathans carrying rifles with fixed bayonets. This gave Ogilvie a strong awareness of a prison, but this feeling was to some extent suspended when he entered the apartment itself. This was high and spacious, and there was a luxurious bed – a real four-poster with rich hangings, that looked as if it had come from England. Another article of furniture with nostalgic overtones of home was the wash-stand, its marble surface bearing a gold-decorated china basin and jug and soap-dish; and a glass water-bottle with a tumbler over its neck. There were three tall, narrow windows, little more than light-giving slits, with that long drop below them and the distant view across the high mountains rolling over Waziristan.

Healey gave a sudden chuckle and said, 'Just look at the ceiling, old boy. That'll give you erotic dreams, all right!'

Ogilvie looked up. The ceiling was covered with a rich painting, a scene that was reminiscent of some debauch of ancient Rome. Dark-skinned men, naked but for their turbans, chased peached-skinned nymphs, and caught them, and performed upon their willing bodies strangenesses that had never entered Ogilvie's well-brought-up imagination. The painting was beautifully executed, and the colours were sharp, the immense detail well defined and startling. There was a sense of action, of real movement in it; it was a depiction of a sensualist's cavorting fantasy but it possessed life.

'Pretty extreme, isn't it?' Ogilvie said.

Healey grinned. 'Not very British! But healthy.'

'*Healthy?*'

'Of course.' Healey swept a hand upward. 'Damn it, these people were realists, they had no bloody silly inhibitions. It all came out, insteady of turning inwards on them. We in Britian have forgotten how to live, all our natural feelings have been battened down by our ghastly Victorian morality. All the things we'd like to do, we daren't do. Sometimes we don't even know we *want* to do them, not consciously, and that's bad in itself, because what's there in us,' he said, pressing the palms of his hands to his chest and staring at Ogilvie, 'has to show itself in one form or another, and quite often it goes bad on us and turns us into extremely nasty people. Absolutely free sexual expression is as good for one as a purge. Better – because it's natural.'

Ogilvie followed his glance upward again. 'Or unnatural!'

Healey shook his head impatiently. 'There's nothing unnatural in any of that, old boy. It's only the teachings of the moralists that makes us believe that.'

Ogilvie was visited by a sudden thought of Andrew Black. Black, to his knowledge, was awkward with women, though on occasions his hot look, a lascivious look when he fancied himself unobserved, had given away his desires. Very likely he was a frustrated man, one of Healey's victims of morality, and equally likely he might show a different side to his character if only he could break through the layers of all that had been drummed into him by stupid, well-meaning parents, sadistic schoolmasters and hidebound nannies. It could indeed explain a great deal.

'There are other things to be explained too,' Ogilvie said aloud.

'I beg your pardon?'

'Oh – just thoughts.' Ogilvie flushed. 'But there *is* something I'd like explained, Healey. How the devil did you come to hear about Mrs. Archdale?'

Healey laughed. 'Why assume it was Mrs. Archdale?'

'There's no one else. It *was* her, wasn't it?'

'Yes.'

'Then how?'

'My dear old chap, you bear a name that's pretty well known in India – oh yes, all the way to Ootacamund, as if you didn't know!'

'But—'

'There isn't any but, old boy. There's only the two G.O.C.'s in the field, and one's your father. He's in the limelight and so, to an extent, are you, because of him.' He threw up his hands and grinned. 'That's all there is in it. Long tongues. You know India. Vast, yes, but there aren't really so many of us British. We take a ridiculous interest in one another's affairs—'

'A damned impertinent interest—'

'Oh, I don't know! It's quite a useful interest at times – isn't it?'

'You mean now?' Ogilvie hesitated. 'If it comes off.'

'It will. But my own interest in the Ogilvie clan has had another use just lately. It's proved to me, right from the start – after you said who you were, that is – that you're on the level. You see, I've met your father, or anyway I've served under him at a distance – and you're really very like him, old boy. Looks and manner both. And believe me, that's a compliment.'

'Thank you. Talking of trust, though, Healey ... how is it that Nashkar trusts you as much as he obviously does?'

'It's my job to be convincing.'

'Yes, but—'

Healey held up a hand. 'Again I say, no buts. I meant what I said. If he didn't trust me, I'd consider I'd fallen down on my job. I've put a devil of a lot of work into it, you know. My background is authentic, my command of the lingo is perfect – my credentials are in order.' He fingered his ear-holes. 'Then there's these, and my nose, of course. I came through the fire, Ogilvie, and was not found wanting. The Pathans set a lot of store by that.'

'I'm sorry.'

'Oh, don't apologize! It's natural you should want to know, since you owe Nashkar's trust in you largely to my own word. If I'm bowled out, old boy, so are you – but I don't need to remind you! The fact is,' he added, 'Nashkar likes me. We see eye to eye on a good many things. If a Pathan likes you, you're in. It has something to do with the second law of *Pukhtunwali*, you know. *Melmastia.*'

'Hospitality?' Ogilvie remembered being instructed in this by poor dead Jones.

'Exactly. On occasions, it even supersedes *badal*. It's so strong that even your worst enemy must be given it sometimes – even to the extent of giving him refuge against anyone who's after his life. A sort of sanctuary – like the church in the old times. Not that I mean to draw an exact parallel with my own case, of course. It's just that *melmastia* has – well, in a sense disposed Nashkar to look kindly upon someone he already likes if you follow. It's not very well put, perhaps.'

'It'll do! Aren't you afraid the *sadhu* will smell you out, though, and tip Nashkar the wink?'

'That old charlatan?' Healey laughed. 'He talks about a sign, but damn it, old boy, he doesn't know a sign from a fried egg!'

'When does he signify the off, then?'

Healey shrugged. 'Don't ask me. He dreams something up. Say a thunderstorm – or something. Not a thunderstorm actually, since the rains are well over. Perhaps a ... a strange light over the mountains! I wonder he didn't take my man-made earth tremor as being the voice of Mahomet, really.'

'So we have to watch the weather now?'

'We have to watch every bloody thing,' Healey said, 'but first, we'd better get down to that message. Or you had. It would be wiser, I think, if I left you to it, though we'd better agree on the general lines – on what we want to produce as an end result, that is.'

Ogilvie asked a little blankly, 'What *do* we want to produce?'

Healey said, 'An attack, of course.'

'D'you mean a rescue?'

'No, I don't mean a rescue, old boy, I mean what I say – an *attack*. An attack in strength before it's too late. I feel it in my bones that things are now on a knife-edge. If he doesn't signify soon, our holy man's going to be dead of starvation anyway. In my view, it's vital your lot in Peshawar attack before the sign comes – before Nashkar's absolutely wholly ready himself, and so we, instead of him, can use the element of surprise. Also, don't forget you need an arms shipment inside Waziristan double quick, if you're to survive yourself. All right? Just ponder along those lines. By the way,' he added, moving for the door. 'Nashkar said you would have the freedom of his palace. He meant just that and no more. It'll include the grounds, but not Maizar or anywhere else, so don't try to get out. There's no freedom outside! So long, old boy. I'll be back anon.'

When Healey had gone a soft-footed native came in with writing materials. Ogilvie went across to one of the slit-like windows and stared out over the hills, thinking about the message he had to compose. It was going to be extremely tricky, indeed the whole plan was full of dangers. What he wrote would, first of all, have to pass Nashkar Ali Khan. Then it would have to be strong enough to send Mary straight to Cunningham – not too much difficulty there, of course – and it would have to give Dornoch, when it reached his hands, the whole gist of what Healey had suggested. What Dornoch would make of a request for arms to be sent into Waziristan – what Fettleworth would make of it – Ogilvie could only guess. Very likely there would be an earth termor in and around Divisional H.Q.! And if dither and procrastination were to be the order of the day, if Bloody Francis flew into a tantrum and decided to ignore the message as being the work of a half-wit, then he, Ogilvie, could kiss the world good-bye.

He took a deep breath and, moving back from the window, went across to a writing-desk to make a start on what could turn out to be either a reprieve or a death warrant.

'It ought to be all right,' Healey said, frowning over his shattered nose. 'Quite good, really. Come on and let's face His Highness – we don't want to give an appearance of collusion by being together too long. All set?'

'Yes.'

They went out into the corridor, along the thick carpet and past the armed guards at the end. Healey led the way to a great staircase, wide and shallow, descending gracefully from the landing, past a half-landing where there stood a marble sculpture of a well-breasted naked woman and an enormous and unexpected alabaster bowl of exotically-scented flowers. They went down into a great central hall over which stood a high dome of clear green glass, through which the afternoon sun struck to give the hall itself the feeling of an aquarium. Healey went towards a big door, which was flung open by a brigandish guard on duty outside.

They went in.

Nashkar Ali Khan was there with a woman, whom he instantly dismissed. She went, averting her veiled face from the two men, her buttocks visible as a divided creamy blur beneath the thin material of her flowing dress.

'Highness, Wilshaw Sahib has written the message.'

'Bring it to me.'

Healey took the message and handed it to Nashkar Ali Khan, who gestured them both to sit – or rather, squat uncomfortably upon cushions, half a dozen of which were arranged about the Pathan. He read the message aloud in English, rather haltingly, which made it sound stilted and unnatural, in Ogilvie's ears, pointing up its many imperfections, its lies, half-truths and evasions. It had not been an easy message to write; now it sounded lethal.

The Pathan read: "*Go to Mr. Cunningham. Tell him I am negotiating satisfactorily and require delivery of total stock to Maizar soonest possible. He will understand and act in accordance with instructions. Am totally trusted and Cunningham's khel units not deliberately endangering reception of caravan vehicles en route.*'

Nashkar looked up when he had finished. 'What is its meaning?' he asked. He tapped the piece of paper. 'The last sentence puzzles me.'

It would also puzzle Lord Dornoch, Ogilvie hoped. He said, 'Cunningham Sahib has charge of one sector of our operations – that is to say, Highness, certain of the *khels* come within his supply and accounting procedures. It is a matter of book work. I think it best to assure him that these *khels* will not expect to receive, or perhaps to commandeer, his caravan themselves – though there may be some who will feel themselves entitled, until they have received your instructions not to do so.'

'Such instructions will be given at once, Wilshaw Sahib!' the Pathan looked down again at the message. 'Now, why do you find it necessary to indicate that you are totally trusted, which I take to mean by myself – and which is not entirely the truth, and will not be so, until the arms delivery is safely made?'

'I am sorry, Highness, if I have presumed too much. I think it important to assure Cunningham Sahib that I am fully competent to issue these instructions and that due payment will be made. You have not forgotten, Highness, that I came into Waziristan as a new representative in these parts, under the wing of Jones Sahib?'

It was a tricky moment; to remind the Pathan of Mr. Jones might have an opposite effect. But all was well. Nashkar Ali Khan shrugged and said indifferently, 'I had not forgotten. You believe that this Cunningham Sahib may be doubtful as to whether you have established yourself?'

'I think it important, Highness, that he should be left in no doubt of my standing with you.'

'Very well. The delivery, however, will not be made to Maizar. You will alter the message, Wilshaw Sahib. The delivery will be to a point on the provincial boundary that runs to Thal from a little east of Parachinar. Ten miles west from the village of Sikandar, which itself is five miles westward from Thal, there is the entry to a pass. The delivery will be made here.'

'As you say, Highness. And your people will bring the caravan to Maizar?'

'If I tell them to, they will,' Nashkar answered enigmatically. 'Go now, and write the message again, and then come to me again with the new message. Earless One, a word in the side of your head!' He laughed indulgently, reaching out a hand to Healey.

Ogilvie left them, returning to his room. There was no doubt about the fact that Nashkar and Healey had some kind of a *rapport*, something that they alone shared . . . back in his room Ogilvie rewrote the message for Mary Archdale, looking upward at the entwined figures in their sexual orgies as if seeking inspiration for some way in which he might be able to improve what he was writing; but decided that to do any more might tempt fate too far, since Nashkar seemed to have accepted not only the message but also the hidden sting in the tail.

The promised delights came, and gave Ogilvie the uncomfortable feeling that he was fiddling while Rome burned. That night there was a magnificent banquet, with heaped food in overflowing bowls along the table, and much – very much – strong liquor. Healey drank only sparingly, but Ogilvie, after two glasses of an excellent French wine, a Montrachet that he would not have expected to find gracing the table of a Pathan, found himself beginning to mellow into a real desire to enjoy all that was being offered. You needed a long spoon to sup with the devil, he thought, but here was he in captivity and he might just as well make the most of it because it could all end very suddenly and very bloodily. So he drank deeply; Nashkar Ali Khan drank considerably deeper without showing any signs of it; so did the other guests, some of them from the palace, some from Maizar, and some, it seemed, from farther afield – all trusted henchmen of their leader. The laughter grew louder, and talk more free, as the meal progressed. There was much general enthusiasm about Kaspaturos, with the semi-drunken diners roaring out the name as though the very word itself were the promise and guarantee of victory, of the imminent advent of the promised land itself. But there was no specific mention, in this context, of Peshawar. Kaspaturos could have been sited anywhere in British-held India; but in point of fact it mattered little, Ogilvie believed, since the broad objective was so obviously the toppling of the Raj. Kaspaturos could be solidly identified later on. Ogilvie heard the forthcoming attack being discussed in some detail, and formed a picture of spearheads striking out from the Waziri border – striking out, it seemed, from three main places: from between Thal and Bahodur Khel, from the part, between Gumatti and Bannu, where he had come in with Mr. Jones, and from Jandola into Dera Ismail Khan.

The columns attacking by way of the two northerly routes would head for Peshawar and then press on towards Nowshera, whilst the one through Dera Ismail Khan was to strike through towards Rawalpindi. Eventually all these columns, consolidating as they went and being reinforced more or less continually from Afghanistan, would converge on Murree, being joined by that time by fresh columns pouring down from Bajaur and Buner. In the meantime the main Waziri force, the great bulk of Nashkar Ali Khan's invasion army, had been assembled now and was being held in readiness in the central hills between Maizar and Gumatti, encamped and waiting and eager to go. Indeed the only fears expressed were that it would become increasingly difficult to hold the tribes from independent action if they had to wait much longer for the *sadhu* to speak. Somewhat to Ogilvie's surprise in these circumstances, abolutely no suggestion was made from any quarter that, since all was ready otherwise, the force should march as soon as Wilshaw Sahib's arms arrived, and that the holy man be disregarded. The *sadhu's* hold upon their minds, upon their intelligences, seemed complete. Nothing would be done without him.

Once again Ogilvie thought: no sign, no rising. That, also, would be written. He had another thought as well, an equally unhelpful one – that he would have liked to have incorporated in his message the plans he had overheard. But in any case it was too late for that; the message was already on its way to Peshawar.

Drunk, or nearly so, James Ogilvie went later to his apartment. He was not surprised when, soon after he had lurched into the huge bed, a native girl came to him, smiling and snaking her hips. She appeared, though he knew this could not be the case, to have four breasts . . . He had drunk enough, and had looked for long enough at the scenes above his head, to have none of the qualms that had come to him when a woman had been offered by the *malik* in one of the villages en route. He enjoyed that night; the girl – she could not have been more than seventeen or eighteen – was experienced and clever; she taught James Ogilvie a great deal. But the morning came, the light of dawn stealing through the window slits, and the girl left him, and the dregs of the wine did not. Ogilvie felt as he had felt that first time with Mary Archdale, only much worse, and for a different reason: this time he felt dishonoured, as though he had let down a woman upon whom he was relying to bring him help, a woman who would play her part because she loved him.

The message went, very much as Nashkar Ali Khan's message, supposedly in Ogilvie's name, had gone earlier. Its route was as circuitous, but rather faster, for now time was shortening towards action – it must be so, the *sadhu* must surely speak soon! Wrapped around a stone, the message was duly flung with good aim through Mary Archdale's open window. There, for some while until it was found by her native servant, it remained, for Mary Archdale, sick with worry in a situation that could not be resolved since no one would tell her anything, had gone to Murree to find out all she could for herself. When the native servant found the message, which had come adrift from its stone, he scanned it in some doubt and then, because he could not read the writing but felt that it might be important to the memsahib, he placed it carefully on the top of her bureau under the secure weight of the image of a heathen god, a brass Buddha that burned incense.

Then, more or less conscientiously, he carried on with his work.

CHAPTER ELEVEN

'YOU are making a great mistake in coming here,' Sir Iain Ogilvie said. He said this firmly but kindly. A man who had as much of an eye for a pretty woman as Fettleworth – a man who had admired his visitor more than once in the past – he was always somewhat embarrassed by women; and on this occasion more so than ever. Worried himself, desperately worried, and anxious about his wife's reaction, for she was still blaming herself, he could offer no comfort to Mary Archdale. There was no comfort in the truth, which he could not tell in any case; there was no comfort in what she seemed to know instinctively were palliatives and lies. 'I would advise you, most strongly, to press your business no farther, Mrs. Archdale. To do so will not help and may well lead to great unpleasantness for you.'

'In what way, Sir Iain?'

'The G.O.C. fiddled with a pencil, wishing the woman away to hell and the devil. A temperamental explosiveness added to by his own deep anxieties made his answer sharper than he had intended. He said, 'You will not wish it to be said that you are throwing yourself at my son.'

Close to tears, she shook her head. 'Talk, Sir Iain! What do I care about talk! God knows I've had plenty of that. All I want is to know James is safe. I feel sure something terrible is happening.'

He looked at her face closely. 'You're fond of him – are you not? Deeply fond of him?'

'Oh God,' she said in a low voice, 'did you ever doubt that, Sir Iain?'

'Yes,' he said. 'Oh yes, Mrs. Archdale, I did! A widow, and a young subaltern . . . a subaltern younger than his years owing to certain factors in his life . . . and you seven years the elder. By God, you should have had more sense! Do you call *that* love – to jeopardize his career, all his prospects? Damn it, when first you grew what you call fond of him, your own husband was alive! Do you not know India better than that, Mrs Archdale? You should have sent him packing from the start. A word would have done it. I think you are a selfish young woman, and that's the truth.'

'No,' she said. 'I love him. Perhaps I am selfish to that extent. Can't you *see*?'

Sir Iain lifted his arms in despair, sighed heavily and began to sweat. He looked at the woman in front of him – little more than a girl against his own years – and tried to interpret the white face, the hollow eyes, the shaking shoulders and the way the small neat hands were twisting and twisting at a rag of a handkerchief in her lap. It was love of a sort, however misguided and ill-begotten and futureless. It could be self-pity; but he doubted if self-pity would have driven a woman all the way from Peshawar to Murree by way of Dornoch and Fettleworth (for he had heard all about *that*). Answering her question to the best of his ability he said quietly, 'I can't be sure what I see. It may be love – the fact that you believe James to be in danger may have made you feel it to be love—'

'Oh, no!'

'—but if this is so, my dear girl, I do assure you, the best way you can show your – your love, is to pursue this matter no farther.' He mopped at his forehead. 'May I suggest you leave it to me?'

'To you, Sir Iain?' Her voice, suddenly, lashed like a horsewhip. Her head was up, her eyes flashing. 'Would that not be like handing him over to Pontius Pilate?'

He was staggered. Blood rushed to his head and he felt suffocated. While he stared and gasped, she went on, 'It was you who sent him – wherever he has gone, and I'm certain now that I know where that is, and what he was sent to do! *You* sent him, your own son – it would never have been ordered without the consent of the General Officer Commanding – you sent him away from Peshawar, *because of me*! Oh yes, Sir Iain, I know India well enough! I know its devious ways – and its dirty filthy tricks, the way the whole *beastly* army is run on – on personalities and likes and dislikes and intrigue. You're responsible for what happens to James, Sir Iain, and you did it for those purely personal and very spiteful reasons!'

Panting, she stopped, pressing a hand to her mouth now. She had gone too far, would have liked to withdraw. She had been cruel and she could see the hurt in the General's face. But he gave her no time to say more. 'You overrate your importance, ma'am,' he said in a deadly cold but even voice. 'Had I felt as strongly as you suggest, you would have been very quickly dealt with, I assure you, and with but little trouble to myself.' He stood up, drawing himself to his full height, impressive in scarlet and gold. 'You have had enough ropes Mrs. Archdale. Go now, before you hang yourself.

For a moment she sat on, with a high colour; but, before Sir Iain sent for his A.D.C. to escort her out, she went. When she had gone the G.O.C. dropped back heavily into his chair and sat gazing unseeingly out through the window, at the cool green of his garden. He felt giddy, and his heart was thumping oddly; he had seldom been conscious of its beat before. Sweat poured from him, soaked into the collar of his uniform tunic, and he felt, as he had felt when the woman had been speaking, suffocated. She had spoken in temper and anxiety but she had come so much closer to the truth than even she perhaps had realized. His alone was the ultimate responsibility; he could quite easily – so very easily in retrospect – have sunk Fettleworth's scheme without trace even before it had begun to blossom.

Eventually he rang for his A.D.C. Telling the young officer that he wished not to be disturbed until he signified otherwise, he went to share his trouble with his wife. Fiona was always a soothing influence in times of real trouble, and she did not fail him on this occasion. He was glad of her arms around him, of her repeated and insistent assurances that he need not blame himself and that he was big enough to disregard entirely a vicious woman's tongue.

'Not vicious, Fiona,' he said unhappily. 'Worried – as we are. It was that that made her say those things. I do believe she does love the boy – or thinks she does.'

'Thinks, possibly. But as a fact, it's nonsense.' She kissed him. 'Forget the whole thing, Iain darling. As for me, I've nothing but contempt for that woman now. She ought to be *horsewhipped* out of India!'

She looked like an angry monarch, her husband thought, as imperiously angry as Boadicea hurling her chariot against the Roman legions.

Back in Peshawar, almost at her wits' end now, in abject misery of spirit, Mary rang for her servant and abruptly ordered him to prepare a *chota peg*. Not normally a solitary drinker, she needed one badly now. The journey alone had been terrible, a hideous ordeal for a woman alone of slow, swaying railway coaches and jolting bullock carts, of heat and dust and flies and demanding beggars and occasionally the ghastly ring of the leper's bell. She was physically exhausted and mentally drained and when the whisky was brought she clutched at the glass avidly and threw the contents down her throat.

'Another,' she said.

'As the memsahib wishes.' The servant, an elderly man who had for many years been house-boy to a succession of British military families, looked at his young mistress in some concern. He had seen the results of whisky and gin on Western women and a start was a start, whatever the stress that brought it on, and there was undoubtedly stress here. But it was none of his business and memsahibs in his experience did not welcome servants getting above themselves. So he said nothing, but prepared another *chota peg*.

Then he remembered the message.

'Memsahib,' he said, 'while you were away, a letter came. A letter of a *sort*, wrapped around a stone.'

'Letter? Wrapped around a stone? What on earth do you mean? Fetch it.'

He brought it from the bureau, from beneath the guarding figure of Buddha. Drinking the whisky, she read it. The signature – she had not understood one word until she came to that – was 'Ernest Wilshaw'.

Her head spinning and a strange sensation gripping her bowels, she read the message again. And again and again, before she began to get its drift.

The ham-like hand of Regimental Sergeant-Major 'Bosom' Cunningham slammed to the salute, quivered for a moment, then snapped down to lie neatly alongside the kilt of the Royal Strathspey. It was a sweltering evening, the declining sun seeming to have left most of its heat behind to boil the men like so many kettles as it rose from ground and buildings. 'Ma'am! I'm told you wish to see me.'

'Yes, Mr. Cunningham. It's – important.'

'Sit you down, ma'am.' Cunningham came forward with a chair and motioned the Orderly Sergeant out of the office; he sensed that this was private. 'You don't look well, Mrs. Archdale. Will I get you a glass of water, or something?'

'No, thank you, Mr. Cunningham.' She took a grip on herself

and came at once to the point. She produced the message, which she had soon seen was so clearly in James Ogilvie's writing, and handed it to Cunningham. There was comfort in that large Scot, comfort even in the precisely waxed moustache. She was feeling better. She said, 'Please read that. You'll see it refers to yourself. At any rate, I can think of no other Cunningham. Do you happen to recognize the handwriting?'

He said, 'I do. Mr. Ogilvie. I should say, Captain Ogilvie. Well, now, what does all this mean, I wonder? It's signed Ernest Wilshaw.'

'Yes,' she answered. 'Mr. Cunningham, it can only mean that certain rumours are the truth, and not rumours at all!'

'Aye.' Cunningham rubbed an end of his moustache between thumb and forefinger. He sat for a moment in deep thought, troubled thought. From neighbouring lines came the haunting throb of the pipes and drums as an Irish battalion, the Connaught Rangers, beat retreat. Something stirred in the R.S.M.'s heart; he had a strong feeling that very soon now the regiments would be on the march again behind those pipes and drums, beating into the hostile hills. This was a sorry business about Captain Ogilvie and he did not understand it. He said, getting to his feet, 'Ma'am, we'd best go at once to the Colonel.'

'Cryptic's scarcely the word,' Dornoch said. 'What d'you make of it, Sar'nt-Major?'

'Little enough, sir, except that I recognize Captain Ogilvie's hand beyond doubt.'

'So do I.' The Colonel paced the room, hands clasped behind his back, his face grim now. Then he stopped and said, 'Very well, now I'm going to tell you both the facts. They're to go no further – you understand, Mrs. Archdale? I *must* tell you now, in order to prevent more rumourmongering – and positively to ensure your making no comment on the matter publicly. I want your assurance that you'll respect my confidence, Mrs. Archdale.'

'You have that, Lord Dornoch.'

'I need hardly press the point with you, Sar'nt-Major.' Dornoch smiled. 'Now, then. It is the fact that Captain Ogilvie was sent into Waziristan on a secret mission. It appears that he has been taken by the enemy, though in the light of this—' He broke off. 'He was posing as the agent for an armaments firm. That's all I can say. I don't pretend to make head or tail of this message, but possibly it will convey more to the Political Officer. In any case, this is now a matter for Division. Thank you both for bringing it to my attention.'

'Yes, sir. Orders, sir?' This was Cunningham.

'Orders, Sar'nt-Major?' Dornoch's mind was elsewhere.

'For the regiment, sir. Pending word from Division.'

'Ah – yes, I see! Will you be good enough to ask Captain Black to speak to me, and Major Hay? For your private ear in the meantime, Cunningham, I'll be asking them to bring the regiment to immediate readiness to march.'

A swinging salute came from Mr. Cunningham and his body gave the appearance of swelling in anticipation. 'I'll have the two gentlemen here immediately, sir, he said, and turned about.

'But what the devil d'you expect me to *do*?' Fettleworth demanded excitedly, approaching a tantrum brought on by sheer indecision. 'The blasted feller's asking me to send arms to the damned natives – that's how I read it!' He fumed and fuzzed. 'Never heard such a thing – never!'

'There must be more in it than that,' Dornoch insisted. 'We must surely credit Ogilvie with enough commonsense not just to ask for weapons to be sent in—'

'Not even to save his life?'

Dornoch coloured. 'I resent that, sir, as a slur on my regiment – and an unworthy insult to a first-class young officer. I would be obliged if you would withdraw it.'

'Oh, stuff-and-nonsense, I never—'

'Instantly,' Dornoch snapped.

Fettleworth opened his mouth again, angrily, saw Dornoch's set expression, remembered that this was no ordinary Colonel but, as a Representative Scottish Peer in the last parliament, an aristocrat very close to the House of Lords and thus a man of much influence in the highest circles of the land. He changed what he had meant to say, 'Oh, very well, very well, if it pleases you, I withdraw. Now. Tell me what you think I should do.'

'Do as Ogilvie asks, sir.'

'I'm damned if I'll do that! What d'you take me for? Think I'm anxious to be Court Martialled – impeached even, I shouldn't wonder – for sending help to the enemy? Bah!' He hunched his shoulders in fury, and glared.

'Then I can only suggest we wait for Major O'Kelly to turn

up, sir. I think you'll find he'll discover something in the message that escapes us.'

In a frosty silence, they waited.

'I'm awfully sorry, sir,' O'Kelly said. 'I'm afraid I don't see the point. Why Cunningham, anyway? Who's he?'

'My Regimental Sergeant-Major,' Dornoch said, 'and that part's obvious. He was to be used as a step on the way to me, and thence Division.'

'Oh.'

'Well, come on,' Fettleworth said testily.

'*Cunningham will understand,*' O'Kelly murmured, deep in thought. 'Did he, Colonel?'

'No! I doubt if he was meant to.' Breath hissed down Dornoch's nostrils. 'I think we can discard Cunningham from the point at which he brought the message to me – don't you?'

'Well, I wouldn't be too sure. *He will understand.* Then it says he'll act in accordance with instructions. Colonel, what sort of man *is* Cunningham? Please answer carefully.'

'Dependable – a tower of strength. He's a fairly typical Sergeant-Major of the old school.'

'Go on.'

'What else can I say?' Dornoch pondered. 'Devoted to the regiment – has a high regard for Ogilvie, too. He's a grand fellow, as a matter of fact. A real fighting soldier.'

'A man of . . . attack?'

'Undoubtedly.'

'There I think perhaps we have it, sir,' O'Kelly turned his sideways look half-left towards Fettleworth and stroked the monkey, Wolseley, perched on his shoulder. 'It's possible Captain Ogilvie was indicating in such ways as he could that an attack of some kind should be mounted . . . very likely under cover of his suggested arms delivery.' He shrugged. 'That's the best I can do.'

'What about all this business at the end – about Cunningham's *khel* units?' Fettleworth pushed distastefully at the much-handled piece of paper, which in truth smelt of its various native bearers. 'What does all that mean – hey?'

O'Kelly confessed defeat. 'I really couldn't say, sir. It could perhaps be a blind to throw his captors off the scent—'

'Captors, man? Why *captors*?' Fettleworth blew out his cheeks.

'I'm making that assumption,' O'Kelly said with another sideways look, as crafty as his marmoset. 'Aren't you, gentlemen?'

'After reading this, I no longer think it follows,' Fettleworth answered, 'but if in your opinion it does ...' He gave Lord Dornoch an I-told-you-so look.

'Yes, General?'

'Oh, never mind. I was assuming he was still operating as an arms peddler, I suppose. Asking for stock, you see, to preserve his safe cover.'

'Ah, but I think we have to read this message in conjunction with the earlier one, sir. I feel confident he's a prisoner, and has been made to write this – made to disobey my orders, I might point out – and that naturally it was censored before despatch.' O'Kelly screwed up his eyes, then metaphorically pounced. 'Just one moment, sir. The message, if you please, and a blank sheet of paper!'

Fettleworth pushed them across, and waited. O'Kelly brought out a stylographic pen and wrote, pursing his lips. He scanned what he had written, looked pleased, and said, 'I have it, by jove!'

'What have you, O'Kelly?'

'Sir, this last sentence – *Am totally trusted and Cunningham's khel units not deliberately endangering reception of caravan vehicles en route.* We've agreed it doesn't make sense, and it's not intended to.'

'Yes, yes—'

'A moment, sir. If you put the first letters of each word together – you see, it's a very primitive kind of code, the only one he could use – it reads *attack under ocver.*'

'Under *ocver*? What's ocver?'

'Cover, sir. Under cover – presumably of the arms caravan. No doubt Captain Ogilvie had to accept the odd spelling – he probably couldn't think up a sentence that quite fitted.' The Political Officer coughed discreetly. 'My first thoughts were correct, you'll notice, sir.'

Fettleworth snorted in disparagement. 'It's a futile suggestion anyway, in my opinion! Might as well have saved his effort. What good could such an attack possibly do – hey?'

'Little indeed, I imagine, sir. But there may be some deeper purpose yet.'

174

'Deeper?' Fettleworth laughed, irritably. 'I've observed no depth at all so far.'

'Ogilvie may be in possession of more information than he's been able to get into a short message, sir. You'll appreciate how difficult it will have been for him to convey his thoughts within such a compass. He will have had to leave a great deal to us. We must read his mind, sir.'

'Yes, yes. What d'you think, then, O'Kelly, and do get that blasted animal out of the way of your face, no wonder they say you fellers are as artful as a cartload of monkeys.' Fettleworth laughed; no one else did, but O'Kelly looked hurt and shifted Wolseley. 'What's this deeper purpose?'

'Well, sir, he may intend to meet the arms delivery himself and pass more information verbally, or he may be trying to convey the necessity of a *full-scale* attack. He may be suggesting that a large expeditionary force should be sent in, to mount an offensive, rather than that we should wait to be attacked at a time chosen by the tribes themselves.'

'H'm. That's your considered opinion, O'Kelly?'

'It's by way of being a first reaction at the moment, but I doubt if I'll find any reason to change it. I've had a good deal of experience of the Frontier, with respect, sir, and I think I can say I know the tribal background. I would not be at all surprised if Ogilvie has come to the conclusion that we would have a better chance in an attacking action than in a defensive one.'

'Why?'

'You must remember the *sadhu*, the holy man. The influence of such men is enormous – so enormous that it is difficult for any Western people to appreciate it fully. Ogilvie will have seen for himself. If we attack in strength before the *sadhu* has completed his hot-gospelling, then Ogilvie may believe the effect, the psychological—'

'Psychological pish.'

'I apologize for the jargon, but it is something that is being discussed these days. Ogilvie may have come to believe the psychological impact could be really, really immense. I would not say he was wrong.'

He sat back, with a triumphant glance around the other officers in the group. Brains had solved a puzzle and had given their solution neatly, and now it was up to the men with the strong right arms. Fettleworth hummed and ha'ed for a moment, then uttered. 'Of course,' he said sagely, 'I take your point, O'Kelly. But it's a damn big thing, y'know, to send in an expeditionary force when one doesn't know *for certain* that the tribes mean to attack us at all! I'm always against actually stirring up border trouble – there's quite enough of it that needs no stirring. Yes, it's a big decision, but,' he added almost smugly now that he saw he was not called upon to act, 'not one that I am authorized to take upon myself. This now becomes a matter for the General Officer Commanding in Murree. I shall refer it to Sir Iain Ogilvie forthwith.'

Dornoch asked, 'And Captain Ogilvie, in the meantime?'

'He, like I, must wait upon Murree now. That's all, gentlemen.'

The wheels of command ground as fast as possible, which was all too slow. In Murree Sir Iain Ogilvie studied Fettleworth's fresh despatch and grew increasingly anxious. He found himself in agreement with O'Kelly, whose comments Fettleworth had faithfully and honestly set down in full, noting that there was sound commonsense behind them. But, like the Divisional Commander, the Army Commander's hands were tied as well and by no means could he despatch an army corps to rescue his own son. To Brigadier-General Leith, Chief of Staff, Sir Iain said the only words he could say: 'It's beyond my powers, Leith. This has to go to Calcutta.'

In Calcutta the clerkly Civilians, duly consulted by the over-all Commander-in-Chief in India, Sir George White, sat upon it hard. The British Raj defended itself – always. No dispute about that! But they did not attack, they did not stir up trouble, they did not oppress the natives – ever. This was an extremely serious proposal and, whilst due weight was naturally to be given to the opinions and advices of such distinguished soldiers as Lieutenants-General Ogilvie and Fettleworth, the final answer could be given only by the Viceroy, the noble Earl of Elgin himself – indeed, and more officially, by the Governor-General of India in Council. Such would take time; many, many words would have to be spoken and written, many files of precedent consulted, many learned arguments listened to by the administration and the executive. Such a weighty matter might even have to be referred to the Secretary of State in far Whitehall, and he would have to consult the Prime Minister, who would have to consult the House, who would thereafter advise Her Majesty . . .

'Please treat this matter as one of the greatest possible urgency,' Sir George White pleaded. 'If we do not act speedily and decisively, the whole Frontier will be in flames. Not least, a young officer remains in danger of his life while we talk, and talk, and talk . . .' and the Civilians nodded, and agreed, and decided in their hearts what they would recommend to the Council.

'It's damnable!' Dornoch burst out. 'Utterly, filthily damnable!' He paced his office, up and down like a tiger. 'This time it's not Fettleworth's fault, unlikely though that sounds. It's these damn popinjays in Calcutta, prinking themselves in their damn boudoirs and pimping around Viceregal Lodge, licking the Council's collective backside . . .' He paused in the angry flow of words. 'I shouldn't have said any of that, Cunningham. Forget it.'

'Yes, sir. But begging your pardon, sir, it's right. It's what I've been wanting to say in the Sergeants' Mess, sir.'

'But haven't?' Dornoch eyes twinkled.

'Well, sir – yes, I have, in a general way, without revealing what I know, of course, sir.'

'Then good for you, Sar'nt-Major. And it *is* right, I agree.'

'Aye, sir. It's hard, to think of Captain Ogilvie—'

'Hard! It's driving me mad.'

'Aye, sir,' Cunningham said again. 'Of course, it's not for me to say, and maybe no real good would come of it, but—' He broke off, gazing down over his vast chest towards his boots.

'Go on, man, go on, we're old friends, you can speak your mind as I've spoken mine.'

'Thank you, sir. There are times when a small force can achieve results out of all proportion to its size, sir. I think you'll agree with that.'

'I do.' Dornoch looked hard at the R.S.M. 'Cunningham, are you suggesting a cutting-out operation – a rescue?'

'I am that, sir.'

'You're an old rascal, my dear Bosom.'

'Why so, sir?'

Dornoch laughed; it was an edgy laugh. 'Why, because you know as well as I do Division would never approve such a thing, so it's pretty obvious what else you're suggesting, isn't it?'

'Aye, sir, I suppose it is. But Nelson got away with it.'

'In a somewhat different situation, yes. He was already in action. By God, Sar'nt-Major, I'd be with you like a shot if it wasn't for one thing: Captain Ogilvie may be – must be – working to a plan. I can't possibly risk upsetting it!'

'No, sir, that's true, of course. But I'm thinking his plan must be set around what he asks for in his message – that is, an arms caravan.'

'He's not going to get it, I'm afraid.'

'Aye, sir, and if the arms are not to come, then his plan'll go agley in any case, sir. And then, if I'm not mistaken, he'll die.' He shook his head. 'I'd not like to stand by in Peshawar and hear of that happening.'

'No more would I.'

'Then you'll get the drift of what I'm saying, sir.'

'Damn it, man, we don't even know where he is, other than all Waziristan!'

'No, sir, but we know where the arms consignment was to be delivered. I don't doubt the Pathans who take it over will be knowing where to take it, and there's at least a chance Captain Ogilvie will not be far away from where that is, if he's still being, as he says he is, trusted as an arms representative.'

'It's not possible,' Dornoch murmured, as if to himself. 'Not possible at all.'

'Well, maybe not, sir. With your permission, sir, I'll be going. I have much to see to.'

Dornoch gave him a searching look. 'You'll do nothing without my permission, Sar'nt-Major. No Nelson touches – if you don't mind! Be sensible, man! You're right on the heels of your pension.'

'Fourpence a day, or little more,' Cunningham said in disgust. 'Do you think I'd weigh that, or all my years of service, against Captain Ogilvie's life?' He hesitated, then said, 'Och, don't fret yourself, sir, I'll no' be quite so foolish as to commit any act of mutiny and risk the men's lives by leading a platoon into Waziristan. But the regiment, now, that would be different.'

'Away with you!' Dornoch said peremptorily.

'Aye, sir. But with respect, sir, will you think the matter over?'

'No,' Dornoch said. 'Of course I'll not!'

That night, which was a guest night in the Mess, he was very silent, very preoccupied, unusually taciturn with the junior officers and the senior ones as well. The senior officers, who knew the facts, understood; Lord Dornoch's regiment was his life, and all his officers and men were his family. That was a fine thing in a Colonel, but it was perhaps a pity to carry it too far. Life went on, however many sacrifices were made. There was really no need to spoil the party, as Mrs. Colonel Bates acidly remarked.

CHAPTER TWELVE

HEALEY said, 'Nashkar's worried. There's still been no word from the border – no sign of any arms caravan. Something's gone wrong, old boy.' They were walking together in the palace courtyard, and Ogilvie knew he was being carefully watched, not only by the quarter-guard at the great gateway, but also from the windows of the palace itself. Trust had not yet entirely evaporated, but had tended to diminish over the last few days. Word had filtered back that his message had been delivered to Mary Archdale's bungalow but from that time on there had been total silence.

'Do you know what he means to do?' Ogilvie asked.

'Nashkar? No, I don't. I only wish I did – though in all conscience, Ogilvie, there's dashed little we could do about it if I did! All I can say is, I've done my damnedest, my very best, to get it across to him that he must wait for more arms before he moves. I'm pretty sure I've made him think hard, but it can't last forever. If our people don't play up, well ...' He shrugged.

Ovilgie said, 'I can see their point of view. Fettleworth's point of view. After all, I'm expendable – like poor Jones. So are you, though I don't suppose they even know you're here. We can both be written off.'

'We didn't exactly initiate that message with the sole intent of saving our own skins, Ogilvie.'

'No, but that was part of our hope, wasn't it? We must face the fact that Fettleworth may see it as just that – a way of getting ourselves out while there's still time.'

'Man's an ass if he does,' Healey said briefly.

Ogilvie grinned. 'A considerable body of opinion in Peshawar thinks that's just what he is. Anyway – have you any ideas as to what we do if that message is disregarded?'

'At the moment, none. We just have to wait and see, old boy. Isn't that a large part of a soldier's lot? Hang around, hold your fire till you see the whites of the bastards' eyes, stand and be

shot at, or stoned by the mob while you grin and bear it ...
turning the other blasted cheek in case you provoke 'em?'

'You're full of platitudes this morning, Healey.'

'I apologize, most humbly.' They stopped talking as they
came closer to the quarter-guard of liveried but still wild-looking Pathans, grim bearded men with dirty rifles. 'Sooner them
than me,' Healey said when they had turned and were pacing
back across the courtyard. 'Those rifles. As likely as not, they'll
blow up in their faces when they fire 'em!'

They parted soon after that and Ogilvie climbed alone to the
battlements and leaned through one of the embrasures to stare
out across the desolate, light-brown hills rolling to eternity. He
thought of the British garrison far away to the north-east
beyond the Horizon's undulating rim. It was not, in fact, such a
tremendous distance to Peshawar in terms of miles; but it was a
cruel country to cross and the passes were very, very few and
difficult of access. Indeed, to a man who did not know the
territory well, as Jones had done, there was virtually no pass at
all below Thal. However, there would undoubtedly be men in
Peshawar or Nowshera to act as guides ... if only the high
command would move! By now Ogilvie was having the
strongest doubts of anything happening other than his own very
bloody death, and then the massacre. He knew his father well
enough, his father who was the vital intermediary between
Fettleworth and Calcutta. He appreciated the terrible quandary
in which his father would now be placed. How could a General
ever order out men, to risk their lives to save his son? If, in that
message, there had appeared the smallest suggestion that the
proposal was intended as a personal appeal, then it would have
to go unanswered. There was the additional complication of
Mary Archdale's involvement. When Healey had made that
carefully interpolated suggestion, it had seemed a brilliant
scheme; now, Ogilvie was not so sure. Mary would at once
introduce the personal note, and the mere fact of her forwarding
the message was bound to influence his father. He felt convinced of that now. The whole thing would have been badly
misunderstood. Then there was Mary herself. She would be
desperately worried about him since the arrival of the message;
it had not been fair on her either. There could be nothing worse
than to have to sit at home and wait for news; and she would
know well enough what the Pathans were capable of inflicting
on prisoners. Ogilvie had been up there on the battlements for

some half an hour, deep in his thoughts of Peshawar, when he heard the thin wail of a native pipe stealing up to him from the inner courtyard of the palace; and, just for a wildly insane moment, he could fancy it was the fifes of some gallant English battalion approaching through the waste of hills. He felt the more alone when the moment had passed.

That evening he spoke again to Healey. 'Nashkar's left the palace,' Healey said. 'Riding alone.'

'Where to?'

Healey said on a note of pessimism, 'He's gone to have a word with the *sadhu*. This I do not like.'

It was full night when Nashkar Ali Khan reached the foot of the track leading from the pass to the heights. Beneath a bright moon, he scrambled up the rocky path, seeing the silvery outline of the age-old man above him. Some men said that he was one hundred and twenty years old, but Nashkar privately doubted this. Of a certainty, however, he was close upon a hundred, and it was a miracle in itself that such an old man could continue to live on his high perch, almost unclad in the cold night air and with no food to sustain him. It could be only the direct intervention of Mahomet that was keeping him alive, Nashkar knew this beyond any doubt. The hand of the Prophet fed him with heavenly dew, warmed the scraggy body with celestial fire. It was all written, yet it was none the less miraculous. The Pathan leader hastened up the track as fast as he could, his vision of the *sadhu* leading him on like a lodestar. His heart seemed to burst within his body, not from the undoubtedly stiff climb, for he was a fit and vigorous man, and hard as steel, but from a sense of boundless pride that he, Nashkar Ali Khan, was the selected instrument of Mahomet, via the *sadhu*, to implement Mahomet's own purpose of extending Islam to the total exclusion from the Frontier lands of the infidel British.

Arriving upon the rock ledge, Nashkar prostrated himself before the death-still figure that seemed cleft in permanency to the mountain. His beard swept the rock close to the *sadhu*'s bony feet, upon which the spread toes sat like claws, yellow and horny.

'Holy One,' he intoned. 'Master, mouthpiece of the Prophet. May you live a thousand years.' He paused, awaiting a response. When none came he lifted his head just a fraction, opening an eye to peer anxiously at the mask-like features above his bent body. Surely the old man was not dead, surely Mahomet – in what, of course, would still remain his undoubted wisdom – had not withdrawn his spirit to that other world and left his earthbound servant without communication? Surely this could not be! He spoke again, more loudly: 'Holy One, Master, mouthpiece of the Prophet. May you live a thousand years.' The last sentence was uttered very loudly indeed, and Nashkar was filled with an intense relief when his opened eye saw a slight wiggle of the *sadhu*'s toes. The old man was not dead, he had fallen asleep – that was all.

'May you also live a thousand years, my son,' the creaky old voice said. It came from afar off, it seemed to Nashkar, even from the sky itself, a thin, frail sound like the workings of an untended water-wheel.

'Is there anything you wish for, Holy One? Some comfort... perhaps some food?'

'No, my son, my fast will not end until the sign is seen, and comfort is not necessary.'

'And the sign, O Master, O Holy One?'

It took some while for the answer to come. Nashkar waited in trembling impatience. 'It will come, my son. Never fear.'

'When?'

'In a short time now. A few more risings of the sun, a few more settings. Then the shadow will come, casting itself before the event... and I shall know, and I shall inform you.'

The Pathan nodded submissively; on the way up, coming past the place where the Englishman had been imprisoned, he had passed the watchful runner, the man who would start the vital heavenly message on its way to Maizar and the east. 'I shall wait, Master, with all the patience at my command.'

'Do this, my son. Why did you come to see me?'

Nashkar felt humbled, despised his own shortcomings, his unworthy desire to see for himself that all was well on that mountain peak, his nagging and wicked feeling that it was perhaps possible for even Mahomet to nod on occasion. He said, 'O Master, I came to see if you had any word for me in the meantime, any command.'

'I have none.' Now the voice was like the gentle sighing of a breeze; undoubtedly the old man was very weak. 'You will know, as soon as I shall know. Go now, my son.' The toes wiggled again; this time they seemed to hold a message of impatience, and Nashkar took the hint. He got to his feet, only faintly aware of the terrible smell that emanated from the *sadhu*, for he was accustomed to such smells arising from the open drainways of Maizar, and bowed his way from the presence. As he made his way down once again to the pass, he was conscious of another unworthy but none the less worrying thought: how terrible it would be if the *sadhu* should be asleep when the sign came!

The officers came in ones and twos, casually, to Lord Dornoch's quarter in cantonments, drifting from the regimental lines as if bound for nowhere very important. Word had been discreetly passed to this effect; and only Andrew Black saw fit to proceed at a marching pace, stiff and straight as ever, his dark face scowling with an intensity of disapproval. The thing, in his opinion, was monstrous, quite monstrously outlandish and unorthodox – and highly dangerous. He had never heard the like and he had no intention of taking part. He had not yet gone as far as saying this to the Colonel, having merely expressed his strong objection when Dornoch, half an hour before, had spoken privately of his mad scheme to Major Hay and himself. But he would do so, for Dornoch had already said it would be a case of volunteers and no pressed men, even though, once they had volunteered, they would come under his orders and the responsibility would be his alone.

Black entered Dornoch's quarter, placed his helmet smartly beneath his left arm and, with his kilt swinging, stalked to the Colonel's study. Curtly, Dornoch told him to sit down and wait till everyone was present. Dornoch's eyes were strangely alight, strangely feverish. He had passed a restless night, a night of real torment after the Mess guest night festivities were over, and had suffered agonizing indecision during the morning also. But then decision had come, final decision, the more irrevocable because it had not come easily. He had weighed everything and there was no doubt left. He was risking his men – that was most important and the hardest part of the decision – his appointment, even his career. This could end in Court Martial; would most certainly do so if he failed. But he would not fail, he felt that very strongly. And in any case he could not, *would* not, leave Ogilvie in the hands of the damned heathens! If he did, if he lifted no finger to help, he could never live with the memory afterwards ...

'All officers are present, Colonel.' This was fatherly old John Hay, Major and second-in-command, an unimaginative but intensely loyal subordinate whom Dornoch would like to see take over the battalion from him in due course, but who would possibly never be seen quite as command potential by the brass hats.

'Thank you, John,' Dornoch said. He sat back in his chair and smiled round at the officers over-filling his study. There was one Warrant Officer present – Bosom Cunningham, taking up the room of two. Dornoch took in Black's disagreeable face and thereafter tried to forget it. There, he knew, was one who would not come and who would not be missed either. He said, 'Now, gentlemen, I'll not beat about the bush. I have some hitherto confidential and perhaps surprising information for you.' As briefly as possible he told them all the facts as known and when these had sunk in he said, 'We're going in to get Ogilvie.'

There was, as he had expected, a stir, and an exultant one. The subalterns especially were jubilant, and Dornoch lifted a hand at once to stop any noisy demonstration. 'I see I have your support,' he said. 'Thank you for that. But I want you to bear in mind that this will be no flag-waving expedition and there will be no jingoism. It'll be just – a tough slog, that's all. The next thing I have to say is this: I want volunteers, from both officers and men. And N.C.O.s of course,' he added, turning to Cunningham. 'I'll leave that to you, Sar'nt-Major.'

'Sir!'

'Company commanders will sound out their companies the moment they leave here. I want the whole battalion to move out if possible, but there's to be no pressure on any man. I must make it clear we're about to commit what is virtually an act of mutiny – or I am. At the least, it's acting without orders.' He paused. 'Well, gentlemen? Who wishes to leave?'

Black moved forward. 'I do, Colonel. I shall have no part in this. I wish that to be clearly understood, and duly noted in orders.'

'Very well, Andrew, it's entirely up to you. Before you go, I think it only fair to the others that you should have an opportunity of publicly stating your reasons for not volunteering.'

'It's not that I have any personal fear—'

'No suggestion that you have, Andrew. There's not a stain on your military character!' Dornoch smiled, a little whimsically.

'Thank you, Colonel. My objections are these: I have a distaste for flouting the wishes of higher authority, even if those wishes have not been expressly communicated by way of orders. We all *know*, I think, that General Fettleworth does not wish to exacerbate the Frontier situation. Secondly, I can see no use in what you propose. You are unlikely to reach Ogilvie – you are more likely to cause him to be put to death the moment you cross the border.' He gave a loud sniff. 'In short, Colonel, I believe you are about to commit an act of the gravest military folly! You may end by involving, and unnecessarily involving, the whole of the British Army in India, and the native Indian Army also.'

Dornoch inclined his head. 'Is there anything further, Andrew?'

'No, Colonel, there is not.'

'Then perhaps you wouldn't mind withdrawing now. There's just one thing,' he added, as the Adjutant shouldered his way to the door. Black stopped. 'I don't want this discussed outside this room. That's to say, Andrew, if you'll forgive me, no reports to the Staff. Do you understand?'

'I understand very well, Colonel,' Black flared, 'and I consider it my duty to go straight to Division—'

'That's enough!' Dornoch got to his feet, his face hard. 'A word in your ear – outside.'

In the hall Dornoch said, 'Andrew, I'm about to do something I seldom if ever do, and that is, to pull rank and connections on you. I want your word that you'll say nothing to Division or anyone else. If you refuse to give it, I'll put you in open arrest under the charge of Captain MacKinlay. And if you give your word and subsequently break it, by God, Andrew, I'll see to it that not only does the 114th get a new adjutant the moment I return, but I'll also see to it that you're drummed out of India so fast your feet won't touch ground on the way to the troopship. I'll still have the power. Understood?'

Black ground his teeth in fury. 'Understood!' he answered viciously. 'You have my word on one condition, Lord Dornoch. That is, that you'll put it in writing that you used threats to ensure my silence, that I have been threatened into not doing my duty!'

Dornoch nodded. 'Yes, I'll do that, Andrew, gladly, for it's certainly the truth! I have your word?'

'You have my word.' Saying no more, Black swished about

and stalked off. Dornoch, his eyes shining even more brightly with that strange inner light, went back into his study. There was no doubt about it, the atmosphere was thoroughly against the adjutant; but Dornoch felt that he should deal with the points raised by Black as publicly as Black himself had been permitted to raise them.

'The exacerbation of the Frontier situation,' he said. 'Since the Frontier has been in a state of exacerbation from the days when first I knew it, I do not feel we can allow such a consideration to stand in the way of what I mean to do. It seems fairly clear that the tribes mean to attack in any case, whatever the views of Division may have metamorphosed themselves into, and I see no harm in bringing matters to a head earlier – if that is the effect our expedition has. As to the possibility that an intervention may mean Ogilvie's death – yes, I agree that could be, but I believe he is in the gravest danger as it is and that when his request for arms is not met – as it will not be – then he will surely die in any case. We can make things no worse in that respect. If nobody has any further observation to make, I'll go straight into the orders for the march and the entry into Waziristan.' He paused. 'No comments?'

None came.

'Very well, gentlemen. The battalion moves out at full dark, that is to say, at midnight. We shall naturally be observed from the adjacent regimental lines, but I have informed Division that I intend conducting a night exercise. No uniforms will be worn, and the men's skins will be darkened with boot polish. They will improvise any kind of native dress, such as would be worn by bearers in a baggage train, no matter how rough and ready provided it gives an *initial* impression of natives rather than of British soldiers. If the boot polish wears off, that's too bad. Remember, a lot of the Pathans are light in their colouring, and many are almost Western-looking. That fact should help us all the way along. Ammunition wagons, six in number, will be taken, with all regimental markings removed, and all rifles and machine-guns are to be stowed in these – no arms of any description will be actually carried. Iron rations and water will be taken. We shall head for the Waziristan border – some way beyond the village of Sikandar west of Thal, where Nashkar's men will be waiting in expectation of an arms caravan. That caravan, gentlemen, will be us – the Royal Strathspeys. We shall overpower the native force, whose strength is unlikely, I

think, to be very great. We then make all possible speed for
wherever it was the arms were to be taken, which we shall have
to find out, and we try to find Captain Ogilvie. A fast spear-
head, an extended rescue force, will if necessary be formed by
men acting as Mounted Infantry and riding the horses unharnessed from the ammunition wagons. From the moment we
enter Waziristan our advance will be highly dangerous, and we
must expect to be under continual if distant observation from
the peaks. My hope is that our dress will fool the enemy at such
a distance and that we shall not too readily be known for what
we are – and thus, with luck, not reported ahead. Questions,
gentlemen?'

Throughout the remainder of the day the preparations went
ahead; with a certain amount of jocular glee the men, of whom
all but a handful had volunteered to take part, made ready the
disguises that were to take the place of spit-and-polish. The
wagons and horses were brought out and the wagons loaded
with the battalion's small-arms and with rations and water.
Black shut himself in his room, and sulked with a bottle of
whisky. In the early evening Pipe-Major Ross sought an interview with the Colonel.

'What is it, Pipe-Major? Or do I know already?'

'I've a feeling you may, sir. Will we take the pipes and drums,
sir?'

Dornoch laughed. 'Do men who sell arms to the tribes march
in style behind the band?'

'No, sir. I was not meaning that, sir. I meant to hide them
away in the wagons, so they would be there should we have the
opportunity. And the pipers' and drummers' uniforms, sir.'

'Well, Pipe-Major. Far be it from me to refuse a request like
that! I can see no harm in it.'

'Thank you, sir.'

'One thing, Ross. Don't let their enthusiasm run away with
them. There's not to be one squeak of wind unless and until I
myself give permission. Secrecy's the keynote for as long as it
holds out.'

'Aye, sir, that's well understood. Till the time comes, sir, the
pipes and drums'll be the dirtiest-looking blackguards of the
lot!'

Ready on time, the battalion moved out of cantonments at
midnight, passing the lines of the regiments bedded down for

Will you have enough for the 'extras'?

The little things that make life worth living
certainly won't cost less when you retire.
But it's easy to plan ahead for your comfort.

£10,000 when you retire

can be provided simply and cheaply by
taking out a Prudential Endowment
Assurance now. For further details,
complete and return this card.

The value of the Prudential

The value of Prudential policies has
been more than proved over the years, as
is shown by these examples of payments
on claims under with-profits endowment
assurances taken out in the U.K. and
maturing at age 65 on 1st April 1973.

Age at entry	30	40	50
Sum Assured	£5,000	£5,000	£5,000
Bonuses*	£7,390	£6,015	£3,780
	£12,390	£11,015	£8,780

*Bonuses on future maturities cannot be guaranteed to
be of this amount.

CN/5/73/1220/FP(3630)

BUSINESS REPLY SERVICE
LICENCE No. K.E. 1511

The Chief General Manager
THE PRUDENTIAL ASSURANCE CO. LTD.

142 HOLBORN BARS
LONDON EC1N 2NH

the night, going on their supposed night manoeuvre. Once clear
of the military area they broke ranks and shambled along fast in
their curious assortment of evil-smelling garments, smeared
with boot-polish, their skins gleaming beneath the moon. Lord
Dornoch, at their head with John Hay, was as ruffianly in appearance as anyone, with his blackened face and dirty turban
and a robe like a dressing-gown. After a forced march, and
shortly after dawn, having made a detour so as to appear to
have come down from the north, they dropped down on the
border west of Thal and continued with their wagons to skirt
Sikandar and make the rendezvous at the mouth of the indicated pass into Waziristan. Two hours later, they saw the wild
men on the heights ahead in the distance, the advanced scouts
of the enemy, of the force that had come to make its collection
and had had a long wait in the process.

As the disguised Scots approached, the scouts were seen to
descend into the pass itself, waving their rifles; and a few
minutes later, as the caravan of wagons came into the mouth of
the pass, upwards of a hundred tribesmen were seen scrambling
down the hillsides on either hand.

The caravan went on calmly, moving into the middle of the
reception committee. Watching the faces of the Waziris, waiting for the dawning of suspicion, Dornoch gave his order with
seconds to spare; and when he gave it twenty black-faced Scots
with rifles and fixed bayonets leaped down from each of the six
covered ammunition wagons. Only four shots were fired; four
of the Waziris died. The rest were surrounded; it was over
almost before it had begun.

Dornoch had the leader brought before him, and questioned
him in Pushtu, asking him where the arms were to have been
taken and where he would find the English seller of arms, Wilshaw Sahib. He had expected no answer, and he got none. He
sent for Cunningham. The R.S.M.'s incongruous salute was
purely automatic. 'Sir!' He looked a thorough-going desper-
ado.

Dornoch stared at the native leader. 'This man is truly ferocious,' he said, indicating Cunningham. 'If you refuse to speak,
it will go very hard with you. Take over, if you please, Sar'nt-
Major.'

'Sir!' Cunningham moved forward and laid hold of the
man's shoulder, throwing him forcefully against the side of a
wagon. The man staggered, steadied himself against a wheel,

and remained with his arms stretched out sideways against the wooden side, his eyes flickering to right and left. From somewhere in the folds of his filthy native dress, Cunningham produced a shining claymore. 'Answer the questions, you bloody heathen!' he roared, 'or I'll have your head off your shoulders and sowther it to your backside!'

Not understanding, the man shook his head.

'By God, you'll talk!' Cunningham used Pushtu now. His claymore gave a close sweep that made the man's head rock instinctively away. The steel nicked the throat, and blood ran. Dornoch felt a little sick, but it had to be done. The man was clearly terrified, and Pathan though he was, gave every appearance of weakening. Cunningham must have his head until he did so. Back in Peshawar Brigadier-General Preston had made the point to Fettleworth that a Waziri never talked. To an extent this was valid, but there was an element of exaggeration. A Waziri would not talk under the more-or-less gentlemanly methods of persuasion used by the Political Officers at Division – this was true. But here in Waziri territory no kid-glove tactics would be used; and there was the difference. Many times before, Lord Dornoch had seen Pathans break under ruthless cruelty, and Cunningham, when needs be, could be savage. The R.S.M. reached forward and grabbed the man's clothing, bunching it in his fist and then bringing the claymore down across the material. A few more cuts, and the man was in rags, which Cunningham ripped from his body until he stood naked, his eyes blazing and flickering, a man at bay. 'Now talk,' Cunningham said. 'Or else I'll unman you first, and leave the parts to be eaten by the vultures, while you will be taken back to Peshawar to be paraded naked before many women . . . and then your entrails will be cut out, and fed with your head to the barrack pigs. This I swear.'

Sweat poured down the man's face. Cunningham pushed his claymore forward, touching the body between the thighs. The man gave a scream and moved convulsively; it may have been his movement or it may not, but blood poured down his right thigh. Cunningham laughed. 'Talk now,' he said. 'Or the next cut will do the trick.'

'I will guide you!' the man cried out. 'Stop!'

The claymore remained in position. 'And Wilshaw Sahib?'

'There is talk of an Englishman at the palace of Nashkar Ali Khan.'

190

'Where's that?'

The man nodded towards the north. 'Outside the town of Maizar, a long distance.'

Dornoch said with relief, 'All right, Sar'nt-Major. Thank you. Nobly done!'

'*Ig*nobly, sir, begging your pardon.' Cunningham wiped sweat from his own face. 'But I know what you mean, sir. I suppose it's all in the day's march, as you might say, sir.' He added, 'Maizar's a long way, as he says.'

'It is, but we'll get there, Sar'nt-Major, and, I trust, in time.' He spoke then to the Waziri. 'How far is our destination – the place where the arms were to go?'

'In the hills this side of Maizar,' the man muttered. 'All this way the arms must be carried, for no wagon will make the journey.'

'I thought as much, Sarn't-Major, you'll have to loose the horses and we'll leave the wagons. With the regimental markings gone, no one who finds them will be any the wiser. Distribute the food and water among the men if you please, and the horses among the officers and senior NC.O.s.'

'Sir!' His grotesque garments billowing, Cunningham swung round and marched along the line of men and wagons, giving his orders. The distribution was quickly complete and the long column set off for the southward, with the Waziri force under heavy guard, their weapons removed, marching between two ranks of the Royal Strathspeys whose bayonets were itching for a probe into native flesh. As Dornoch remarked to John Hay, any watchers along the route, at a distance as they would be, would take them for a purely native force bringing in the caravan with the addition of more tribal levies to join Nashkar's army.

'True, Colonel, with one provision – that this morning's proceedings were not under observation from the hills.'

'And that's true too, John, though I don't believe we were seen. I think the whole bunch came down into the pass. At any rate – let's hope so!'

They rode on, with nine hundred-odd men of the battalion, and the captured natives, trudging on behind. They pressed ahead with all possible speed, the loud voices of the Colour-Sergeants chivvying their companies along, sparing no one.

Some hours after its crossing of the border, the supposed

arms convoy was indeed sighted from one of the crests, where a hawk-faced Pathan warrior lay concealed. He saw the large body of nondescripts snaking along the pass below him and adjudged it to be carrying the expected weapons, the caravan that was to be strictly left alone by the *khels* so that its burden might enlarge the arsenal of Nashkar Ali Khan himself. That order of non-molestation would be rigorously obeyed, all along the line to Maizar. A little after this the abandoned wagons were found in the entry to the pass. Two and two were put together when these intelligences converged, and the answer arrived at could have been three or five but was certainly not four. And an erroneous but happy report was sped on its way by means of the mysterious bush telegraph to Nashkar Ali Khan in Maizar.

'The tidings are good,' Nashkar Ali Khan announced when, two days later, this report reached him. 'Bring Wilshaw Sahib to me.'

'Wilshaw Sahib,' he said, when Ogilvie was brought in, 'I have word that your arms are now well inside Waziristan, exactly as promised. I am indeed grateful.' He placed his arm through Ogilvie's. 'Now my trust is restored and is complete. I wish to show my pleasure, Wilshaw Sahib.'

'You are very kind, Highness.' Ogilvie's heart beat fast. He had some difficulty in hiding his sheer exultation in the certain knowledge that a British force must now be on the march for Maizar, or for the arsenal close to Maizar anyway; the only imponderables now were its strength, its composition, and its present whereabouts. He asked, 'How far off is the caravan, Highness?'

Nashkar pulled at his beard. 'I cannot say this with much accuracy, since my reports must of necessity be behind the event. But I shall expect its arrival within, let us say, two days from now.'

'We have not yet agreed a price,' Ogilvie reminded him.

'You shall name your own, Wilshaw Sahib,' the Pathan said magnanimously, 'but first, let us see what has been sent, and of what quality.'

'I dare say that might be as well,' Ogilvie murmured; he was glad Healey was not present, for he was certain he would never have kept a straight face as he said that.

'Then we shall discuss the payment on arrival. For now, Wilshaw Sahib, what is your pleasure, what can I do for you, to

192

show the gratitude that fills my heart to overflowing?'

'You have given me everything, Highness. Food, drink, women, all the pleasures of your palace. For that, I am grateful in my turn.' He hesitated. 'Yet there is one more thing, Highness, and this is freedom.'

'Freedom?'

'I am thinking of the woman in Peshawar, the one to whom I sent the message, and who has also been of assistance to you, Highness. When your forces move against the British, when they enter Peshawar, things may go badly for her.'

'I shall give my personal order for her complete protection, Wilshaw Sahib. That will be obeyed on pain of instant death.'

'I was thinking more, perhaps, of the British troops. If anything should come out ... British India is a web of gossip, Highness. I would fear greatly for her safety.'

'But she will have been most circumspect, and will continue to be so?'

'Oh, yes, assuredly, most circumspect, Highness! I still fear, however.'

Nashkar looked at him shrewdly. 'Yes, this is natural, but until we march, I can offer no help, Wilshaw Sahib.'

'Quite. No direct help.' Ogilvie hesitated, frowning anxiously. 'If I were to be permitted to cross into Tirah, Highness, I believe I could get her away from Peshawar before the fighting starts, which would mean complete safety for her.'

Nashkar smiled but shook his head. 'Wilshaw Sahib, I am grateful, but I am not a fool. Certainly I trust you as I have said. But if you were to be captured by the British, if you were to be seen coming out of Waziristan ... no, the risk is much, much too great! You would be tortured, and made to talk. I am sorry, but this cannot be.' He let go of Ogilvie's arm, and paced for a while alone, up and down his apartment, between tall stately pillars of marble, across a marble floor, dappled by shafts of sunlight coming through the high windows. Then he came back to Ogilvie and once again took his arm in a friendly fashion. 'A little of this freedom, however, you shall have — freedom to go into Maizar, freedom to move around our beautiful hills and valleys, the finest in all India. You shall go in freedom with the Earless One, Wilshaw Sahib, and an escort of my horsemen, whenever you wish.'

'Thank you, Highness,' Ogilvie said. Again he had difficulty in suppressing his exultation. Expectant, really, of no bread at all, this was certainly a very good half loaf indeed.

'. . . no one, I gather, but the 114th adjutant, one Black, more than a little drunk, and a handful of private soldiers and clerks and storemen with a Lance-Corporal named MacDunt,' Brigadier-General Lakenham finished. 'Otherwise, the lines were empty. Empty!' He threw up his arms. 'They had no *orders*, sir!'

'Damn it, I *know* they had no orders!' Fettleworth shouted, and slammed his fist down on his desk. 'Didn't anybody see them go, man? Or did they evaporate?'

'The Connaught Rangers' sentries saw them go, but assumed it was merely Lord Dornoch's night exercises that were—'

'Night exercises be damned! They'd have been back long ago, unless they've all been butchered by a raiding party, and that's not very likely without Division hearing something about it!' He fumed and raged. 'You know what Dornoch's done, don't you? He's taken his confounded Scots into Waziristan – a pound to a penny he has! Damn clansmen! No better than natives themselves, half the time. I could see the way he was thinking, at that last conference. Lakenham, I'll have his crown and star. I'll have his appointment. I'll have his damn commission. I'll have him brought before the Commander-in-Chief – and – and – and I'll have him arraigned at the bar of the House of Lords! Damn it, Lakenham, you can start drawing up Court Martial papers now – at once!'

'We don't know that he's—'

'Oh, fiddlesticks. Don't we! I know Lord Dornoch,' Fettleworth said grimly. 'I wish to very *God* you'd told me about his request for a night exercise! I'd never have allowed it, I can tell you. You may be my Chief of Staff, Lakenham, but I do like to deal with important matters *myself*.'

'I didn't regard the matter as all that important, sir.'

'Well, you know better now, don't you.' He bared his teeth like a gun-shy artillery horse. 'Now we have to decide what's to be done about it, and frankly, I don't know! Oh, I could send out a force to intercept – but it's too late, of course. He'll have crossed the border by this time, and we don't even know where! Still, it might be worth trying – just in case he's been delayed.' Fettleworth's jaw came forward. 'My compliments to the Colonel of the Guides, Lakenham. He's to send four squadrons immediately, to cover the Waziri border from Bannu to the Durand Line.'

'Very good, sir. And the orders?'

'Well, what the devil d'you imagine the orders are,' Fettleworth barked. 'To instruct Lord Dornoch to return immediately to cantonments with his regiment, what else? My *personal* order, Lakenham, to be disobeyed at his further peril.'

'I think, sir—'

'See to it *now*, if you please.' Bloody Francis rapped on his desk, sharply. Brigadier-General Lakenham left the room, returning a few minutes later to assure his General that the order had been despatched. Fettleworth nodded. He said frenziedly, 'It'll do no good, it'll be like bolting the stable door after the horse has gone, I realize that only too damn well!'

Lakenham, still intrigued by Fettleworth's reference to Dornoch's 'further peril', for Bloody Francis seemed already to have run through a fairly comprehensive list of retributive measures, agreed; and added that in any event there was nothing else to be done, at least for the moment.

'Really – really! Nothing in the way of *action*, perhaps, but there are other things.' Fettleworth drummed his fingers hard, beating out a tattoo on the desk top. 'Sir Iain Ogilvie must be informed at once—'

'But of what, sir?'

'Of the facts!'

'But what are the facts, sir? We have nothing to go on, absolutely nothing except what you *think* Dornoch is doing. In my submission, that is not evidence enough to form the basis of any useful report to Murree.'

'We can report that he's made off with a whole damn battalion, can't we? What more do you want?'

'I think Sir Iain will want a reason, sir. Or at least the result of your attempt at interception. Would it not be advisable to wait for some report from the Guides first? This could all turn out to be a storm in a tea-cup.'

'Oh, balls, Lakenham – balls!'

Lakenham said stiffly, 'I realize you don't agree, sir. But would you not agree at least to wait for Captain Black?'

'Ah – now, that's an idea! Why didn't you think of it sooner – hey, Lakenham? Get hold of Black at once and I'll talk to him.'

'I doubt it, sir. If you remember, I said I'd been told he was more than a little drunk. In point of fact, the Staff Captain who made the report to me said he was incoherent. It seems we must give him a little time.'

'Time? Give him coffee, hot and black and strong, and as many buckets of water as necessary. Get him here – d'you hear, Lakenham? *Get him here!*'

Black's face was flushed a deep red with the drink he had taken, and looked swollen. He appeared almost in a state of apoplexy as he walked into the Divisional Commander's presence, but somehow or other he managed to maintain an upright stance and his salute was impeccable.

'Sit down!' Fettleworth snapped, eyeing him with displeasure.

Black sat.

Fettleworth barked suddenly, 'Well, where are your damn manners? Take your damn helmet off this instant.'

Black made a curious sound in his throat and obeyed. 'I'm s . . . sorry, sir.'

'All right, all right. Now. I want a fully detailed account of what's been going on in the 114th's lines. To start with, where is Lord Dornoch, where is the battalion, and why the devil aren't you with them – hey?'

'I . . . didn't wan' to go.'

Fettleworth raised his eyebrows. Cowardice was cowardice, notwithstanding a Colonel's contempt of authority. 'You are afraid to face the enemy, Captain Black?'

'What?' Black's face suffused even more. 'Who said . . . who said . . . anything about the enemy?'

'I did!'

'Oh, did you. I don't know anything about the enemy. And I'll tell you this, General or no General – sir – I'm never afraid to face shot and shell or cold steel. By God I'm not.'

'Oh, very well.' Breath hissed down Fettleworth's nostrils angrily, but he knew better than to delay the possible helpfulness that might emerge from Black by indulging in drunken arguments at this stage. 'Then I apologize, and salute your bravery. Come now, Captain Black. The facts, if you please, and quickly!'

Black shook his head. 'I don't know any facts . . . sir.'

'Damn it, you must!'

'I know I must *not*, sir.'

'D'you realize who you're talking to, sir?'

'Yes, sir.'

'Who, sir?'

There was a snigger. 'Bloody Francis, sir.'

Once again, in the interest of information, Fettleworth held on to his temper; but there was a look in his eye that said Black had gone too far, and irrevocably, this time. 'For the moment I shall overlook your confounded rudery and lack of breeding—'

'I'm well enough aware I'm not a gentleman—'

'Yes, yes—'

'Oh, so you agree, do you, General Fettleworth?' Black half lifted himself from his chair, but the effort was a trifle too much and he lurched back. 'May I ask what's wrong with an officer's family being in trade, when—'

'I'm not interested in . . . Oh, God give me strength!' Fettleworth lifted his arms in despair and fury. 'Kindly do me the courtesy of paying attention to what I have repeatedly asked you, Captain Black. What are the facts of Lord Dornoch's apparent abandonment of his lines?'

'I can't say anything about that,' Black said with a drunk's obstinacy, 'for I've given my word, and even if I'm not a gentleman, I don't break—'

'I'm giving you an order, man! Never mind your word – do as you're told! What's all this about giving your word, anyway?'

'I have been th . . . threatened by my Colonel, sir. Yes – threatened. I must not reveal anything to you. I'll give evidence at his Court Martial – yes, certainly – but at this moment I am saying nothing. I trust this will be properly no . . . noted in your records, sir. Nothing . . . nothing will I say. No.'

'You will tell me—'

'Nothing.' Black waved his arms. 'I tell you nothing.'

'I absolutely insist upon—'

'I may not be a gentleman in the sense that my family—'

'I—'

'—never did a hand's turn in their lives to soil their lily-white hands, or in the sense that my f . . . forbears grabbed their lands and castles by pinching them from the peasantry, but my word's my—'

'Take him away!' Fettleworth roared at Lakenham. 'I can stand no more. Get him out of my sight. He's to be held in arrest and I'll see him when he's sober. Get the doctor to him! Damn it, the man's certainly *not* a gentleman!' he added as the Chief of Staff took Black's arm and led him from the presence of his General. Black went more or less unprotestingly, feeling somewhere inside his whisky-drenched brain that he was a clever fellow who had made his point, kept his word, and out-manoeuvred his Divisional Commander, and all in spite of the fact that he wanted very badly to see Dornoch condemned. This was not a feeling that was due to last for very long, but for the present it floated him out of Fettleworth's sight on a wave of confidence. He was taken to a spare bedroom and put to bed, and the doctor was summoned. When this had been done, Laken-ham returned to face Fettleworth's mottled rage, and this he made the worse by somewhat tactlessly saying that he had an idea the General may have stirred up a very large hornet's-nest indeed.

'Hornet's-nest be damned. What the devil d'you mean?'

'As yet, sir, I repeat, we have no facts – or very few. I think we should be cautious and not pre-judge Lord Dornoch's actions and motives. I think—'

'I'll get him back. I'll have him—'

'Steps have already been taken to recall him, sir. At this stage we can do no more, and I would—'

'No more! Lakenham, I've a damn good mind to send out the whole Division!' Fettleworth was shaking with the strength of his emotions, seemingly quite beside himself and liable to commit almost any act of folly to relieve the pressure. 'Yes, I've a damn good mind to do just that.' He gnawed feverishly at the trailing ends of his moustache, his light-blue eyes protuberant in a scarlet face.

'I repeat, sir, I advise the strictest caution. If you're right about Lord Dornoch's intentions, then by this time he may well be inside Waziristan. You know the Scots, sir, as well as I do. You know their intense loyalty, and their fighting spirit. If they have gone in to rescue Captain Ogilvie, there is a chance they may succeed. I doubt if Dornoch is foolhardy enough to lead his regiment into a risk which he himself sees as hopeless – we must allow him that. In my opinion we should take no action that might operate against possible success, and the most I would advise is that we hold the Division at instant readiness to march in support if required. In point of fact, the Division *is* ready to move out, as you know. If you think it necessary, we could move the troops to strategic positions along the Waziri border. Indeed I think this would be a prudent precaution, sir, always provided we leave Peshawar adequately garrisoned.'

'I've a mind to cross the border in full strength, Lakenham.'

The Chief of Staff shook his head. 'I advise against this, sir. We can't commit the whole Division against the Waziris alone, since they're only a part, if a central and vital one, of the likely tribal rising.' He paused. 'I think, for the time being, the Waziris could well be left to the 114th.'

'One battalion, Lakenham? Are you mad?'

'No, sir, I am not. I am suggesting that if Lord Dornoch can bring off this rescue, it will have an immensely strong psychological effect on the Pathans in Waziristan, and indeed all along the Frontier. The psychological—'

'That word again! Do we now fight all our battles with the aid of witch-doctors?'

Lakenham disregarded the question. He said earnestly, 'Sir, we must leave the situation alone for the moment, except for a movement of Division westwards. Then we shall be ready to act when necessary – and not before.'

Lakenham's advice was followed, albeit grudgingly; orders were despatched to the various Brigade headquarters, and thence to the regiments, and almost within the hour the British troops were moving out for the Waziri border with their transport and supply trains kicking up the dust behind while the drums of the infantry battalions beat out the step ahead. Three long columns of route were formed to march respectively on Parachinar, Thal, and the general vicinity of Bahodur Khel in Kohat. In the meantime Murree had been informed and Sir Iain Ogilvie's approval obtained for the movement; and reinforcements of the Peshawar garrison had been requested as a matter of the greatest urgency.

There was no one in all the Peshawar cantonment area who could remain unaware that a movement was in progress; and Mary Archdale watched the soldiers march out behind their beating drums and their colours, a long line of men in stiffly starched khaki-drill tunics with rifles and side-arms gleaming under the hot Indian sun. She was one of many British women who waved as the regiments went by, one of many others whose hearts went with the men as they moved towards the flame and the smoke of war, marching once again to enhance the glory that was the British Raj, to keep the rule of the Queen-Empress in being and to preserve by battle the Pax Britannica. They went on their way singing, eager enough to play their part, and the sounds rolled back from the cantonment buildings as the columns marched away. *'We're soldiers of the Queen, my lads ...We're part of England's glory, lads ... The Queen, my lads, the Queen, my lads.'*

It faded into the distance at last. Mary Archdale's eyes were wet and shining, much as were frequently those of Her Majesty Queen Victoria herself on the occasions when she rolled in her open carriage past the review lines of her beloved soldiers drawn up for her inspection in Hyde Park or Windsor or on the Horse Guards' Parade. But that regal little woman in the black bonnet had never had the ache in her heart, the personal involvement with one man among so many, that Mary Archdale felt on that hot Indian day as the drums and the singing and the marching feet and the rumble of the transport wheels dwindled towards the North-West Frontier.

CHAPTER THIRTEEN

NASHKAR ALI KHAN'S escort kept close as they rode out that first time from the palace, but tended to fall a little behind as the ride progressed. It was possible for Ogilvie and Healey to talk openly from time to time.

Ogilvie asked if there had been any further word of the arms supply party.

'Not yet, old boy, though I rather gather they're not so far off Maizar now – at least, that's Nashkar's estimate. He hasn't told me of any definite report from his scouts.'

'Anything about the main movement?'

'The rising? Again, nothing definite. I have the feeling there's something about to break, though. I doubt if we've got much longer, Ogilvie. Touch and go, now.'

'Can you be more precise?'

Healey shook his head. 'Fraid not. It's just a feeling. I know these people. Nashkar's getting cagey, and that's a sign in itself.'

'Talking of signs . . .'

'Yes, indeed!' Healey grinned. 'Talking of signs, as you say – the *sadhu*'s still as mute as an egg.'

'Then are you suggesting Nashkar's going to jump the gun?'

'No. I'm pretty sure he wouldn't do that. I think he has a simple premonition the *sadhu*'s going to utter shortly.' He paused. 'The thing is, what do *we* do?'

'That's soon answered! We break from the escort and join the supposed arms caravan as soon as they arrive, and we fight our way out across the border and report in full to my Divisional H.Q. How's that?'

'It's all we can do, though *I* shan't be with you that far, old boy—'

'But—'

'No buts, Ogilvie. Oh, I'll be doing all I can to help, of course, but I'm not leaving Waziristan just yet. Remember, I'm a Political Officer. I can still be more use here than in Pesh-awar.' He waved a hand around the hills. 'This is my parade ground, old man – and Nashkar's palace makes a pretty comfortable Officers' Mess! I'm well content, and I don't want old Nashkar to lose his trust in me, you know!'

'But that's what he's going to do, isn't it, the moment I ride out on him? After all, you vouched for me.'

'It's a chance I'll have to take. I think he'll allow me one mistake.'

'I wouldn't be too sure! Honestly, Healey, I don't feel I can let you down like this – just ride out and leave you to it, you know.'

Healey laughed and reached out to clap his shoulder as the horses jogged along close together. 'Don't give it another thought. We both have our duty, and we both know we have to do it.'

'You're a brave man, Healey.'

'Rot. I just happen to know my duty, that's all, and I like my job. Besides, I've no entanglements, no dependants . . . no one to worry me or to worry *about* me either. Single and fancy free. Parents dead. My life's India, and by India I mean the native states – which is why I went into the Political as soon as I could. Much more interesting. Look at the light on those hills.' He reined in his horse and Ogilvie, doing likewise, followed his pointing arm. 'Those shades of light . . . the browns and the purples and the yellows. You've seen the sun rising and setting out here often enough. What d'you think of it?'

'Pretty spectacular.'

'That's all?'

'Well . . . yes.'

Healey shook his head. 'No poetry in your soul, that's your trouble! It all does something to me. In a way I'm like the *sadhu*, I suppose – I feel closer to my Maker in this kind of country. In a physical sense, of course, I am, literally. But it's spiritual as well.' He looked into Ogilvie's face. 'You're a High-lander. Surely you can feel something?'

'Well, yes, I do, but I happen to prefer Scotland!'

'Yes, I can understand.' Healey's voice softened and he stared into the distance. ' *"From the lone shieling and the misty island, mountains divide us and a waste of seas . . . but still the blood is pure, the heart is highland, and we in dreams behold the Hebrides."* '

'I rather like that, Healey.'

'So do I. It's probably how you feel about Scotland, in your heart . . . and if you had enough soul, you'd say so! It's certainly how I feel about this particular part of India. No, you really needn't worry about me, I'll take what comes.' He laughed. 'I'm feeling in the mood for poetry today. Care for another quote about your native land, old boy?'

'Go on.'

'Right, I will. "*Let me feel the breezes blowing, fresh along the mountain side . . . let me see the heather growing, let me hear the thund'ring tide.*" Here are my breezes, Ogilvie, and here are my mountain sides. And there's the ling – what you call heather. I can do without the thund'ring tide, and to take its place I have the distinctive smell of the Orient! And there's something for *you*.'

He pointed.

'What?'

'That hill, the one standing out by itself just beyond Maizar on it. See the one I mean?'

Ogilvie looked, across the clustered white buildings inside the walls of the town below. 'Equidistant between two higher peaks?'

Healey nodded. 'Correct – you have it.'

'Well?'

'That's your goal. Journey's end – or journey's start – for you. Nashkar's arsenal was below that hill, and it's there your fake arms caravan is heading for. Now, we've done enough talking for the present. Let's ride. Come on – I'll race you!' Healey sent his horse plunging ahead fast along the track. Small rocks flew as Ogilvie rode after him. The escort, taken by surprise, galloped up from behind, calling out angrily, clearly scared. But Healey pulled his horse up some four or five hundred yards ahead, laughing gaily. It was quite a good gambit; when the time came, the escort would understand that the Earless One and the English arms salesman liked to pit their riding skill against each other.

A little later they all returned to the palace.

The Regimental Sergeant-Major rode along the line of rock-scrambling, disreputably-dressed Scots, making his way to Lord Dornoch at the head of the column. 'Sir!'

'Yes, Sar'nt-Major?'

'I have been questioning the native leader again, sir. He reports that we're now little more than a day's march from Maizar.'

'Thank God for that!' Dornoch lifted a filthy hand and mopped the sweat from his eyes. 'I trust the palace will have a bath in it!'

'Are we making direct for the palace, sir?'

'No, Sar'nt-Major, we can't do that. I'll head for the arms dump and consolidate there. Once we're in possession, I'll send out my Mounted Infantry to scout. After that – we'll see.'

'Aye, sir. I trust our luck'll hold.'

'So do I, Cunningham, so do I! We've used up rather a lot of it the last few days. Nevertheless, we're going to succeed, I have no doubts about that.'

'Nor have the men, sir. They're in good heart, all of them.'

'Thanks to you, Sar'nt-Major.'

'I have good Colour-Sergeants, sir, the best.'

'I know that too, Sar'nt-Major. Keep 'em that way!' There was a smile in his eyes, tired eyes now, as he went on, 'And keep a tight rein on the Pipe-Major's natural enthusiasms!'

'Sir?'

'The pipes, man, the pipes! I've already told him one premature squeal means he'll be hanged, drawn and quartered the moment we reach Peshawar on return. But seriously, Cunningham, I want you to see to it that there's absolutely no relaxation after we reach the arms dump. The charade has to be kept up right the way through until further orders from me.'

'Aye, sir. I'll be seeing to that, sir.' Instinct began to lift Cunningham's right hand to his helmetless forehead as he prepared to turn away; recollection of the charade kept it in place at his side. No clues must be given to the watchers on the peaks. It went against all training and all tradition of the Queen's Own Royal Strathspeys to do so, but the Regimental Sergeant-Major managed somehow to make even his horse shamble, rather than walk, towards the rear.

Again the following morning, and yet again in the early evening, the escorted ride of freedom took place. Healey and Ogilvie rode down almost to the gates of Maizar on that evening ride, enjoying a slight breeze that blew from out of the north, bringing a welcome touch of cool. They halted only some two hundred yards from the gate in the town wall. There was a

curious hush about Maizar, the townspeople seeming subdued —
or expectant. Through the gateway's arch, Ogilvie watched
them curiously, forming the strong impression that they were
waiting for something to happen. Crowds of them were sitting
in the narrow roadway that led to the gate, sitting in silence
and, except for the occasional scamperings of children, very still.

Healey said, 'I see you notice it too.'

'Yes. Something in the air, very definitely. It's almost as
though they've moved ahead of us in time ... as if they know
something we don't.'

'They do, old boy. It's a kind of telepathy. Many of the
primitive peoples have it. I suppose we all had it once, but
we've become too sophisticated now, too much so to have any
trust in our feelings and instincts. I told you yesterday – Nashkar himself has the feeling that the sign is about to show
itself.'

'And you, Healey?'

'I told you, I too.'

Ogilvie grinned. 'Primitive – aren't you?'

'Possibly. I prefer to think of it as my *affinity* with these
people.'

'Same thing.'

'You may be right,' Healey said indifferently. He turned his
horse. 'We'd better be getting back to the palace. That's where
the fount of all news is! Come on, Ogilvie.'

He moved back along the track, and Ogilvie followed. The
sun was low now, a red orb in the western hills, spreading one
of those magnificent sunsets of which Healey had spoken,
throwing great splashes of rainbow-colours over the land.
Climbing, Ogilvie looked back. The old town of Maizar was
bathed in a curious purple light, shadowed with deep black
between the close-set buildings, while the domes and minarets
of its mosques, standing above the purple, were cascaded with a
glowing orange. It was a remarkable and strange sight, and
impressive – almost as though the odd juxtaposition of colours
in the one place, and from the one sun, in itself might have
constituted the long-awaited sign.

'Come on,' Healey said. 'We'll race again. I've a strong feeling this'll be the last of the heats!'

'Did you see those colours?'

'Yes.'

Ogilvie said, 'You know, one way and another, I'm absorbing

that premonitory feeling of yours, Healey. I'm not sure the moment hasn't come already.'

Healey raised his eyebrows. 'The sign? I doubt that, old man. If that were so, Maizar would be making the welkin ring! The townspeople would have sensed it.'

'I didn't mean the sign itself, Healey. I meant – well, it's time to act. Time for *me* to act. O'Kelly said the sign hadn't to be allowed to materialize and that I would have to deal with the holy man.'

'So you've told me. Well?'

Ogilvie said, 'I think the time has come for that *sadhu* to die, and I've got the chance to see to it now. If I ride out for the peak – I believe I can find the pass all right – I may be able to stop the whole thing happening. And I've a feeling it would be better to do that now, rather than wait for the arms caravan and its escort to turn up.'

'You have a point,' Healey said slowly. 'Yes, you have a point . . . but I wasn't expecting action this night, I must admit! It's a trifle sudden.' He paused, bringing his horse down to a walk. 'How would you propose to go about it, old boy?'

'It's darkening fast. I've noted that our escort's already getting restive, Healey – they'll be chivvying us back to the palace in a moment. Well, darkness is the best cover I'm likely to get. If I can get into the hills before the moon's up, I'm half-way home. Are you going to come with me, Healey?'

'I told you, I still have a job to do. No, I'll not come. I'm not sure you wouldn't do better to come back to the palace and then, when the time's right, make your getaway and try to join up with the arms party. It's not a good thing to make last-minute changes in plans, old boy, not always.'

'Surely it's a principle of war? One must be flexible.'

'Pliable's another word for it, remember.'

There was a sudden harshness in Healey's voice; all at once Ogilvie had the idea Healey's mind was not in fact wholly made up as to whether he wished to remain behind, and that he was resentful of being forced into an unexpectedly swift decision, a sudden decision that would be irrevocable. Ogilvie said, 'But changed circumstances call for changed plans to meet them. You've convinced me that the sign's imminent—'

'I could be wrong.'

'Of course you could, but I've come to see that some kind of a build-up of feeling is going on, and I don't think we can risk being too late off the mark, Healey. I'm sure that the vital thing, now, is to deal with the *sadhu* before the sign comes. The rest can wait. It must be a case of first things first. You see that, don't you?'

He waited anxiously for the answer. Healey's co-operation was as vital as the inhibition of the sign itself. But then Healey, whether or not he agreed with the change in plan, would scarcely hinder him by refusing his help.

Ogilvie said as much.

'No, no, I'll not hinder, old boy. You'll go your own way, I suppose, and I won't say it may not turn out right. I'll give you cover.'

'Thank you, Healey. I appreciate that.'

Healey laughed. 'Don't sound so damn British, so stiffly polite. This isn't the R.M.C. and I'm not a Gentleman Cadet who's just promised to lay off your best girl. We're both going to be in danger of our lives this night, you mark my words! Not that I haven't been ever since I set foot in Waziristan, or you either. But tonight things are going to sharpen up to a very fine point. But wheesht now, as I believe you say in Scotland, for our escort are doing as you prophesied, old boy, and coming in for a little urging, a touch of the spur.' He turned in his saddle as the Pathans rode up close, and there was a conversation in Pushtu. Healey agreed to ride ahead faster, and the wild men went on, pushing past to lead the way now, leaving one behind to act as rearguard. When they were all out of earshot Healey said, 'Now listen, if your mind's made up to go and kill that poor old holy heathen on the heights . . . is it, by the way?'

'Yes.'

'Then so be it. So is mine – and I'm staying. No – no argument on that point, if you don't mind. Just listen.' Healey's voice was very quiet now. 'About a mile ahead, there's a defile leading off to the right of the track, north-westerly. If we don't go too fast – just fast enough to keep the escort happy – it'll be nicely dark by the time we reach that defile. When we do, you nip into it, fast. If you keep going right ahead, it'll lead you smack into the pass you were brought along from that hole. When you reach the pass, turn westwards and there you are. You certainly can't miss the *sadhu*, he's like the signpost on the Great North Road saying Scotland and The North . . . but you know that, of course. However, don't underestimate the dangers. Nashkar's going to know very well where you're heading, and he'll do everything he can to cut you off along that route. That's obvious. As—'

'Not really. He doesn't know who I am, and he trusts me. You've said yourself – and it's been plain enough – he has no suspicions left now. He may think I'll just head for the border and away, to save my own skin – just in case.'

'When you're being, as you say, trusted?' Healey shook his head. 'You wouldn't do that, old man, not when you're on a good wicket. No, he'll assume the worst – that you're a British agent after all and heading for the *sadhu*. Naturally, I'll be doing all I can to cause delay and confusion and give you a start. You can count on that.'

'Thanks, Healey. And you'll cover my actual getaway when we reach the defile?'

'Certainly I will, old boy. But you must cover me as well. You throw me to the ground when I give the word, and you dash off, after which I'll do what I can to mislead the immediate pursuit. Don't expect miracles, Ogilvie, old boy. I did warn you it was dangerous! There's a strong chance you won't get a hundred yards.'

'That was always a chance I had to take – there's no difference now. But can't we stick to the idea of a horse-race? That way – if we belt off now – we'll be moving fast with the escort well behind us—'

'Yes, I think you're right. We can have a nice little pile-up. But d'you really feel your horsemanship is up to a night race in this kind of country, Ogilvie?'

'No. But again, it's a chance I have to take.' Ogilvie tried not to look too closely at their surroundings. To the left rose high rock, seeming to reach to the very sky, sheer and smooth and black in the swiftly-gathering darkness. On his right the ground fell away quite steeply, dropping towards another rise into hilly country scarred by defiles such as the one he would take, and valleys, with the rearing crests stretching away into Afghanistan. The track itself, the one they were on, was smooth but dotted with small rocks that had fallen from the heights above, and smashed, to endanger the horses' feet with their treachery. It would, in fact, be the very devil of a ride. He said, 'I'm ready when you are, Healey.'

'Then we won't delay.' Healey shouted ahead to the escort, and they halted. A moment later Ogilvie could just see them coming back. They stopped in front of Healey.

'A race,' Healey said in Pushtu. 'Wilshaw Sahib wishes to test his skill against mine at night.'

'As the Earless One desires.'

'Then ride behind us, that the way may be clear.'

They obeyed what was in effect a command, peremptorily uttered – all along it had been clear that the escort was there not to guard Healey, but to assist him in guarding the supposed Wilshaw Sahib. Already now Healey was counting for the off. They raced along the track, deliberately keeping neck and neck so far as possible. Stones and small rock fragments flew from beneath the horses' hooves, occasionally striking sparks from the track. Ogilvie's hair and tattered clothing streamed out along the wind made by their passing. It was a thoroughly madcap ride and they were soon well ahead of the escort – who were excellent horsemen without a doubt, indeed far better than either Healey or himself, but more prudent men, horsemen too good to risk breaking their horses' legs or their own necks in a pointless endeavour to keep, as they appeared to believe, unnecessarily close. Ogilvie grinned to himself; within the next few minutes those Pathans were going to be right up against a very pointed point indeed!

He heard Healey's voice: 'Coming up to it now ... three openings at the foot of the slope. Take the centre one. Can you see where I mean?'

'No, it's too dark.'

'Then turn off when I yell, but knock me down first. Use the darkness as cover and sniff around when you hit the foot of the slope. Stand by now!'

A few moments after this Healey spoke again. 'Don't think too badly of me, old boy,' he said enigmatically, and then he gave his yell. It was beautifully done, a yell of sheer surprise and alarm and sudden pain. In the split second that the yell came, Ogilvie leaned sideways and struck out hard at Healey with his bunched fist, taking him heavily on the right shoulder, then he pulled his horse off the track sharply and belted down the slope. Before leaving the track he was aware of Healey smashing sideways into the rock face on his left, and of flailing hooves, and then, as he reached the foot of the slope, with his horse's hooves sliding and slithering in the rolling debris and the animal itself practically on its rump, he heard the yells and cries that told him Healey had unseated the escort.

He could only hope Healey hadn't had his skull smashed in the process.

He found the defile – or he hoped it was the right one – more quickly than he had feared might be the case. He rode down it fast, scattering more general rock debris, feeling safer as he penetrated into the lee of the high, enclosing sides. Before he had reached the defile wild shots had come down in his general direction, although he was certain he could not be seen from the track. He had heard the pursuit behind him, no more than two horsemen he fancied, which must mean the rest of the escort had been satisfactorily injured; but that pursuit had not come at all close, proceeding, he judged from the sounds, up the wrong channel. He had lain low for a little while, and then, when he had heard the horses moving away, he had gone ahead. He had ridden as fast thereafter as he could manage in what was virtually total darkness, darkness in which he could make out nothing whatsoever more than half a dozen feet distant, except as vague blurs. All he could see distinctly were the high peaks, stark against the sky that was a degree lighter than the confines of the lower slopes of the hills. He had no idea whether or not he had indeed taken the right defile, though he believed he had followed Healey's somewhat imprecise instructions faithfully. Time alone would tell him the answer; he had no route indications to follow, no guidelines, no landmarks. If he picked up the main pass leading to the *sadhu*'s peak, then it would be a case of so far so good; if not, not! He fancied that, given a little kindly light from a moon that seemed reluctant to rise, he would be able to identify the pass from his previous journeyings along it though even of this he could by no means be certain.

Soon after this, that reluctant moon did appear, stealing up over the mountains' high rim to spread a silvery radiance over the terrible desolation. Now he could pick up his surroundings with the greatest ease. They stood out like a ship at sea on moonlit waters, stark and black and menacing against the silver. Ogilvie rode on, feeling his heart pumping hard at every small night sound, at the very slither of lizards among rocks, at the occasional sudden cries of the night birds, at the swish of wings as shadows flitted across his tricky path. He went on, finding no pass crossing that track, which just led ahead and upwards, slowly climbing to the skies.

Some hours, as it seemed, later, the moon, a full one, and riding high now, well clear of the mountain peaks, began to present a slightly different appearance. It was difficult at first to define this difference, but something about it intrigued Ogilvie as he made his way along as fast as he could manage. It was a difference of colour and of brilliance. It was as if something had cast a veil over the light, dimming it down progressively with more and more veils, so that it was becoming a reddish brown. Ogilvie thought fancifully of the man in the moon, and of green cheese . . . of the excellent cheese made at Stilton, kept too long so that it turned brown. It was very curious. Gradually the moon was becoming fainter and fainter, a red-brown ball sailing back through space on some heavenly errand, deserting its mother Earth.

When, later than it might have done, the truth came to him, Ogilvie felt a cold sweat break out on his body. Never before in his life had he witnessed an eclipse of the moon, but he had expected it to be similar to a solar eclipse – an extending wedge of dark spreading across. But this must be a lunar eclipse . . . and what better sign to a superstitious people than a deepening darkness spreading over that friendly light to snatch it from the sight of men?

CHAPTER FOURTEEN

FROM his lonely mountain peak the aged *sadhu* had seen the
fading and discoloration of the cold, disdainful orb riding
across the night sky, and he had begun to shake throughout his
whole skinny frame as he waited for the hand of Mahomet to
obscure further the moon's surface. For this must be the hand
of the Prophet; on other occasions during his long life the *sadhu*
had witnessed similar happenings, similar defacements of the
moon, and even of the sun – sometimes in the sun's case these
defacements had been partial, sometimes they had been total,
but always, his memory told him, sun or moon, they had been
followed by some act of Mahomet for good or ill, something
that could be ascribed, by any devout believer, only to the intervention of the Prophet.

This time, therefore, it was perfectly clear. Mahomet had
spoken, Mahomet had revealed his mind to his servant, the long
awaited sign had been manifested at last. The duty of Mahomet's servant was as plain as the sign itself, the shadow that was
slowly diminishing the silvery radiance of the moon. The
significance must now be communicated to Mahomet's war
leader upon earth that the tribes might rise as one, and march,
and storm down upon the British citadels, upon the mighty
garrison at Peshawar, to win back the ancient city of Kaspaturos for its own people, and in so doing avenge the wrongs
and insults and depredations of a thousand years.

Creakily, swaying like an old tree in the mountain breeze, the
sadhu climbed miraculously and with much difficulty to his feet
and lifted his outstretched arms towards the moon, and then
with further difficulty got down again and prostrated himself
before Mahomet, murmuring many prayers. After this he rose
again and, standing statue-like with arms once more outstretched, he sent a long-drawn keening cry echoing out across
the mountains. Below him, the waiting runner heard it, the
runner who had also been staring at the hand of the Prophet

and feeling strange movements in his bowels as he did so, movements of anticipation of excitement and glory to come. Gathering himself for the descent into the pass and the long road to Maizar, he remained for a moment staring in wonder and adoration at the age-old holy man, whose cry had now stopped but who was still, with arms uplifted, gazing into the diminishing face of the moon.

Ogilvie also heard that cry faintly from the distance – heard it from the pass which, by the grace of God, he had at last found ahead of his horse. Hearing it, he interpreted it correctly, and wondered what he should do. After a moment of indecision he came to the conclusion that since, on his own, he could do nothing else, he must continue towards the place where he had last seen the *sadhu*. The holy man was scarcely mobile enough to move very far on his own account, and his death might yet have some effect on the tribes. Notwithstanding the fateful fact of the sign's revelations, part of O'Kelly's instructions held good still: the *sadhu* must die, much as Oglivie revolted from the thought of lifting a hand against so old and frail a man. And then his body must be well concealed where no Pathan would ever find it. His very absence at a crucial time might cause some dismay, some upset, in the tribal ranks.

It was all that could be hoped for now.

Ogilvie rode on, fast, dangerously, obsessed now with the one thought and aim: to reach the *sadhu* before Nashkar Ali Khan could get his hands on him.

The eclipse of the moon was seen, naturally, over all Waziristan, though the long wailing of the *sadhu* was heard only in his own sector of the mountains. The great concourse of the tribal levies down towards Gumatti saw it and, like the *sadhu* himself, saw in it the hand of Mahomet. Around the camp-fires of the watchmen, the talk grew loud, the excitement mounted. Soon now the order would come from Maizar – the order to march upon the hated British. Kaspaturos was much in the air, and the older men told once again often-repeated stories, handed down from father to son through the centuries, of the glories and war endeavours of the past. Well-known as they were, these tales were avidly listened to afresh, and wild faces grew wilder, eyes shone more brightly in the flickering fires that dotted the great marshalling area between the hills; steel was sharpened yet again and loaded rifles dangerously flourished in the air.

In his palace outside Maizar Nashkar Ali Khan saw it, and then waited impatiently for confirmation of its meaning to reach him before he sent word on to his levies.

'The significance is as obvious as the nose upon your face,' he agreed with his principal adviser, 'but until word comes from the *sadhu* I shall not move. This will mean no delay of any consequence, and it is most important that the tribes should be assured by the voice of the *sadhu* of the sign's validity. Bring me the Earless One again.'

When Healey was ushered into his presence Nashkar Ali Khan looked at his bloodstained shoulder and leg, at the injuries Healey had sustained when he had crashed against the hard rock side of the track during Ogilvie's escape from the escort. The Pathan said, 'Soon now you will have your revenge, Earless One, upon the English arms seller, for I believe the sign has come. You have seen the shadow over the moon?'

'Yes, Highness.'

'An eclipse, of course, a natural phenomenon, but sent with special purpose tonight by Mahomet.' Nashkar Ali Khan took Healey's arm and led him across to one of the great windows. He stood for a moment in silence, looking out over the still faintly moonlit peaks. Then he asked, '*You* believe this to be the sign we have been waiting for, Earless One?'

'It is not for me to say, Highness. The *sadhu* alone can pronounce. You have said, and rightly, that an eclipse is a natural event, predictable before it comes. Doubtless an eclipse is written ... but the writing may not coincide with the wishes of Mahomet. When the *sadhu* speaks, the truth will be known. Until then, we cannot be entirely sure.'

The Pathan leader nodded. 'Truly spoken, Earless One. Yet the great majority of our peoples will see, not an eclipse at all, but the sign.'

'They have not all been given your knowledge of the skies, Highness.' Healey bowed his head, to hide the irony in his expression.

'You flatter me, Earless One. I was not boasting; I was saying this: I could use the eclipse as a sign, and give the word, and *not* wait for the *sadhu*, even though I have already told my chief minister that I shall do so.'

214

'Why so, Highness? Why not wait?'

'Because, Earless One, the Englishman may reach the *sadhu* before my men ... and if he does, then the word will never come.'

Healey said, 'This I doubt, Highness. The runner from the *sadhu* will be already on his way if indeed the sign has come, and even if the Englishman's intent *was* to reach the *sadhu*, a thing of which we cannot be certain at all, then he will be too late. Besides, the men you have sent may have killed the Englishman by this time. Having themselves witnessed the punishment by death of the defaulting escort, they will use their very best endeavours, Highness!'

'Then you think I should wait? This also, I confess, was my own first thought.'

'A good thought, Highness. Yes, I think you should wait for the final confirmation, and then with a satisfied heart make it known to all Waziristan.'

'Very considerate of our Maker,' Lord Dornoch remarked to the R.S.M., riding at his side. He had failed to recognize the work of Mahomet in organizing the eclipse, which had so reduced the silver radiance that the Mounted Infantry striking force was now much less susceptible to any snipers that might be lurking outside Maizar. At Dornoch's other side was Rob MacKinlay, still commanding B Company of the Royal Strathspeys but now detached as second-in-command of the Mounted Infantry, who were using the horses unharnessed from the wagons left behind at the arms dump. The rest of the M.I. was made up of a Colour-Sergeant and two Corporals, with fifteen uncomfortably-seated privates, raw – in more than one sense – blaspheming Scots quite at home in highland country but only so long as they were firmly upon their own two sturdy feet. 'At the same time, of course, it does make it harder not to run into all these damn boulders,' Dornoch added testily as he steered his horse round a particularly big one that had been lost in the shadows. Knowing nothing of the long-awaited sign, he yet felt a certain sense of unease, he didn't know why. He said abruptly, 'We must move faster, Rob. Sar'nt-Major, pass the word to the men. We must reach Maizar and this damned palace before it's too late!'

Cunningham still dressed, as they all were, in his execrable native rags, wheeled his horse and made his way to the rear. It

215

was while he was doing this that there came, like a thunderclap in the still night, the sound of a single shot from ahead, from where the advanced scouts were riding to protect the main body of horsemen. Close on its heels there came another, and another, and then a fusillade. By this time Lord Dornoch had called out the order to advance, and was himself sending his horse fast ahead, risking the treachery of the jagged boulders and smaller rocks. One of the scouts, he found, was coming back to report.

'Well?' Dornoch demanded. 'What was that?'

'Three natives, sir, mounted and heading north-west . . . they came suddenly from a defile to the left, sir—'

'What's the result?'

'All killed, sir.'

'And ours?'

'Private Crummel, sir, dead. Shot through the throat.'

Dornoch nodded, and turned in the saddle as Cunningham rode up. 'Burial party, Sar'nt-Major,' he said curtly. 'All bodies to be concealed beneath the rock. There's no time for digging a grave for Crummel, but no evidence is to be left behind uncovered.' He swung round on the scout who had reported. 'First I'll see the bodies of the tribesmen,' he said.

He rode ahead with the scout, and dismounted by the three corpses. With MacKinlay's help, he examined them thoroughly, going right through their clothing. Straightening, he said, 'No help there. They could have been anybody, going anywhere. Merely bandits. Yet I'd doubt that.' He sounded puzzled. 'Yes, on second thoughts I'd doubt it.'

'Why so, Colonel?' Mackinlay asked.

'I don't know, Rob, it's just a feeling. Just a feeling . . . it's the clothing for one thing. Pretty smelly – but too good for bandits, and besides, it has the look of a uniform, or a livery. Do you agree, Rob?'

'It could be, Colonel. But if so, what . . .?'

'I don't know,' Dornoch said once again. He looked around at the dark rearing hills, at the peaks that cut against the lighter sky which was darkening fast as the shadow of the eclipse deepened. '*If* they're uniforms, however scruffy, these men could be from the palace.' He pointed back down the track, towards the entry to the defile which they had now passed. 'I should say, I think, from our maps, that that's the way from Maizar or thereabouts. And I'm wondering why three armed horsemen should be riding out from Maizar, and possibly from Nashkar Ali Khan's palace, at this particular moment of history!'

'I don't understand, Colonel?'

'Rob, the eclipse! You know these people – I've been bothered by that eclipse, I confess. The hillmen like to be guided by Mahomet, don't they? Don't you see? Who deals with heavenly signs in these parts?'

'Soothsayers, I suppose . . . holy men.'

'Exactly! *Sadhus*. There's been talk of a *sadhu* being the king pin being this rising. The eclipse comes and Nashkar sees it as a sign, or a possible sign. He wants to find out what the portents are – very naturally! So he sends men to seek out the *sadhu*. How's that?'

'Wouldn't the *sadhu* be at the palace, Colonel?'

'Not necessarily. Usually these holy men like to be on their own. I suppose Mahomet is more likely to reveal himself to them in solitude! Besides, they're solitaries anyway, ascetics – they don't inhabit palaces willingly. Not for them the flesh-pots and the women, Rob!' Dornoch laughed, and there was a mounting excitement in his laugh. 'If we follow where those men were going, I've a feeling we might come upon the *sadhu* – and I believe it's worth a try.'

'Colonel, we've come to find Ogilvie,' MacKinlay said.

'That's true, and we're going to. But there was always a very big doubt that we'd be able to get inside the palace – and out again with Ogilvie. It was a risk we were all prepared to take, but if a better way offers itself, then we should think again. If we can get our hands on the *sadhu*, then we have a very effective hostage to secure Ogilvie's release. Now do you see, Rob?'

'By God I do, Colonel! Do you think we can bring it off?'

'There's no knowing, Rob, but the chances are no worse than they would be if we stormed the palace. And if we don't find the *sadhu*, we go back to the first idea.'

'With some time lost, Colonel.'

'Time has always been one of the imponderables anyway, Rob.' He looked back at the waiting men. 'Move 'em forward, Rob, the moment the dead are covered. Straight through the pass – and warn 'em all to keep their eyes skinned and their rifles ready, more than ever now!'

217

Twenty minutes later, with the evidence of the encounter well hidden, they were on the move once more.

Somebody was scrambling down the side of the mountain, coming fast for the pass itself. Ogilvie, who had the *sadhu* in sight now – the old man was standing like a beanpole on his flat piece of rock – stopped dead, then moved for cover.

There was deep shadow all around, but he fancied he saw the movement on the slope; he could certainly hear the fall of stones dislodged by the hurried descent. Clearly, it must be the runner, bound for Maizar. Somewhere around, though he couldn't yet see it, the runner's horse must be tethered.

Still upon his own horse, he waited, motionless. Having no weapon, he would have to rely on being able to ride the man down when he reached the pass. That shouldn't be too difficult. When that had been done, the *sadhu* would be easily enough dealt with, always provided the task was not interrupted by any of Nashkar's men from Maizar. Ogilvie listened intently, but could pick up no sounds other than those made by the runner in his rapid descent into the pass.

Reaching the foot of the incline, the man headed away from Ogilvie, going, no doubt, for his horse. Ogilvie saw the outline of a rifle. He came out from cover, riding straight for the shadowy figure, and the man turned sharply, hesitated for a moment, then darted to one side and, as Ogilvie came on, reached out and laid hold of his leg, and pulled. Cursing, Ogilvie slid from his horse and hit hard ground. Twisting himself onto his back, he saw the man leaping at him, and he lashed out with both feet; he caught the man's heavily bearded face but failed to deflect him. The tribesman merely gave a grunt of pain, dropped his rifle and fell upon Ogilvie's body, hands reaching for the throat and getting a tight stranglehold. Gasping, Ogilvie tore and beat with his hands, feeling foul breath in his nostrils until the squeezing fingers stopped his own breathing. Overhead, the eclipse had by this time virtually extinguished the moon behind the earth's shadow. Ogilvie was close to passing out when suddenly the holy man uttered once again, giving that strange long cry. It penetrated the drumming sounds in Ogilvie's ears, and he was aware of his attacker looking upward at the peak, his attention on the *sadhu* but his fingers never for an instant relaxing their grip.

Then, as suddenly as it had started, the cry stopped, nipped as it were in full voice.

There was an instant reaction from the runner.

The man gave a startled sound and let go of Ogilvie as though he no longer mattered, and scrambled to his feet, seizing his rifle and staring upwards, and making a low sound deep in his throat, like an animal at bay. Ogilvie, lying flat on the ground still, found his vision clearing; and he saw the tall figure of the old *sadhu* outlined starkly against the sky, arms lifted as if in supplication to the eclipse-obscured moon, or to Mahomet in his heaven.

The skinny body was swaying alarmingly, leaning like a windbent branch over the long drop onto the jagged rocks of the pass.

Ogilvie pulled himself up.

By now the runner was kneeling in prayer, making obeisances, arms and torso lifting and falling again. His backside was presented to Ogilvie, excellent target for a hefty kick, and his bayoneted rifle was by his side. As quietly as possible Ogilvie advanced, but to his surprise and alarm more shadows flitted from out of the sides of the pass, and there were more cries. There was a cold wind now, blowing around the *sadhu* and eddying down into the pass.

The runner, hearing the new arrivals, ceased praying and leapt to his feet, turned, grabbed his rifle again, and made a rush for Ogilvie behind his long, rusty bayonet. At the last moment Ogilvie dodged aside; as the steel slid past his body, he brought a fist down with almighty force on the back of the man's neck. The runner collapsed in a heap, his face smacking into the rocky ground.

As the other men, four swift shadows, closed in, Ogilvie dived for the rifle. From the corner of his eye he saw two more shadows scrambling up the path that led to the *sadhu*.

They were too late.

There was one more long-drawn keening cry from the heights and the *sadhu* swayed outwards, arms lifted still.

Then, with an appalling scream, he toppled.

He fell clear over the edge as the scream echoed off the mountains. The men halted. As the skinny old body vanished from sight, they uttered loud cries of alarm, and there were sounds of moaning, of terror and distress at being in the vicinity of a holy man's death. Seconds later there was a dull, grisly thud from a little way along the pass, followed by driblets of falling rock fragments. Ogilvie saw where the body had landed: it was a whitish blur against the black of the lonely pass.

The cries from the other men continued.

The runner, back on his feet again, pointed towards Ogilvie.

'The Englishman has killed the *sadhu*. It is he who has caused him to fall. For this he must die a thousand deaths, my brothers!'

'It was not I.' Ogilvie felt a cold sweat trickle down his back. This was a terrible and lonely place to die, a place of ghosts and dereliction and greedy vultures' beaks. 'The *sadhu* was struck down by Mahomet himself!'

This brought cries of anger.

'Yes, truly, it was Mahomet.' Ogilvie did his best to make his voice carry strength and conviction. 'Mahomet killed the old man, struck him down because he had done a wicked thing, because he had poisoned men's minds . . . because he had mis-interpreted the will of Mahomet and had misread Mahomet's sign. Do you not see?' He glanced upward, briefly; the red-brown ball that was the moon in eclipse appeared not to have darkened any further. The natural phenomenon might now have reached its height, and it could be worth taking a pro-phetic risk. 'The sign is coming to its end, and soon the moon will reappear, to show all men that Mahomet is displeased with the *sadhu*, whom he has killed!'

'The Englishman speaks only lies,' a voice said out of the darkness. 'Let us kill him, brothers!'

'I speak truth. What Nashkar Ali Khan thought was written, was not written! Is not the very death of the *sadhu* himself a more potent sign than any for which the *sadhu* was waiting?'

To minds orientated towards superstition there must surely be much more than a touch of godly wrath in that terrible fall from the heights in the very hour of what should have been the *sadhu*'s triumph! Surely, the symbolism couldn't fail to regis-ter!

There was no direct reply to what he had said, though he caught a muttered word here and there, a sound of hostility and anger.

Then, with no more warning, the attack came.

Howling like wolves, intent upon pulling the Scotsman limb from limb, the shadows, all seven of them now, advanced upon

220

him. Ogilvie did the only thing he could do, which was to retreat along the jagged pass, and hold the bayonet steady in front of him, and hope to kill at least some of them by steel and bullet before the end came. In his retreat he almost stumbled over the shattered remains of the *sadhu* lying in the pass. Then his back was literally to the wall, and the men were closing in.

He pulled the trigger of the rifle.

Nothing happened. He worked the bolt again and again.

Cursing viciously, he made a swift thrust with the bayonet as a man came close, a thrust right into the rib-cage. A wrist-wrenching twist dragged the blade clear just in time to deal with a second man.

Five left now.

They drew back a little way, and talked among themselves in low voices. As they did so, a little more light touched the scene: Ogilvie glanced upward at the moon's brown outline. It was more visible now. 'See,' he called out. 'Now Mahomet is withdrawing the sign. It is as I myself prophesied. Mahomet is displeased.'

Whether or not they were impressed, Ogilvie could not tell; but there seemed to be some hesitancy in the air now, though this could be due merely to a wonderment as to whether the Englishman should be held safe until Nashkar Ali Khan's personal guard could take him over, or another attempt be made to kill him now.

At all events there was a delay; and in the end they delayed too long.

The first touch of dawn in the sky showed up the *sadhu*'s corpse, with one leg twisted up around the trunk, and the skull broken and shedding its contents; and somewhere in its violent bouncing off the hillside a jag of rock must have gashed and penetrated the gut, for this too was rent asunder and spilling, to the satisfaction of the busy vultures who were no respectors of *sadhus* and who were currently profaning the remains.

But that early dawn showed up something else, away down the pass: two horsemen, like advanced scouts, keeping one on either side of the track. And then, behind them, a considerable number more. They were natives, Ogilvie saw – more Pathans.

And yet, as they came closer, Ogilvie found some odd and

unexpected familiarity and a wild hope grew. A moment later the men guarding him, evidently suspicious also, began to run – and then the firing started and the horsemen came pounding on in a dangerous gallop, and Ogilvie realized that Lord Dornoch was calling to him, and that he had been found by a detachment of the Royal Strathspey.

It seemed like a miracle. His mind had been full of Mahomet, and now God had turned up to redress the balance.

CHAPTER FIFTEEN

'I HAD not come specifically to attack,' Lord Dornoch said. He lifted a hand to shade his eyes from the climbing sun, shining through a gap in the eastern hills. 'My objective was to find you, James, that and no more.'

'Yes, Colonel. Nevertheless, there is that Pathan striking force, down in the hills beyond Maizar. If that could be destroyed, or at any rate dispersed—'

'By one battalion?'

Ogilvie said, 'Not precisely that, Colonel.'

'Then what, man?' Lord Dornoch shifted restlessly, irritably. 'Out with it! Time's short, as you should know as well as I.'

'Yes, Colonel. I was thinking . . . it should be perfectly possible, the way things have turned out, to convince the runner that the tribes are not onto such a good thing as they've been believing. He's intact and functioning, but he'll be having plenty to think about at the moment – with the *sadhu*'s death, and the apparent withdrawal of the sign, and your own arrival here.' He hesitated. 'Colonel, I believe we may be able to make him spread the gospel.'

'Kindly be more explicit!'

'Yes, Colonel.' Ogilvie took a deep breath and came out with his suggestion. 'I think we could try to disaffect the main army, Colonel. You see – the symbolism of the death, at that particular moment! The fact it may have registered with the runner, however, with just one solitary tribesman – that's not enough! We need to communicate it, and undermine Nashkar Ali Khan's personal authority. Do you not see, Colonel?'

'By God!' Agitatedly Dornoch moved his horse a few paces away, then came back again. 'James, that's a bold stroke, is it not? Disaffect an entire army – and as likely as not be torn to shreds before we could open our mouths?'

'Yes, Colonel, but I'm sure it could work out. We can show them the actual body of the *sadhu* while keeping ourselves in a defendable position until the word has spread – and use the runner to substantiate the fact that the *sadhu* died when the sign appeared. You know the Pathan mind, Colonel ... don't you agree it could work?'

Dornoch frowned; there was a battle light in his eyes and he had his regiment not too far away, and fighting was in his very blood, was his whole training. He said, 'It might – it might! When all's said and done ... a sign's a sign!'

'Very much so, from my observation, Colonel.'

'And a botched sign – which we might consider this to be – could cause grave doubts in native minds?'

'Yes, Colonel.'

'It's the devil of a march to Gumatti!'

'But a faster ride, Colonel. And my information is that the tribes are encamped well this side of Gumatti. The distance from Maizar to the camp is no more than about twenty miles, in fact.'

'Which is still a long way in this kind of country, and would take us at least a full day's forced marching – and we have still to get back to that arms dump to rejoin the battalion. Not that that's so far.' He stared along the pass, then turned to Mac-Kinlay at his side. 'What think you, Rob?'

'I'm all for finishing the job, Colonel.'

'H'm. James, time is of the essence now. And you talk of riding – I haven't horses for the whole battalion!'

'No, Colonel. But I have one, and so has the runner.'

Dornoch stared. 'My dear young man, you're not suggesting you should go to this camp alone, are you?'

'I shall have the *sadhu* with me, Colonel.'

'You're wasting my time,' Dornoch snapped.

'No, sir.' Ogilvie sounded obstinately determined now. 'If you will allow me to go in ahead of the battalion I can handle it, and handle it better in the first stages alone. I can sow the seed, Colonel, work on their superstitious fears, and get them worked up into a – a frenzy of doubt. That's the point! I'll tell them that if they don't take the *sadhu's* death as the sign it was meant to be, and disperse, then the British will come, that they'll be hoist with their own petard and invaded. That should at least delay the start of Nashkar's march across the border! There'll be plenty of argument – but I'll bet they'll never move out when there's the slightest possibility the signs may be against them rather than with them! Remember, Colonel, the whole thing depended on a sign right from the start—'

'True, true—'

'And once I've done my work, Colonel, you arrive with the battalion – spread out to give the impression of an army corps!'

This time Lord Dornoch laughed. 'By God, James, you think of everything! Rob?'

MacKinlay said, 'There's sense behind it, Colonel. If we mean to try to inhibit the rising at all, it's the only way. To attack without this sort of preparation would be suicide, that's certain. This idea may be crazy, but if we *can* bring it off, well, General Fettleworth's going to have to destroy an awful lot of anti-Scots bumph he'll have been making ready since we sneaked out of cantonments!'

Dornoch laughed again, and there was a tinge of real excitement in the laugh. The idea, Ogilvie saw, was beginning to appeal. The Colonel moved his horse, riding slowly a little way along the pass, thinking deeply. Coming back, he said, 'One condition, James, for your part of the expedition. I give my approval on the clear understanding you make no damn silly attempt actually to penetrate that army, to get *inside* the camp. This must be done from the outside in, if you follow me?'

'Yes, Colonel.'

'I know the kind of country – not unlike this, hilly. You must find a vantage point, much as you yourself suggested, it'll not be hard, and use it the best way you can until I come up with the battalion. Understood?'

'Yes, Colonel.'

'There will be no heroics, no throwing away life. Shout your persuasion from the hilltops – but remember your backside and make certain it has a nice clear route to the rear. And another thing. Although I realize well enough the urgency of speed, of your reaching the camp before Nashkar moves, you must compromise to this extent, James: you will *not* put too great a distance between yourself and the regiment. It will be vital that I am not too far behind you, as I'm sure you'll appreciate. All right?'

'Yes, Colonel.'

'Very well, then.' Lord Dornoch turned again towards the men. 'We're an infantry battalion, just under a thousand of us all told, against God knows how many of the heathen – but we'll not be making history, for that part of it has been done before now, and successfully. Remember that. Remember another thing of importance. We're not just an infantry battalion of the British Army, we're a Scots regiment of Highlanders – and there's no prouder thing than that on all the face of the globe!'

The *sadhu*'s body did not, after all, accompany Ogilvie; Lord Dornoch considered this too dangerous, for the sight of that mangled body could well cause the tribesmen to jump to hasty conclusions before listening to the truth, in which case Ogilvie's death, torn to shreds by a shrieking mob, could be considered a certainty. The *sadhu* would therefore make his final earthly appearance at a more appropriate, more propitious time – with the advance of the 114th Highlanders once the ground had been prepared by Ogilvie. Also, Ogilvie did not in the event go alone with the runner. He went with a mounted escort of ten native-dressed Scots privates, and Bosom Cunningham, wild-looking ruffians who could still fool any hilltop snipers, sure to be encountered along the way. Cunningham guaranteed that he would prime the runner in his part and see that there was no talking out of turn. The runner would give the evidence of what he had genuinely seen, and no more.

Before Ogilvie's group left, the whole party moved back along the pass as the sun came up. They had gone a couple of miles when native horsemen were seen ahead, horsemen who came on in surprise but not in suspicion. The party, whose members looked anything but British, could have been levies coming in from Afghanistan. The bitter truth was learned when Lord Dornoch gave the order to fire; and Cunningham thereafter used his extricatory talents to prise out of the survivors the information that they were a second group to have been dispatched by Nashkar Ali Khan to find Wilshaw Sahib and the *sadhu*. Nashkar, they said, was worried and upset, and also angry. It was rumoured that he planned to ride out for the encamped tribes, together with the Earless One. With the dead concealed, the survivors rode along in the centre of the British files; and a little to the north of Maizar, the two sections parted company, Lord Dornoch taking his men back towards the main body of the battalion at the arms dump, and Ogilvie – himself now in the disguise of native dress – heading east towards

Gumatti with his escort, following the directions of the former runner, who now seemed only too anxious to placate those who, so strangely, seemed to have become the elect of the Prophet. As they made their way along, passing to the north of Maizar, keeping south of Miram Shah, they were aware now and again of men watching from the peaks, men of that eternal band of snipers that roamed the Waziri hills, indeed all the hills along the Frontier, the majority of them bandits pure and simple. But, keeping strictly to the tracks, they went by unmolested. They formed a reasonably strong force, and they were clearly armed, and would give a good account of themselves if attacked; and besides, it was well-known that levies were coming in from Afghanistan and to fire upon levies riding to join the great army outside Gumatti would be to invite the most terrible reprisals from Nashkar Ali Khan . . .

'The Colonel's taking a devil of a chance, Sar'nt-Major,' Ogilvie remarked soon after they had parted company with Dornoch.

'In what respect, sir?'

'Why, bringing the regiment across the border without orders.'

'Aye, sir, a great risk it is indeed, and certain to lead to a Court Martial.'

'He must have known that.'

'Of course, Captain Ogilvie, sir, he knew it well, and so did all of us, but it'll be a Court Martial without disgrace!' Cunningham spoke with some heat; his big face was angry, but there was anxiety beneath the anger. He, of all the men in the regiment, knew the army and its ways. The Nelson touch was a fine thing and there were still senior officers around who appreciated the grand gesture – one of them being Sir Iain Ogilvie himself. But the Nelson touch and the grand gesture had to result in total success; that was the essential thing! Failure would lead to professional ruin for the Royal Strathspeys' Colonel and even Sir Iain might well be powerless – *would* be powerless – to prevent it. Cunningham, who had a profound respect and a personal devotion for Lord Dornoch, could not bear to think of failure; and was filled with bitter thoughts that it was he himself who had started the ball rolling down the slippery slope of acting without orders. It had perhaps been a foolish thing to do, and no doubt His Lordship had also acted foolishly, but he had acted as a man, a Scot and a brave battalion commander who would not stand by and see anyone of

227

his regiment left to die as a result of incompetence and bloody-mindedness and a lack of feeling in high circles. And, as Cunningham had just said, no *disgrace* would attach afterwards, to a Court Martial on a charge of impetuously engaging the enemy. Lord Dornoch had shirked no duty, had chosen no easy option. He would go out of the British Army with his head held high, an officer and a gentleman who had preferred not to skulk behind the golden tassels and cocked hats of the Staff.

'With one proviso,' Cunningham said aloud.

'I beg your pardon, Sar'nt-Major?'

'I'm sorry, sir. I was speaking some thoughts aloud.'

'Then a penny for them, Sar'nt-Major!'

Cunningham shook his head. 'They wouldn't help, Captain Ogilvie, not at this moment. But there's one thing I'll say, and it's this: I hope you'll do your persuading well!'

'You mean, make the most of the *sadhu*?'

'Aye, Captain Ogilvie, I mean just that. They say there's upwards of sixty thousand tribesmen ready in Waziristan, and maybe a great deal more by this time. The 114th are but a thousand men, just under. There must be no massacre ... no wiping out of the regiment. And you'll do me the honour, Captain Ogilvie, of understanding that I speak from no personal fear of battle—'

'Of course, Sar'nt-Major. That goes without saying.'

'Thank you, sir.' Cunningham wiped the back of a hand across his forehead; it came away dripping with sweat. 'I fear for the Colonel, that's the truth. His name would not survive the massacre of a regiment, sir – in the circumstances. You have his honour in your hands now, Captain Ogilvie.'

'I know,' Ogilvie said quietly. 'By God I know, Sar'nt-Major!'

There were halts for rests, to ease the strain on men and horses and also to ensure that they did not too far overshoot Lord Dornoch and the main body of the regiment. Water-bottles were used sparingly, though there was a good hope of replenishing them from the rivers along the way, for the rains had not been too long over for the water-courses to have dried, and cold water was still trickling down from the melted snow on the highest peaks. Iron rations were handed out, also sparingly, and were eked out by fruit that the men picked along the track as they began to descend into the valleys. Ogilvie and

Cunningham spent a good deal of time during these respites in priming the native runner in the part he was to play when Nashkar's army was reached. Cunningham left him in no doubt as to what would happen to him if he said too much, or if he failed to be convincing of the truth. The man, his dark eyes flickering as he followed every move Cunningham and Ogilvie made, was mostly silent, merely nodding when asked if he understood. It was only too obvious that he couldn't be trusted an inch, but Ogilvie formed the impression that he had a due regard for his own life and could probably be made to function just so long as he was firmly in their hands. Moving on, coming farther towards a valley, they entered a more fertile district, with more fruit for the picking, and signs of scattered habitation, and a cluster of huts in the distance, forming a *khel*. As they rode along they could see men coming out from the huts to stand and stare, men who would have seen last night's lunar eclipse and would now be awaiting word to join the concourse of tribesmen towards Gumatti. But they did not come down from their *khel* and made no contact with the riders. Perhaps, Ogilvie thought, they were the old men, the ones who would be left behind. The fighting men may already have left for the assembly zone. By this time that assembly must be complete – and certainly they had seen no movement of armed men anywhere along the way. Waziristan, ready for war, was in a state of suspension, a state of pause and inaction that could be released either way depending upon whose interpretation of last night's events would in the end prevail.

Ogilvie gave a sudden shiver. The day was fine and bright, with long views across the mountains, and the air was invigorating, the wind cold; and Ogilvie, after a whole night with no sleep, was very tired now. But the shiver was not a shiver of cold or weariness; it was the kind of shiver that makes men say that someone is walking over their graves. He was visited by an unnerving sense of failure ahead, almost a premonition of evil and of doom. Suddenly, the whole of their endeavour, all Lord Dornoch's impetuous disregard of the high command, seemed utterly pointless, wasteful and insane.

When another night's full darkness had settled on the mountains and valleys Nashkar Ali Khan, who had come from Maizar by way of a different pass, still accompanied by the Earless One, rode in to join the great gathering of war-bent

Pathans. He entered the arena to the sound of reedy native pipes, and rifle shots, and a wild acclaim. Men surged around him, yelling, chanting, praising, knowing now that the time had come, that their leader had come to announce the meaning of the sign they had all seen, that by the morrow's light they would be rolling across the Waziri borders in a tumultuous rush upon the British.

Nashkar, apparently supremely confident, every inch the war leader, sat his horse surrounded by his advisers, both military and civil. His dress now was splendid. He wore a magnificent sky-blue turban that shone in the light from the many camp-fires, and a long cloak of brilliant red that fell across the rump of his horse, which was also regally caparisoned. His eyes were bright, seeming to reflect the glow of the fires, as he rode slowly through the throng of warriors and the shouts of war, the shouts of '*Kaspaturos ... death to the British, death to the infidel invaders ... death and destruction ... Kaspaturos!*'

Smiling and waving, Nashkar Ali Khan rode towards a low hill, a central point in the gathering. Way was made for him, and with his staff he rode to the top of the gentle incline, remaining mounted, sitting for a while looking out over the flickering fires and the sea of faces that were turned towards him, over the steel of swords and lances and bayonets, the dull gleams from the wooden butts of the rifles; and, listening to the roar of sound, of sheer enthusiasm and pent-up, centuries-old anger and hatred that over the months he had fanned into this strong flame that now burned before him, he was convinced his was an unstoppable force, bound for immense and shattering and final victory.

He stood in his stirrups, lifting a hand. 'The Prophet has spoken,' he said in a loud, carrying voice when the tumult had eased. For a while he could go no farther; the tumult was at once intensified, echoing off the surrounding hills, back and forth like a million tongues. When he was able to speak again he said, 'My people, I have promised you Kaspaturos, and this promise I shall keep, with the help and guidance and strength of Mahomet to lead us on. You have all seen the sign of the Prophet ... his sign to us that all is in our favour and that our cause is just. You have been waiting long, and patiently. I, also, have waited – for the sign, without which we could not move. Thus it is written. Now the long wait is finished, or almost so. Shortly before the next setting of the sun, we shall march. One more day's patience, for it is better that we cross the borders under cover of the full night, when the British are largely sleeping, and their sight is dimmed.'

There was a roar of approval, and more shouts of Kaspaturos, the watchword of the campaign to come. Nashkar's face was full of emotion, but he was under complete control as he turned to Healey. 'A most excellent fighting spirit, Earless One,' he said through the din. 'If the British could but hear the shouts, they would tremble in their beds this night, knowing the truth, which is, that within but a few more sun's risings, the Frontier will have become the grave of the Raj and the grave of all its upholders. So be it! It is written.'

'It is written, Highness. The will of Mahomet shall prevail.' Healey, who had caught only fragments of his speech, paused, his face gleaming with sweat in the fires' light, his naked earholes battered by the rising crescendo of sound that filled the immense natural arena. 'Yet we must still have a care, Highness.'

'Earless One, you must speak much louder, for I cannot hear.' Nashkar waved his arms for silence, and his staff did likewise, standing in their stirrups to demand peace for their leader. Healey himself had been unable to hear Nashkar's last words, but had guessed their meaning.

As the noise decreased, Healey spoke loudly: 'Highness, we must yet have a care. *We do not know where the sadhu is, nor what his interpretation.*'

The words fell into something approaching quiet; by no means a silence, and they were unheard more than a couple of yards away. But Healey had spoken quite loudly enough for his words to be caught by men in the front of the crowd pressing close to the leader. Nashkar, who was far from being a fool, realized this, and realized that the Earless One had committed a rank indiscretion. Fury gripped him like a vice; his face suffused and hardened, and without further thought he struck out viciously, knocking Healey from his horse with the one blow. At once, he realized that another indiscretion had been committed, this time by himself. He controlled his mounting fury, and slid from his horse. Bending, he lifted Healey to his feet and embraced him. 'A thousand pardons, Earless One,' he said loudly. 'I have sinned against my closest, most trusted adviser and friend.' His tone was friendly, placatory, but there was steel beneath. He embraced Healey again, very publicly.

'You will forgive a thoughtless act, brought about by the strain of the long wait for the Prophet to send his sign?'

Healey bowed; they understood one another perfectly well, with crystal clarity. In a loud voice Nashkar Ali Khan said, 'The *sadhu* is safe and sends by me, his servant, the tidings that the Prophet has given the sign. Kaspaturos awaits our coming, and we shall not disappoint the glorious city of our fathers!'

There were cheers and cries, but a good point had been made and overheard nevertheless, as Healey could see, and Highness was going to have a devil of a job working his way clear of *that*. He hid the gleam in his eyes, noting the wondering conversations that were going on in the vicinity, and the outward movement of the warriors, pressing away to pass the word, the shattering word that, unaccountably, the *sadhu* seemed to have vanished without confirming Mahomet's message in person and Highness was trying to gloss this vanishment over. It was very strange; at this moment of all moments, any believer would indeed have expected the *sadhu* to appear and give the message personally. Within ten minutes, by which time Nashkar Ali Khan and his staff were making their way towards a richly ornamented tent being set up by their retinue, there was a noticeable restlessness in the air, and a growing murmur of wonderment. Tongue was given to this restless wonder by the time the leader was about to sit down to a meal. The tongues, growing louder and more numerous every second, were now shouting a different refrain:

'*Where is the sadhu? Why is the sadhu not here? Where is the sadhu? Tell us, O Lord Nashkar, tell us!*'

Seeing the malignant look of fury in Nashkar's eyes, and feeling the hand of death touch his shoulder, Captain Healey bent his face towards his food and smiled inwardly.

Back, angrily, upon the low hilltop, Nashkar Ali Khan once again addressed his tribesmen. 'May the wrath of Mahomet fall upon you if you continue to disturb my due rest, doubters of my word! I tell you, the sign has come and that is all that matters now.'

'*Where is the sadhu, O Lord Nashkar, highest in the land?*'

'The *sadhu* is old, and he is resting. He has had a long fast and he is weak.' The Pathan paused. 'He is in my palace, outside Maizar. He is safe and well, but he is tired, and too old a man to face such a multitude after the loneliness of the hills.'

His face hard, he turned away, striding back through a cleared lane towards his tent. He would say no more; he was not a man much given to explanation. But he grew more disturbed as he heard the noise rising around him, saw the shaken heads and the doubting looks. Savagely, beneath his breath, he cursed the very existence of the *sadhu*, whose unknown fate, though he had allowed none except the Earless One to see his anxiety, had been causing him worry ever since the sign itself had come but had not been reported from the *sadhu*'s lonely peak. It was possible, of course, that the *sadhu*, knowing full well that the sign would have been seen all over Waziristan, had in the event felt no need to signify further. Yet it was most unlikely; he had had the runner for the express purpose of sending his confirmation ... and the men whom Nashkar had dispatched subsequently had not yet returned.

The answer, of course, to any reasonable man, must lie in Wilshaw Sahib.

Back in his ornate tent, Nashkar Ali Khan strode up and down restlessly, deeply concerned now. In anger he listened to the mob-sounds outside. The sign had come, had been so clearly manifested to all, and he, Nashkar Ali Khan himself, had given his confirmation of its meaning! Who were the tribesmen, to doubt him and to demand further evidence? Who indeed! They were a rabble – but he could achieve nothing without them. And, being a Pathan, a man of ancient race, with the same deep, inborn faith, the same superstitious link with a remote past, he could not but understand and, in understanding, tremble for the implications.

'It was you, Earless One, who induced me to trust Wilshaw Sahib,' he said bitterly. 'This makes me ask myself why it was I grew to have trust in you!'

'Highness, I have done nothing to lessen your trust. I was as deceived by Wilshaw Sahib as you were, and we do not know that he went towards the *sadhu*.'

'Then where is the *sadhu*, where is his messenger, Earless One? And one thing we do know, and this is, that it was you who talked too loudly of the fact that the *sadhu* had not personally spoken. I shall remember this. If my ambitions are frustrated, Earless One, I shall know where to turn for my revenge!' Nashkar resumed his restless pacing, watched by Healey. Healey recognized the leader's dilemma. Of a certainty more men could be sent to the west, to seek out the *sadhu* and discover, if they could, what had happened to the men sent to him earlier. But if something *had* happened those fresh men would see it, and would return with bad tidings, and the tidings would spread like wild-fire, and that, indeed, would be the end of the affair.

Healey left the tent while Nashkar prowled; and in his own way continued the good work, by nods and winks and shrugs and a mournful face when questioned by the anxious tribesmen. The *sadhu*, he confirmed again and again, had indeed not signified, and no one could say where he was. It was very strange, and very disturbing, and the omens were now far from good.

Ogilvie had halted his troops some while before, with the encampment distantly in view.

'I've no doubt they'll have posted sentries,' he said. 'We'll keep well outside the perimeter for the time being. Mr. Cunningham, if you please?'

'Sir!'

'Keep the men in cover – we'll do a little scouting on our own account before we move on. D'you see the lie of the land?'

'It looks as if they're in a kind of bowl, sir, hemmed in by the hills.'

'Yes. And this track leads right in. I think we'll have to climb, Sar'nt-Major. Get into the hills, and look for that vantage point to address them from as the Colonel wanted – somewhere defendable, for preference!'

'Aye, sir. It's true we'd not stand a chance if we rode straight into the mass. I'll detail scouts right away, sir, and accompany them myself, with your permission.'

'Thank you, Sar'nt-Major.'

Cunningham wheeled his horse, walking it away as quietly as possible. Ogilvie heard his low voice, issuing orders to the men. As those not required for scout duty moved silently into such cover as they could find beside the track, and dismounted, Ogilvie sat his horse and stared ahead towards the enemy's distant camp. It was an uncomfortable feeling, to be so close, in such miniscule numbers, to that immense fighting force of fanatical Pathan warriors. They could be overwhelmed in an instant, hacked to pieces almost before they had had a chance to sight their rifles, if events should go against them now. As he sat in the stillness, the awe-inspiring silence of the lonely hills gripped him, seeming to press down upon his ears like a blanket. But after a while he became aware of some curious distant sound, one that at first he could not identify. It was a kind of murmur, low but continuing, a sound that could perhaps be the shouts of very many men, a sound of war and fervour. The tribesmen were being whipped up to a frenzy, evidently. It was not a healthy sound.

Dismounting after Cunningham and the scouts had moved away, Ogilvie led his horse back towards his hidden troop. He had a word with each of the soldiers, reminding them that there was to be no firing, whatever the provocation, unless and until he gave the word. The lives of all of them, he impressed upon them, hung upon a total avoidance of fighting. They would come upon the vast encampment as men bearing information, not arms. They had to be seen to come in peace, at any rate until the regiment arrived and deployed around the perimeter.

'It'll merely be the bigger slaughter when that happens,' a private named Mauchline said.

'Come, Mauchline,' Ogilvie said sharply. 'You didn't speak that way, when you made contact with me back in that pass, did you?'

'I've had time to think a wee bit more since then, sir.'

'And time to get cold feet?'

'No, sir. A wee grain o' sense, that's all!' He spat at Ogilvie's feet, mutinously. 'We'll all be dead by sunrise and you know it, Captain Ogilvie.'

'I know no such thing!' Ogilvie felt his face whitening with anger. 'You'll stop talking like this at once, Mauchline, and you'll obey orders as a soldier of the 114th, or I'll have you before the Colonel the moment we return to cantonments, on a charge of insolence.'

'I've no' said a word that's insolent, sir!'

'The army's not yet finished with the charge of dumb insolence, Mauchline, as well you know,' Ogilvie reminded him. 'But now I'll tell you something else: if you continue undermining morale, *you*'ll be dead by sunrise without a doubt, for I shall exercise my prerogative as an officer in command of troops confronting the enemy, and I shall shoot you.'

'You don't mean that, Captain Ogilvie!'

Ogilvie gave a grim laugh. 'I hope you'll not be trying to find out,' he said, and turned away. He was conscious of the thud of his heart, of a dryness in his mouth. Never before had he made such a threat; until now, he would not have believed himself capable of it. But he had spoken in temper because he had the feeling, very strongly, that the imminent events would be decisive, that on the efforts of his small force could well depend the future of the whole of the British Raj, or at the very least the fragile stability of the North-West Frontier. A grandiose thought, perhaps; but a valid one. Empires in the past had hung upon as gossamer a thread. The repercussions of a wholesale slaughter in North-West India would shake the British Empire badly, would rock the foundations of Windsor Castle itself, probably topple the Viceroy in Calcutta and the Government in Westminster. It was a huge responsibility for a mere Captain of Infantry in his twenty-third year; but it was possibly an even greater one to shoot a defenceless private, to commit what under other circumstances would be a cold-blooded, premeditated murder. Ogilvie's anguish was real enough as he sent up a prayer that Private Mauchline would not force him to face up to his threat.

They waited. They waited in silence mostly now, with Ogilvie's ears attuned to the sound still coming, more strongly he fancied, from the distant camp. It was more than an hour before Cunningham returned with his scouting party. 'There's a route to the north, sir,' the R.S.M. reported. 'It's a difficult climb, and the horses'll not make it, but I believe it will suit our purpose. There's a tongue of rock jutting out, so far as I can see – projecting close to the perimeter of the camp.'

'Did you get near the camp?'

'Not too close, sir. I thought it best not to risk being seen—'

'Quite right—'

'—but near enough sir, to hear a deal of racket. You can hear it even from here.'

'So I've noticed. What is it, d'you think, Sar'nt-Major?'

Cunningham shrugged. 'It'll be the blood-stirrers at work, sir, the fanatics. They'll be in a high state, sir. We can only hope it'll not be so high they'll not listen to what the runner has to say.'

Their eyes met; Ogilvie looked at Cunningham's strong features, saw him lift a hand to twirl at the once-waxed end of his moustache, which was now drooping down his chin like a Chinaman's. In a low voice, as they stood apart from the rest of the men, Ogilvie asked, 'What d'you make the chances, Sar'nt-Major?'

'Oh, we'll get by, sir, never fear!'

'Yes, but I want to know, Sar'nt-Major.' He repeated his question. 'What are the real chances?'

'Chances, Captain Ogilvie?' Cunningham looked back along the way he had just come, towards the camp and the flickering night-fires that were now being lit as darkness started to come down. He reached out a hamlike hand, which he placed with rough affection on Ogilvie's shoulder. 'The British Army's well used to long odds, sir. A touch of boldness has often enough won the day, long before now. I told you – we'll get by! It's a custom we have.' He hesitated. 'But just in case we don't all come out, sir, I'll wish you luck. You've always been a credit to the regiment, sir, if I may say so – and to your father.'

He reached out a hand. Ogilvie took it, and gave it a warm clasp. 'And the same to you, Bosom – if I may say so!'

Without further talk, Cunningham, assuming what the order would be, turned away and roused the men from their cover, forming them up to ride as far as the northward-leading track he had found. 'We'll need to leave the horses once we reach the incline, Captain Ogilvie,' he said. 'We must chance them being found.'

'Right you are, Sar'nt-Major. I'll leave a man on guard, for what good it'll do. We may be in need of those horses!'

'Aye, sir.' They moved out, heading through the increasing darkness for the invasion army's perimeter, quietly, carrying their rifles at the ready. Within ten minutes they had reached the foot of the climb, within fifteen they had moved all the horses up as far as they could go, and had left them under guard on a small plateau off the track. As they climbed from there, Ogilvie gave orders for the men to collect what wood they could find en route. 'I've an idea a fire would help,' he explained to Cunningham. 'It'll attract attention – that is, if we can light it.'

'I have matches, sir.'

'I thought you would, Sar'nt-Major! Where d'you keep them, in that rig you're wearing?'

'Uncomfortably, sir – in my loin-cloth. We must hope they're not sweated through.' They went on, climbing, scrambling up, dislodging rocks and stones and debris from the hillside. The moon was visible now, eclipse-free; there was a little cloud coming up from the north-west, and there was wind that freshened as they gained height. After some ten minutes Ogilvie saw the jut of rock described by Cunningham, distantly protruding towards the dotted fires that illuminated the bowl of the hills. The sounds were louder now, though spasmodic, for the wind was taking them and flinging them away into the emptiness from time to time, as it gusted fitfully. A little more climbing and the way flattened out, becoming a good deal easier. They made good speed after that, going farther ahead now than Cunningham had gone earlier, still seeing no sentries. This Ogilvie did not find especially surprising, in spite of his caution in halting his troop in cover in case there should be any posted. Nashkar Ali Khan would scarcely be expecting any sudden forays by the British Army or indeed anyone else; any men who came along this way would have the sole intention of joining his levies for the forthcoming attack. Another short, fast march brought Ogilvie's small force to the verge of the long tongue of rock, and thereafter they moved with greater circumspection, falling, in due course, upon their stomachs and creeping painfully onward like snakes in the night, carrying rifles and the gathered wood with difficulty. The moon was bright now, spreading silver over all; Ogilvie could see the assembled tribesmen plainly, and the immensity of the gathering appalled him. Now the cries were filling their ears with a sound of sheer menace. There was a hate-fed fury in those almost animal cries and yells, more hate in the rifles that were being brandished in the air. Nashkar Ali Khan must be having his work cut out, Ogilvie thought, to hold these wild hillmen in check until he was ready to march – and wondered, indeed, why he had not marched before this. With that howling mob tearing through the passes and bounding down on Peshawar and Nowshera and Murree, no one was going to have a chance. And behind them, when Nashkar called for their support, would come the Afghan hordes from beyond the Khyber, riding past the forts at Torkham, and Ali Masjid high on its rock, and Landi Kotal, and Jamrud ... passing hell-bent into British India with fire and sword.

Slowly, carefully, as yet unseen, they crawled forward towards the end of the tongue of rock, a tongue that Ogilvie soon saw ran right against the perimeter, in fact pressed into it like a sword against flesh, forming a natural stage for the performance he was about to put on, an apron stage lifted some twenty feet above his audience, with steep, sheer sides falling to the floor of the bowl. Still some way from the end, Ogilvie called a halt. He looked through field-glasses towards what appeared to be the central point of the great arena, where a tent stood. There was a strong guard around this tent and so far as Ogilvie could make out, the tribesmen were being kept back, held outside the ring of guards.

Puzzled, he passed the glasses to Cunningham.

'What d'you make of it, Sar'nt-Major?' he asked.

After a long and careful scrutiny the R.S.M. said, 'It's hard to say, sir. It could be enthusiasm. But to me it has not quite that look.'

'Nor me. Let's have the glasses again.' Ogilvie once again scanned the scene below, running the lenses over the fires and the farther perimeter and the seething mass of armed, shouting men. Those shouts didn't seem to be all enthusiasm, either. He said, 'I've a feeling something's gone a little wrong.'

'Aye, sir, and so have I!'

'Then this could be the moment to make it go more wrong still – don't you think, Sar'nt-Major?'

'I do, sir.'

'Then have the runner brought up, if you please, Mr. Cunningham. We'll take him forward between the two of us from here. Have you the matches ready?'

'Aye, sir.' Cunningham slid backwards on his stomach, returned within half a minute at a crouch, with the runner ahead of his claymore. The man sat on his haunches, rolling the whites of his eyes and plucking at his beard. Ogilvie, speaking in Pushtu, told him he would be required to make his announcement shortly now. The runner was shaking badly; he was a very scared man indeed, torn between the present threat to his life and the worse threat that would develop if his own countrymen should get their hands on him once he had brought down their high hopes of conquest.

'Hold tight to him, Sar'nt-Major,' Ogilvie said. 'And two men behind him. If he attempts to break away, a bayonet in his buttocks. No firing from any of you, as I've said. Not unless I order it, or Mr. Cunningham if I'm killed. We'll all go forward from here at the run – no more crawling. I doubt if anybody's looking this way in any case. When I halt you, I want the fire prepared and lit as soon as possible. Are you all ready?'

There was a murmur of assent. Cunningham put the two

men behind the runner and Ogilvie gave the word to advance. They went ahead fast, with two shining bayonets pricking into the Pathan runner's backside and Ogilvie's and Cunningham's hands gripping his arms. In three minutes they had reached the end of the jut of rock, and, apparently, had still not been seen. 'Right, the fire!' Ogilvie snapped. He was shaking himself now, shaking with impatience and a sudden hope, a feeling that this was going to work out. No one could fail now to recognize the note of anger and dismay in the continuing din below. Quickly the men built up the gathered wood, and Cunningham bent and struck his matches, shielding the flames in cupped hands against the cold wind, trying to catch the smaller twigs. At last, with the aid of a scrap of paper and some of his own filthy clothing, he succeeded. The tiny flames curled upwards through the network of dry wood, growing larger and larger until the whole fire was crackling and throwing out a welcome enough heat. Now it must be clearly seen.

With Cunningham and the runner, and the watchful men with the bayonets in rear, Ogilvie stepped to the edge of the rock, where they were outlined in their native dress against the leaping flames. Lifting an arm, he called down.

'*Men of the tribes. I have word for you!*'

There was no response; there was too much din for his words to be heard. He called again and again until he was hoarse with the effort; then the Regimental Sergeant-Major lifted his voice in a parade-ground bellow, with no more effect than Ogilvie as it seemed at first. But a few moments later the racket did seem to die away just a little, and there was some rifle fire, though no shots came close to the men on the jut of rock. In this lull, the R.S.M. shouted again, and they noticed that many faces, more and more of them, were turning in their direction at last and the tribesmen were coming towards their sector of the perimeter.

When there was a little peace, a lull in the vicinity at any rate, Ogilvie repeated what he had called out earlier: 'I have word for you.' Below, the interest clearly quickened; the tribesmen gave the appearance of listening intently. Ogilvie shouted, 'I come from the peak . . . the peak where the *sadhu* kept his long vigil. The *sadhu* is dead. The *sadhu* died in the moment that the sign was given, struck down because he was misleading you.'

He paused, trying to gauge the effect so far.

Another sound was rising up now; a sound that was hard at

this stage to interpret – a low but increasing murmur that could be of concern or could be of hostility. Rifles and swords were brandished; quarrelling broke out. Ogilvie waved his arm again, and he and Cunningham dragged the reluctant runner closer to the edge. He shouted, 'Peace, O brothers, and listen to the truth. I say again, the sign was wrongly explained by the *sadhu*. Unguided, you do not wish for war! You wish to live in peace and happiness, that you and your families may not be killed, for assuredly, if you cross the borders with hostile intent, you will be conquered, vanquished for all time, and your race decimated. It is written. You cannot succeed . . . and as a sign, Mahomet has slain the *sadhu*. Listen now to the words of the *sadhu*'s own messenger, who with his own eyes witnessed the *sadhu*'s death.'

Cunningham jerked the runner's arm savagely, thrusting him forward, and, with his free hand, slamming his claymore against his spine. 'Talk, you bastard,' he said, 'and talk just as you've been told!'

The man opened his mouth. By this time a complete hush had fallen in the immediate vicinity, though there was still plenty of noise from farther off, where their presence had not yet been especially noted. 'Come on!' Ogilvie snapped. 'All you have to do is to tell the truth.'

The man, shaking like a leaf, began. 'Brothers, what you have been told is true. I saw the *sadhu* die. As the sign sent by Mahomet faded from the face of the moon, the *sadhu* was struck down from the peak, to fall and die in the pass far below. Truly, the *sadhu* is dead.' There was no doubting his sincerity.

There was a momentary gasp from the mob, followed by another hush; then pandemonium broke out. Men shouted and called out, brandished weapons, fell upon their knees; then broke away to the rear, calling the terrible tidings – the confirmation of the rumour that had already run like wildfire through the mass: '*The sadhu is dead, the sadhu is dead, and Mahomet is displeased . . . the sadhu is dead!*'

Ogilvie stepped back, his head swimming and sweat pouring from his body like a flood. Within the next ten minutes, the whole arena was a bedlam. The British stood their ground, watchfully, waiting for the next development. As Ogilvie said to Cunningham, they couldn't leave yet. Someone, surely, was going to demand proof. He was right; soon a mounted procession was seen coming through the yelling, screaming mob, the mob that was so clearly no longer an army in the full control of its leaders. Through the field-glasses Ogilvie recognized the figure of Nashkar Ali Khan, with Healey alongside him, and some of the officials from the palace outside Maizar. They were being hustled along for their own safety but still guarded from the hands of the infuriated tribesmen. They were escorted close to the foot of the rock, where they halted. Nashkar Ali Khan's eyes blazed up at Ogilvie; his face was still proud and unafraid, arrogant, even splendid in what must be approaching defeat and soon after, most probably, death at his followers' hands. Captain Healey's face was impassive, giving nothing away. He was a strange man, and inexplicable Ogilvie thought . . .

Nashkar Ali Khan called up: 'So we meet once more, Wilshaw Sahib. What is this nonsense about the *sadhu*? You come with lies to my people, you, who are a British spy! The *sadhu*, as I have explained, is safe in my palace, but is old and tired, and cannot come here. Why do you lie, other than to save your British imperialists?'

Ogilvie said, 'I do not lie. The *sadhu* is dead. The runner saw this, and confirms all I have said.'

There was a smile on the Pathan leader's face now. 'Then where is the body?' he called in a strong, confident voice. 'Produce the body, and we shall believe!'

He was game right to the last, Ogilvie reflected. It was a dangerous bluff, for the body could easily enough have been up there on the rock, ready to view. But as it happened, of course, Nashkar's bluff was a good one. Ogilvie mentally saluted a brave and still wily and dangerous man. He hesitated, then caught Cunningham's eye. Cunningham nodded and said, 'I'd let them have it straight, Captain Ogilvie. It'll all help to addle their minds for them – or maybe sort them out! And a little exaggeration wouldn't come amiss, sir.'

'Right!' Ogilvie lifted his voice towards the tribesmen: 'You must be patient. Proof will be given soon. The body of the *sadhu*, destroyed in anger by Mahomet, is on its way. It is being brought by an escort . . . an escort of four divisions of the British Army who are marching upon you now from your rear, and who will drive you across your own borders into the guns of the British Raj, waiting for you beyond the passes.'

He stopped, and moved back from the edge. There was a burst of firing, probably from the leader's personal bodyguard, but no one was hit. Before he had stepped back Ogilvie had seen the look of fury in Nashkar's face, and the curious smile that twisted Healey's mouth. As they all moved back from the end of the stage, Cunningham said, 'Now, sir, we're in for a dirty night!'

They formed a watchful square in the old tradition of the British Army, all the rifles facing outwards, ready for attack from any quarter, with the native runner safely in the centre between Ogilvie and Cunningham. They were rock-steady, even Private Mauchline now, as they began the last long wait for the arrival of the battalion or their own deaths. They listened to the noise from the great arena, noise that rose and fell and rose again. From time to time Ogilvie crawled on his stomach towards the edge, and looked down. Each time he saw Nashkar Ali Khan and Healey, in the middle of the loyal body-guard. It seemed they had not been allowed to move away. Nashkar was maintaining his proud, arrogant bearing, gazing around disdainfully at the tribesmen and their menacing aspect; but it was as clear as the sun at noon that the control had passed right out of his hands. Everywhere fiery, bearded men were addressing the tribes, each with his little, or big, band of listeners. Already some of the men had streamed away, taking no chances on being caught by British enfilading gunfire in the confines of the bowl in the hills. Ogilvie could only guess what theories, what advices were being offered by the various tub-thumpers in the arena. No doubt some would be for waiting to see if the British really did arrive, some would be for Nash-kar still, ready to remain and fight to the last man if the divisions came in. Others, like those already gone, would go either soon or when the first British soldier made his presence known. Decisions would be made, and reversed, and made again, and then reversed again, as each would-be leader made his point and lost it to a louder, more appealing voice. It was, and would remain, the most fluid of fluid military situations.

Nashkar's voice alone was the totally disregarded one now.

The first attack on the British position came at a little after 2 a.m. Ogilvie himself was the first to spot the movement along the inward end of the jut of rock, and was quick to order the rifles into action. The attack was held off, but two of the Royal Strathspeys died. In the next attack, they sustained two wounded, only lightly. In the third, which came after a pause of almost three hours, the native runner was shot through the head and died, and Cunningham received a flesh wound in his upper arm. After this there was some sniping, as the dawn rose in spectacular colours over the eastern rim of the hills. All told the Royal Strathspeys accounted seven men dead, including the two first wounded; and including Mauchline, who thus himself fulfilled his own prophecy in the end. Ogilvie, remembering his threatened 'prerogative', was particularly moved by this casualty. The problems and self-recriminations of command were endless, though a good officer, perhaps, would not dwell on the self-recriminatory angle, except in so far as he could learn a little from his heart-searching. Ogilvie had no personal knowledge of Private Mauchline, who was not one of his own company, but he had been a mature enough man to have had a wife and children – somebody, at any rate, who cared enough about a Scottish soldier to have his or her life now laid in ruins by what had happened on this remote Waziri hillside.

'My God, when's the battalion coming up?' Ogilvie asked, and almost failed to recognize the sound of his own voice.

'They'll be here, sir, never fear.' It was Cunningham who answered, Cunningham with a blood-stained strip of shirting tied round one arm. 'Meanwhile we have another visitor. Look, sir.'

He pointed.

Ogilvie looked. Three men were coming out from the inward end of the rock, one of them carrying a white flag tied to a pole. 'A flag of truce! Sar'nt-Major, it looks as if we've done it—'

'Not so fast, sir. I'm thinking they want only to talk, to parley. Listen, sir. The man's calling out.'

Ogilvie listened, a hand cupped to his ear.

The Pathan, a tall man with a heavy beard, called, 'We wish the Englishman to come back with us alone – Wilshaw Sahib. He will not be harmed.'

'If I were you, sir, I'd stay right here,' Cunningham said.

'Wait. What do you want with me?' Ogilvie called back.

'One of our leaders, a *malik* opposed to Nashkar Ali Khan, wishes to hear your story face to face.'

'Then why does he not come here?'

There was a pause. 'This cannot be done, Wilshaw Sahib. Do as we ask and you will be safe. Refuse, and all your soldiers will be killed.'

Ogilvie blew out his cheeks. 'I'll have to do as he says,' he told Cunningham. 'I'll not risk the men.'

'You'll be foolish to believe the bastard,' Cunningham growled. 'I'd not go, sir.'

'You would if you were in my shoes, Sar'nt-Major, and you know it! I've got to go. I repeat, I'll not risk the men.' There was still pandemonium below. 'This may help. If I can persuade one of the *maliks* personally . . .'

'Why not wait for the battalion to come up, sir?'

Ogilvie grinned. 'I don't believe the foreign gentleman's in a waiting mood, Sar'nt-Major, that's why!' Without further argument he stood up and moved away from the small, decimated square. He lifted his hands above his head. 'I come,' he called out. 'Alone and without weapons.'

His heart beating fast, he advanced towards the waiting enemy delegation.

It was a terrible scene, below in the huge arena. There was fire and death and fighting, wild surgings to and fro of the rival factions. His own escort was attacked more than once, but each time some tribesmen sprang to their aid, and wielded their weapons, and more men died. Over all was the noise, the cries, the shouting. In his heart Ogilvie wished he'd heeded Cunningham's words of wisdom. He was, in truth, mortally afraid now, and realized he had done a foolish thing, though he had seen little alternative in view of the threat to his small force, if it could be called a force any longer. Away in the distance he could see Nashkar Ali Khan still, surrounded by wild men – and then he saw Captain Healey, leaving the Pathan's side and fighting his way through on horseback, a sword whirling above his head, laying about him from side to side, savagely.

Healey was coming towards him. There was no sign so far of any *malik*, anyone who appeared anxious to talk to him. Healey, dripping blood from many gashes, pulled up his horse in front of Ogilvie and his escort. As the animal reared on its hind legs, its front hooves almost beat out Ogilvie's brains.

'What are you doing here?' Healey demanded.

'I was brought.'

'What for?'

'To talk to a malik—'

'You'll talk to no *malik*, old boy. Get to hell and gone this minute! Go on, clear off!'

245

'Easier said than done, isn't it – old boy?'

Healey grinned and, from the back of his horse, gave a small bow. 'Your servant, my dear sir.' He headed his horse right into the escort, leaned down, and almost nonchalantly sent his sword slicing through one of the necks, then another. The third man, the one with the white flag, threw down his burden and fled. Healey said, 'It was a trap, old boy. Take your chance now, and get out, back to your men. Here – take my horse.' He slid to the ground and handed the reins to Ogilvie. Fighting surged around them still; they were in a kind of oasis, if only a temporary and highly dangerous one. 'Now – ride out, Ogilvie. And don't worry about me. Rejoin your regiment, and may God go with you till you do.'

'But Healey—'

'Off with you! Are you like me, old boy – no ears? Can't you *hear*?'

In bewilderment Ogilvie listened to the mixed sounds of fighting, the cries of men and the neighing of the horses; already Healey had moved away on foot, and seemed to be looking out for another mount. Ogilvie swung himself into the saddle of Healey's horse and then, losing no more time, headed back along the way he had come into the arena, digging his heels in and riding like the wind. And as he sped like an arrow through the milling hordes, the by now utterly confused hordes of tribesmen, dodging bullets and bayonet thrusts and the whirling, slicing swords, he began to hear the sounds, so faint at first, so thin, so reedy, so insubstantial, the distant but closing sounds of the pipes and drums of the 114th Highlanders borne along the wind as they marched to relieve his tiny force. Soon the sounds came stronger, bringing a lump into Ogilvie's throat as the regiment came on, the words drumming through his head:

> *The Campbells are coming, they are, they are*
> *The Campbells are coming, hurrah, hurrah*
> *The Campbells are coming to bonnie Loch Leven*
> *The Campbells are coming, they are, they are!*

The tribes began to hear it. The men on the jut of rock had told the truth and the British Army was coming in. There was a fresh stir in the arena, an instinctive movement away.

The head of the regimental column wound into view from

the rock, snake-like as it twisted along the pass below. Behind the pipers and the drummers, now in full uniform and resplendent, Lord Dornoch was riding, still in native dress, and behind him marched the companies with their officers and Colour-Sergeants and Corporals – marching smartly in their weird assortment of clothing and marching proudly. Across the horse of one of the officers a white-wrapped bundle was laid. Cunningham turned to Ogilvie, who had now rejoined. 'That'll be the *sadhu*, sir.' He added, 'This looks much like victory, though I'd sooner have seen the Colonel come in in darkness than now, for the size of the force will soon be seen, and they'll know we exaggerated, sir.'

'It won't matter. The regiment could be merely the van . . . and I don't believe they'll wait to see in any case! Just look at that, Sar'nt-Major!'

Cunningham looked down into the great bowl of the assembly arena. There was sheer panic as the bulk of the once confident native levies strove to get clear before the expected British guns reached the surrounding crests and opened. For now the arena had become in their view a rat-trap and would become a slaughter ground once the British troops had climbed to the heights. It was a rout now, or almost. A fairly large number of the tribesmen were in fact standing their ground – but, as soon became evident, they were doing much more than that.

They were standing guard over Nashkar Ali Khan.

The Pathan and his staff were sitting their horses in the centre of this guard while a cloud of dust swept across the bowl, dust stirred up by the thousands of milling feet. Ogilvie turned away and sent two of his remaining privates down to act as guides to the Colonel, informing him that Ogilvie advised the bringing of the *sadhu*'s body to the rock for final display. Then he smiled across at the R.S.M. 'Last act coming up,' he said.

Wordlessly, Cunningham nodded. Ogilvie looked down once more, looked down towards Nashkar Ali Khan in his finery. He noted that Healey had not rejoined the Pathan leader, was nowhere to be seen. He recalled Healey's words, the last he had spoken just before he, Ogilvie, had made his escape from the palace escort: *'Don't think too badly of me, old boy.'* Strange last words, those! What was the truth about Captain Edward Healey, late the Bengal Lancers? As Ogilvie had remarked on their very first encounter, Healey was a little off his normal beat around Ootacamund – in fact some fifteen hundred miles off it, though of course he'd had an explanation for this. Yes — strange!

Cunningham broke into his thoughts. 'You know what is going to happen now, sir?'

'Yes.'

'It's not pleasant to have to watch such things.'

'I know. Nashkar was only fighting for what *he* believed to be right — just the same as us. I wonder if the world will ever learn?'

'It will not, sir, it will not! Our trade will last till the day of judgment.'

'One day, it may be our turn to be thrown out of India.'

Cunningham was shocked. 'Never, sir! Never! With great respect, sir, that's not a sentiment for a British officer to have.'

'No, you're right, Sar'nt-Major, it's not.' Ogilvie lifted a hand and rubbed wearily at his eyes. 'There's a lot of cruelty in the native States, and we do our best to clean the place up and bring some kind of justice to bear. I don't know if we really succeed or not. Here they come, Sar'nt-Major.'

They turned as the sudden increase in the volume of the pipes and drums announced that they were emerging into the open from the cleft in the hills. On the peaks around the nearer sector, heads were already appearing, and bayonetted rifles. Coming onto the rock projection was one half-company of the Royal Strathspeys, led by Rob MacKinlay with Lord Dornoch ahead of him, on foot now. In the lead were the pipes and drums, their kilts a splendid splash of bright colour amidst the barren brown of the hills and the blown dust of the arena, as the tartan of the Royal Strathspey swirled around the knees of the men. In the centre of the half-company two privates, in front of a Colour-Sergeant, carried the white-shrouded burden, the *sadhu*'s corpse.

They marched straight down the rock as if on parade at Invermore in Scotland, the pipes and drums beating out in succession The High Road to Gairloch, The Heroes of Vittoria, and the Old 93rd. Ogilvie felt a surge of pride as the notes of war beat off the hills; so, obviously, did Cunningham. The R.S.M. was standing stiff and straight, his big chest thrust out against his rags; and Ogilvie fancied he caught a moist gleam in his eye as the battalion marched swinging up, to the tune now of Farewell to the Creeks, to halt on the Colonel's order, smartly and together. The pipes fell silent, and the Regimental

Sergeant-Major, helmetless though he was, gave an almost fierce salute; so did Ogilvie.

Lord Dornoch looked out over the arena below. 'All's well, Captain Ogilvie?'

'We're still here, Colonel,' he answered inadequately.

'So I see, so I see! Casualties?'

'Seven dead, Colonel.'

'That's bad – but not as bad as it might have been, God knows! I have a feeling of victory. Your arm, Sar'nt-Major?'

'It's nothing, sir, just needs a wash and a decent bandage.'

The Colonel nodded. 'Your report, James, if you please.'

'Yes, Colonel.' Ogilvie made his report in full and added, 'The levies have largely gone, as you can see, Colonel. I think they know already they've had the truth about the *sadhu* after all!'

'So it would seem. But having brought him all this way, he must still be made to play his final part, James, and dispel any lingering doubts! And we'll lose no time over it.' Turning, he signed to the Colour-Sergeant in charge of the corpse. The Colour-Sergeant and the two privates moved away from the half-company, carrying their burden to the edge of the rock. From the arena, every eye was watching them. The air now was very still, and there was a tense silence and expectancy; even the brooding hills seemed to be an integral part of the drama, seemed to be watching and waiting.

Dornoch nodded briefly, and the Colour-Sergeant flipped away the shroud at his feet. The two privates hoisted the skinny, almost disembowelled corpse to shoulder height, and walked with it to the brink. The sightless eyes of the old holy man stared across the arena, and on his shattered skull a few wispy hairs moved slightly in a waft of breeze.

For a moment the dead silence held.

Then, low at first but increasing, a murmur arose, almost a keening, a sound of total despair that quickly changed to hostility and menace. Around Nashkar Ali Khan, around the Earless One, the mob suddenly seemed to explode inwards, pressing, yelling, fighting. The personal escort, whether or not they remained loyal no one could see for certain, were overwhelmed. Nashkar Ali Khan was jostled, seemed for a moment to be lifted high above the mob, his brilliant red cloak hanging now in strips and the sky-blue turban awry, and then a sword flashed in the strong sunlight and came down on the leader's neck, slicing through it. The severed head lifted in the air, then fell into the midst of the infuriated mob, and at that moment the firing started. Bullets swept the rock, and the Royal Strathspeys flattened to the ground behind their rifles as they returned the fire. Simultaneously the rest of the battalion, disposed around the one sector of the arena, also opened fire with rifles and machine-guns. The Maxims were deadly. In the confusion, in the rout that this firing brought down upon the shaken, disillusioned remnant of the tribal levies, Lord Dornoch executed a rapid withdrawl from the rock, leaving the *sadhu*'s body behind. Looking back, Ogilvie fancied he caught a glimpse of Captain Healey laying about himself with a sword and spurring his horse towards a gap in the hills, but he could not be sure. Later, when the battalion had re-formed and was marching in column of route behind the pipes and drums, right across the arena to the east which, as the Colonel said, was the quickest way home, he saw no sign of Healey among the few living and the many dead.

'I'd *like* to Court Martial him!' Fettleworth snapped. 'But how the devil *can* I? He's a – a blasted hero! So is that young Ogilvie. I suppose you've read Sir George White's telegraphed comments, and the Viceroy's?'

'Yes, indeed,' the Chief of Staff said.

'Well, then! Oh, tear the damn Court Martial papers up!' General Fettleworth wriggled furiously beneath his uniform tunic. 'And Lakenham!'

'Sir?'

'You've treated this particular matter in confidence all along, of course?'

'Of course, sir.'

Fettleworth drummed his fingers on his desk; there was an absent yet furtive look in his eye. With only his Chief of Staff and his aide-de-camp, possibly one or two others, aware that he had started a Court Martial file, something might yet be saved. He fizzed and fussed, trying to think the matter out sanely. Dornoch had done well – so had Ogilvie. Very, very well. He, Fettleworth himself, had been responsible for sending Ogilvie in on that mission. Ha! He preened a little, feeling happier . . . but of course the same couldn't quite be said about the movement of the 114th Highlanders . . .

Not without a little covering up, anyway, a few little fibs. It was extraordinary what could be achieved, quite extraordinary, by a word here and there, a hint, a nod, a tactful silence. A good deal could be made to rub off, as it were, on a Divisional Commander one of whose regiments had done so splendidly. And perhaps a very straight talk to that fellow Black about his drinking habits might be better than the publicity of a Court Martial? Yes.

'Interesting — what you've told me about Healey,' O'Kelly said, fondling the hairy body of Wolseley.

'Yes, isn't it.' Ogilvie was damnably tired and was finding concentration difficult and O'Kelly's suave manner irritating. 'He said you were at school with him, by the way.' Then he added, 'You were wrong about Kaspaturos being Peshawar, I fancy, Major, although Healey had an idea that could turn out to be the case. As a theory, I never heard it advanced by Nashkar Ali Khan or anyone else ... though I suppose it's possible the *sadhu* might have come out with it if he'd lived.'

'Well, it doesn't much matter,' O'Kelly said. 'So long as Kaspaturos was somewhere around these parts, it'd have been good enough to suit Nashkar's purpose of tribal inflammation. In fact, I gather from your report it *was* good enough.'

'Yes ...'

'Healey, now. Yes, I was at school with him.' O'Kelly leaned back in his chair and lifted a glass of whisky to his lips, thoughtfully. He frowned. 'Curious chap — very. Odd, you know. Never quite *saw* him in the service — not in the cavalry, anyhow—'

'He was a good horseman.'

'Oh, I know, but I don't mean that, old boy. I mean, he's not the sort to *fit*. He was never a really *pukka sahib*, hadn't the conventional outlook at all. Really, he was a bit of a case.' The Political Officer gave Ogilvie a long, hard stare. 'I don't see why I shouldn't tell you in the circumstances. Damn it — you're entitled! Mind you ... it's supposed to be secret.' He cleared his throat and stroked Wolseley. 'Healey disappeared from Southern Command about a year ago. No one knew what had happened to him, and for various reasons it was never made public that he'd gone. He was written off as missing, believed killed on duty. But you see, I *knew* Healey as well as anyone ever did know him. I suppose you didn't know he was a *chi-chi*?'

251

'No!' Ogilvie was startled.

'Well, only remotely. His grandmother was a Pathan woman . . . the grandfather, who never actually *married* her, was a Major on Sir Henry Havelock's staff in Afghanistan a long while ago. It's a long story – he told me it all once, when he'd had a good deal to drink. In a way, the army being what it is, it's a wonder he was ever commissioned. But he's got a damn good brain, you know. Never made the most of it.'

Ogilvie asked the question direct: 'Was he loyal, Major?'

O'Kelly lifted his eyebrows. 'Funny you should ask that. I used to have my doubts. Still have. I think his loyalties were divided, that's the best answer I can give. I know what you mean, of course – having heard your report, you see. Sometimes he seemed to be acting for us, sometimes he could have been acting against us. Right?'

'Yes. There was the blowing up of the arms dump, but . . .'

'Yes, the buts. Oh, I know! That's Edward Healey. Same at school – take too long to explain.'

'I wonder what's happened to him.' Ogilvie frowned and bit his lip. 'He wanted to be left behind, but I feel hellish guilty about that.'

'You needn't.' Surprisingly, O'Kelly closed his eyes and recited what seemed to be a verse, and after the first line Ogilvie recognized it as being a follow-on from what Healey himself had quoted to him back in Waziristan: ' *"Be it hoarse as Corrievrechan, Spouting when the storm is high, Give me but one hour of Scotland, Let me see it e'er I die."* And you see, Ogilvie, the Waziri hills were Healey's Scotland. He often quoted that verse, as a matter of fact.' Suddenly he became brisk. 'Enough of all that,' he said. 'Tell me – would you care to take up this work, transfer to the Political, old boy?'

'No,' Ogilvie said, and laughed. 'Sorry, but it's not for me. I've got my company now, and I'm sticking with it.'

'That's your final word?'

'Yes.'

O'Kelly shrugged. 'Oh, well! *Chaqu'un à son goût.* Personally, I'd detest the bloody infantry. How's Mrs. Archdale?' he asked suddenly.

'Well, thank you.'

'She played a big part in this.'

'I know.'

'Of course, you'll see more of her if you stay with your

regiment than if you were liable to be whirled off in disguise into Afghanistan or somewhere at any moment, in the Political.'

Ogilvie snapped, 'I wasn't thinking of that when I gave you my answer. I was thinking of – other things. Poor old Jones, for instance. He did well, too.'

'Yes, indeed. Far be it from me to denigrate the useful Jones. Nevertheless, he was expendable. His was a *dirty* trade, too!'

'Isn't yours?'

O'Kelly looked startled. 'Look here, old boy, I wouldn't be heard saying that outside this room if I were you. I'm broad-minded. Others may not be. And don't go around with a long face because of Jones, for heaven's sake! What did you expect for him – a retrospective military funeral and a gun carriage?'

'It's just that no one's so much as mentioned him since he died,' Ogilvie said, mentally contrasting that bouncing, bloody trunk with the image of a dignified funeral and military honours – horses, firing-parties, full dress and muffled drums. 'It doesn't seem right.'

He got to his feet.

'Where are you going?' O'Kelly asked.

'I've an appointment with Mrs. Archdale.'

'Give her my regards, won't you, old boy.'

Ogilvie went out into hot sunshine, into the military atmosphere of Peshawar and its marching men, its drilling defaulters, its loud-voiced Colour-Sergeants, its brilliant uniforms and its beating drums. And its peace and security. He returned to his room in cantonments before keeping his appointment with Mary Archdale, and as he went past the Mess he saw Andrew Black sitting with a glass of whisky and a heavy scowl; sitting quite alone. Ogilvie had been back in cantonments for only a few hours, but he had noticed that something more than usual was bothering the adjutant. He had done nothing but scowl, and mutter, and avoid people. Especially the Colonel. After what MacKinlay had told him, Ogilvie was scarcely surprised. It seemed that Captain Andrew Black had wilfully deprived himself of taking part in a march that could have helped his promotion prospects no end.

THE END

Further adventures of James Ogilvie of the Queen's Own Royal Strathspeys by *Duncan McNeil*:

DRUMS ALONG THE KHYBER

Two generations of Ogilvies have served – and in their time commanded – the 114th Highlanders, the Queen's Own Royal Strathspeys. James Ogilvie, the third generation, is pitchforked with mixed feelings first into Sandhurst, then into the family regiment, with which he finds himself in 1894 a subaltern en route for India.

The passage out teaches James many things about the army the hard way, and his initiation is not eased by the vindictive attentions of the adjutant, Captain Black. Viceregal India has lessons of a different sort for a young officer, but action brings new emotions and a new testing, as the Royal Strathspeys are sent through the Khyber Pass to contain the rebel Ahmed Khan outside Jalalabad ...

0 552 09364 5   35p

LIEUTENANT OF THE LINE

James Ogilvie's career as a subaltern with the 114th Highlanders, the Queen's Own Royal Strathspeys, offers him ample proof of his superior officer's observation that the Queen's service isn't a damn bunfight for old ladies. Especially when after a severe reprimand for the grim consequences of a disastrous patrol, James is sent on another during which, it is hoped, he will redeem himself. Yet although this results in what is apparently ignominious failure, it brings an unexpected recruit who, in the ultimate confrontation before Fort Gazai, can help make all the difference between defeat and victory ...

0 552 09365 3   35p

A SELECTED LIST OF FINE NOVELS THAT APPEAR IN CORGI:

☐ 0 552 09218 5	A SEASON WITH EROS	*Stan Barstow* 35p
☐ 0 552 08506 5	A RAGING CALM	*Stan Barstow* 35p
☐ 0 552 09274 6	A KIND OF LOVING	*Stan Barstow* 40p
☐ 0 552 09277 0	THE DESPERADOES	*Stan Barstow* 30p
☐ 0 552 09278 9	JOBY	*Stan Barstow* 30p
☐ 0 552 09156 1	THE EXORCIST	*William Peter Blatty* 40p
☐ 0 552 09089 1	THE HORSES OF WINTER	*A. A. Davies* 45p
☐ 0 552 08963 X	CAPE OF STORMS	*John Gordon Davis* 40p
☐ 0 552 08108 6	HOLD MY HAND I'M DYING	*John Gordon Davis* 40p
☐ 0 552 09364 5	DRUMS ALONG THE KHYBER	*Duncan Macneil* 35p
☐ 0 552 09365 3	LIEUTENANT OF THE LINE	*Duncan Macneil* 35p
☐ 0 552 09366 1	SADHU ON THE MOUNTAIN PEAK	*Duncan Macneil* 35p
☐ 0 552 09230 4	BUGLES AND A TIGER	*John Masters* 40p
☐ 0 552 09142 1	THE DECEIVERS	*John Masters* 35p
☐ 0 552 08832 3	THE ROCK	*John Masters* 50p
☐ 0 552 09256 8	THE LOTUS AND THE WIND	*John Masters* 40p
☐ 0 552 09291 6	THE ROAD PAST MANDALAY	*John Masters* 40p
☐ 0 552 08582 0	RAMAGE AND THE FREEBOOTERS	*Dudley Pope* 35p
☐ 0 552 09258 4	RAMAGE AND THE DRUMBEAT	*Dudley Pope* 35p
☐ 0 552 08887 0	VIVA RAMIREZ!	*James S. Rand* 40p
☐ 0 552 07954 5	RUN FOR THE TREES	*James S. Rand* 40p
☐ 0 552 09295 9	WE, THE ACCUSED	*Ernest Raymond* 65p
☐ 0 552 08716 5	THE LONG VALLEY	*John Steinbeck* 25p
☐ 0 552 08459 X	THE PASTURES OF HEAVEN	*John Steinbeck* 25p
☐ 0 552 09356 4	THE RED PONY	*John Steinbeck* 25p
☐ 0 552 08325 9	THE WAYWARD BUS	*John Steinbeck* 25p
☐ 0 552 08326 7	TO A GOD UNKNOWN	*John Steinbeck* 25p
☐ 0 552 08327 5	CUP OF GOLD	*John Steinbeck* 25p
☐ 0 552 08993 1	ONCE THERE WAS A WAR	*John Steinbeck* 25p
☐ 0 552 09108 1	THE BRAVE CAPTAINS	*Vivian Stuart* 30p
☐ 0 552 09053 0	THE VALIANT SAILORS	*Vivian Stuart* 35p
☐ 0 552 09323 8	HAZARD OF "HUNTRESS"	*Vivian Stuart* 35p
☐ 0 552 08866 8	QB VII	*Leon Uris* 50p
☐ 0 552 08091 8	TOPAZ	*Leon Uris* 40p
☐ 0 552 08384 4	EXODUS	*Leon Uris* 50p
☐ 0 552 08385 2	MILA 18	*Leon Uris* 40p
☐ 0 552 08389 5	ARMAGEDDON	*Leon Uris* 40p
☐ 0 552 08521 9	THE ANGRY HILLS	*Leon Uris* 30p
☐ 0 552 08676 2	EXODUS REVISITED (Illustrated)	*Leon Uris* 50p

All these books are available at your bookshop or newsagent: or can be ordered direct from the publisher. Just tick the titles you want and fill in the form below.

CORGI BOOKS, Cash Sales Department, P.O. Box 11, Falmouth, Cornwall.
Please send cheque or postal order. No currency, and allow 7p per book to cover the cost of postage and packing in the U.K. (5p if more than one book), 7p per book overseas.

NAME ....

ADDRESS ....

(NOV 73) ....